# Carousel

## by
## Kimberley Rose Dawson

authorHOUSE™

1663 LIBERTY DRIVE, SUITE 200
BLOOMINGTON, INDIANA 47403
(800) 839-8640
WWW.AUTHORHOUSE.COM

*First published by AuthorHouse 2/16/2006*

*ISBN: 1-4259-0817-9 (sc)*

*Printed in the United States of America*
*Bloomington, Indiana*

*This book is printed on acid-free paper.*

Based on the true story of Elizabeth Burgess' addiction to men, alcohol, and abuse.

*This book is dedicated to a dear friend and soul-mate*

*Valerie Thompson*

*(Darlene)*

*born November 21, 1944*

*died February 8, 1997*

# Acknowledgements

I'd like to thank:

Linda, for encouraging me and helping me to re-write the first edition;

My editor, Clelie Rich, for all her good advice;

Carol, for giving me a computer and correcting my punctuation and grammar;

My daughter, Brandy, for encouraging me when I wanted to quit;

Gina for being the first to read Carousel and say "This is a really good story, Mom.";

My dear friend, Nancy, for saying "The book is excellent. It would make a good movie.";

Sharon and Shannon for all the proof reading;

Joe for all the photocopying;

Val for her encouragement after it was finished;

And, special thanks to my daughter, Brandy, her friends, Khyley, Nicky, and Crystal, and my granddaughter, Ashley, for listening to the chapters over and over and over again until I got them right.

*Carousel: A merry-go-round, repeating the same rotations, covering the same ground over and over again.*

*Liz's was a carousel of painted white steeds, garlanded with flowers and ribbons, with smiles on their faces. Promise of happiness and potential for love was contained in their beauty. As they turned, their smiles turned to sneers. Quickly as they go round and round, look, they are smiling, look again they are sneering.*

*Look again, these horses are drunk on their mad turning round and round. Look again? No! She's getting off.*

# Prologue

"Could we open this meeting with a moment of silence for those who have helped us and for those whom we may help?" the chairman's solemn voice quoted.

As the crowd stood, Liz, looking beaten and forlorn, stumbled to her feet. She found the silence to be deafening and the moment to be an eternity. Without a drink in her system to deaden her thoughts her sick and broken mind easily raced back across the shattered years of her life.

Some of the memories were so ugly and painful that she couldn't bear to think about them. But try as hard as she might, she couldn't block them out. Horrific scenes from the past flashed through her mind.

"*Mom, what happened? You should see the big hole in the wall.*" Jimmy's shocked voice echoed in her memory. Her chest tightened as she saw the vision in her mind's eye. *Her three kids came thumping down the stairs. Then there was a terrific blast through the stairwell. She ran up the stairs to check the damage. There was a small hole where the bullet had entered the wall on the right side of the stairs. Then her eyes bugged out in horror as she surveyed the damage on the left wall. There was a hole two feet wide.* Beads of perspiration broke out on her forehead. She fought to change her thoughts. Another scene quickly flashed.

"*I've done the worst thing that you could possibly think of.*" The drunk voice echoed in the confines of her mind.

She heard her own voice echo. "*Did you kill someone?*"

"*No, worse than that.*"

She squeezed her eyes shut as tight as she could trying to blank out the memory. With all her strength she turned her thoughts to rehearsing what she'd say when it came her turn to speak.

*My name is Elizabeth and I am an addict. I'm addicted to love and alcohol. This is my story.*

She reflected on the broken years once again. Her mind screamed out to her, *Why?*

The chairman looked compassionately in her direction and said, "Would you like to say anything?"

She nodded and opened her mouth to speak; she uttered like an automaton the words, "My name is Elizabeth and I'm an alcoholic." All of a sudden from the depths of her soul a cry escaped her lips, and she shook with sobs. She had plenty to say, but she was unable to speak a word. Finally, she had come home.

# Part I
# THE CAVALIER

## Chapter 1
## Little Turtle

The room was suddenly dark and still. It was deathly quiet too, except for Alicia's intermittent outcries. The lightning flashed, briefly illuminating the doctor's huge, tense form. The thunder cracked, splitting the night. The storm had knocked the power out.

"Get a Lantern, quick!" the doctor cried. "I can't see a thing. I'm afraid I'm going to have to use the forceps; she's not delivering properly."

John rushed with the coal oil lantern, but he was too late. The forceps had gripped her the wrong way and Elizabeth Burgess was born with a cauliflower ear, perhaps indicative of the constant pounding her life would bestow upon her. The ominous day was September 2, 1944. It was just before the end of World War II. Liz was a Baby Boomer. She was also the baby of her family.

The doctor tied and cut the cord, wrapped the babe in a blanket and handed her to John while he tended to Alicia. John grasped her wee head in one large hand. The length of her body didn't even stretch to the crook in his arm. He held the tiny, pale bundle in his arms. She was so small and frail looking.

He stared down in awe at a perfect little face with a rosebud mouth. Tears started to well up in his eyes. "Damn!" He cursed under his breath in an attempt to gain his composure. "Is she gonna make it?" He asked with a slight quake in his voice.

"I think they're both gonna be fine, but I would keep a close eye on that babe. She was early, ya know. She looks a touch underweight too. I'll want to see her regularly," the doctor sighed.

For the first few months Liz was a very sickly infant, and Alicia wasn't much better. She was feeble and depressed so with the exception of nursing Liz, Alicia left most of her care to John. Because Liz was so frail, John kept a constant vigil by her side. He would often hold a little mirror under her nose to see if she was still breathing. She was so white and still, like a wax form in her little wicker basket. But she was a fighter. John coddled and nurtured her with the patience of Job. He spent so much time with her that a very close bond developed between the two right from the start.

But not so with Alicia. She'd had a very difficult pregnancy and a dreadful birthing. Besides, she really hadn't wanted Liz. She had followed too closely after Allen's arrival. With the depression years and then the war, a sixth child was a further burden.

The family had lived through many hard times and Alicia was left very stressed by it all. During the war the government gave out ration books of food stamps for each member of the family, but the stamps soon ran out, and several times the family was left with only tea, peanut butter, and bread for all their meals. There was no money for new clothes, let alone any recreation for the older children, although they did get to see a movie at the Odeon theatre once in a while, if they were fast enough. Money was sparse everywhere, and people couldn't pay to see a movie so in order to eke out an existence the theatre owners admitted anyone who offered a potato or a piece of coal. Of course, the family had no extra potatoes, but if the kids got to the railroad tracks before all the other kids in the neighbourhood they could grab up the stray pieces of coal that fell off the coal car of the old locomotive.

It broke Alicia's spirit to see her brood struggling. Trying to cope with all the pressures of the depression, along with the fear of John having to go off to war, Alicia had become severely disheartened. With the hard pregnancy and birth and a sickly baby to care for she became even further discouraged and found it difficult not to harbour a little resentment towards Liz for bringing her more grief.

Alicia's pregnancy with Allen, born two years earlier, on the other hand, had been a pleasure and the birth good so Alicia felt a certain closeness to Allen that she never developed for Liz. As Liz grew, Alicia tried to love her, but because the two had gotten off to a rough start there was a gap between them that could never be bridged. As a matter of fact, some days Alicia could hardly stand to be in the same room with Liz, and try as hard as she might to conceal it Liz was well aware of it. So she tried to stay out of Alicia's way as much as possible which meant long lonely days until her papa came home from his new job.

Every day Liz would sit on the steps of the big wooden front porch until she spied John coming around the corner at the end of the block. Regular as clockwork he would turn the corner at precisely 5 o'clock.

On one of those days she wiggled her little, round bottom off the step, all excited, and shouted, "Here he comes!" John swung his black metal lunch bucket back and forth as he walked jauntily down the street towards her whistling the tune "Blow The Man Down, Johnny Blow the Man Down." He looked like Charley Chaplin with his little black moustache and his black curly hair parted on the side. He wore a tweed cap pushed back so that his curls tumbled down on his forehead under the peak. Like Charley Chaplin he wasn't very big, but to Liz he was a giant of a man. His face lit up as he saw her running towards him with her short, pudgy legs going as fast as they could. He stooped low as she reached him and scooped her up to chest level in one solid arm. She snuggled into his thick flannel shirt and breathed in his rich musky male smell. "I love you, papa," she whispered in his ear.

"I love you too, princess," he whispered back. "And have I got a surprise for you. Tomorrow we're going to Toronto Island on a company picnic. There is a huge carousel there, and you're going to ride, ride, ride." He twirled her around as he chanted the words.

Liz's eyes bugged out with excitement, and she clapped her pudgy hands together. Then, she stopped, looked at her papa, and asked, "What's a carousel?"

John laughed as he answered her. "A carousel is a merry-go-round with horses and music and it's lots of fun, you'll see. He started to whistle cheerily again as he carried her the rest of the way home.

Saturday dawned in a blaze of glory and so did Liz. The family quickly prepared, caught the bus on the corner of Pharmacy and St. Clair and headed to downtown Toronto to catch the ferry.

Wind and spray licked at Liz's face as her papa held her close in the front of the boat. When they docked, John put Liz down and she ran headlong towards the carousel squealing with delight. "Wait, wait, I've got to get a ticket," John laughed as he ran after her. The lilting music coming from the centre of the merry-go-round caused his own heart to quicken as he chased her.

After getting the ticket, he picked her up around the waist, jumped up, grabbed onto a pole, and swung her up on a white horse. As he held her close he could smell her popcorn breath. His heart warmed. She was the light of his life.

And Liz's heart soared as the carousel spun her round and round until she was dizzy with delight. Oh, how she loved the warm wind in her face. She looked at her papa. Oh, how she loved him. She rode over and over again. She couldn't get enough. But too soon the day was over.

The sky was beautifully painted with pinks and mauves as John carried a sleeping Liz over his shoulder, her little hand clutching the string of a red balloon. And Alicia marched proudly with Allen at her side as they headed for the ferry and home. The momentous day would be forever ingrained in Liz's heart.

As the years passed and the children grew, Alicia constantly remarked to everyone that Allen was a very good boy. Without realizing it Alicia was causing Liz to wonder if, by contrast, this meant she was not good.

Alicia wasn't completely right about Allen though. Oh, he was a good boy as long as he was in her sight, but once out of her sight he was mean. He picked up on Alicia's intolerance of Liz, and he played on it.

So one hot August day Allen and his playmate, Larry Spencer, lured Liz away from home with the pretense of playing soldiers with her. They shoved her down a deep hole that was bulldozed for the foundation of a new house.

"Lemme out! Lemme out! I'm tellin' Papa!" Liz cried, terrified.

"You're never gettin' out of there," Larry yelled in a mean voice. "You're our prisoner, right, Allen?"

"That's right." Allen agreed, smirking.

Liz struggled up the side of the excavated basement on her tiny, four-year-old legs. Her head whirred with confusion and fear.

Whoosh! Larry pushed her back in. She rolled to the bottom; gravel and sand tumbled down with her almost burying her.

After several attempts to get out and Larry pushing her back in again she finally wailed, "You gotta let me out. I gotta go pee." Tears rolled down her pudgy cheeks. She was all dusty and bruised. She squeezed her little legs tight together as she danced around in the hole.

"You're just sayin' that!" Larry yelled. "You're the prisoner. You gotta stay in there." He held up his wooden sword, as he spoke.

"That's right," Allen agreed.

Liz shuddered as she felt the warm liquid running down her legs, turning cold as it hit the air.

"Hey, Larry, we can let her out now. She's gonna be in big trouble for wetting her pants."

Larry wacked the ground with his sword and moaned, "O-o-o-kay." He walked away muttering, "Just when I was having fun."

Liz scrambled up the side as they left. She was shaking. She dusted herself off. She felt waves of guilt and shame as she walked home like a penguin, the cold wet panties chafing her legs. She was afraid; Allen was right she *would* be in trouble for wetting her pants.

But by the time she got to the house, her papa was home from work. She was so relieved. The wet pants could have meant a spanking if Alicia had been there to meet her.

Once again her papa was her hero. Not only that, he had a surprise for her as well. His arms were hidden behind his back and with a big grin on his face, he said, "Where's papa's girl? Come here, Lizzy-Tish and see what I've got for you."

He reached out with one arm and swung her up to his chest.

"Hey, you're all wet!" he cried. "Papa's little girl have an accident?

At that precise moment, Allen appeared in the doorway. He stopped dead in his tracks. He glanced sideways toward Liz with eyes bugged out. *Would she tell on him?* She caught his look. She never said a word.

"Let's get you changed," John said.

When John and Liz came back from the bedroom he picked up the two little children's books he had set on top of the ice box. Liz loved books and he knew it. One of them was the turtle book.

Changed and dry, she snuggled next to her papa as he read the story. The little turtle was feeling hemmed in by his shell. He wanted to romp through the meadow and play free like the other animals, but his shell was too heavy. It always slowed him down. But every time he thought of taking it off his mother's voice would echo in his mind, "Never take off your shell!"

Then one sunny, summer day the yearning to be free was too much to bear. Once out of his mother's sight, he quickly removed his shell and found out just how exhilarating it was to be without it. He had a wonderful time racing through the huge field of daisies chasing King Billy butterflies. Without his shell he just flew.

Then suddenly a terrifying thunder storm blew up. The black clouds boiled. The lightning sliced through the sky. The wind whistled and whipped dust and leaves and branches around. Thunder roared. Then came big splats of ice cold rain bouncing off his back and piercing his delicate skin. He was in the middle of the meadow. Now what would he do? He was terrified. He ran with all his might to the edge of the meadow where an old deserted house stood. He crawled under the porch behind a protective wall of lattice. Amongst the dead leaves, he shivered and sobbed uncontrollably wishing he had listened to his mother.

Liz was spellbound. She snuggled deeper into John's side. His arm tightened around her. He could feel her fragile, little bones under her warm skin. He sighed deeply. A sudden fear of losing her rippled through his body, and he hugged her closer as he continued with the story.

Liz's heart went out to the poor, little turtle as John finished the tale. She had listened intently not realizing at such a young age that this poignant story was to become a metaphor for her life.

With the passing of time she became that turtle. She longed to get the heavy shell off that restricted her movements. Inside she was a wild and free spirit. Alicia was Liz's shell. She was a stern and strict woman, and she believed thoroughly in discipline. Her father had used a leather strap on her and her siblings to keep them in line. On becoming a parent, Alicia followed suit. With six kids and a soft-hearted husband she felt she had to keep order herself. The years of hard times had taken their toll on her and left her with very little patience so she often lost her temper, especially with Liz. Liz was always getting into trouble. She didn't mean to. She just had such a strong desire to have fun and enjoy life that she didn't always think of the consequences.

Thus, when Liz trudged home from school one rainy spring day all muddy and wet from running through the puddles with the other kids, she was greeted with the full force of Alicia's ire.

"Look at those clothes," Alicia cried, anger rising in her voice. Her eyes were wild, and Liz quivered as her mother's voice rose. Liz was always terrified when Alicia gave vent to her anger. Liz, like her papa, had a gentle and caring nature, and she hated Alicia's angry outbursts.

"How many times have I told you, don't get your good clothes wet and muddy?" Alicia shrieked, as she grabbed for the leather belt.

The belt connected with Liz's back with several well-directed blows. She stiffened and bent over and braced herself for each wack. She never muttered a sound and not one single tear fell from her eyes.

"Now you know where you're going, don't you?" Alicia muttered.

Allen smirked as he looked out from behind Alicia. Liz knew where she was going alright -- to the cold, dark basement. Alicia would shut her down there out of her sight when she got so angry. Liz was scared, but she never let it show. She had smuggled a little music box down there when Alicia wasn't around. The music box, which her papa had given her, gave her comfort as she cried alone in the dark. It wasn't so much the beating that made her cry. It was the fact that her mother didn't seem to love her.

Alicia believed thoroughly in "Spare the rod; spoil the child", but somehow the application was wrong. Liz hated the anger so consequently she didn't learn the lessons Alicia was trying to teach. But she did learn to fear anger and become immobilized by it.

Not only was Alicia a stern woman, she was very head strong, and she ruled the roost. She was always ordering John around. Being a soft and gentle man, he would just give in. So when Liz heard the terrible disagreement between her mother and father she knew her mother would win. What she didn't know was that it was to alter her entire life.

She heard her name mentioned several times but didn't fully understand what the argument was about. She didn't know Alicia was jealous of John's intense love for her. Alicia wanted John to pay more attention to the son that she so adored, so she devised a way to get John to stop spending so much time with Liz.

As the argument intensified, Liz stopped playing with her dolls, sat still and quiet and listened.

"I don't care John, you're too close to Liz. She's getting older now."

"What do you mean?"

"You shouldn't be holding her on your lap. A man shouldn't get too close to a little girl. It just isn't right."

"B-but Liz is so special to me. You know I would never hurt her. Besides, she's only five."

"She'll soon be six. You mark my words. It's just not proper. You don't want to ruin her life, do you?"

"Well no, but..."

"Then you better do what's best for her. Don't pick her up or cuddle with her anymore. Just leave her alone."

John loved Liz and he would never have hurt her, but to keep peace he agreed even though it nearly killed him. Not only did it nearly kill him it was a major turning point for Liz. Her father's love and attention had been the one thing that made her feel worthwhile.

After the confrontation with Alicia John crept into the living room looking like a beaten pup with his tail between his legs. Liz went and climbed on his lap. He looked at her sadly and lifted her off and sat her on the floor at his feet. Looking up into his face she said, "Papa, Papa, what's the matter?"

John didn't answer. He didn't know what to say. He just stared into space.

"Please talk to me, papa. I love you, papa." Liz cried as she attempted to crawl back on his knee.

"No, Liz, you have to stay down." His voice cracked as he spoke. "You go play with your dolls now." He gently pushed her away from him.

His face turned to stone and his eyes were haunting. It was as though something inside him died. On that dreadful day a little part of Liz died too.

For days after she tried to hug him, but it was always the same he would turn away from her. Believing that Alicia knew better than he did about raising little girls, he just kept pushing Liz away, but it was taking its toll on him. Not only was it taking its toll on John, it was destroying Liz . She longed for him with an intensity that made her ache in the pit of her soul. But John remained totally untouchable. Allen was secure, he was the apple of Alicia's eye, but now, Liz had no one to comfort her.

Several weeks later she stood behind the closed living-room door in the empty hallway at the foot of the stairs. Alicia had sent her to bed. She had walked right past her papa sitting in his old wicker chair. He hadn't even looked up.

In the dark, a tiny tear wended its way down her cheek. An inner-struggle was tearing at her. She wanted to run to him and kiss him goodnight. She fought with her reluctance to go to him with every fibre of her being. Her heart so longed to be close to him again, but fear of his rejection held her back. It was her last attempt to get close. She lost the struggle and climbed the stairs with her chin on her chest. The light that lit up her world flickered out.

# Chapter 2
# Margie

It was the end of June, 1957, and Liz was charged with excitement. The family was on the move and she had high hopes that the move would somehow change things for her. She had survived the early years without her papa's love and affection, but she was left with a haunting emptiness inside that screamed out for male attention. The location they were moving to offered possibilities of providing that attention.

They were relocating from Scarborough to a home in the country about forty miles north near Bradford. The Holland Marsh, a dried up lake, was located on the *southern* outskirts of Bradford. Immigrants from Holland, utilizing their techniques from the old country, had drained the marsh, using canals to channel the water. The soil was black as coal and fertile. Anything would grow there. Bradford was called "The Heart of Canada's Vegetable Industry". The packing plants there packaged the vegetables that ended up on the tables in the homes of most of eastern Canada. The lucrative industry drew lots of young men from all over Ontario. Liz had heard tell of this, and she was thrilled. Even though she was not quite fourteen, she was already enthralled with the opposite sex. She was almost obsessed. Ten huge packing plants full of young men was a very exciting prospect.

But after settling in their new home Liz's enthusiasm soon fizzled out. They were five miles *north* of Bradford, living in a country house. They were totally isolated. They were no where near the packing plants.

So severe loneliness enveloped Liz once again. Oh, she wasn't alone, but she might as well have been. Her older siblings had long since married and left home. So that left her, Allen and their parents. As for John it was as though he had died inside. For years he hadn't talked to anyone except Alicia, who had become his mediator. Liz had given up trying to get close to John a long time ago. And as for

Alicia, she had never had time for Liz and still didn't. She was always too busy with Allen. Besides, Liz was a burr under Alicia's saddle. She just wouldn't conform to the rules so Alicia felt the less time spent together the better.

And then there was Allen, who was filled with the need to be good, for Alicia. He had no time for Liz either. That didn't really bother Liz because he was very serious-minded while she was filled with a passion for living life to the fullest. Besides, he had been mean to her in her early years and she hadn't forgotten. Yes, Allen was very serious-minded. He was the scientific type, using his telescope to see the stars while Liz, on the other hand, saw only the stars that twinkled in the eyes of the boys.

Allen was always sending away for things advertised on cereal boxes. He had deep sea divers that were propelled through the water by baking soda. He loved the way things worked; Liz loved the way things felt. She was a romantic dreamer, full of expectations, in awe of the world around her. She was brimming with enthusiasm. The two were worlds apart in personality. Other than their parents, they had nothing else in common. They definitely were not close.

So with the isolation and no one in her family to relate to, Liz was plagued with loneliness and always left to her own devices. She escaped to the woods as often as she could to be by herself amidst the stately pine and elm trees to dream about finding that special someone who would love her. Without any close human contact, that summer was an eternity for Liz.

So when school finally started in September she was ecstatic. There would be new people in her life! She loved people in spite of the fact that she had developed a timid shy side. But even though she was very excited about starting school, she was still a little apprehensive. She was starting grade nine at the young age of thirteen because she had completed her last two public school grades in one term. She was smart beyond her years.

On the first day of school she was scared because she didn't know a soul. She had a wild, adventurous spirit, but her mother's harsh discipline, over the years, had suppressed it somewhat, and her father's rejection had left her with low self-esteem. Not only that, she was very small compared to the girls in her class. To start with, she was small in stature and she was more than a full year younger. She longed to be bigger, taller and older. She felt very out of place. Then, she met Margie Leighton and her whole world spun right around. She was sauntering down the hall at odds with herself when she heard some well dressed, pretty girls tittering. They were pointing at a large dark haired girl. Liz thought the girl was kind of pretty in her own way, but she was huge. Just then one of the girls unkindly hollered, "Hey Hippo," and all the girls began to giggle.

The large girl tilted her head up with dignity and began to walk faster past them. Liz raced after the girl and said, "Can I walk with you?"

"Thanks. What a bunch of jerks, eh?"

"Yeah," Liz said, shyly.

"They're all like that at this school. A bunch of snobs. Think they're better than everyone else. Hey, my name's Margie Leighton, what's yours?"

"Liz Burgess," Liz said smiling and the two walked off together to embark on a very exciting relationship. In the beginning it was Liz's empathetic side that drew her to Margie. But in the end, it was Margie's very daring way with the boys that kept her drawn.

Liz was raring to go like a young thoroughbred filly, but was just as nervous. She hungered for male attention, but at the same time she was scared to pursue it. Margie on the other hand was very bold. She was not afraid to approach the boys and go joy riding with them. Liz was thrilled. Margie was exactly what she needed. Margie's dad had died; Liz's was totally withdrawn so they both sought out boys to fill their innermost needs. It was the beginning of Liz's fascination with the male world.

But trouble was brewing on the horizon because Liz's relationship with Margie was no secret to Alicia. And one evening after the dinner table was cleared and Alicia and Liz were doing the dishes together Alicia brought up the subject.

"I understand you're hanging around with Margie Leighton."

"Yeah, why," Liz said, defensively.

I haven't heard anything good about her. She has a bad reputation, and she's very bold. She doesn't have a father and they're so poor.

Why can't you hang around with some of the nicer girls at school? The ones that come from families that are better off," Alicia answered.

"Mama, I don't care if she's poor. She's not bad! She's the best friend I've ever had. She's the only friend I have. Please don't make me stop seeing her. Besides, what you call the *nice* girls are really just a bunch of snobs. They're not very nice, and they're so catty."

"Oh, Liz, you're just imagining things."

"No, I'm not!" Liz said, stubbornly.

In spite of Alicia, Margie and Liz became inseparable. Liz was not giving her up. Margie had the same zest for life as Liz and they had a common interest that cemented their relationship -- boys.

Liz always craved excitement, so when Margie pulled into Liz's yard with her older sister, Mary, and asked Liz to spend the night at her house in town, Liz begged Alicia to let her go. Finally, after Liz had nearly driven Alicia crazy with her pleading, Alicia relented and the girls drove off in a cloud of dust in Mary's black 1950 Ford.

Margie's mother worked evenings so Liz and Margie were free to do as they liked. Margie was older and more experienced. She knew all about makeup and what to wear to draw the boys. In spite of her large frame, she could work wonders and make herself very attractive. She used some of her magic on Liz and the results were stunning. Liz's beautiful, dark brown, fawn eyes were accentuated by a touch of brown eye shadow fading to white by the brows. Margie had plucked the brows to a fine arch. Liz's chestnut hair was piled high which made her look taller. Just a touch of copper lip gloss detailed her rosebud mouth. Margie even knew how to apply darker makeup to shorten the nose that Liz hated because it was a slight touch too long. After dressing and putting the finishing touches on the makeup that was designed to make them look older, the girls headed downtown. Liz was excited. She felt so grown up. She was frolicking free without her heavy shell.

As the girls stood at the four corners of Bradford a car load of handsome boys from the packing plants pulled up. Liz's whole being pulsed with excitement.

The driver stuck his head out the window and said, "Hey, girls, wanna go for a ride?"

Then the young man in the passenger's seat said, "Yeah, come on girls we'll show you a good time. Do you like to sing? Look, Terry's got a guitar in the back."

"Oh, Margie, I love to sing, let's go!" Liz cried.

"Sure. Where are you guys from?" Margie responded.

The driver answered, "We're from Lloydtown. My name's Clay. What's your little friend's name?"

"Liz and my name's Margie."

"This here's Nick and that's George and Terry in the back. We gotta pick up Nick's girlfriend in Schomberg, but we can have a good time singin' on the way over there."

The girls went to climb in the back seat and Clay reached over and grabbed Liz's arm.

"*You* get in the front beside me." He smiled warmly at Liz and she smiled back.

They drove through Bradford, laughing and singing, then out toward Schomberg where they stopped and picked up two more girls. Liz had never had such fun. Then the party ended up in a gravel pit outside of town where there were lots of young people gathered around a big bonfire. The gang all piled out of the car, and everyone paired off, heading in different directions. Of course, Liz was singled out by the driver, Clay. He was older -- 18, and he was so handsome with his sky blue eyes, blond hair, dark tan and broad smile. Liz was dazzled by him. His attention made her swoon. He flirted and teased with her making her feel so important and liked. His eyes were electric and as they held Liz's in a steady gaze, she started to feel a very pleasant spinning sensation. The feeling was vaguely familiar. Then a scene flashed in her mind. The carousel ride she'd had with her dad. She could almost hear the music. She could definitely feel the warmth, the love. All of a sudden she felt very close to Clay and his slick ways soon convinced her to slip off to a field, away from the others.

"C'mere. How about a kiss. A good lookin' girl like you deserves to be kissed."

Liz felt flattered. He leaned over her and his lips barely touched hers as he brushed past to her cheek, then nibbled further reaching her ear and neck. Liz's heart skipped a beat. She liked what she was feeling, so she didn't stop him.

His lips found her mouth again. This time demanding, hot. He forced her mouth open and started to probe with his tongue. His tongue touched hers, and instantly her mind replayed a scene. *Two very small girls experimenting, touching tongues. Then suddenly, her mother ripping her up by the arm and beating her with the leather strap across her backside.* Liz shuddered as she remembered the terror.

She started to feel ill at ease. She tried to push him away. He gripped her harder. Then his hand went to her developing breast; she pushed his hand away, uncomfortable with the touch.

An alarm went off somewhere in the centre of her. Fear crept through her. In spite of the fact that she was vibrating inside with the need for attention and affection, she had a powerful misgiving about sexual things. Her mother's words echoed in her mind. *Bad girls do bad things with the boys. Don't you ever let me catch you doing things like that!*

She was naive. She was innocent. She knew nothing about a man's strong need for sex. No one had educated her. All she knew was that she craved the love which she had been deprived of by her father. She just didn't understand what kissing might lead to.

"Aw, c'mon," he said, continuing to kiss her neck and pinning her hands down with one of his. Groping, his other hand slid down between her legs. She jumped and tried to get away from him. He grabbed her tighter and then with his weight heavily leaning forward on her, he pushed her to the ground. She began to panic with this new assault. She tried to squirm out from under him as he pressed his full weight down on her. She felt smothered. She fought but she was no match for him. She couldn't budge him. She couldn't throw him off. He was just too heavy.

Her heart sank. She was a fighter but there was nothing she could do. Conscious that her skirt was up to her waist, she twisted under him as hard as she could trying to escape. In the acute sensitivity of slow-motion panic, she was aware of a rock in the middle of her back pressing pain through her. He kept her pinned down as he fumbled with the front of his pants. Sheer terror raced through her as a scream tore from her throat. She screamed and screamed, but no one came. Then, she begged.

"Stop, please stop!"

He tried to penetrate her with several thrusting motions; he was panting, his hot breath pulsed on her neck. Just when Liz thought she was going to lose her mind with fear, he shuddered, went limp and rolled off her. Scrambling to her feet, she quickly straightened her clothes, feeling hot tears of fear and anger stinging her cheeks. She turned away. Then, she turned back to look at him. She lowered her face in shame. She felt cheap, dirty. Her mind raced with vivid sights of what her mother would do if she ever found out. *She must never find out!*

Seeing her fear and confusion Clay said, "C'mere." He tried to put his arm around her and soothe her.

She shrugged off his arm, shaking with anger and stomped back to the car. She wiped the tears from her cheeks with the backs of her fists.

She had just wanted a little affection, a little kissing. Evidently, Clay expected a good deal more. She was relieved, though that he hadn't been able to take her innocence before his body betrayed him.

She had just wanted to have some fun. She was too young and inexperienced to understand. She was the little turtle, caught out of her shell, and the heavy downpour had pierced her delicate skin. Her craving for male attention had taken her down a path that nearly ruined her. The carousel had begun to turn. Liz was on it and didn't know enough to get off.

# Chapter 3
# Kindred Spirits

Liz had lived eight years without her papa's affection and attention, and she thought she could replace him with another male, but after her terrifying experience with Clay she gave up on that notion. So she was left just screaming inside. She craved human contact. Margie filled the void to some degree, but not completely. Then in the spring of 1958 Alicia finally got her way and even her relationship with Margie came to an abrupt end.

Margie's mother had given her a brand new 17 jewel Bulova watch for her birthday. Liz's parents were out, and Margie came to visit. She bragged to Liz about her "17 jewels", and Liz insisted on seeing them. Margie told her they were inside the watch. Liz didn't believe her, and so the girls commenced to take it apart at which time it ceased to function.

On the very same evening, Margie persuaded Liz to let her call her new beau on the telephone. The call was long distance, and Margie talked for over an hour.

Inevitably, Margie's mother called to demand payment for the watch, at which time Alicia had plenty to say about the long distance call, the end result being the girls were forbidden to see each other. So Liz was left alone and feeling empty again.

There was, however, one reprieve from her sentence of loneliness. Saturday night was show night. John would drive Allen and Liz to the theatre in town. Then he would come to pick them up after the movie was over. They waited for him outside the Holland Theatre.

At first, alone and bored, Liz sat with Allen. Then she started to sit by herself for freedom from his watchful eyes. She would meet him outside after the show.

One ordinary Saturday night, Liz was in the washroom at the theatre when she heard someone come in. She came out of the stall and found herself face to mirrored face with a beautiful, young girl with long black hair and violet eyes. She appeared to be about five foot two. She had the tiniest waist Liz had ever seen. As she greeted her, she was amazed at how much the girl looked like Elizabeth Taylor. She was a beauty alright, but the violet eyes lacked sparkle. They were dull as if they were masking something. On a long silver chain around her neck hung a man's signet ring of black onyx.

"I really like your ring," Liz said.

The girl's face lit up, her smooth, curved lips turned into a warm smile as she reached for the ring and fondled it. For a second her eyes brightened and met with Liz's. Their eyes locked as they searched each other's hearts. Liz's heart warmed in a way that it never had before. She caught a glimpse of the kindest expression she had ever seen. Then the light faded, and the dullness returned. It was as though the girl was lost in a world of memories.

"Thanks," she muttered, "It belonged to my boyfriend, Ed."

"Aren't you with him anymore?" Liz asked sympathetically.

"No."

"Oh, what happened?" she asked cautiously. She hoped she wasn't being too intrusive, but she wanted to carry the conversation further. She had instinctively developed a keen interest in this girl. She wanted to be her friend.

"He was killed in an accident," the girl said sadly.

Liz was crushed. She wished she hadn't pried.

"Oh, I'm so sorry," she said as she touched the girl on the forearm.

Then, she quickly introduced herself and learned the girl's name -- Carol Simpson. The conversation continued, and Liz listened intently as Carol told the story of how Ed had been killed while rushing to see her. Her family had moved up north to Elliott Lake for awhile and Ed had missed her terribly. He finally got some time off work and was in a hurry to see her. He was zooming along the open highway on the new motorcycle he had purchased to make the trip when the car ahead braked abruptly. He braked and skidded. With his tires squealing, he careened into the back of the stopped car. He was thrown thirty feet and killed instantly.

Liz's heart sank. It was a tragic tale, and it was evident to Liz that Carol was still grieving. Such a devastating loss at such a young age caused Liz's empathetic side to make an instant link with this beautiful girl. They made a bond that day that could never be broken. Carol Simpson and Liz Burgess became forever friends.

Carol was two years older than Liz. She had one sister, Darlene, who was Liz's age and in her class at school. Totally opposite to Carol, Darlene was tall and blonde with gray-green eyes. She had the German look about her, which she came by honestly from her Germanic ancestors. She was handsome. She had a shyness about her, but her eyes mirrored a warmth that went right to her heart, and she had a very witty sense of humour that delighted Liz. By their looks Liz would never have guessed that Carol and Darlene were sisters. The girls had two younger brothers, Nathan and Tommy.

Liz learned to love Carol's whole family including her mom, Vera. She spent many happy hours sitting around Vera's old, round, wooden table. The Simpson's Drury Street house was a haven for talk and laughter, which they pursued for hours on end. Vera treated the girls as equals and not as kids. Liz would often hear her quote her two favourite sayings. *You've got to walk a mile in another man's moccasins. If you want to have a friend, you have to be a friend.* That was the recipe for success in Liz's relationships with her new friends, Carol and Darlene.

A feeling of belonging that Liz needed in the very pith of her soul was satisfied by Carol's family congregated around the table and nurtured by Carol's mom, Vera.

Vera was not tall, but she was a very handsome woman who at one time had been a real beauty. There was, however, good reason for her stooped shoulders. In a real way, the weight of the world was on them and it showed on her aging and tired face. It was no wonder she looked the way she did. She was the nurturer, the mother, the glue that kept it together when Carol lived through her tragic loss. Raising four kids on her own and doing a fine job of it, Vera faced the slights of people who were neither neighbourly nor kind.

Liz had first heard about the Simpson family through the *nice* girls at school. They had talked about Carol and her family and had not been very kind. Liz was sickened by their gossip. She felt sad for Vera's plight. Vera had been left by an alcoholic husband to support her four children. As a result the family was poor and ridiculed by the so-called good families.

Vera worked at Harry's Restaurant, the local "greasy spoon" for $15.00 a week. She maintained a home for the four kids on that. Unlike Liz's cool, stern mother Vera was very patient, warm and compassionate. She absolutely won Liz's admiration.

Vera's home became Liz's second home; Vera became her second mother, and Carol and her siblings became her sisters and brothers.

Vera's place was a magnet for lots of kids. She didn't seem to mind; she was always very hospitable and kind. Liz began to spend a lot of time there. Every school lunch hour she was eager to walk Darlene home. The three girls, Liz, Darlene and Carol, became inseparable.

It was at one of these noon-hour rendezvous that Liz met Sheryl Morris. Sheryl's blue eyes sparkled with mischief as she and Liz were introduced. Liz knew instantly that she would be a lot of fun, and she wasn't wrong. Not only was she a lot of fun, she turned out to be a loyal friend as well.

Sheryl was tall like Darlene. The two towered over Carol and Liz. Her long blond hair and big, blue eyes, complemented her full lips. Sheryl was a beauty in her own right even beside Carol's dark loveliness, Liz's petite figure, and Darlene's handsome Germanic looks.

Sheryl was one girl in a family of five boys. Her oldest brother, Clancy, was handsome. He was gifted with a good singing voice and was very talented on the guitar. Clancy hoped to be another Elvis Presley. Darcy and Dan were the twins who didn't look a bit alike. Darcy was quite tall with brown hair and brown eyes. Dan was short, blond, and blue eyed. Peter, the youngest, was also quite handsome, probably the best-looking of the six. Willy, on the other hand, really got gypped. He was a little guy with a Durante nose that definitely did not match his stature. In spite of his outward appearance though, he was very good humoured and kind.

Liz grew to love all the Morris kids as well as the Simpson kids. But she kept her new relationship with all of them a secret from Alicia. She was afraid of losing them like she had lost Margie. It seemed every time Liz found someone to love or be close to, they were ripped away from her. She knew Alicia would not approve of her associating with poorer families so the only time she saw her new friends was at school noon hours and on Saturday night when she would sneak out of the theatre to be with them.

After a few months Carol started to heal nicely from her grief. Her friendship with Liz helped tremendously. The girls were like two peas in a pod; they shared the same adventurous spirit and the same sense of humour, and on one occasion Liz learned that they both liked to walk on the razor's edge as well.

Carol's eyes sparkled as they raced from the theatre down the street to her friend Murray's car.

"Wait'll you see what I've got in store for you," Carol exclaimed.

Liz chased behind her, and they both climbed into the front seat of Murray's '54 Ford.

"Murray, will you take us to the eighth line and let us do what I did the other day? Ple-e-e-ase," Carol pleaded.

"I don't know Carol. It can be dangerous."

"C'mon Murray don't be a stick in the mud."

"Alright, but you take your chances."

They drove out to the eighth line and once they were out of sight of the highway Murray pulled over to a stop.

"C'mon, Liz, follow me," Carol said as she climbed out of the car.

She hopped up on the hood of the car and instructed Liz to get on the other side.

"What? You're crazy," Liz laughed.

"No, come on. Try it."

Liz climbed up on the hood giggling nervously. They laid back against the windshield. Murray slowly pushed the gas pedal until he reached a speed of about thirty miles an hour. Liz looked over at Carol and grinned. She felt totally exhilarated with the warm wind blowing in her face. She imagined she was a beautiful headpiece on a grand ship sailing full speed ahead on the open ocean.

The girls smiled warmly at each other and grasped hands. Just as they did, Murray, upset that Carol had refused to be his special girl, stomped on the gas pedal and roared down the road at speeds of sixty to seventy miles an hour. Carol and Liz gripped with fear held on desperately to the little quarter inch rim above the windshield until their fingers bled. It was the only thing there was to hold on to.

Finally Murray slowed to a stop. Carol jumped off the car and ran around to Murray's side. She was furious. "You're crazy, Murray! I told you I'm not ready to be anybody's girl yet. You couldn't wait, could you? Just being friends wasn't enough. Well, now, I don't even want to be your friend. You better take us straight back to town or I'll, I'll, I don't know what I'll do, but you better just take us back to town right now."

Liz was shaking as she climbed back into the car. When the girls got back to town they jumped out of Murray's car and raced down the street holding hands. When they got around the corner out of Murray's sight they hugged and laughed uproariously. "Wow, that was a gas," they shouted in unison.

The white and pink blossoms that had dotted the roadways had been replaced by luscious green leaves. The tall maples and elms were in full leaf as well. The spring sun was warm on Liz's back as she walked down the highway to town with Sheryl and her brothers. The boys walked several feet ahead of the girls.

"Who do they think they are leaving us behind?" Sheryl asked. "Watch this!" she said as she picked up speed. She took a running leap and landed on Clancy's back. Then he took off running and twisting at the waist trying to shake her off. She clung to his back shaking with laughter. Then he started to laugh too as he wrapped his arms around her legs and ran with her. Liz smiled weakly. She felt an uncomfortable twinge inside. Sheryl had a special rapport with her brothers that Liz envied.

Liz so longed for that kind of closeness with a male. She would never have behaved in that fashion with Allen or her papa. She had learned to stay away from her papa, and as for Allen he'd been so mean to her over the years that the distance between them was unbridgeable. As he got older he stopped being mean, but there remained a sibling rivalry that could never be mended. No, such shenanigans would never happen in her family, and since the incident with Clay, Liz had become afraid to seek any other close male companionship. So she tried to satisfy her emptiness with her new girlfriends, Carol, Sheryl and Darlene, but a hollow feeling was still there, buried just beneath the surface.

She spent as much time with the girls as she could in the hopes that the emptiness would eventually subside. When they weren't sharing time at Vera's, they gathered at Jack Pong's Chinese Restaurant. All the kids in town hung out there.

It was an old building with scuffed hardwood floors. There were several wooden booths, painted yellow, down each side of the room with a jukebox in the centre. At the front by the window was a counter with round, leather stools.

The rain was pouring down as Liz, Carol, Dar and Sheryl raced through the door and scrambled into the front booth where they always sat so they could see who was coming in. They were soaked.

Liz laughed as she whipped her jacket off and shook the rain out of her hair all over Sheryl.

"Hey watch it!" Sheryl laughed and wiped her wet hands on the dry sleeves of Liz's blouse.

The girls straightened up as Jack Pong approached the table. He was a very small Chinese man. He wasn't any taller than Liz. He had beady eyeballs under his slanted lids and a round face that always looked very sad. He wore black, bell-bottom trousers, a clean, white shirt, and a long white apron covered in soup, gravy, and ketchup stains. The suspenders on the pants pulled them up high causing a deficiency on the other end. He wore the same thing day after day, after day.

He stood with a note pad, which was ludicrous, because every time they came in, the girls always ordered the same thing, one plate of fries and gravy, lots of ketchup, and four forks. He shuffled away from the table with their order written in his little note pad.

"Hey, Dar, how come you sewed your black leotards with white thread?" Liz questioned as she looked down at Dar's leg.

The girls wore uniforms to school which were made up of very short navy blue tunics, white blouses, navy blue bloomers, and black leotards.

Dar started to giggle. "Well it used to be black. You see, we couldn't afford to buy two spools of thread so I bought white because most things I have are white. This is my last pair of leotards, and I got a run in them. I sewed them this morning with the white thread then I rubbed black soot from the wood stove on them, but it looks like the rain washed it all off."

Liz just roared. "Tell you what I'll smuggle a spool of black thread out of our house for you," she said as she looked up to see who was coming in the door. Her head swivelled; she looked at Carol, at Darlene, and then at Sheryl. They all had the same astonished looks on their faces and then in unison they burst out with gales of laughter.

"What the heck is this!" Sheryl squeaked out between giggles.+

Lo and behold, right there in their midst stood Elvis. Clancy had dyed his light brown hair and side-burns black and had pencilled his eyebrows with black. He shook the rain out of his hair, did a little gyration with his hips and squeezed into the booth next to them to share their fries.

Jack returned to the table with the same sad look on his face, set down the fries and gravy, the bottle of Heinz ketchup, and four forks.

"Jack always looks so sad," Carol said.

"Yeah and he always wears the same things over and over. I bet he's poor just like us. He probably can't afford any new clothes," Sheryl piped up.

"Ah, I doubt it. He owns a restaurant," Clancy said as he dug into the fries.

" Yeah, but look at this, five of us in a booth and only one plate of fries. No profit in that. He's a really kind man too. He never chases us out even though we never buy anything else. I feel sorry for him," Dar chimed.

"Yeah me too," Carol agreed.

"I don't know. It's a mystery to me, but he only has one outfit that's for sure and that's sad. I feel bad for him too," Liz added.

"Yeah, me too," said Sheryl.

A few days later the rain cleared up, and the sun was shining beautifully as the girls walked through the back alley on their way to the restaurant. They looked up and spotted the clothes line at the back of Pong's apartment. What they saw made them look at each other and simultaneously go to pieces. They bent over with laughter, they pointed upwards, then doubled over with laughter again.

There, on the line, were about ten pairs of black, bell bottom trousers and about ten white shirts hanging neatly in a row. "I guess Clancy was right," Sheryl muttered between giggles.

Not only did the girls share a common sense of kindness, they also shared a common sense of humour. They were related, not by blood but by common bonds. They were kindred spirits. They enjoyed a closeness beyond Liz's wildest dreams. Liz prayed Alicia would never find out about them and forbid her to see her newfound friends.

But like Margie, Liz's new friends didn't completely fill the emptiness in her. In spite of their closeness and all the fun they had, a tumultuous storm was brewing inside Liz. Something was still missing.

# Chapter 4
# Golden Sunbeams

The hot summer sun blazed down on Liz as she wandered away from her country home. She headed up the side road to the highway. She was wearing lime green pedal pushers, a white peasant blouse that revealed bare shoulders, and a lime green neckerchief that hung down loose on either side of her chestnut pony tail.

She felt proud of her blossoming, hour-glass figure and very chic in her new clothes, but it was all wasted, walking up the eleventh line. Who would ever see her? She was totally alone. Since school had let out for summer vacation and she wasn't spending lunch hours with her friends, that nagging feeling of emptiness plagued her even more. She'd had a fear of boys ever since Clay tried to rape her, but now the demanding void inside her was causing that fear to rapidly subside.

She felt pretty and perky, but she was bored with the isolation of country living. As she walked aimlessly, she daydreamed about that special someone. Then whoosh out of the blue came a cream-coloured 1954 Ford full of young boys. The car surrounded her with a cloud of dust, but in spite of the dust she saw the look in their eyes. Message sent; message received. She was feeling saucy and flattered. Instantly a thought flashed, *Surely every boy isn't like Clay.*

A few days later sauntering down the same road, hoping to see that car again, she spotted two jaunty figures strutting their way towards her. As they came closer she recognized Sheryl's brother, Willy Morris. He was accompanied by a strange looking little guy who looked as though he belonged in a comic strip. His front teeth were huge and protruding, his eyes were too close together, and he had a little button nose that twitched. He, and Willy with the "Durante" nose, made quite a pair. For sure neither of them could be her special someone, but Liz was pleased to run into them nonetheless. Company in her isolated world.

She was even more pleased to hear what they had to say.

Willy spoke up, his eyes were big as saucers, "We know somebody who likes you."

"Yeah," said the little guy giggling.

"Who? And who's this?" Liz asked.

"Oh, this is Bugsy Harlson," Willy replied.

Liz looked at "Bugsy" and chuckled to herself thinking his name was certainly appropriate.

Willy continued, "Edmund Brooker told us he saw a new girl in town. Seems he and his friends were driving around the other day, and they spotted a girl walking down the eleventh line. He said she sure was c-u-u-ute," Willy teased, grinning from ear to ear.

"I'm not new," Liz said. "I've lived here for a year."

"I know," Willy said impatiently, "but Edmund doesn't. He's been away working for his uncle in Toronto. He just got back in town. Anyway he wants to meet you."

Liz's interest was sparked so she agreed to meet Edmund.

Saturday show night, Liz sneaked out of the theatre after she made sure Allen was engrossed in the movie. Her heart was in her throat as she left. It always was with the fear of being caught, but tonight it was doubly so. She was going to Jack's to meet Edmund for the first time.

She flew across the busy street dodging cars. She pushed the heavy glass door of the restaurant open and spotted Willy grinning like a Cheshire cat as he stood behind Edmund poking his forefinger towards the back of Edmund's head and mouthing the words, "This is him, this is him."

Liz was dazzled. Her heart skipped a beat. All of a sudden she felt totally inadequate. He was so perfect with his black hair combed back on the sides and tumbling loosely over his forehead. His skin was bronze and his eyes! His eyes were snapping black, and full of devilment. He had a handsome ski jump nose and a very sensual, pouty bottom lip. He wore a white tee shirt, light blue jeans, a black leather Jacket and black motorcycle boots.

He looked towards her as she stood frozen by the door. He drank in her petite figure clad in light blue jeans, navy blue brotherhood jacket and white bucks. Her long chestnut hair just gleamed. She looked like a small frightened deer with her big fawn eyes. His heart beat rapidly in his chest cavity. His mouth went dry, and he knew instantly he loved her.

As he surveyed her she wanted to bolt, but she couldn't move. He stood and moved towards her, and as he did she was drawn to him like iron filings to a magnet. She was out of control, her own control that is. She came under his spell as their eyes met. She already loved him too. As he moved closer to her she saw that he felt the same way about her. It was mirrored in his eyes. Willy, Jack, all the customers, and the restaurant disappeared, and they passed into a magic world all their own. There was an instant unspoken bonding. It was as though they had always known each other as they drifted through eons of time. The carousel slowly started to turn as the room spun around them.

From that moment on Liz and Edmund became one in the universe. But the only time they could be together was on Saturday show nights. Allen always thought he knew where she was, but he really didn't. She was meeting with Edmund while Allen watched the movie. After the show, she would find Allen outside and be there for their father's arrival. No one was the wiser

Edmund and Liz, together with the gang of Morris and Simpson kids, would pile into Clayton's car and drive around. Clayton was unique. He was very dark-skinned with a high cheek-boned face and beady eyes. He had big lips, severely bucked teeth and skin that was laden with deep pock marks. Liz thought he was an old man. Actually he was only twenty-eight. At first she was frightened by him, but Edmund reassured her that he was just a lonely misfit who was very grateful for their company. He was harmless and was thrilled that they were willing to spend time with him.

So the gang rode around with Clayton often, laughing and singing. Clancy would play his guitar, and they would all sing. Liz loved to sing. They knew all the words to songs like *Bye, Bye Love* and *Pick Me Up On Your Way Down*. But Edmund's favourite song was *Geisha Girl* by Hank Locklin. It was G5 on Jack's juke box. Liz had memorized that and she played it for him every time he came in the restaurant. She was totally smitten with him. He was nothing like Clay. As a matter of fact, he was so shy that he had not even held her hand, let alone kissed her.

That is until that fateful Saturday night. Liz and Edmund were squished between Willy, Clancy and the guitar in the back seat of Clayton's car. Carol, Dar, and Sheryl were all squeezed in the front seat with Clayton. The girls took turns sitting on the edge of the window with the top half of their bodies outside the car. The warm, summer wind blew their long hair straight out behind them as they laughed and banged on the roof of the car with the palms of their hands to the beat of the music.

"Liz, this is wonderful!" Sheryl squealed. "Try it!"

"Yeah, come on, just climb over Willy and squeeze out through the window. It's fun," Dar said.

"Yeah," said Edmund as he pushed Liz towards Willy. She sat on Willy's knee as she wiggled the top half of her body out the window. The wind hit her instantly almost sucking her out. "Whoa!" she cried and grabbed the roof of the car. The wind blew her chestnut hair into the air as it warmly caressed her face. Sheryl was right it was wonderful. She glanced over at Sheryl on the other side of the car roof and they started to sing *Hang down your head Tom Dooley* as Clancy plucked on his guitar. Liz felt like she was on top of the world.

After a short time she pulled herself back in and squeezed beside Edmund. Her cheeks were pink from the wind and her face was lit up like a small child's, alone inside a candy factory. Edmund's heart did a flip as he looked at her. He was overcome by the pleasure he saw reflected on her face. He turned to Liz, their eyes locked, and she was swept away by his gaze. Her world started to spin. The carousel whirred with delight.

They were drawn to each other, slowly, gently. Her face came closer and closer to his. Their lips met. She had never felt such a sensation. His lips were like warm silk. He was so gentle. It was nothing like her experience with Clay. Warmth flowed through Liz's body as he held her close. She was reeling, dizzy with delight. He clung to her unable to let her go. That was it! They became one!

Then Willy giggled nervously. "Are they gonna be alright? Hey, you guys, you better come up for air."

At that Edmund let Liz go, but the tingling continued on and on. She was floating. She had never experienced anything so perfect. Her pain was gone. Her haunting emptiness filled.

It was true love. Liz spent as much time with Edmund as she possibly could. They looked for every opportunity to be together. She was sure they would be forever.

With the passing of time, Liz learned that Edmund's family came from the wrong side of the tracks and they were dirt poor, but that made no difference to her. She did not adopt her mother's criteria for class.

She knew Alicia wanted her to be with kids from the so-called *good families*, but Liz just didn't want to be with them. They were snobby and too serious. They never enjoyed the fun that she and her friends did. She loved her kind, down to earth companions, and besides Edmund was very special to her. Where he came from didn't matter. She knew one thing for certain though, no matter what, she had to keep him a secret from Alicia because she needed to be with him. He filled the emptiness.

He was so handsome in his black leather jacket, blue jeans, black motorcycle boots, all obviously second-hand, and no underwear (so he said -- she never found out). He told her that poor kids didn't wear underwear because they couldn't afford it.

But the difference in economic status didn't stop Liz from going to Edmund's house. They lived on a hill at the edge of town where a new subdivision had sprung up all around them. At one time they had owned a large farm but had slowly sold off the property, acre by acre. Now their house was an old decrepit duplex in the midst of brand new homes. Sheryl Morris' family lived in the back of the duplex. The Morris's called the place, *The Mansion on the Hill* after the song of the same name. It was no mansion for sure and the well-to-do neighbours would have liked to squeeze them out.

The first time Liz went to meet Edmund's family she discovered how exciting their place could be. His mother, Leona, put the kettle on for a pot of tea and then sat at the table opposite Liz. She just kept smiling at Liz. It was obvious she was pleased with Edmund's choice. As a matter of fact, everyone seemed to be. Liz glanced around the table, and all eyes were on her. Edmund's three siblings were smiling widely. They were all looking at her as though she was some kind of supernatural being, and it unnerved her. It was obvious they were all as shy as Edmund because none of them spoke. They just kept smiling at Liz, and Liz just kept smiling back. Then the whistle blew on the kettle, and Liz nearly jumped out of her skin.

Edmund's mother made the tea, and then while they were sipping away at the kitchen table an explosion rocked the whole room. Liz gasped and threw her hand across her chest. The lids of the wood stove blew up in the air spewing out thick, black plumes of smoke while the dog took off from his corner chasing the squawking chickens and pigs away from the front door. The kids all snickered as Leona almost came right out of her skin, dancing around the room.

"What the hell was that?" Edmund asked between chuckles.

His mother looked hilarious. Her big brown eyes were bugging out and her black hair was standing on end as if she'd put her finger into a wall socket.

"I dunno," Leona squeaked.

"Now, what did you put in the stove, Ma?" Edmund asked.

"My empty hair spray can?"

"How many times I gotta tell you? Don't put aerosol cans in the stove."

"I forgot," Leona muttered.

Edmund put his arm around Liz and smiled warmly down at her. His eyes twinkled with mischief, and she started to just howl. She laughed so hard tears started to run down her cheeks. Before long Leona and the kids joined in her laughter.

Liz found out it was never dull at Edmund's house, and that was right up her alley. She craved excitement. She was addicted to it. She got a full dose of it at Edmund's.

Liz was at Edmund's as often as she could be. It was fun, and as poor as they were there was a closeness that she never experienced in her own family. She kept looking for a sense of belonging. At Edmund's she belonged.

The fun they had that summer of 1958 would be forever ingrained in Liz's memory. They played hide and seek in the golden wheat fields at the back of Edmund's place. The wheat was waist-high on Edmund and good for hiding in. Playing with the gang of Morris kids, Edmund and Liz would hide together. They didn't particularly want to be found. Shielded by the long wheat grass, they would kiss and hold each other as if there was no tomorrow. They shared a common emptiness and longing for love that they satisfied in each other. Liz was happier than she had ever been in her life. And not only was the emptiness filled, but there were all kinds of adventures.

One lonely Saturday while Liz's parents were away shopping Edmund showed up at her house unexpectedly. She was thrilled. Edmund had observed her parents for weeks and learned their schedule. He knew they would be away for hours, and he couldn't wait to surprise Liz. He came with Bugsy and Willy. Edmund was riding his chestnut horse, Sundance, with Willy behind him. Bugsy had his own horse. Being a city girl Liz had never ridden a horse before. Her adventurous spirit kicked in. "Can I ride?"

"Sure but you'll have to ride bareback. I had to sell my saddle." Edmund's face reddened with embarrassment. He hated being poor.

Liz stood on a fence post while Edmund helped her get on Sundance's back. How very warm the horse's smooth body felt underneath her. No sooner had she started to relax than Bugsy hit the horse's rump with a heck of a wallop. Sundance took off, hell-bent for leather. Edmund took a swing at Bugsy; Bugsy ducked, and Liz rode, fast and furious.

It was a sight, for she had never ridden before, and she was bouncing all over the place, holding on for dear life to Sundance's mane. Then, everything came together. As Liz tuned into the rhythm of the horse's stride, she gained confidence and was able to stay on. Soon they were moving as one. She rode high with the warm wind caressing her face. They galloped and galloped. Finally, of his own accord Sundance slowed down and turned around to return to Edmund. Liz never liked Bugsy Harlson much, but she was ever grateful to him for that ride.

Edmund kept Sundance at Granny Brooker's place. That was another home where Liz felt welcome. Granny Brooker lived down the road from Edmund's in a dugout shack that seemed to be rooted in the very earth. The floors, in fact, were dirt, but always swept clean. Liz was amazed at how Granny Brooker survived the freezing cold Ontario winters in her shack with no proper flooring.

She was a tough old gal, with her leathery brown skin and steel grey hair. Although pulled back in a bun, her hair was always wild around her face, poking out here and there. She was scary looking. But in fact, she was very kind, and she loved Edmund. That was good enough for Liz.

Liz had come to know Edmund's family quite well. Bob Brooker, Edmund's father, had the longest chin you ever saw on a human being. The kids called him "Lantern Jaw". Edmund's mother Leona looked worn out and old, probably from the life that she led with Lantern Jaw, and the effects of raising four children in a poor environment. Edmund was the oldest, followed by Gord, Edith and Edna. They were close in age, each only a year apart.

Leona showed Liz a picture of a beautiful young nurse holding a bouquet of red roses. It was the picture of her graduation from nursing school. Liz could hardly believe that the young woman in the picture was Leona. Always interested in others, Liz listened intently as she told the story of how unkind the years had been to her. Liz suspected that Bob was unkind also as he was a drinker, very explosive, and he certainly frightened her. He was seldom around, but when he was he consistently yelled at Leona and the kids.

Bob had his moments, however. He bought Edmund a blue and white 1949 Pontiac. Edmund wanted so badly to take Liz for a ride in it, but his father had forbidden him to take it out until it was properly licensed. Bob was away one day. Edmund and Liz sat on a stump staring at the car. They looked at each other, grinned and bolted towards the car.

On their way down the hill, they met an old man nicknamed Cinnamon Bun. Liz imagined it was because of all the grooves in his face. He actually looked like a cinnamon bun. He was a sight. A wizened-up old guy with skin like a withered potato, and he wore a long overcoat buttoned right up under his chin, in spite of the 80 degree temperature. He had no teeth so he sprayed as he talked. Edmund pulled up beside him with a big grin on his face and said, "Hey, Cinnamon, do you want a ride downtown?"

Cinnamon, spitting and sputtering, answered, "Edmund, what are you doing with that damn car out? You know Lantern Jaw's gonna kill you. No way am I gettin' in that car wit' you guys. You're crazy.

You better get that car home right away. You can't drive anyway." He spent about five minutes yelling, spraying from his toothless mouth the whole time, that there was no way he was getting into that car with them.

Then all of a sudden, he stopped. He looked up in complete silence, deep in thought. After a few moments of reflection and concentration, Cinnamon spat out, "Hey, Edmund gimme a ride downtown, will ya?" Liz and Edmund laughed so hard that the tears ran down their cheeks as Cinnamon pulled up his big overcoat and piled in the back.

They dropped Cinnamon Bun off where he wanted to go, then turned around and headed for home. They felt so grown up. Liz snuggled closer to Edmund and placed her hand gently on his arm. He smiled warmly at her. His eyes twinkled making her melt.

They got back to Edmund's house to find his father had come back. Like a raging bull he came towards the car. Edmund no sooner got out of the car than his father's big fist connected with his jaw. Edmund cried, and Liz seethed with anger and shuddered with fear. She wanted so much to run and protect him, but she was afraid.

Blood trickled from the corner of Edmund's mouth as they walked quickly to Granny Brooker's, a place of sanctuary. Granny loved Edmund and that's where he would find healing for his split lip and his bruised spirit. She reached into the old cupboard and got out a bottle of whisky to make him a hot toddy. She dispensed her love along with the medicine. Having witnessed it all, Liz's heart felt his pain, and she was grateful to the wild-looking woman in her old shack with the dirt floors.

Liz enjoyed some of the wildest, funniest, and happiest times of her life with Edmund, the Morris kids, Carol, and Darlene. They were very poor but they were the kindest, warmest, most fun loving people she had ever met. These kids had to make their own fun because life was so hard for them. They included Liz. She belonged. She loved them dearly. She had found her place as long as she could keep them a secret from Alicia.

Liz and Edmund had their Saturday night rendezvous precisely timed. She didn't know whether Allen knew and didn't say anything, or just didn't catch on. It worked perfectly. Then there was a Wednesday night show that Allen wanted to see. Liz was ecstatic. She could see Edmund during the week. She met him at Jack's. All went well until her return to the theatre. On Saturday nights, they had perfect timing. She was always there to meet her father when he came to pick Allen and her up. This was a Wednesday and somehow she missed him. The show was over and they were gone. Liz was *scared*. She was upset about missing her father, but mostly she was afraid of Alicia finding out about Edmund.

"Now What am I going to do?"

"You can stay at my house," Edmund suggested.

She couldn't go to Edmund's. If Alicia found her there, all hell would break loose. So instead Edmund took her to a barn on the north edge of town. They slept there that night. Liz soon forgot her fear as she totally relaxed, cradled in Edmund's arms in the hay. They didn't make love. Just being together, clinging to each other for comfort was all that mattered to them. Liz easily drifted off to sleep with his arms around her. Morning came too quickly.

*Where am I?* She thought as she stirred. The stirring released a strong sweet aroma of mown hay which slowly enticed her to consciousness. In the first moments of wakefulness, she was aware only that she was warm, nestled into warmth, Edmund's warmth.

Eyelids fluttering, she became instantly aware of a magical scene. As though framed in slow motion, the black velvet of the previous night was replaced with golden sunbeams pouring through a thousand places. The slotted spaces between the boards in the big barn emitted warm rays of sunlight. A thousand diamonds sparkling became her romantic stage; tiny particles in space were twinkling all around in the sunbeams. Liz sighed and snuggled deeper into Edmund as she became more and more aware. Caught on the same carousel, her cavalier smiled down at her. All was well. Nothing could touch them. They were in a world apart, and all their own. It was a world of golden sunbeams and sparkling diamonds for a cavalier and his lady. The words of Johnny Mathis' song playing in her mind were "Wonderful, oh so wonderful, my love."

C-r-e-a-k, the barn door swung open.

"Edmund! Edmund! This is not very nice, you know. You get out of here before I call the police." The angry farmer's gruff voice instantly shattered the magic, stopping the carousel. Of course, he assumed the worst. Shot through with fear, they quickly crept away from the big barn and the angry farmer.

*Now what do we do?* Liz thought.

As though reading her mind, Edmund said, "Come to my house; my parents won't mind, maybe you could stay there with us forever."

She smiled slightly feeling somewhat consoled by his words, but could she shuck the turtle shell completely? She knew this wouldn't be possible, but Edmund's words were a comfort. She knew her parents would be looking for her and Alicia would be very angry especially if she found her with Edmund. She was torn between doing the right thing and what she really needed. She couldn't possibly lose Edmund who was filling an emptiness in her that had existed since she was that little girl who desperately wanted to kiss her papa.

They had no where else to go so she finally agreed to go to Edmund's house. In a way she hoped her parents would never find her, but she knew that was too much to wish for. Edmund was right; his parents didn't mind her being there. One more didn't make a difference to them. For Liz it was a dream come true being with Edmund for one whole night and day.

Meanwhile back at Liz's house Alicia was ranting and raving to John. "I just don't know what to do about that girl. I'm sure she's seeing a boy, I see all the signs, but I can't prove it. She just galls me. She's so headstrong. I know she's hanging around with those Simpson and Morris kids. She's thinks I don't know, but I do! That's probably where she is right now. Any boy she'd see with them would be no good for her. From the wrong side of the tracks the lot of them. She needs a boy from a family that's better off. I don't know why she won't hang around with the kids from the good families like I told her to. She makes me furious, but there doesn't seem to be anything I can do about it short of beating her half to death and if I don't give myself time to cool down that's exactly what I'll do."

Edmund's mother was a simple person, but she was good to Liz. All day Liz was torn in two, enjoying time with Edmund, but living in fear of when her parents would come. The whole day went by, and they didn't come. She was somewhat relieved, but she knew it would eventually all come to an end, and Alicia would be furious. She hadn't had a beating from Alicia since she was nine or ten and was feeling somewhat cockier. Alicia had sort of given up on her. Liz was as headstrong as she was, and she just exasperated her. But what would happen now?

Night fell, and Liz was not sure what the sleeping arrangements would be. She supposed that she would sleep with one of Edmund's sisters. At least, that was the way it would have been in her house. To her surprise Edmund's mother said, "You two can sleep together, but keep your clothes on." That seemed strange to Liz. She wanted to be with Edmund, but somehow it didn't seem right to bunk up in the same bed in his parent's home so after everyone went down for the night they slipped out and went to Morris' in the back.

It was never a dull moment in the Morris family either. There were two parents, six kids and only one bedroom. The beds in the one bedroom were all crammed in cheek by jowl, and the family slept in shifts. Willy knew every nocturnal activity by heart. While half the family slept the other half sat up drinking tea at the table with Willy verbalizing his thoughts.

"Oh, Dad's gonna cough now."

And sure enough old Clancy would hack.

"Mom's gonna roll over."

Followed by a squeaky bedspring. It was uncanny, and Liz was amazed. They spent the whole night there with Liz curled up in Edmund's arms in a big old easy chair.

The next day Liz's parents arrived on the doorstep, and Alicia was still very angry. They had found out where Liz was from the farmer. She and Edmund had been seen going into the barn. John and Alicia had found out the day before, but Alicia was so furious that she was afraid she would kill Liz. So she took some time to cool down, but the time only reinforced the sense of abandonment that Liz already felt. It was as though she was in her family but outside the family circle. This episode confirmed those feelings and made her more determined to be with Edmund even though she knew Alicia was going to forbid it.

Liz loved her parents in spite of the fact that they didn't see eye to eye. It broke her heart that they didn't seem to love her. She wished so much that they could understand her. As much as they didn't understand her, she didn't understand them. They thought it very important to be upstanding citizens in the community and mingle with the well-to-do families. Liz thought it was more important to be loved and have fun.

Her aged straight-laced grandmother who lived with them was always sticking her two cents worth in. She said that Liz was nothing but a *party girl*. Now, seeming to confirm her grandmother's worst opinion of her, here were her parents picking her up from the home of a boy they did not approve of. Liz was sure she was the bad seed.

"Come on, young lady. You get yourself out into that car immediately. Wait til I get you home!" Alicia barked.

Liz sat with her head drooping all the way home. She didn't know what was in store for her, and she was missing Edmund already.

When they got home Alicia sent Liz to the bathroom with instructions to strip down to her underwear. Liz did as she was told and stood waiting, wondering what her mother was up to.

Alicia ripped the door open. She had a can of Raid in one hand and a brown, paper grocery bag in the other. Without warning she started to spray Liz from head to toe. Then she grabbed Liz's clothes off the floor, threw them in the bag, stuck the hand holding the Raid can into the bag, closed the top with the other hand and sprayed. Liz was flabbergasted. How insulting! She could not believe what her mother had just done. Alicia was pushing her farther and farther away.

"Now that's that. That should kill anything you might have picked up. Honestly, Liz Burgess, I just don't understand why you insist on hanging around with such riff raff. I never liked that Margie, and I don't like the one's you're hanging around with now. You think I don't know what's going on, but I have my ways. I just don't know what I'm going to do with you Liz. There are lots of decent families in the community. Why can't you choose some of them to associate with?"

The Raid scene was bad enough, but the worst was yet to come. Liz was grounded. She was not allowed to go to the show. She wouldn't be able to see Edmund. She would rather have taken six kicks than be parted from him.

She had survived all the years without her father. She had survived standing back and watching her mother and Allen growing closer and closer, heads together in deep conversation, laughing together without her. She had survived those years but they had taken a toll on her. They had left her with an emptiness inside that was unbearable. She knew what it felt like not to be wanted. She would do almost anything to kill that pain. Edmund killed the pain. Before he had come along she had just lived with it. She had developed a callous over her heart. But since she had met him and he had taken the pain away the callous was softened and now the pain was even more difficult to bear.

So she sat in her room rocking back and forth on her bed holding her pillow close to her stomach. That's where the pain was. Right in the middle of her. A tear trickled down her cheek. Her stomach literally ached. It was an overwhelming sadness that sucked her breath away. She felt hollow. By forbidding her to see Edmund Alicia had ripped a six inch valley through the middle of her soul.

Her mind drifted back to the early years when she and her papa had been close. She could see it as clear as if it was a moving picture in her mind. On a swing under a huge maple tree sat a pudgy little girl.

"Fwing me papa, fwing me!"

Her dad chuckled with pride. He smiled warmly at her as she twisted around on the swing. Little helicopters fluttered down from the tree. Sunbeams streaked through the branches. She was as happy as she could be.

Then it was gone. Emptiness took it's place -- hollow, she was hollow. The weeks went by slowly. It was an eternity. Liz thought she was going to die.

But after a month the weekly show times and rendezvous were resumed. Even though Liz was threatened by her mother to stay away from Edmund she just couldn't. He was her lifeline. Their first night back together she clinged to Edmund as though she'd never get enough of him. She made an oath to herself that she would never suffer through the emptiness again, no matter what the cost.

# Chapter 5
# "Cool Hand Luke"

Liz recovered nicely from her bout with loneliness once she was seeing Edmund again. Eventually Alicia gave up trying to fight Liz. It was a stalemate. Alicia knew how deeply Liz loved Edmund and her friends. She was furious, but she was afraid she would have to beat Liz half to death before she would give them up. She was at her wits end as to what to do about Liz so she did nothing for the time being. Liz won that round. A year passed quickly. In a month Liz would be sixteen so begrudgingly, to keep peace in the family, Alicia gave in to Liz's begging and allowed her to date and go to town on her own, but Alicia was just seething inside.

A new chapter began in Liz's life, and she was thrilled. There was an onset of a new era in Bradford as well. Work was scarce on the East Coast. They had a saying in the East, "Goin' down the road", which meant that the young men had to leave home to earn a living. Bradford had a drawing card for these young, transient workers so they came to the town where the vegetable packing plants offered work.

Being far from home and not knowing anyone, these young men would hang around Jack's to dispel their loneliness. That's where Liz and her friends met them. The kids were looking for someone to drive them around; the young men were looking for companionship. Of course as soon as they saw Carol, they wanted her to be one of the car group. She was the prettiest girl in town.

That's how Ben Buchner came to be sweet on Carol. Even though Carol drew boys to her like bees to honey, she didn't necessarily return their regard. However, she was smitten by Ben and a whirlwind romance began.

A Prince Edward Island boy, Ben was handsome, but tough-looking, like Paul Newman in "Cool Hand Luke". It was not so much his looks that were like Newman's, but his nature. He wasn't that tall, but he was solidly built with tightly curled brown hair cropped short and sea-blue eyes. They were laughing eyes, and he loved to tease. Carol and Liz loved his down-east accent. "Roll up your windys fellers!" or "I'se da by from da bay." he'd say, and the girls would just come unglued.

Ben boarded at Brooker's, so he and Edmund became hard and fast friends. Ben was older, so Edmund looked up to him as an idol and tried to be just like him. The two were just as inseparable as Carol and Liz. So the couples double-dated every chance they could get. Liz had a special friend and a cherished love. The carousel turned incessantly.

Then suddenly things changed. After Ben moved out of Brookers and was established in his own apartment, he and Carol had a disagreement. Carol and Liz were at Ben's place when the fight broke out. Liz was immobilized by the angry vibes in the room. So when Carol left in a huff, Liz just stood there with her mouth gaping open. Ben begged Liz to stay. His pride was hurt, and he didn't want to be alone. Liz didn't really want to stay. She was always a little uncomfortable with Ben. He seemed so tough in contrast to Edmund who was gentle and innocent. And he was so cock-sure of himself that it unnerved her. She realized that Ben was still angry over the fight as he reached into the kitchen cupboard and brought out a bottle of whiskey. He poured two glasses, and Liz stuck her hand up immediately and said, "No Thanks!" He insisted. She wanted to bolt but her feet were anchored to the floor. She was so frightened by his anger; she felt like she was five years old again, having to do as she was told.

She brought the glass up to her nose, sniffed and wriggled her nose at the sharp aroma.

"Go on, drink it. It's good fer what ails ya. It'll put hair on yer chest," Ben said as he winked and took a big swig from his glass, swallowed hard, shook his head and made a face .

She put the glass to her lips and looking over the rim at Ben the whole time, she slurped a small amount. The whiskey was silky smooth as it entered her mouth. Then the amber firewater burned as it slid down her throat. She shook her head and made the same kind of face that Ben had and instantly felt a warmth quickly spread through her from the middle of her being. She started to glow. She took another sip and went through the same process of silky smooth liquid, burning firewater, and warm glow and kept repeating the procedure taking a little more into her mouth each time. She finished the glass and held it out for more. Ben laughed as he poured.

Before long she wasn't afraid of Ben anymore. She felt braver than she had ever felt in her life. Her timid, shy side disappeared along with her low self-esteem. She felt full of confidence. She was on top of the world. Nothing could touch her.

They finished the bottle. Then they left the apartment and staggered down the street, arm in arm, singing "Pick me up on your way down, when you're blue and all alone". Completely oblivious to the rest of the world they became the best of friends.

"You know what?" Ben asked.

"What?"

"I really like you. You're a lot of fun. You're more fun than Carol. She won't drink. I like to drink and Carol doesn't, but you do." Ben slurred. "How about going out with me tomorrow night to the drive-in."

In her inebriated state she felt flattered and answered immediately, "Sure."

Then the fun was over. *What have I done?* she thought. In her foggy mind she knew that yes wasn't the right answer, but it was too late. Fear enveloped her and broke through her drunken armour. *How can I say no to him now that I've already said I'd go. He'll be really mad. But I have to. Carol and Edmund would be so hurt. I can't possibly hurt them. They're my whole world.*

"Uh, Ben..."

He turned to her with a scowl on his face and barked, "What?" He knew she was about to change her mind and he was having none of it. He knew he could bully her and she would be intimidated. He had her now and he wasn't about to let her spoil his plan.

Fear prickled up her spine; once again she felt five years old. "Uh, nuthin'," she muttered. "It's just, uh, I think I better get home now." She turned and ran to Jack's to try to sober up before catching the bus.

She was just sick. She realized, too late, that the whiskey had played a dirty trick on her.

The next day, chastised and sober, she panicked when the drunken words from the day before echoed through the confines of her mind. *How about going out with me to the drive-in tomorrow night? Sure. -- I don't want to go with Ben; I've never wanted to go with him. Oh, my god. What have I done. I can't go with Ben. I love Edmund. And Carol. I can't hurt them. Oh, Damn. I hate Ben. He's so tough. I bet he'll be mad, really mad if I say no. Oh, man I just can't say no to him. What am I thinking? I've got to say no to him.* She cringed. *He'll be so mad. I bet he'll be mean. I just couldn't stand that. Oh, what am I going to do? I just can't stand to think about this right now; I know, I'll paint my nails instead.*

Then she thought about the time she had been sitting on the toilet and heard Allen climbing up the ladder outside the window. He was going to work on the roof. The toilet was just under the window. She didn't have time to get up. She froze. He was going to catch her with her pants down. She couldn't move. It wasn't until he got to the top and yelled at her to shut the curtains that her brain began to work again. It was so simple. Why hadn't *she* thought of shutting the curtains? It was always that way for her. When she got into a panic her brain just wouldn't function properly.

This was the same. She was in total panic. It was simple. All she had to do was tell Ben she couldn't go. All she could think of was that she was trapped. She had given her word, and now she had to do it. She sulked around her room going over and over it in her mind the whole day, but every time she thought of saying no to Ben, she pictured him being really angry with her, and she just couldn't deal with that. She had grown up with a very angry mother and had learned quickly how to appease people to keep their anger at bay. She couldn't possibly say no to him. But the thought of hurting Carol and Edmund was tearing her apart. She tried to think of a reasonable way to get out of the commitment and couldn't seem to come up with anything. Finally, unable to think of a way out of her predicament, her fear took over, and she resigned herself to the fact that the only hope she had was to do it and not get caught. That way she wouldn't have to face Ben's anger and no one would get hurt. Feeling a little better about it all she reluctantly decided to go with Ben to the drive-in.

Liz climbed into Ben's car that night. Ben smiled warmly at her. She gulped and weakly smiled back. She felt just sick about what she was doing. She closed her eyes and hoped with all her heart they wouldn't be seen. It was really risky, but she figured it all out. If they went straight from her house to the drive-in, there was a good chance no one would see them. And at the drive-in the darkness would conceal them. She just wouldn't get out of the car. Then coming home it would still be dark, and no one would see them for sure. So the only chance they might be spotted would be when they drove through town to the drive-in. She felt like an ostrich burying her head in the sand hoping no one would notice, hoping it would be over quickly, and everything would go back to normal with no one the wiser.

She breathed a big sigh of relief as they passed through town and headed out the other side without being seen. Then all hell broke loose. Ben yanked on the steering wheel, pulled a U-turn, headed back through town and drove down the block past Carol's house on purpose. It was part of his plan. He wanted Carol to see them together. Liz knew then she had been used and she was ripping mad. She had hoped she could get away without hurting anyone. But sure enough, there was Carol walking uptown.

When Carol saw them both in Ben's car her face mirrored her pain. She turned on her heel, did an about face, and hurried back to her house. Liz was crushed. She wanted to run after her and explain. Then she wanted to smack Ben. She had been trapped and deceived by her own fears. She slumped down in the seat and pouted, thinking it couldn't possibly get any worse.

But it did. Next they ran into Edmund on Main Street. Edmund was stricken. His eyes opened wide and his mouth gaped when he saw them. His head turned and his big eyes followed them down the street with the saddest look Liz had ever seen in her life. The silent sound of his heart breaking deafened her. She leaned way up in the seat and turned and looked longingly over her shoulder as they passed. She wanted to scream. She wanted out of that car in the worst way. She felt like she was being kidnapped as Ben sped up and left town. *What am I doing here? I've just betrayed the two people I love most in the whole world because of my own stupid fears. Why do I have to be so afraid? Why couldn't I stand up to Ben? Why couldn't I tell him no?* She asked herself these questions over and over and couldn't come up with any answers.

At the drive-in, "Seven Brides for Seven Brothers" with Jane Powell was playing. Liz had longed to see it at one time, but now she didn't care. She stared straight ahead, pouting. Ben offered her a beer, but she quickly and very firmly refused. Alcohol had got her into enough trouble already. Silent tears slipped down her cheeks while Ben knocked back several pints of beer. His head was drooping as the realization of what he had done hit him. His plan had backfired. Finally he said, "This is stupid, let's go." She agreed, and they left. Liz was miserable. She felt as if she was the worst person in the world.

After a short detour to look for more beer, Ben took her home. Once there she had to face herself. How could she deal with this mess? She went upstairs to her room and sobbed her heart out. She hated Ben. She wanted to turn back the clock. More than she hated Ben, she hated herself.

After a few days of brooding over the situation, she mustered up the courage to call on Carol. She apologized profusely.

"You really didn't want to go," empathized Carol, "You just found it hard to say no, right?"

Liz was amazed. How did she know?

Carol knew Liz. She knew about her inner fears. She knew how she was so afraid to displease anyone. How grateful Liz was. Carol's perceptiveness made a bond that would last a lifetime. Liz was relieved and so was Carol. She knew Liz's heart was good and didn't want to lose her friendship either. The two hugged and smiled warmly at each other, and Liz was determined she would never let anything come between them again.

Now, Edmund! How could she possibly mend things with him? The astonished sad look she had seen on his face haunted her. She just had to fix the mess she had got them into. It was vital to her. From him she got the human contact she desperately needed. She knew he needed her, too. How could she have been so foolish?

She went to Jack's in search of Edmund. He was there and reluctantly agreed to meet her outside so she could talk privately with him. She glanced over her shoulder as she went out the door. He was pulling a crumpled two dollar bill out of his tight blue jeans. Her heart melted as she watched the simple act. She was desperate to make him understand and prayed that he would take her back as Carol so readily had.

By this time she knew she couldn't live without Edmund. It became a matter of life and death that she convince him. He filled the void in the centre of her and kept her from feeling hollow. She needed him as much as she needed breath and blood.

She stood on Main Street waiting for him. The few minutes seemed like an eternity. Finally, he sauntered through the door, hands tucked into his jeans. His eyes no longer danced with mischief. His warm smile was gone. Pain tugged at Liz's heart strings. A big Greyhound bus was just pulling out. The roaring engine was making so much noise she wouldn't have been heard, if she did speak. As a matter of fact she was speechless so she was grateful for the bus. It passed and disappeared around the corner. The silence was deafening. Where should she start?

"I'm sorry," she muttered. It was hardly audible.

Edmund didn't say a word. He shuffled from one foot to the other as if he were bored. His indifference devastated her.

*Why doesn't he just yell at me or something and get it over with?*

She made another attempt to speak. Nothing would come out.

His head was bowed. His chin resting on his chest. He raised it slightly and glanced towards her. The look in his eyes crushed her. It was a look somewhere between pain and disgust. It nearly killed her. She longed for that familiar twinkle and that warm smile that ignited the part of her that had died so many years ago.

"I don't know how to explain," she said.

"What's to explain? You want Ben, go for it. Nuthin I can do." His eyes looked cold.

"I don't want Ben!" she said stomping her foot in frustration. "You don't understand."

"Oh I understand all right. I understand what my eyes see."

He took his hands out of his pockets, crossed his arms and looked into her eyes. His gaze was cool. She glanced back briefly, ashamed to look too long. But in that instant she saw a slight glimmer of hope. A little warmth still there for her. He couldn't hide it. It encouraged her to go on.

"I didn't want to go with Ben at all. I was afraid to say no to him. That's all it was. Honest."

"Oh, sure."

"I'm telling you the truth. Why won't you believe me? You're just being stubborn."

"I'm being stubborn. I'm not the one who did the wrong here."

"I didn't do anything wrong. I didn't even kiss Ben. He didn't even put his arm around me. He doesn't even like me. He loves Carol. He was just trying to make her jealous."

"Oh, and so you went along with it? Some kind of friend you are."

"I told you I was afraid to say no to him. Carol understands. Why can't you? I love you Edmund. I always have. I always will. We're special together."

"Yeah, right, that's why you went out with my best friend."

"Oh, what's the matter with you. Why do you have to be so stubborn? Why can't you understand?"

"Yeah, right, make me the bad guy."

"Edmund I don't know what else to say to you. I love you, and I'm sorry. I need you to forgive me. Ple-e-ase.

He stood with his head down kicking at a piece of loose concrete on the sidewalk. He wouldn't budge. He wouldn't speak. He wouldn't even look up.

Finally, out of frustration, Liz raised her voice, "Well, do you want to go with me or not?" She was at the end of her rope. She didn't know what else to do. He didn't want to give in. His inner turmoil was evident on his face. Shuffling his feet, kicking at the sidewalk, head down, he finally did answer reluctantly, "Yes, I do."

Liz grabbed him around the neck and kissed him warmly. He shyly returned her kiss.

The breech was mended, but Edmund was a little insecure. It took a while for him to completely trust Liz again. Liz was nervous too. She tried hard to show how much she loved him and to make him feel secure. She was with him every opportunity that she could be. She showered him with cards that professed her love. She promised faithfully she would never do anything like that again, and she kept her word. She even carved his initials in her upper arm with a razor blade to prove her bravery and her undying love for him.

Eventually, things went back to the way they had been between them. Liz was relieved and so was Edmund. He hadn't wanted to lose her anymore than she wanted to lose him. The rest of the summer was a dream come true. Liz had learned a valuable lesson. She would never betray her friends again, no matter how scared she was.

Ben and Edmund were best friends and so were Carol and Liz. So after the bridges were all mended the foursome ended up double-dating again.

Lazy days of summer swiftly swept into blustery days of winter. Liz was in town at Jack's restaurant with Edmund, Ben and Carol eating Chinese food when Ben said he wanted to get Liz and Carol home because he had to leave early in the morning to go to Toronto and look for work.

The incident with Ben and Liz left Edmund with a constant awareness that he could lose her so he was always reluctant to let her go home when it came time. Because it was still quite early, Edmund asked Liz to stay longer. He said that he would get her a ride home later as he knew some people who lived on the eleventh line about a mile from her place. He promised to walk her home from their house. Liz was as eager to stay as he was to have her stay so she agreed.

The Grayson's did give them a ride, but by the time they left the bar, loaded Edmund and Liz into the car, and headed into the country, a blizzard had blown in.

Winter blizzards in Ontario could blow up suddenly with such a force of wind that drifts four feet deep would soon block the side roads. The weather got so bad as they drove that night that when the

Grayson's pulled into their driveway there was no way they would let Edmund and Liz walk the mile to her place. Liz and Edmund knew they were right so they agreed to stay.

After the Grayson's showed them into a room off the kitchen, Liz and Edmund closed the door and once again wrapped themselves around each other for the comfort and love they both craved.

In the morning the sound of the ploughs scraping snow in huge piles beside the road woke them up. Liz shuddered at the sound. She knew the roads were cleared, but she didn't want to go home. She was afraid of what Alicia would say. She knew Alicia was not happy about her seeing Edmund and after the last overnight episode Liz was very concerned. She had got off easy that time, but she didn't know how far Alicia would be pushed. She was afraid of being parted from Edmund. She remembered her oath to herself not to suffer the emptiness ever again. She was very attached to him. Edmund had become her "family".

"I guess I better get you home," Edmund said, looking forlornly at Liz. He knew what that could mean.

"I'm not going home," Liz said, head cocked to the side, determination written all over her face.

"What do you mean? You have to go home."

No, I don't! If I go home you know what will happen. I'll be grounded again and probably for a lot longer this time. Besides my mother is looking for any excuse to separate us, and, Edmund, I just can't be away from you."

"Well, what can we do?"

"I don't know. I only know one thing I won't be parted from you again."

"Well we can't go to my house. Your parents would only find you there and make you go home."

Edmund 's brow wrinkled as he thought deeply. Liz reached over and put her hand on his arm and squeezed. She gazed at him with love in her eyes waiting for him to take charge.

Finally, Edmund looked up with a smile that warmed her heart. "I know, I have an uncle in Toronto. We could hitchhike there. We will have to wait until tomorrow though. I need to talk to my folks and get them to call him. By that time it will be too late to leave today. It gets dark early, and I don't want to hitchhike with you at night. It's too dangerous."

"What can we do until tomorrow?"

"Kenny's got a motel room just out of town. He'll be heading home soon. I'm sure he'll let us stay with him."

Kenny was an older friend of Edmund's who had stayed at the Grayson's as well. He called a cab, and they got a ride into town with him and went to his motel.

Kenny's place consisted of two large adjoining rooms, a kitchen/ sitting room with a large couch and a bedroom with a large double bed. Edmund and Liz stayed in the bedroom while Kenny bunked in the other room.

Very little planning went into their plot. Liz was nervous. She sat very still on the edge of the double bed, staring into space.

Edmund took her by the hand. "Are you alright? You don't look very happy."

Liz smiled faintly and squeezed his hand. "I am. I'm happy to be with you. It's just, it's just..."

"Are you afraid?"

"I'm not afraid to be with you. I've just never been away from my parents before. They will be really worried about me and never mind that, how will we live?"

"I'll get a job. There's lots of jobs in Toronto. My uncle said it's okay if we stay there until I find one."

"I know, it's just Mom and Dad. I don't want to hurt them. I feel like I'm being pulled apart. I love you Edmund. I want to be with you. I couldn't stand it if we had to be separated again. But do I have to hurt my parents to do that?"

"Well it seems to me that there is no other way. You know they don't care for me and after last night they are going to be ripping mad. I can guarantee it. I don't know Liz. There doesn't seem to be any other way. The decision is yours. I can go. My parents don't care, but whatever you decide is okay with me. I just want you to be happy."

"I want to be happy too. That means being with you. But I'm scared. I don't even know your uncle. My parents will be just sick about this. They aren't young any more. Oh, I wish Carol was here she would know what to do."

"I can go and get her."

"No, I don't want to be here alone with Kenny. I don't even know him."

"Oh, Kenny's okay. I've known him a long time, but if it makes you feel any better, I can get Kenny to go and get her."

"Carol wouldn't come to a motel with a guy she doesn't know. I know, I'll give Kenny the ring you gave me. Then she'll know for sure I'm here."

They sent Kenny and Carol came right away. She thought it would be best for Liz to go home and face the music. Almost as soon as the words were out of her mouth, someone knocked loudly on the door. Rap! Rap! Rap! The anger communicated by the vibrating door startled them all.

"Sh-sh-sh!" Liz put her finger to her lips, looking from Edmund to Carol, her eyes bugging out with fear. Kenny opened the door just a crack, concealing the girls' presence. Liz could hear the anger in her Mother's voice. Chills as cold as ice trickled down her spine.

"My daughter's in there," Alicia shouted, "I want her out *now*! We know she's in there," she repeated with fierce determination. "the cab driver told us."

"Uh, they've left," he said quickly shutting the door.

Safe for the moment, they had to think fast. Liz was torn in two, fraught with fear. She was confronted with two faces of fear. Fear of her mother's anger was ingrained in her. She thought of the times when Alicia's livid rage meant a beating. The other face, fear of losing Edmund, was more than she could bear. She had vowed she'd never be parted from him again. How could she live without her heart and soul? Edmund owned them.

Which way should she go? She was being ripped apart. She really wanted to obey her parents, but she wanted to ease that ever-gnawing, black void in the very centre of her that made her feel hollow, the emptiness that had plagued her all those years. The one that Edmund filled.

Minutes turned into a century, an eternity. What to do? Which way to go? Insanity!

Then Edmund took over. Nervously taking her hand, he said, "By the sounds of your mother's voice I think we'd better make a run for it."

Assailed with doubt, she reluctantly agreed. She let him make the decision. He was her cavalier.

As they opened the door, they spotted her father's light green '55 Chev parked in front of the motel.

"Run!" Edmund cried out as he grabbed her hand and took off across the field to the bush behind the motel. They ran together side by side. But not fast enough, hot on their heels was Allen. *Traitor!* Liz thought bitterly as she slipped in the snow, losing her footing. In a flash, Allen grabbed her arm just as she was about to fall.

"Keep going," she called to Edmund. He had stopped ten feet ahead and had looked back with a sad and confused look on his face.

Before Edmund could do anything Allen was dragging Liz back to the car.

She felt like the little turtle in the storybook her father had given her. She had shucked her shell and enjoyed the marvelous freedom; she had ridden the carousel, but now the thunderstorm loomed in the shape of her mother's rage.

It all happened so fast, but she caught a glimpse of a look in Allen's eyes. It was a look of confusion, of "sorry". In the clear thinking that sometimes comes in the midst of confusion, she felt empathy for him. Allen was caught too. He was the good boy. He was obedient to Alicia, but he knew what was in store for Liz, and he had outgrown his mean streak.

Hauled back by her arm to the car, Liz shrank as her mother came out of the passenger's side with a vengeance. The two years of Liz going against her grain had finally caught up to Alicia. She had been seething for months. She knew the only way to stop Liz was to beat her silly. She had come to a boiling point, and that's exactly what she was about to do. She would make that girl conform come hell or highwater.

All clear thinking ceased as Liz was gripped in a vice of fear. She could see that Alicia was crazed with anger. In one quick move Alicia grabbed Liz by the hair and yanked. Chunks of hair ripped loose, leaving Liz's eyes watering and her scalp throbbing. Alicia doubled up her fist and drove it right into Liz's face. Through the pain Liz was conscious of blood dripping down from her nose, warm and sticky, to her lips. Then she was pushed head first into the back seat of the car by her mother's rage. Alicia was screaming, but her words were not penetrating deep enough to register in Liz's frightened mind.

Through the frenzy, Liz totally lost sight of Edmund. Not only had she lost sight of him, she had lost him. She knew he was gone as surely as she knew that she would never be the same again.

All the way home, her mother and father bantered back and forth about what should be done about her, as though she wasn't even there. That was the way it always was, as though she wasn't even there. John felt bad about what was happening to Liz, but being a timid man, he was as frightened of Alicia's rage as Liz was.

Her Father parked the car in the yard at home. Liz was the first to get out wanting to retreat to her room to lick her wounds and to pine for Edmund in private.

Thud! Thud! Thud! Her Mother's heavy black purse connected with her head with several well-directed blows.

"Get out of my sight before I kill you!" Alicia screamed.

Renewed terror spurred Liz on and she took flight as fast as her weak legs would carry her. Through the kitchen, up the big flight of stairs until she found refuge in the bathroom with the door locked securely.

She heard rather than saw the wood splintering as the door was ripped open. She saw rather than heard the screws being pulled apart from the door. Sheer terror gripped her as Alicia lunged through the door grabbing her arm and beating her at the same time with a large stick. She scrambled away, crawling across the floor, and cowered in the corner with her arms up over her head to protect herself.

"You'll do as I say or else. No more hanging around with riff raff. I'll have my way if it kills me."

Whack! Whack! Whack! Would it ever stop? Then all of a sudden, quiet. It was finally over. Her mother was gone. When did it stop? *What's this? I'm all wet. How did I get wet?* She looked down at her skirt and realized to her horror that she had wet herself at some time during the beating, but was totally unaware as to when. She had been so terrified that the muscles in her bladder had failed to work. In shame, she skulked to her room to change her clothes.

Liz shared her room with her older sister, Jane, who had moved back home because of a broken marriage. Now Jane was embroiled in the problem between Liz and Alicia. Their angry voices carried up the stairs to Liz's ears.

"You can't do that!" Jane yelled.

"Oh yes I can. I'm going to call Dr. Blackman tomorrow and make an appointment for her to have an internal to see if she's still a virgin. If she's not that boy is going to pay big time. I will have him arrested." Alicia shrieked.

"Mother don't do that, please. She's only 16. It would be so humiliating for her. Why don't you just ask her if anything happened?"

Liz ran to the top of the stairs sobbing and shouting, "I *am* still a virgin! I'll hate you forever, mama, if you take me to the doctor for that! I love Edmund, mama, and he loves me. It's not like that you don't understand. You never do and you don't even try."

The voices from the kitchen died down immediately and Liz skulked back to her room.

Liz never meant to be bad. She just wanted to be where she was loved. She and Edmund had not been intimate, at least not physically. Theirs was a relationship of soul-mates. Edmund filled the void. Her mother *didn't* understand.

When Alicia cooled down, she brought Liz a bowl of hot milk and bread for her supper. Liz ate it even though she didn't want it. She was afraid of making Alicia angry again. She didn't need hot milk and bread. She needed Edmund.

Alicia never did take Liz to the doctor which was a great relief to her. She would have been devastated. She was grounded for a year. She was forbidden to ever see or even talk to Edmund again.

This was worse than the beating. Better to take her breath away than to deprive her of him. Edmund's heart must have broken. He phoned time and again. Her mother wouldn't let her speak to him. He would get others to phone for him, but to no avail. Liz was completely forbidden to talk on the phone to anyone. She was not even allowed to see Carol, Darlene, or Sheryl at lunch time anymore. Liz was only to go to school and straight home again. No more show night. Liz had won a battle or two, but Alicia won the war.

Liz cried and cried for Edmund, but she was too young to do anything about it. She felt herself too weak to face another beating even for Edmund. Alicia had beaten him out of her.

The carousel stopped. The faces of the carousel horses turned sad. They halted their magnificent ride. Would Liz ever see Edmund again?

# Chapter 6
# Broken-Hearted Melody

Liz's spirit was broken from the bathroom beating. They say that life's events change a person. Liz was certainly a different person. Not only that, she had that void, that hollow feeling, back inside again, but now she was afraid to do anything about it. She just suffered with it. She would lie on her bed hugging her pillow trying to make the pain go away. It would gnaw at her. Visions of her father and her together would eat her up. Visions of her and Edmund together were impossible to bear. She had sworn when she was parted from Edmund before that she would never go through it again, but her determination was shattered. The wild adventurous side of her had suffered a death blow.

Without Edmund, Liz had to restructure her life. At first it was unbearable. Then she found herself spending a lot more time with her family. She was still an outsider, but getting to know Jane was fun. There was twelve years between them which meant that Jane had been married before Liz had started school. Now 28 years old, Jane had returned home with two daughters, Lois age 7 and Debra, age 5.

Of all Liz's brothers and sisters, Jane and she looked most alike. They were like two peas in a pod. The budding of their relationship began when Jane returned to her parents' home. She became an ally for Liz. She was a lot younger than John and Alicia, and she was full of life, not solemn like Allen.

The summer of 1960 was a time of healing for both Jane and Liz. Losing Edmund was like a death. Liz grieved for him. She desperately needed something to fill her hours. Jane, hurting over a broken marriage, needed distraction, also. Their common bond of woe laced them together as did their favourite songs, Sarah Vaughn's "Broken-Hearted Melody", Johnny Mathis' "Twelfth of Never", and the Fleetwood's "Come Softly To Me". Tunes that tapped into their innermost feelings seemed to help somewhat.

When Alicia complained that the laundry was just too much work for her with Jane and her two girls home, Jane and Liz would go to the new laundromat in town. That in itself was not terribly exciting but Jane always made it an event. She seemed to make everything fun. She was always joking around and laughing. When Jane pulled Liz's angora sweater out of the dryer, and it was the size of a baby sweater they just roared until the tears ran down their cheeks. Liz wasn't even upset about her sweater.

She missed Edmund desperately, but Jane being there was like a buffer. She was the only one who provided relief. She took Liz's side. She became her friend. When her mother and Allen were engaged in deep conversation, Jane would come to Liz's side with the Eatons catalogue and they would talk about what clothes they would like to buy. Jane would let Liz borrow her best clothes from the new wardrobe she had acquired from her new job. When Alicia became irritated by Liz and picked on her, Jane came to Liz's defence. It lit a spark of hope inside Liz. Finally, she had someone on her side. She was not alone anymore. They did everything together. They shared a room, and every Saturday they would curl each other's hair, paint each others nails and just hang out and do girl things. Liz grew to love Jane. Of course Jane would never be able to take Edmund's place, but she was, indeed, a buffer.

Jane did help, but there was still a great sadness in Liz as though something had died. Her life had become an echo of the song, "Broken-Hearted Melody".

When she wasn't busy with Jane, she was listless. She didn't sleep very well, she tossed and turned. Then when she finally did sleep she had terrible nightmares, nightmares of being alone, being abandoned, being unable to take care of herself. They haunted her. She lost her appetite and started to lose weight as well. The emptiness was all-consuming. It was like an addiction. She could hardly think of anything else.

But she was afraid to do anything about the deep, black void inside her that was eating her up. Doing something about it would involve Edmund. He was the only one who had ever made the pain go away. But since the beating, she was too terrified to even think about seeing him.

Once Willy Morris approached her in town to relay a message from Edmund that he needed to see her real bad. She wanted to see him too, but she quickly walked away from Willy in fear that somebody would see her with him and tell Alicia.

She felt incomplete, half a person. She craved for the day when she would be whole again, when she would be old enough to be with Edmund. The big fear was would he wait for her, the even bigger fear was *could* she wait for him?

# Part II
# THE IRISH ROVER

## Chapter 7
## The Tender Trap

The spring and summer of 1960 passed very slowly for Liz, but time heals all wounds, so the pain of not being able to see Edmund subsided somewhat, but Liz still couldn't forget him.

And Edmund, having tried unsuccessfully several times to see Liz, finally gave up trying. Heartbroken, he went back to his uncle's in Toronto to seek work because he couldn't bear to run into Liz and not be able to be with her. He still loved her, and she still loved him, but she took his leaving as a sign that he had given up on her. After he left she was beyond grief, so when fall arrived, and school started up again, she was relieved. She opted to take a commercial course. She decided to throw herself into her schooling as her social life had been terminated. She hoped it would help her get over Edmund and the all-consuming emptiness.

Then one brisk fall day Liz's sister Jane came home and said, "You should see the new boy in town, is he a looker."

Liz knew Jane was only trying to cheer her up so she nodded her head slightly to be polite, but she really wasn't interested. She was still pining for Edmund.

A few days later Darlene and Liz were walking downtown on their lunch hour from school. Through a store window, Dar caught sight of the most handsome boy she'd ever seen.

"That's got to be him," she said as she grabbed Liz's arm.

"Who?" Liz questioned.

"The boy that all the girls in town are talking about."

"He must be the one Jane was telling me about."

Liz *was* impressed. He *was* good-looking with his Irish eyes, green as emeralds, and his coal black hair -- black Irish. He had to be at least 6 feet tall. But impressed or not, she just wasn't interested. Edmund still filled all her thoughts. She turned around, stuck out her tongue at the boy and made an ugly face. He accepted the challenge.

At home a few days later, the phone rang.

"Hello, yes this is Burgess's. Who? I'm afraid she's not allowed to date. Why, yes I think that would be just fine. Saturday would be good. I'm sure Liz won't mind," crooned Alicia. She hung up the phone.

"I wouldn't mind what?" Liz asked as she looked up from her books.

"Oh, that was Brian O'Shea on the phone."

"Who?"

"Brian O'Shea. You know that new family that moved into town from Toronto. His father is a big boss at the Department of Highways. I think they are quite well off. It would be a good opportunity for you to get to know some of the better families."

"What do you mean?"

"He asked if he could come over and see you Saturday. I told him that would be fine."

"*You did what*? How do you know I want to see him."

"I think it's a good idea. You've been moping around here long enough. He comes from a good family, and I don't think you should pass up this opportunity."

"But I'm grounded!"

"I know. That's why I wouldn't allow him to take you out. He's coming here on Saturday and that's that."

Liz hung her head; she was devastated. How could she be unfaithful to Edmund. He was gone, but her heart was still his. She knew she wouldn't be able to get out of seeing Brian, though, because her mother was determined, and she knew her mother's determination. Not only that, she had lost all of her spunk since the beating. Lately, she was doing just what Alicia told her. So she resigned herself to seeing Brian, but it would be nothing like her relationship with Edmund. Nothing ever could be.

The carousel was turning again but not for Liz. Brian would not rest until he had her. He showed up right on time Saturday. He was as polite as could be. Her parents were impressed. Liz was impressed to some degree. She thought he must really want to see her, if he was willing to come to her house to court her and he *was* very handsome. She was polite.

A boy from a well-to-do family was exactly what Alicia wanted for Liz. Now, Liz had someone that her mother approved of. In the beginning Liz's heart was elsewhere, but Edmund was gone, and Liz thought that he had given up on her. He hadn't, but she had no way of knowing that. So, reluctantly, she convinced herself to try to get along with Brian.

He spent the fall of 1960 and winter of 1961 courting her at home. Although she was constantly comparing Brian to Edmund, Liz grew to care for him somewhat. She could never give her heart completely though because it still belonged to Edmund. Nonetheless, she appreciated the effort Brian made to see her.

Under the close supervision of her parents, they visited in the big front yard. He would entertain them with acrobatics. He was very well built and muscular and could flip frontwards and backwards all over the lawn. He played with her nieces, paid attention to her grandmother and respected her parents. He was courting the whole family.

Coming from a similar family background to Liz's, his parents thought their relationship was great. He was from a family of three boys and three girls, like hers. His dad worked in Toronto, like hers. His mom stayed home and looked after kids, like hers. The families were perfectly matched and Alicia was thrilled.

Even though Liz still loved Edmund, a little part of her was proud to be seen with Brian. Every girl in town had wanted to date him including Darlene. Every girl that is, except Carol. Carol, always very perceptive, knew he wasn't right for Liz. She cringed when Liz showed her the friendship ring Brian had given her, but she remained silent.

All Liz knew was she didn't want to be alone anymore. Edmund was gone, and the emptiness was unbearable. Brian was fun, outgoing and very energetic. Her mother liked him. He seemed to have good work habits. He was working for Spence's Lumber Company. He was polite, prompt, and reliable. So Alicia relaxed her discipline and once again, Liz was allowed to date. She was sure that Brian cared for her, and she tried very hard to care for him. It wasn't anything like being with Edmund, but it was all she was allowed.

They double-dated with Brian's brother, Wayne, and his fiancee, Ona. As good looking as Brian was, Wayne was not. He sported one solid bushy eye brow that went straight across his forehead and squishy lips that looked as though they had been inherited from a mackerel. Ona was a little Polish girl with the same kind of lips. They made a perfect couple. Wayne's disposition matched his looks so there was always tension between him and Brian. But even though there was a sibling rivalry between them, they still double-dated because Wayne had a car and Brian did not. Brian's father could well have afforded to buy him one, but he had worked hard to get where he was and felt the boys should do the same. Someone else's car always meant that Brian and Liz automatically sat in the back seat. Alicia assumed that double-dating meant a chaperone. Not so. The back seat of Wayne's car became the tryst spot for their love-making.

Wayne and Ona were making out in the front seat, so Liz and Brian followed suit in the back. Brian was much more experienced and bolder than Edmund had been, and Liz found it ironic that she was not allowed to see Edmund, and yet Alicia trusted her with Brian. So Liz, in her own small way, was getting even with Alicia by allowing Brian to go as far as he wanted, short of the actual sex act. Liz wanted to save that for marriage.

At first, it was just kissing, then heavy necking and petting. With the close contact with Brian, Liz became infatuated. She thought that she was in love. She thought Brian loved her.

She was lonely. She was still in love with Edmund. Without realizing it, she was trying to replace him with Brian. She tried to rid herself of that horrible empty feeling. Brian did fill the void somewhat; the carousel was turning, but the horses weren't smiling.

Brian was nothing like Edmund. All Brian was thinking of was *How can I have my way with Elizabeth?* instead of *How can I make her happy.* As a result they rarely talked seriously, but Brian made sure they did neck and pet seriously. Because of their closeness Liz thought all was well so she was shocked when a side of Brian that she had not seen before came to light at the Beeton Fall Fair.

Beeton, about 15 miles northwest of Bradford, was the hub of activity in September. It held the largest fall fair in the county. Skipping school, Liz and a lot of other students hitchhiked to the gala event. It was a yearly occurrence that they wouldn't have missed for the world. The teachers just turned a blind eye because over half the school was missing.

Liz was thrilled when Brian took the day off work to accompany them. When they got there, he showed off his talents by playing all the games. He was good at them, and he won big prizes for her. She was impressed.

Then at a ball-pitch booth Brian tossed the ball and knocked down all the wooden milk bottles. "Yes! You did it again!" Liz squealed with delight and stood waiting with wide eyes to see which prize the tough, dirty-looking carny guy was going to give them. He reached into a big box and pulled out a pink plastic comb.

Liz stuck her hand out to take it with an astonished look on her face. Then Brian grabbed her arm with a death grip. She looked up at him, and his eyes made her heart quicken with fear. She had never seen such a look in anyone's eyes before. His eyes were intense and demonic. She watched spellbound as he glared at the tough carny guy who instantly threw the comb back in the box and reached up to the top shelf for a big stuffed panda.

Was Brian someone she should be afraid of? True, the carousel was turning, but she caught a glimpse of the horse's faces. They were grotesque and evil looking, shivers ran down her spine. It was only a glimpse, though, and the image disappeared when Brian put his arm around her and smiled sweetly putting the panda in her hands. The rest of the day was fun, but Liz was left with a nagging doubt that put a black mark on the relationship.

After the incident at the fair, Liz found herself thinking more of Edmund again. She thought she was over him, but when she heard that he was living with a girl named Gail, and they were having a baby, it hurt more than she could say. Edmund, having heard that Liz was dating Brian, had totally given up and with a broken heart tried to go on with his life. She had only dated Brian because she thought Edmund had given up on her. The sad thing was she had no way of knowing that he hadn't.

With that sorrowful news her heart felt a sad longing, but with genuine caring she wished him well. She did love him, but she had to go on as well. Would the star-crossed lovers ever meet again?

Fall leafed its way along and after the mishap at the fair Brian showered Liz with all kinds of attention and affection and won her over again. Then came October 10, 1961 -- Wayne and Ona were getting married. No one was more surprised than Liz that Ona picked her to be her maid of honour. Liz was all caught up in the thrill of the wedding preparations. She wore a strapless, yellow net and nylon evening gown. The ensemble was completed with brown velvet heels, elbow-length gloves of the same colour, and a brown pill box hat with a veil. Looking so grown up, Liz felt like a princess in the gown with its shirred bodice and voluminous belled net skirt.

After the ceremony the wedding party drove to Ona's parent's house in River Drive Park where the reception was being held. Brian climbed out of the driver's seat went around the car and took Liz's hand to help her out. At the same time Wayne and Ona climbed out of the back seat. Ona's beautiful long lacy white gown ballooned out as she pried herself through the car door.

"Run! Papa's going to throw the whiskey," she cried, just as her father threw a large glass of whiskey up in the air over top of them. Ona and Liz giggled as they raced across the front lawn holding hands with their men and darting between drops of whiskey.

This was Liz's first experience with a Polish wedding. The air was filled with gaiety as the accordians played lively polka music, and everyone from the oldest to the youngest bounced around the room to the beat of the music, clad in beautiful bright colours. Liz's heart beat fast with the excitement. Everyone was drinking even the youngsters were sipping a little wine. Liz had not touched alcohol since her bad experience with Ben. She was afraid of it.

Ona's papa grabbed her empty glass and laughing with his big belly shaking, reached over top of her and poured her a glass of whiskey. "Come on everyone toast the bride; everyone toast my little Ona."

Liz pushed the glass away.

"Come on the bridesmaid must toast the bride."

She squeezed her eyes shut, took the glass to her lips, tipped it up and swallowed. Fire burned all the way down her throat and then it was there again, that beautiful warm glow that she had enjoyed with Ben before it got her into trouble.

Once she started there was no stopping. The music pulsed. She danced. She drank. She laughed until she slowly sunk to the floor waving a chicken leg around in the air, slurring the words, "Thish ish the best shicken I ever ate." Then it was lights out.

Brian's mother was afraid of what Liz's parents would say if they knew, and feeling responsible for her, she quickly whisked her out of there. Brian carried her out, and Liz awoke to find herself at the O'Sheas' big rambling farm house on Highway 88 just west of Bradford.

Brian carried her upstairs to his bed, and left her there; the room was swimming. Then he and his mother rushed up the stairs with a large glass filled with a white liquid. Liz was so woozy that she was too disoriented to resist as Brian and his mother insisted that she drink the brew. Obeying their instructions, she drank down a glass of cooking oil topped with a touch of milk. Liz gagged and bolted from Brian's arms that were holding her upright on the bed. She held her hand over her mouth as she raced for the bathroom. She didn't make it. She spewed white cooking oil all over the floor and the walls. She immediately swore off alcohol of any kind.

Liz and Brian's courtship carried on, and after Wayne and Ona's wedding they made plans to marry as soon as Liz turned eighteen. Her engagement to Brian brought with it a freedom that she had never experienced before. Finally, she was free from Alicia's restrictive shell, but little did she know that another shell would soon weigh heavy.

Then in June of 1962 Brian was laid off from the lumber company. With wedding plans in the air the young couple needed household furnishings and a place to live, so the job search was on for both of them. Liz had finished her fourth year in high school, and her typing skills were excellent by this time. Brian's mother heard of a job opening in town for a clerk typist. Liz was thrilled when she applied for the job and got it. She went to work for the Gallinas who had a small magazine company. She was seventeen, impressionable, and feeling very grown up.

Liz came to love Mrs. Gallina who was the office manager. She was a feisty little thing. She was the tiniest woman Liz had ever seen and her face was very wrinkled. As a matter of fact, she looked like a wrinkle dog. She had very sparse blue-gray hair that was permed neatly and big round blue eyes that emanated a warmth and kindness that went right to her heart.

In spite of her tiny little frame, she would take on the most challenging jobs. She came to Liz's house to visit one summer evening, and while she was getting out of her car she spotted Liz's dad roto-tilling the garden. She chased after him waving her arms and yelling, "Let me try that, let me try that." With her 85 lb. frame she grabbed hold of the handles and Liz bent over double with laughter as the roto-tiller dragged Mrs. Gallina halfway across the yard.

Not only did Liz come to love Mrs. Gallina, she grew to love the job as well. It gave her a wonderful sense of accomplishment. She was bright, and she learned quickly. Mrs. Gallina trained her and became very fond of her. And not only did Liz love the job and Mrs. Gallina, it meant she could pay her share of the furniture expenses.

Brian landed a good job as well building cottages in northern Ontario. He had to be away for the summer, but they desperately needed the money to get married. Although Liz missed him, they kept their relationship going with letters. But being apart proved to have a down-side for her. She started to feel that emptiness inside again.

With Brian away she felt lonely and bored. So one hot summer evening she decided to go to the Holland Theatre by herself. It had been a long time since she had gone with Allen on Saturday nights and sneaked out to meet Edmund.

She settled down in the thick velvet seat waiting for "The Grapes of Wrath" to start. As she munched on her popcorn her mind reflected on the days when she had been so full of life and risked sneaking out to see Edmund. She smiled to herself remembering the fun they'd had. Then her mind drifted to Edmund. When Brian wasn't around Edmund's image always sneaked in. It irritated her because she was going to marry Brian, and Edmund was with someone else so what was the point? Some days she just didn't understand herself. She shook her head trying to shake the thought away. Just then a young man spoke startling her back to reality. "Is anyone sitting here?" he asked.

"Uh, no," Liz said feeling a little apprehensive. She would have preferred to sit by herself, but she certainly couldn't restrict anyone from sitting anywhere they wanted to. In the dim pre-movie lights she could see he was rather attractive with his blonde curls tumbling down on his forehead, his square jaw and wide eyes. He slumped down in the seat beside her. Liz wriggled in her seat feeling a little uncomfortable with his close proximity. He glanced over towards her and drank in her dark hair and fawn eyes.

"The name's Olly," he said as he stuck out his hand to shake hers. Liz gave him a cool gaze and ignored his hand. Looking very embarrassed, he slowly pulled his hand back. Liz felt bad and wished she had taken his extended hand.

"My name's Liz," she said trying to make up for being rude. He was foreign, and his accent made it obvious he hadn't been in the country very long. Liz assumed he was another lonely transient worker. She felt empathy for his loneliness. But before they could say anymore the lights were dimmed and the show started.

As Liz watched the movie, especially the love scenes, she became very aware of Olly's aura. She could sense that he was attracted to her. His energy filled the air and surrounded her. So when he reached his arm across the back of her seat she didn't move, and before she could stop him, he gathered her in his arms and kissed her. The worst of it was she returned his kiss. It was warm and enticing. She was enjoying his attention and affections, but thoughts were whirling around at top speed in her head. *What's going on? How did this happen? What's wrong with me? I'm engaged to be married in the fall. This is not okay.* The carousel was turning of its own accord. She was puzzled by her behaviour. It was as though something worked inside her beyond her control. Her mind knew it was wrong, but her need to fill the emptiness wouldn't let her stop. She didn't move from where she was sitting. She just stayed there returning his kisses.

Then her mind battled between being decent and giving her heart what it craved. She thought she would go crazy. After the movie was over she left the theatre feeling like a traitor. She took the bus home and walked from the highway in the dark, crying quietly. *What's the matter with me? I feel like a real Jezebel, but I'm not. I'm a decent person. Aren't I?* On the one hand she knew she was a decent, loyal person. On the other hand, she was driven with an insatiable need. She didn't understand what was happening to her.

The truth was that she just didn't love Brian. She didn't know it. Her heart still belonged to Edmund, just as it still belonged to her papa. She had lost them both. Puzzled with her behaviour and plagued with guilt, she never went to the theatre alone again.

So when Brian came home halfway through the summer, she was relieved. She knew she would behave. The subliminal message that she was telling herself was that she wanted a turtle shell of protection to keep her in line. She didn't trust herself to be free. She was too wild. She was glad he was back in spite of the job loss. He told her he quit because he had missed her so much he couldn't stand it. She felt flattered. The truth of the matter was he had been fired for mouthing off at the boss.

But in spite of Brian losing his job they still enjoyed the summer because Jane met a new beau, Gord Bowman, who owned a 1959 red and white Ford Continental Convertible. It was quite a car. The foursome double-dated often and basked in the warm wind and sunshine as they breezed down the road on the wings of frivolity on the soft leather seats of Gord's new car.

One of their weekend excursions took them to Wasaga Beach on the shores of Georgian Bay. "Hey let's rent a boat," Brian chimed.

"Great idea," Gord said.

"Wow, I've never ridden in a motor boat before," Liz said, all excited.

"Never? You're in for a treat," Brian said as he grabbed her around the waist and hugged her.

They sped down Lamont Creek with the throttle full speed ahead. The sun sparkled like diamonds on the surface of the river. The water sprayed up making mini rainbows as the front of the boat lifted. Liz was thrilled.

"Look, a swinging rope bridge!" Brian said as he pointed high overhead. "Let's pull the boat over and climb the stairs up to it and go across."

"Uh, I don't know," Liz said, apprehensively. "I'm scared of heights."

"Nothing to it. I'll be with you," Brian said.

"Yeah come on, Liz, I'll be there too." Jane said, full of adventure.

"Okay, but promise you won't shake it," Liz said, looking into Brian's eyes.

He grinned a wicked grin. "Promise!" she repeated.

"I promise," he said rolling his eyes.

They moored the boat and headed up the stairs with everyone running two steps at a time, that is everyone except Liz, she dragged behind.

"Come on Liz. Where's your adventurous spirit?" Brian yelled back over his shoulder.

"It died some time ago," Liz yelled back, jokingly.

The four of them headed across the bridge with Gord and Jane in the lead. The bridge shook eerily from side to side with Brian and Gord's huge frames. Gord was even taller and heavier than Brian with his six-foot four inch, 240 lbs. Liz was feeling squeamish and beginning to perspire. "Don't walk so fast. It's shaking," she yelled as she grasped Brian's hand tightly. They were 50 feet above the river.

All of a sudden Brian, pulled his hand loose from Liz's, turned and grabbed her around her back with one arm, bent over and with his other arm behind her knees he scooped her up and swung her over the side threatening to drop her. His eyes had that demon look in them again.

Liz screamed frantically. The only thing that kept her from a fall into the deep murky water below was the sheer strength of his arms.

Jane whirled around and taking charge, she yelled, "Put her down -- right now!" He did.

That incident ended their double-dating with Jane and Gord.

Jane now sided with Carol in thinking that Brian was not right for Liz, and she refused to be in his company. She tried to talk Liz out of marrying him. She suggested that Liz go and live with her sister Joy in Toronto. She could have some freedom, look around a little, and experience what it would be like to be on her own for a while. Thinking about the independence, Liz was almost convinced to go. Jane reasoned with her that if her and Brian's love was strong enough they could still get married at a later date. She became convinced.

When Liz mentioned it to Brian, she was totally unprepared for his reaction. He exploded and shouted that he didn't want to wait. He accused her of not loving him. The weight of her shell became unbelievably heavy, but she was afraid of displeasing him. Then she reflected on the bridge incident. Every once in a while, Brian would do something strange like that. Should she be frightened of him? She was sure she was in love with him or was it a habit? Anyway she was going to marry him. She had given her word, and she always kept her word. Edmund was with someone else so it didn't matter to her any more. So she continued to ignore Brian's strange quirks and the wedding plans were a "go". The carousel was turning, but the horses' faces were very sad, and Liz was turning a blind eye to them.

Brian kept Liz isolated from other people as much as he could in order to keep her blinded. As a result she lapsed in her friendships with Carol, Darlene and Sheryl. Then Sheryl met Brad Peterson, and they became a match. Brad was as handsome as Brian, and Sheryl was eager to show him off. So she made a special effort to contact Liz. Brian reluctantly agreed to double-date with them. The foursome spent the rest of that summer together with Brian keeping Liz busy and happy while waiting for the big day.

Then near the end of the summer the Gallinas moved their business to Toronto. It was a very exciting move for Liz. Now she was working on the 22nd floor of the Daily Star Building. When they were just kids Liz and Annie, her "little girl" friend from Scarboro, had daydreamed about being secretaries in downtown Toronto. They would imagine going to lunch together. Now, the reality was that Liz would have lunch downtown at the Sword Tavern with Annie quite often. It was a very swanky place. Annie was single and liked it that way. She was very sophisticated and independent. She wanted to travel the world before she settled down and couldn't understand why Liz wanted to get married at such a young age. Annie almost convinced Liz to wait.

Liz started to feel fulfilled at her job. She was a country girl in the middle of cosmopolitan Toronto. Now, she was in conflict; the wedding was set for September 8th, and she was enjoying her independence in a big city. With this new experience her eyes started to open a little, and at times she wondered if she would do better on her own, without Brian.

However, he fed her addiction. When she was with him she was euphoric, high. When she wasn't, she was empty, sad. Only once in a while did she get a glimpse of the ugly side of her addiction.

There was the incident at the fair when he got that frightening demon-look in his eyes. There was the incident at the bridge when he was so insensitive to her fear. There was the explosive angry fight when she suggested that they wait for a while to get married. All of these were clues to the downside of him, but she subconsciously chose not to see them, not to heed them.

She was on a carousel spinning out of control. She was dizzy, whirling in circles with no way to get off. She didn't even realize that she should get off. It was a one-way ride -- a one-way ride to disaster. She had brief glimpses of the surrounding scenery -- satisfying independence, self-esteem and confidence. As soon as she turned her head for a better focus of the opportunities, Brian's large frame would loom up, blocking her clear vision. The view was too fuzzy to seek actively. She accepted less than she deserved.

The wedding was set, the way chosen; there was no turning back now, no turning aside.

# Chapter 8
# A Tiny Gold Yoke

Liz turned 18 on September 2, 1962; Brian and she were married on the 8th. It was a small wedding with just close friends and family. Presided over by a minister, they tied the knot in her parent's living room. The short ceremony was followed by a small reception with baked goods and wedding cake. That was it; yoked by a tiny band of gold.

Liz's brother Jack and his wife drove in from Toronto for the wedding so they drove Brian and Liz to their new home in the city. Because Brian had just started a new job at Dunham Bush Refrigeration he didn't think it would be wise to ask for time off so the couple spent their wedding night alone in their luxury apartment. Their love nest was neatly filled with their new black leather sofa, chair and ottoman, white rug, stereo, smoked glass and brass coffee and end tables, coloured television, oak dining room suite and their king size bed with matching dressers so Liz was pleased, even though they couldn't go on a honeymoon.

She was a nervous young bride but yet filled with desire. She went into the nicely tiled white bathroom to change into her lacy white peignoir while Brian stripped down and crawled into bed. She checked herself in the mirror. Her makeup was perfect. Her hair looked a little dry, but it was styled nicely in an updo. She was satisfied as she admired herself in the full length mirror. The peignoir hugged her hour-glass figure, leaving little to the imagination.

She entered the bedroom and smiled sweetly at Brian who was laying with his hands behind his head on the bed. The blankets were pulled up to his waist. She admired his upper torso. His arms were thick and muscular and the mass of black hair on his chest pleased her. She sat on the edge of the bed and started to run her finger tips gently across his chest, then looked into his eyes.

But his eyes were cold. Fear prickled up her spine as he grabbed her wrist in a death grip and twisted her arm behind her, revealing the scar of Edmund's initials. "What's this on your arm?" he sneered. Then he pushed her hard onto her back on the bed. "W-what are you doing?" she said, her voice quaking.

He grabbed the neck of her gown and ripped it right down the front. Liz lay back like a frightened pup with her knees locked tightly together. He pried her legs apart with his knee, pinching the tender skin on her inner thigh. Liz squirmed and shrieked, "Stop it Brian! What's got into you?"

He clasped one hand over her mouth to shut her up and thrust himself into her with such a force that her head banged against the head board. Her eyes bugged out as a searing hot pain cut through her lower body instantly bringing tears to her eyes. She tried to scream, but his hand was cupped too tightly over her mouth. She winced with the pain as he continued, finally satisfying himself. Heart broken, she sobbed as she lay curled up in a ball. He left the room and returned with a razor blade in his hand.

"What's the matter with you?" he said, sneering to her shocked and disappointed face. "I waited all those years for you. What did you expect? Now you're mine and you'll wear my initials on your leg." He sat on her middle and carved his initials in her upper leg while she screamed in pain. Then he got up, grabbed a blanket and a pillow and headed for the couch. "I'm not going to listen to that snivelling all night," he said and disappeared around the corner.

The day after they were married, Liz woke up with a total stranger. He was so different, or was he? Images of his previous strange behaviours filed through her mind, and she longed to go back to the safety of her parents' home, back to her safe, protective shell.

The day before the wedding Liz had her hair permed by a novice hairdresser. The girl had left the perm solution in too long and burnt Liz's beautiful chestnut hair. So with her dry hair and red eyes from her dreadful night of crying she looked a sight. Not only did she feel lonely, used and abused, she felt ugly as well.

This was her state when Brian asked her to go to the bank to open a joint account. She really didn't want to go, but Brian insisted. As they walked through the door, she kept her head bowed in shame.

Then when she glanced up and saw the teller, she felt even worse. The teller was a petite, pretty little thing and right under Liz's nose Brian began to flirt with her. His green eyes flashed; the girl responded. *What more?* Liz thought. She felt awful. She wanted to cry with her burnt frizzy hair and her battered feelings.

Liz was too ashamed to tell anyone what had happened to her. She stayed with Brian in their beautiful apartment, but she locked him out of the bedroom for the next week. As time passed though Brian turned on his charm and wormed his way back in. He calmed down and returned to normal, but Liz was frightened of him and kept her distance emotionally. As a result she was again feeling very lonely and empty.

A couple of months after the wedding Brian had some friends over from work. He brought home a 24 pak of Labatt's Blue with him. Liz had sworn off alcohol since Wayne and Ona's wedding, but because Brian started to berate her in front of everyone, she talked herself into drinking some beer in the hopes of getting that warm glow that made her feel so good. It worked! After only two beers she felt very confident. This feeling was in complete contrast with how she felt ever since she married Brian. She had lost what little confidence she had gained from working out on her own. It was slowly eroded by Brian. She began to think she was very ugly and unattractive as the distance between them became an unbridgeable gap.

As the evening ensued Liz became engaged in deep conversation with David, a congenial young man from Brian's plant. She was feeling terrific for the first time in a long time. Was it the beer? Or was it the heady feeling of being considered intelligent and interesting enough to be good company. So thoroughly engrossed were they that she failed to notice that everyone else had gone and they were now alone in the living room.

"Brian must have crashed in the bedroom," she said as she concealed a yawn with the back of her hand.

"Looks like it. Sure is quiet in here except for the music playing."

"I guess the others couldn't keep up with us," she said, suddenly aware of the seclusion.

Then she became very aware of the dim light from the solitary orange lamp. It cast a warm luminous glow in the room. The lyrics from the stereo, "Only love can break a heart, only love can mend it again", struck a resonating chord in Liz's heart.

She shifted her position nervously on the couch as she looked across at him. David was sitting on the hassock, his long legs stretched out in front of him, She noticed his well-fitting jeans. Her eyes travelled from his jeans to his willow-green shirt and then to his face. She hadn't noticed it before but his eyes matched his shirt. She liked green eyes. They were lighter than Brian's but green, nonetheless. He had a smooth mouth, slightly curved up at each side. His light brown hair was tousled in loose curls over his forehead with the sides combed back.

She shifted again as the beer and the man gave her that heady feeling, charging her with warm desire. When her eyes met his the circle was complete. Eyes rivetted, they gently moved toward each other as the room slowly began to spin, the carousel carrying them along. Their lips met in a crushing, searing, hot kiss.

Then just as suddenly as it happened, they recoiled from each other.

"I guess I'd better go," David said shyly.

"Y-yeah," Liz stuttered, still feeling the kiss lingering on her lips. "That's probably best."

It was happening to her again just like at the theatre with Olly, but this time she felt justified. Brian had verbally abused her in front of everyone earlier in the evening. David had seen it all and was sensitive to her needs. But even though she felt justified, she still felt guilty. Thoughts spun around in her head. *What's wrong with me? This is not right, but it feels so good.*

Brian never found out what happened; David never came to their apartment again and Liz was glad. Unhappy as she was, she didn't want the incident to reoccur. She decided to swear off alcohol of any kind. But as a result she was feeling empty again. She and Brian did make love on occasion, if you could call it that. Brian satisfied himself at her expense. Liz found herself thinking a lot about Edmund again. She started to wonder where he was.

Aside from daydreaming about Edmund, her only pleasure was her job. She continued to work for Gallinas whose company sold a package of three magazines and one large bound book. The main office was located in Montreal and she worked in the Toronto office. Part of Liz's job was to translate the French correspondence into English which she thoroughly enjoyed. She was very adept at whatever she put her hands to. So while Brian tore her down, the job built her up.

Then after about three months of being married, Liz found out she was pregnant. In spite of the unhappiness in her marriage, she was very excited about having a little one. When she was alone she would lay on their big bed with her hand on her stomach and sing lullabies to her little embryo.

But morning sickness and overall tiredness were taking their toll on her and got so bad that she started taking a lot of days off work. She didn't tell Mr. Gallina, who was now managing the office, about her condition. She didn't like him. He was cold and callous, not kind like Mrs. Gallina, Liz didn't think he would understand. The end result was that he fired her for taking so much time off. Liz was beside herself with grief, her pride was hurt by being fired, but not only that, the job was the only thing that gave her any confidence.

With Liz no longer working, she and Brian had to live on only one income and it was simply not enough. So Brian decided to take on the job as superintendent of their building and the one next door. He was still working shift work at Dunham Bush, a factory that built refrigeration units, plus he was spending a lot of time away from home so the duties of superintendent became Liz's.

Young, pregnant and most often alone, she took on the task of looking after two buildings with three stories, four apartments per floor, two in the basement in addition to a laundry room and storage lockers. Her job was to keep the hallways clean, the garbage burned in the incinerators everyday and any problems in the apartments repaired.

When Christmas time came that year, Brian had some time off. Liz longed to go home, but they were chained to the apartments. If she could find someone just to burn the garbage, they could go. The nice people next door agreed to do it and away they went. When they got back three days later, they discovered that the neighbours had left unexpectedly and had not burned the garbage.

Every floor of each building had access to a central garbage chute which allowed garbage to fall to the incinerator in each respective basement. So in each building the garbage chutes were jammed to overflowing with holiday wrappings and boxes plus three days of garbage.

As soon as Brian saw their predicament, he made a lame excuse to leave. Liz ran to each floor gazing at the boxes and wrappings sticking out of the chutes. She was overwhelmed. *What can I do? I can't get the garbage back out. There's only one thing to do. Burn it!*

She pushed as much of the garbage down the chutes as she could on each floor, went to the basement and with her tongue in her cheek she lit a match and threw it in the incinerator. Whoosh! She backed up as an inferno of flames licked furiously all around the paper wrappings.

She raced to the second floor to push the garbage down and close the door. When she got there the flames jumped out at her, burning up the wall. She poked the burning garbage down the chute with the shovel she had carried up with her. She ran to the third floor -- the same thing, flames right up the wall. Her heart was racing as fast as the fire; she was afraid the whole building would catch. She ran and grabbed the red fire extinguisher and sprayed white foam all over the wall. The flames were extinguished without much damage, but it was a close call.

Liz slid down the wall and sank to the floor holding on to the fire extinguisher. Tears of fright flowed down her cheeks. Her hands and face were smudged with black.

"Damn, Brian! Damn this apartment! Damn my life!" she cried. The superintendent's job was taking it's toll on her. If it had just been the job she might have been able to handle it, but the way Brian treated her dragged her down. He hadn't got any better since they had first married. He was constantly verbally abusing her in front of others, and he hadn't become any more loving. He remained cold and callous and spent more and more time away from home. She was finding herself constantly thinking of Edmund, but she didn't even know where he was.

Just when Liz thought she could no longer go on with the loneliness she felt, a bright spot lit up her life. On a rainy Friday night while Brian was engrossed in watching wrestling on TV, and Liz was reading the newspaper, a loud knock came at the door.

"Will you get that?" Liz asked as she rubbed her stomach.

Brian grumbled and headed for the door. He whipped it open, but no one was there. He walked out into the hallway in his sock feet and peered up and down. He shook his head and went back to the living room.

"Who was it?"

"No one."

"What do you mean, no one."

"No one," he barked, "No one was there."

A few minutes later another knock came at the door. "You get it this time," Brian moaned.

Liz groaned and pried herself out of the easy chair and shuffled to the door. She opened it. No one! She peered down the hallway the same as Brian had, scratched her head and went back to her chair.

"Who was it?"

"No one was there."

"What? What's going on? Damn kids playing Nicky Nine Doors, I'll bet," Brian grumbled. "Next time I'll get the door alright."

A third knock came and Brian and Liz both rushed to the door and whipped it open. As they peered out into the hallway they heard a fourth knock from inside the apartment. They whipped around and the closet door slowly opened. First Sheryl's grinning face, then Brad's, appeared around the corner of the closet door. They swept out of the closet, arm in arm, shuffling their feet in a soft shoe dance routine as they sang "Way Down Upon the Swanee River". Liz cracked right up and she doubled over with laughter.

Unbeknownst to Brian and Liz, they had sneaked into the apartment and had quietly gone into the closet. Liz was amused immensely by their antics. She was so glad to see them. She hadn't seen them since she got married. The girls hugged each other as they danced around the room grinning from ear to ear. Thus was the beginning of a weekly routine. The two couples spent every weekend together. Sheryl and Brad would stay with them at their apartment or they would go to Brad and Sheryl's on the other side of the city. They went to the theatre, bowled, or just stayed home munched on goodies and watched TV. Their company helped Liz dispel her loneliness on the weekends, but during the week her duties as superintendent still droned on without relief until one day the landlord wanted Brian to get up on the roof to check for a water leak. That meant Liz.

"This is the last straw. I'm not crawling through that tiny opening in the hallway ceiling in my condition," Liz said crossly to Brian.

She was four months pregnant. Brian refused to do the job and the impasse ended by them giving up "their" job as superintendents. Now, they couldn't afford the rent in their luxury apartment so they were forced to move.

An older workmate of Brian's had a basement apartment to rent. It was one bedroom with a combination kitchen/living room, but the real downside was that the sink and the toilet were in a separate part of the basement and there was no tub. What a come down! But They had no choice, the rent was cheap.

As it turned out though, the landlord, landlady, and their seventeen-year-old daughter, Stacy, became very dear to Liz. Liz had a way about her that just drew people to her. The Vance's were no exception so through laughter and tears Stacy became like a sister, and Gord and Florence became like parents. But could Sheryl and Brad or the Vances fill her emptiness? Could she ever forget Edmund?

# Chapter 9
# The Indescribable Silence
# of a Heart Breaking

What a relief it was when Brad and Sheryl came to visit. Liz didn't have to be alone with Brian. She never knew why but Brad's '54 Ford had an odd effect on their T.V. The interference lines across the screen were the signal of their arrival. *Relief!*

It was even a relief when Brian would spruce himself up to go to a Lodge Meeting. He was gone for hours on end, and Liz was left alone. Being by herself was bad enough, but being with him was even worse. The silence between them was deafening. Marriage, by its very nature, is a menage a deux. Liz's was un seul, one alone. Could she live with indescribable loneliness forever or would it drive her crazy in the end? Her mother's words echoed in her ears, *Your bed is made; now lie in it.* She was lying in her bed, but the bed was cold on the other side. The band of gold on her finger had become a shackle.

Then one night after a silent supper, Brian turned to look at Liz with the dazzling smile that she seldom saw anymore. Her heart almost skipped a beat. He hadn't looked at her like that for a long, long time.

"Liz, how would you like to go home and visit your parents for a week?" he crooned. She was ecstatic.

"How can you take a week off work?"

"No, no, Liz, you can go by yourself. I'll stay here and work. You can have a whole week with your family."

She couldn't believe her ears. It was unlike him to be so kind so she readily agreed before he could change his mind. She hadn't seen her family for some time. Home wasn't the greatest, but anything would be better than the loneliness with Brian so she accepted his suggestion at face value not knowing he had plans of his own.

In the next few days, she tidied up the apartment, washed and ironed clothes and packed her bags. Finally she was ready to go.

Getting off the Greyhound bus in Bradford was coming home. She was four and a half months pregnant by this time and quite big. She cautiously stepped down from the big bus. She had decided to get off in town to avoid a long walk down the side road. She planned to phone Jane to pick her up at Jack's Restaurant. She waited anxiously on the curb while the bus driver unloaded her luggage. She was excited. Anticipation was running through her veins like fine wine. She had a heady feeling from wondering who she might run into? The possibilities were endless, Dar, Carol, Willy, Clancy.

After seven months in Toronto, she had lost touch with the old gang. Even before they moved to Toronto, Brian and Liz had kept to themselves. Marriage to Brian was terribly lonely and she missed the caring, she had enjoyed with her old friends. Now she was grown up and married; Alicia couldn't stop her from seeing anyone she wanted to. She felt smug.

Fumbling in her pocket for a dime, she spotted the phone booth on the corner and went to call Jane. That done, she crossed the deserted street and headed for Jack's.

What was it she felt? Hope? Anticipation? Belonging? All of the above.

Hand on the door, excitement was rising in her as she pushed it open. Stepping inside Jack's restaurant was like stepping back into another time.

*Carol!* She was turning around to see who had entered. Eyes rivetted, Liz watched the smile quickly illuminate Carol's face as she stood up from the booth in the back of the restaurant. She too was pregnant, Liz realized as she caught sight of her swollen belly. Another common bond.

Liz was delighted to see her. She didn't think she could have felt better, but she did as her eyes slowly focussed on the dark figure across the table from Carol. *Edmund!* Her heart raced. A warm flush burbled up from the tips of her toes to the top of her head filling her veins with champagne. Her face beamed. She moved towards the booth, irrevocably, as though drawn by a powerful magnetic force.

The silent, still carousel was turning again. The horses were smiling. She could hardly believe her eyes. In the three years before she married Brian, she and Edmund had never run into each other. Edmund had moved away and if he ever did come home, she had never seen him. In fact she had thought he had totally given up on her.

Now, here he was. He had grown some and filled out nicely. As she got closer, Edmund looked up. Their eyes met. Time stood still as the room started to spin. It was the carousel that was moving, carrying them along. Edmund smiled broadly, reassuringly, but it was the twinkle in his eye that put them in a universe all their own; golden sunbeams danced as in days of yore. "Wow! It's so good to see you," Carol exclaimed breaking the spell. Unimpeded by their blooming bellies, they hugged and laughed and laughed and hugged.

"Oh, excuse me," Carol stopped. "How rude of me. This is Louise North."

Letting go of Carol and turning towards the booth, Liz caught sight of the most stunning girl she'd ever seen. The young girl was sitting beside Edmund. Caught up in her reunion with both Carol and Edmund, Liz had been totally oblivious to her. She had beautiful blonde hair, a "perfect" ski-jump nose, "perfect" lips, "perfect" sky-blue eyes, and "perfectly" shaped brows. Liz was completely taken aback by her beauty.

Suddenly she felt uneasy and inept as she slipped into the booth beside Carol, her belly rubbing against the edge. She need not have worried though, for Edmund's eyes never left her face. If eyes are the windows to the soul, his were revealing a love that had never died. What message did Liz send with hers? Nothing has changed. As she glanced back at him feeling less than adequate, she was swept up in the love she saw in his gaze. As perfect as Louise was and as awkard and out-of-place as Liz felt, Edmund gave Liz his undivided attention, flirting openly with her. *Here I am*, she thought, smiling to herself, *pregnant, unloved by my husband, in the presence of a real beauty, yet lavished with his full attention.* Her heart warmed. Edmund had always made her feel good. Yes, she discovered she still cared for him and he for her. Was there a slim chance for them? How quickly the heart schemes when given the setting and the ingredients for love. More importantly, when given the history of a mutual caring evidently undiminished by time and circumstance. Edmund and Liz had had a perfect melding together for only two short years, but their love was still as strong as ever.

Then Liz started to wonder what had happened between him and Gail, the girl that she had heard he was living with. She'd heard they had a baby. But just as quickly as it came, she dismissed the thought so she could thoroughly enjoy her brief encounter with him.

Then, too soon, Jane stuck her head in the door and said, "Are you ready?" Very reluctantly, Liz left the restaurant knowing in her heart that she would see him again. She wanted to see him again. She would make a way to see him again. She was married; he seemed to be involved, but they had been soul-mates, and it was obvious to her that they still were.

She left the restaurant that night with hope in her heart, but as they drove home she developed a strange foreboding feeling that she didn't quite understand. It plagued her, but she was so happy about seeing Edmund that she just shook it off.

In spite of the friction that was always there between Alicia and Liz, Liz was at peace being home. It was a relief to be away from the deafening silence she shared with Brian. Her only disquieting thoughts were those of Edmund.

*How could she arrange to see him? What would happen? What could happen?* Her anticipation of ecstasy was laced with guilt. She was busy mulling these things over in her mind when the phone rang. To her surprise and delight it was Edmund.

"Liz, how are you? You didn't look very happy the other night," he said with concern in his voice.

"You always know how I'm feeling, don't you? I could never hide anything from you, could I?"

"No, I guess we always did dance to the same tune."

"Yeah, I guess we did. How are you doing? I see you're not on your own."

"Oh you mean Louise? She's just a friend. I hang out with her sometimes for something to do. She's too young for me."

"What happened to Gail?"

"That didn't work out. I don't think I ever really got over you, Liz. I thought I loved her, but I realized too late the only reason I went with her was because you were with Brian. I figured I had lost you for good, and I couldn't stand being alone."

"Edmund, I thought you didn't want me any more when you moved away. Brian was my mother's idea, but when you went with Gail I just gave up and married him."

"I only moved away because I couldn't stand to see you and not be with you."

"Oh, damn! I didn't know that. I thought I would die when I wasn't able to see you, but I was too afraid of my mother at that time."

"How about now? Could I see you now?"

Liz's heart skipped a beat. Of course she wanted to see him. Nothing had changed. But she ended up uttering the words, "Edmund, I'm married."

"Do you love him?"

"Don't ask me that," she said. She didn't love Brian, but she was torn because she was having his baby.

"Do you?"

"I-I. That's a hard question to answer."

"Liz, *I know* you don't, you don't have to tell me."

"You always did know me better than I know myself. You're right, but I'm pregnant with his child."

"I don't care. I still love you Liz. I could love your child."

"Oh, Edmund, I don't know. It's such a mess. I don't love Brian, and I don't think he loves me either, but we are married. I just don't know what to do."

"Please, Liz, even if nothing ever develops could I please just see you? Let's not leave it the way it is. I needed you so bad back then I didn't think I was going to live. It was terrible not even being able to talk to you. I still need you."

It was awful for me as well. I really need to see you too." In frustration she finally blurted out, "Oh, hell, pick me up in an hour.

Liz was thrilled. She did still love him. All of a sudden, she didn't care what happened to her and Brian. She needed Edmund. He needed her. They would work out the details later.

Almost four years had gone by, but it was just as though it was yesterday. She hurried around and fixed herself as best she could considering her condition. Then that foreboding feeling hit her in the pit of her stomach again. She waited anxiously, watching the clock. Finally, he arrived. She was so relieved. She grabbed her sweater and bolted for the door.

"Where are you off to in such a big hurry?" Alicia shouted.

Liz answered, smugly, "Just out," as she rushed through the door.

Parked on a side road Edmund took Liz's hand in his, his eyes never leaving hers. Then he slowly let go of one of her hands and gently caressed her cheek. Then they were in a passionate clinch. In spite of her large belly they hugged and kissed just as they had in days past, satisfying their very inner needs. The Carousel spun with ecstasy.

Finally, they let go of one another and then talked for hours and planned their future. Until Liz uttered sadly, "Well I guess I better get home before mama has a bird."

"Yeah, we don't want to push it if we eventually want her blessing, which probably isn't going to be easy."

Parked in Liz's lane, Edmund cuddles her close one more time. "When will I see you again?" Liz queries as she looks up into his velvet brown eyes.

"Soon, real soon, but tomorrow I gotta work on my brakes. They haven't been working very good, and one of these days they're gonna give out on me. But as soon as that's done you can bet I'll be here with bells on," he grinned.

"What? You're driving with brakes that are no good. I don't want to see you again until you get them fixed. Promise? I don't want anything to happen to you now that we are finally together again. Call me when they're done. I'll be here for a week," she uttered looking seriously at him. He grinned. "I mean it," she said as she pried herself away from him and got out of the car.

"I'll love you always," he yelled as she walked towards the house.

"R-i-i-i-ng." The clear sharp reverberation of the telephone pierced Liz's ears, and she jumped. *That's got to be him,* she thought.

"Hello. -- Liz, it's for you. It's Carol," shouted Jane.

"Hi," Liz said excitedly. She couldn't wait to tell Carol about her and Edmund. She would be thrilled. She had never liked Brian.

"Hi," Carol said in a very sombre tone. It sent chills up Liz's spine. It was totally out of character for Carol. Something was very wrong. Alerted, Liz sank down on the chrome chair attached to the little telephone table.

"Uh, listen," Carol stammered, "There's been an accident. There's no easy way to say this, Liz. Edmund was killed last night in a car accident." She blurted the words quickly as if to get it over with.

Silence. Deafening silence. The indescribable silence of a heart breaking.

"Are you there?"

"Uh, yes, thanks," Liz muttered through a fog of unreality.

"I'm not sure when the funeral will be," Carol continued, "Do you want me to let you know?"

"Yes, uh, yes. I've got to go now," Liz stammered incoherently, unable to speak any longer. In a daze she hung up the phone.

Then crystal streams flooded down her cheeks, and she shook uncontrollably as sobs racked her broken mind, heart and body.

"What's wrong?" asked Jane, followed up by Alicia's urgent "What is it?"

She gulped back a sob and cried,"Edmund's dead, there will be a funeral service."

*Would they understand?* Liz wondered as she recalled her mother's reaction to her relationship with Edmund in the past, how she had forbidden her to ever see him again. She stifled her sobs in apprehension.

"Surely you won't go," Jane stated, matter-of-factly.

"No, you mustn't go," followed her mom. "You must think of your babe. You're in a delicate condition. It would be a terrible shock."

*Would be? It already is. Perhaps, they're right, though.* Her confused mind slowly accepted the fact that she shouldn't go as the next thought crossed it. *Edmund in a casket, could I bear it?* She quickly dismissed the morbid thought as an overwhelming sob ripped the breath out of her. She bolted with her hand over her mouth and escaped to her room to be alone with her grief.

*Golden sunbeams, rider on a chestnut stallion, golden wheat fields, Johnny Mathis' "The Twelfth of Never". Never. I will never see Edmund again.* She hugged herself as she sobbed for what should have been. In their hearts they had still loved each other. At least she had found that out. She would hold on to that forever.

She gently caressed white scars on her upper arm. Through tear-filled eyes she looked down at the scar tissue that spelled the initials E. B. She vowed her love would be eternal. She vowed she would be faithful to his memory. Exhausted from sobbing, she finally slept, the memory of the twinkling dark eyes and half smile/half grin indelibly etched on her aching heart.

As she dozed and dreamt she felt a warm comforting sensation. It was summer again. The hot sun was beating down on her. She and Edmund were racing through the wheat fields. She was running, with Edmund in hot pursuit. She laughed as he grabbed her around the waist and twirled her around, sinking with her into the sweet-smelling golden wheat. As she lay on her back she felt as though she could almost reach up and touch the sky. Then the fluffy white clouds and the azure blue expanse slowly started to spin as Edmund's face came closer and closer to hers. He kissed her, oh, so gently, and the sky faded out of sight as she closed her eyes. Then he was gone! All was black. Silent tears plastered her dark brown lashes to her cheeks as they oozed out from under her sleeping lids.

Once again, he was stolen from her. It was the year 1963, the month of April; they were both 18. Liz would *never* forget her first love.

The grief that week nearly killed her, but she knew she had to gather all her inner strengths together and go on for the sake of the little heart beating inside her.

# Chapter 10
# Cheating Heart

With a heavy heart and a sad mind, Liz returned home. She was numb, but still she noticed their basement apartment was gleaming clean. In her despondent mind, she thought it strange. It wasn't like Brian to be so neat and clean, but she was too weary to question.

Stacy and her family, who lived upstairs, were so glad to have her back. They were anticipating the birth of Liz's baby as though it was one of their own. They just loved to fuss over her. Their company kept Liz from going crazy with silent grief. She couldn't speak a word of it to Brian. She didn't tell a soul. It was private. Edmund's love was her's alone to keep in her heart forever.

Weeks went by and during one of their many penny-ante poker games with Vances the real truth about the "trip home" came out.

"My deal," said Joan, Vances' married daughter who was home for a visit.

"Here's the cards," Gord said as he passed them across the table to her. Joan began to deal as Brian turned to Liz and said, "Well, stupid, are you going to watch your cards this time?"

He often verbally abused Liz, but she had learned to shut it out, so she just ignored him. She lived in her heart with Edmund.

"I don't care much for the way you talk to your wife," Joan stated.

Sudden silence.

Brian muttered a "hmmph" and continued to verbalize his discontent with Liz, ignoring Joan.

Seething, Joan continued to deal, slamming the cards down on the table.

"When are you going to do something with your hair, Liz. It really doesn't look too good these days." Brian muttered.

Then Joan blurted out, "You've got a nerve talking to your wife like that." Turning to her mother, she said, "I'm going to tell her."

"You mind your own business," Mrs. Vance said firmly.

"No!" she answered. "He has no right to talk to her that way after what he's done."

Liz's curiosity was piqued, but she was certainly not prepared for what she was about to hear as Joan angrily blurted, "How dare you bring another woman into your apartment while your wife was away?"

Liz thought she was numb beyond compare with her silent grief. But now, she was so livid with anger that she shook involuntarily. There wasn't any love between Brian and her but the deceit was too much to bear. If he wanted out why didn't he tell her sooner. Perhaps she could have gone with Edmund and salvaged something of her life. Perhaps things might have been altered enough that Edmund wouldn't have died. The game was over in more ways than one, and Liz and Brian quickly retired to their little shattered home in the basement.

"How could you?" she screamed. Then her mind raced back to her meeting with Edmund. Intermittent flashes of anger, grief and guilt collided with each other.

After she pleaded with Brian, he finally confessed. The girl had spent the whole week with him in their apartment. *And I feel guilty? For What? For nothing!* Liz thought.

"Her name is Liz. At least, I didn't have to worry about confusing names," he joked, in a feeble attempt to cut the tension.

It didn't work.

So he continued, trying to defend himself, "She works at the plant, she's a secretary there. That's where I met her. I never meant any harm. It just happened."

"Right!" Liz replied angrily. Then she thought of Edmund again. She was torn between anger at what Brian had done and guilt for what she had intended to do. She didn't care that Brian went with another woman, she loved Edmund, but the fact that he had brought another woman into her home, her kitchen, her bed, really infuriated her. Also, along with all his verbal abuse, it was another blow to her self-esteem.

"What does she look like?" she asked, thinking that perhaps if the girl was plain and unbecoming, she could somehow feel better.

"I have a picture," he said, as he reached in his back pocket for his wallet.

*Why am I doing this to myself? What does it matter anyway?* Liz thought. Then she thought, *How strange, this is the most we've talked to each other since we got married.*

She stared at the photograph, and was ignited with renewed anger as she saw a pretty, saucy looking, blond girl pictured there.

"Well, you asked," he said to Liz's crimson face. The girl was pretty, and she wasn't swollen out of shape. Liz felt worse and wished she hadn't asked.

"You're not going to leave me, are you?" Brian asked.

"I don't know." she answered. "How long has this been going on? I suppose all those times you were gone, you were seeing her." Liz wondered why she bothered to ask. In her despondent state she really didn't care, but it seemed the proper thing to do.

Brian hung his head as he answered,"For three months and yeah when I said I was going to the Lodge, I was meeting her, but it's over now. I don't want anything more to do with her. She's crazy. Please don't leave me." he pleaded. "I know you're really angry at me and I don't blame you, but think about the baby. Our baby needs a father.

Liz was disgusted with him, but she didn't know what to do, where to go. She struggled silently, thinking, *What's left for me anyway? Edmund is gone. I'm having Brian's baby. But he slept with another woman. How can I let him touch me again? He lied to me all those months. He doesn't really love me and treats me badly most of the time. But I have no place to go. Make your bed, lie in it,* Her mother's words echoed in her head. She was broken in spirit. Unable to go on alone. At least, Brian provided a home and an income and he was right, their child did need a father.

Brian pleaded with her late into the night and she was bone tired when she finally gave in and decided to forgive him and stay.

Several months later Liz was busy ironing the nice maternity clothes Brian had bought her as restitution for his transgression. She was huge by this time with only one month left to go in her pregnancy. The apartment door flew open taking her by surprise. It was the middle of the day an unusual time for someone to be coming in. Brian burst through the door holding up his right hand. It was cast in plaster to the elbow.

"What happened?" she gasped. There wasn't a real strong bond of love between them, but they had continued their relationship in a mundane manner by tending to their husband and wifely duties. Liz did care somewhat. She had never been a cold and callous person.

"I drove a screwdriver through my hand," he muttered, almost defensively. "I damaged some nerves," he continued "I'll have to wear the cast for eight weeks. I won't be able to work."

His defensiveness sparked the idea in her that perhaps he had done it on purpose to get out of working. She quickly dismissed the thought, chastising herself for thinking it, but she wasn't far off. He really didn't like working, and he got careless. He was bitter that his father, with all his wealth, refused to help out.

"Well, I'm glad you're okay, but what are we going to do for money now?" she asked.

"I'm covered by compensation," he muttered, seemingly annoyed at her question.

She was relieved. Her relief was short-lived though. He applied for compensation but weeks went by with no money. They were in dire straits. Gord Vance, their landlord, said not to worry about the rent which was very kind, but there was still the matter of food.

There was nothing more for it, they needed assistance. So they decided to head back to Bradford to her parents. Liz was going home again, but this time she was burdened with an unemployed husband she did not love, and inconsolably burdened by a broken heart.

The only light in her otherwise dark existence was the beating of the little heart within her. As Brian drove silently to Bradford Liz laid her hand fondly on her stomach and a little heel appeared, crossed her swollen belly, and disappeared again. Warmth flooded through her. Her unborn child was the only joy in her life. But was that enough? Would she ever be in love again? Would the carousel ever turn again?

# Chapter 11
# Tiny Hands Grip Her Heart

Brian reluctantly agreed to stay with Liz at her parents' home, but he was uneasy about it because verbally abusing her had become a bad habit, and he knew abusing her in front of her whole family wouldn't be a good idea. So he had to walk on eggshells and bite his tongue most of the time which took its toll on him.

On the other hand, Liz was flourishing. Since she had married and left home, her relationship with Alicia had improved immensely. Not only that, the grief of Edmund's death was subsiding somewhat as well. Nurtured by her kin, she began to feel alive again. Allen had married and was gone, but Jane and her two girls were still living at home and so was her grandmother so there was a houseful of females fussing over Liz and anxiously awaiting the birthing. She was in her final month.

One very warm August day Liz and her Grandma sat relaxing in lawn chairs in the front yard, safely out of everyone's way. A refreshing breeze wafted over them as they chatted excitedly about the baby coming. Liz felt elated as she always did when given the opportunity to discuss the baby. Then Grandma burst her bubble by saying, "It's not a picnic, you know. As a matter of fact, it's the worst pain you'll ever feel."

Liz became frightened by her words, but soon forgot them in the excitement of the rest of the females in the house. They could hardly contain themselves while waiting for the arrival of the babe, especially Jane's young girls, Lois and Debra.

Liz was relieved to be surrounded by her family while waiting for the birth of her first offspring. But Brian was not overjoyed about being the only male in the house most of the time. Liz's father was gone all day working and Brian was left with six of the gentler gender, at least five of whom were not exactly keen about him.

He was anxious about the situation and started to act none too kindly towards Liz which enraged her family. He soon relieved the tension by obtaining a part-time job driving cab which helped to some degree, but didn't totally alleviate the pressure. In the end he opted to move back in with his parents. So it was that he and Liz were apart when she went into labour.

Liz gaped blurry-eyed at the bright red spot on her pyjamas as she arose on September 13, 1963. She was instantly elated. From what she had heard, and read she knew that it was her "time".

She descended the stairs cautiously, her large belly preceding her, a big smile on her face. As she reached the bottom she started to recite "Today's the day, they give babies away, with a half a pound of tea", a little quip that she had heard her very British grandmother often say.

Alicia and Jane both looked up from the breakfast table, big grins pasted on their faces. Liz was anxious to get going to the hospital and get on with it. Little did she realize she had plenty of time. They tried to call Brian before leaving. No luck. Liz was disappointed, but this blessed event was bound to occur with or without him.

The three women sped to Newmarket hospital in Jane's '55 Chevy hardtop. Jane didn't spare the horses, but it wasn't fast enough for Liz. Once there, she waddled through the elevator doors proudly putting on a brave front in spite of the uncomfortable tightness forming around her middle. Then, apprehensively, she recalled her grandmother's well-intentioned words *It's not a picnic, you know! As a matter of fact, it's the worst pain you'll ever feel.* Fear rippled down her spine.

Then she was too busy to notice the fear as the nurse instructed her. She was very embarrassed by the procedures. She stripped to don a skimpy gown slit down the back.

Then the nurse asked her to lie down while she shaved her. Liz, with crimson face to the wall, thought she would die. She had no idea that births were such public affairs. She had suffered the humiliation of the internal examinations at the doctor's office, but this was almost more than she could bear.

Soon finished, the efficient, pert nurse said, "There you go, my dear, now if I can just get you to roll over..."

What now? Worse embarrassment, then pain, as she was given an enema of soapy water.

"I can't hold anymore," Liz gasped.

"Just a wee bit more," the nurse uttered. "There now, you can go."

Liz ran, if you can call it that, with her knees squeezed together, dams ready to burst, to the nearest facility, expelling the hot liquid out a lot quicker than it went in.

The enema triggered the pain. She was injected with Demerol and through a drug-induced haze, she was aware of the most severe pain she had ever felt in her life. She felt as though she was being ripped apart. Grandma was right. It turned out she was the only one who had uttered the truth. Alone, Liz had nothing to occupy her mind. Her body felt rent in two with the pain, pain and loneliness.

*Why is there no one here with me?* she thought. Liz had experienced loneliness before, but this was ludicrous. She was cursing Brian for not being around and then she realized even if she had been able to reach him, he wouldn't have been able to be with her anyway. Hospital rules. No one but the nurses were allowed in the labour room.

Liz felt lost and frightened in the sterile bowels of the big hospital. She cried out in pain, thrashed to and fro. *How long has it been? What's happening? Where is everyone?*

Finally a nurse and an inspection. "Not quite yet!", penetrated through the dim haze. Another voice screamed out "When?" It was her own.

More thrashing, more pain, more time. Finally, big round ceiling lights flashing past. A man's face so round, so bold. *Is it Dr. Blackman?* Leather straps bound her wrists. *What's this? Do I really care?* Another pain ripped through her.

"Just so you don't fall, dear," a kindly nurse said.

Another voice. "Water, please." It was her own again.

"Not now dear, you've had ether."

"Please!" she heard her own voice beg.

"Just a bit of ice, then." The room swam. Nausea. It passed.

The doctor's voice penetrated the Demerol haze "You can watch. There's a mirror up there."

*Watch*? She looked up.

"Oh! she's tearing." The doctor's voice again.

A lucid moment. *Oh, my God. I'm being cut.* Blood gushed forth as a little wet head popped out. Then she lost consciousness.

"Here's your dinner, dear. It's Friday, fish day."

*Where am I?* Liz wondered as she lifted her splitting head. She glimpsed down a long corridor. There were quite a few beds including hers right in the hallway. To the right she saw a room full of beds. Her head swam as she tried to focus, but it was just too much of an effort and her head fell back down.

"Mrs. O'Shea, Mrs. O'Shea wake up, dear, your baby is here."

Liz sat up groggily as a warm blanket containing what seemed to be a large bean bag was plopped into her arms. Her arms filled with warmth. The warm sensation catapulted the distance to her heart as she felt as if she would burst with joy. Tiny hands gripped her heart. Gentle streams trickled down her face. Fleetingly, she thought of Edmund's words, "I could love your child." She felt a sad longing. But her new babe would help fill her heart. She peered in awe through tiny prisms at the most perfect little face she had ever set eyes on. He was the spit of his father.

*His father!*, her mind jerked back to reality. *Where is he? Where is everyone? I need to share this moment.*

She hoped the fact that the baby was a boy, and that he looked like Brian would please him. He was always displeased with her. Maybe the baby would make a difference between them. *Where is he?*

Down the hall towards her came John and Alicia, the proud grandparents.

"Where's Brian? Does he know?" Liz asked.

"He's coming. We saw him in town."

She thought they looked upset but the thought was fleeting, and then they were busy ooing and ahing over the new little life.

A few minutes later Brian rushed in apologizing profusely. Suddenly, there was tension in the air. You could cut it with a knife. *What is it?* Liz thought, *What's wrong?*

Diverted by Brian's attention to the baby, she became overwhelmed with pride as he stared down at little Brian James Thomas O'Shea.

Too fast came the day of release. Liz had asked the doctor how many stitches she had received because it felt as if she had been pulled tight somewhere in the middle of her being. He said he had lost count. Liz felt very proud as it was something she had heard young women brag about. Medals of Valour for the battle. It had been a terrible ordeal for her because she was so tiny, but she had been brave and was very proud of her new offspring. She left the hospital walking very carefully. She was unable to stand up straight.

This was pretty much the shape she was in when Brian burst through her mother's door a few days later, demanding that she gather up a month's worth of living and leave. Even though Alicia and Jane had trained her in the basics of baby care, she wasn't eager to leave familial safety so soon and she started to balk.

But he was firm and insisted. "Come on, Liz, we're going home. I can't take any more of this being apart. I want my wife and my son at home."

It was already dark out and the baby was sleeping. Liz was very tired, and so she hesitated.

Then Jane, perturbed by his intrusion, shouted, "What gives you the right to barge in here and demand?"

"Shut up and mind your own business. This is my wife and son. I'll do as I please," he retaliated.

"We know that!" she stated curtly.

"What do you mean by that?"

"Never mind," she returned. "Well, if you insist on Liz and the baby leaving, the least you could do is start taking the baby clothes off the line for her. The girl can hardly walk."

Again he said, "Mind your own business!"

"Watch it, B-r-i-a-n!" she said with a deliberate threat in her voice.

Brian and Jane continued to bicker back and forth until she finally blurted out, "Why don't you tell us all about Louise Vickers. How you were on a date with her while your wife was having your son."

A giant pair of hands squeezed Liz's heart. She had hoped that Brian would change. She had hoped they could salvage something of their marriage. He was all she had left. She slumped to the couch. No wonder John and Alicia had left the hospital so soon after he arrived. They knew. They had seen him. She found out later that Alicia had told Brian to get to the hospital to see his wife and new baby or she was going to tell. That explained why he had raced into the hospital with such a concerned look on his face. That explained the tension. That explained why he wanted her out of there in such a hurry.

Liz knew in her heart it was true. He had done it before. Feeling defeated, fatigued and disgusted, she slowly gathered up their belongings. She went about the difficult task of taking the clothes from the line while Brian sat in the car waiting.

*What am I to do?* The thought barely penetrated. She functioned like a programmed robot. She was too weak to fight. She had a beautiful son who needed a father. Worse things happened to people. What worse, she didn't know. Feeling totally beaten down, she piled her 98 lbs, their tiny son and her misery into their black, 1958 Oldsmobile Supreme for the long ride home. What was to become of her? How long could she go on living like this?

# Chapter 12
# The Juggling

Liz resigned herself to staying with Brian for Jimmy's sake. He needed a father. She would stay with him, but she would stay faithful to Edmund's memory. She would never love Brian like she had Edmund, but she would try to be a good wife. Besides, she had become terrified of the carousel. She was afraid of the way it enticed her to behave, and most of all she was afraid of the pain it could inflict. She hoped she would be safe from it as long as she had a husband.

So life returned to their usual mundane routine except for one blissful detail. Now Liz had a star in her life. A tiny bundle of joy with tiny hands that held her heart. Jimmy was beautiful. He had all of Brian's handsome features. The only thing that was like Liz was his brown eyes and chestnut hair. She just doted on him. He was the only satisfaction she got out of life.

Days rolled into weeks, weeks into months. Liz lay in the middle of her huge bed, breast-feeding Jimmy. The radio was playing soft, dreamy music. Her mood was soft and dreamy. Jimmy's little fingers were wound tightly around one of hers as his tiny tongue sucked on her breast leaving her with a warm sensation that melted her heart. She looked down at his sweet face and breathed a big sigh of contentment. *Edmund would have loved you too,* she thought sadly. Suddenly, the radio announcer's urgent voice interrupted, "President John F. Kennedy has just been shot."

"What?" Liz shrieked as tears of shock flooded down her cheeks. "What is this world coming to?" she gasped. She clutched her tiny new babe tightly, feeling intense fear for his future.

Then an hour later Brian returned home from work with more bad news for her.

"Liz, you're going to have to help me," he stated sounding exasperated.

"What do you mean," she said hesitantly, knowing full-well what he meant. The bills were piling up again. When they had returned to the city a plump compensation cheque which more than adequately took care of their back-log of bills had awaited them, but now it was all gone.

"You're just going to have to get a job," he said with a harshness she didn't much care for.

"Oh, no please, Jimmy is too young, how can I leave him with a stranger? Please don't make me," she pleaded. "Is there any way we can cut back?" she asked, hopefully. Liz was dead against leaving Jimmy, but Brian had so berated her over the years that she had totally lost all of her spunk. She found it difficult to balk against him.

"No!" he declared firmly. Then softening somewhat he said, "I could ask for straight afternoon shifts. You could work days, and I'll watch him if Stacy will fill in for an hour or so before you get home."

Stacy, their landlord's daughter, agreed so Liz was placated somewhat, but still her job search was launched with a great deal of reluctance on her part.

With her typing skills and office experience, she easily landed a job with Gold Bond Company, in the purchasing department. The juggling began.

Gold Bond company dealt in merchandise given in exchange for Gold Bond Stamps, received from large grocery chains in the United States. It was a far cry from her previous job with Redfern Publishing Company, where four girls and one office manager, five people in all, made up the docket. Here there were rows on rows of desks as far as the eye could see with women and men seated at them, probably fifty in all.

The male half were extremely handsome, polite and outgoing. Liz wondered if they treated their wives as well as they treated her. She felt pampered and respected. She didn't get that kind of treatment at home. And the female half were gracious and kind which made up somewhat for having to leave her wee babe at home.

She excelled at the job and was even congratulated by the "big boss" for finding an error in the consecutive numbering of the computer printout for the new catalogue of merchandise. Finding that error saved the company a great deal of grief. Mr. Woodworth was impressed and grateful. Liz thought she would burst her buttons with pride for a job well done. She decided working wasn't so bad after all. Her confidence was beginning to grow again.

Her heart still ached for Jimmy every morning though when she had to rush out and leave him. After feeding, changing and cuddling him, she would tear herself away. Sometimes he would still be awake while Brian slept peacefully in their king-size bed beside the crib. She hoped if he didn't get back to sleep that Brian would wake up and tend to him right away. She had no way of knowing whether he did or not. So apprehensively, she would creep slowly out of the room and race to catch the bus on the corner, feeling mother-guilt supreme.

Once outside in the cool crisp morning air, leaves crunching under her feet, she would blink back a small tear, swallow a large lump, take a deep breath and get on with her day. Then when she arrived at work her mind would become so caught up with paper, numbers, letters, phone calls and interactions, it didn't allow her heart space to feel.

During one of those very busy days, one of her female co-workers called out, "Hey, Liz, have you heard? The Beatles are coming to town."

"Eeew, I sure would like to go," said another.

"Chances of getting tickets are probably pretty slim."

"I've got an idea," said the girl sitting at the desk next to Liz's. "Why don't a bunch of us just go downtown to Le Coq d'Or Tavern? Ronnie Hawkins is playing. It's not the Beatles, but we'll be sure to get in."

"Great idea, he's a dream," shouted a girl from farther down the row.

"Hey, Liz, why don't you join us?" Judy offered.

"I, I don't know," Liz stammered shyly as she thought to herself, *not a chance with Brian's attitude.*

Even though she didn't think that Brian would consent to her going, the invitation stirred old feelings in her adventurous spirit. It was as though that spirit had died when Edmund died. Nothing much had excited her since. Now a little spark was ignited.

She was jostled back and forth on the crowded bus by blank-faced city automatons as she made the long trek home from work. She hardly noticed though because thoughts of an exciting evening out with a gang of fun-loving females danced through her head.

The thoughts prodded her enough to finally ask Brian.

"A bunch of the girls at work are going out next Friday night to Le Coq d'Or Tavern to see Ronnie Hawkins," she said timidly.

"So, I suppose you want to go too," he snorted.

"Well, I just thought."

"Well, just don't think," he replied, interrupting her. "You've got a son to look after."

"I'll watch him." Stacy's voice echoed cheerily from the bedroom where she had gone to check on Jimmy.

She was a gem! Brian looked annoyed as his face reddened and his brows knitted together in a frown. He looked as though he was going to explode. Then catching himself, he muttered angrily, "Oh, I don't care, I'm night shift anyway."

Liz knew he wasn't happy so with great effort she stifled a grin.

Friday came before she knew it. Then finally after a very long day at the office, she headed home. Excitement rose in her with every step. She threw open the door of their tiny apartment and greeted Stacy with a big eager smile. She was feeling alive again.

The girls ate supper, then Stacy styled Liz's hair in a coif that made her look older. That was important because the legal age to get in the Tavern was 21 and Liz was just 19.

She donned a dark brown (her most flattering colour) wool suit adorned with fur cuffs and collar. Her chestnut hair, which exactly matched her eyes, was teased back on one side and upswept to the other where it puffed up in curls around her face. She felt like a movie star when the girls arrived to pick her up. Since Edmund's death she hadn't bothered too much with her appearance. Now she was looking and feeling good again.

"Wow, you look gorgeous!" they declared.

Liz's face lit up. She smiled warmly at her new friends.

"You'll pass for 21 easy," said Judy and they were off.

As they crowded around the entrance, the aura that surrounded the little group sparkled with excitement and gaiety mixed with apprehension on Liz's part. They each glided past a handsome young man clothed in sleek black pants, crisp white shirt, black jacket trimmed in velvet and a pert, black bow tie.

"Good evening, Good evening," he chanted as they each passed by.

*I'm in! I'm in!* Liz shouted in her mind while trying to maintain her composure.

"Hold it! Hold it! I need to see some I.D.," he said.

Liz turned in fear as he held his hand up to Judy who had just recently turned 21.

"I don't believe this," she cried and shot Liz an accusing look. Embarrassed, Liz moved along quickly so her red face wouldn't betray her.

It was Liz's first venture into a night club. Her eager eyes drank in the sight, bright red carpeting with black floral patterns and round tables with black and red cloths with candles burning on every one. Pungent odours of alcohol tinged with a collage of perfumes, laced with whiffs of tobacco smoke filled her nostrils.

On centre stage Ronnie Hawkins was belting out "Hey, hey, good lookin', Watcha got cookin'" as Liz strolled past in front of him. She turned to see him smiling directly at her. Her face flushed bright red.

Cinderella was at the ball, there was no Prince Charming and no glass slipper, but nonetheless, she was at the ball. The girls grabbed a table right in front of the stage. Liz was thoroughly entertained by the flirtatious antics of her co-workers and the reciprocation of the famous singer. She felt important and flattered as he paid special attention to their little group.

Too soon the evening came to a close, but having thoroughly enjoyed the well-known entertainer, and the company of her fun-loving work-mates, she headed home with stars in her eyes, glee in her heart and a mind full of memories to cherish in a clear head. She hadn't had any alcohol. She had sworn off it after the incident with David. She had had plenty of heartache, enough to drive anybody to drink, but she had fought against it and won.

Even though she had been a little nervous it was the first time in a long time that she had felt so alive. The event carried her over months of toil. She relived the evening over and over and the thoughts filled her heart with a warmth and satisfaction that she lacked at home. She thrived on it for a while. The carousel had turned once more, if only very slightly.

"Brian you've just got to change Jimmy more often!" She was angry as she saw his bright red bottom. "He's got a terrible rash."

"I'm doing the best I can. I'm tired you know. It's not easy to work til 3:00 a.m. and get up to a screaming baby," he shouted.

"Well, you wanted me to work!" she threw back at him.

Brian ignored her pleas and the diaper rash became severe. Being young and inexperienced and desperately drained of late, she was unsure of what to do about it. She had tried all the methods that she knew and nothing was working. It just kept getting worse. Finally she took a day off work, and Stacy accompanied her to the doctor's office. The doctor was very stern with her and coldly delivered instructions on what to get to heal the rash. Penaten Cream.

After that she decided Jimmy needed a reliable baby sitter. Someone who would properly care for his needs. As a result, she placed him in the care of a sitter who she hired through an agency so she could be sure she was qualified and reliable. But the sitter lived in the opposite direction of Liz's employment. She hated to take Jimmy out but she had no choice.

Fall turned to winter. Winter plodded its way to February, 1964. Liz's evening of bliss had long since past. She was feeling so tired out, and she soon discovered why.

"Brian, I've got something to tell you," she said, her heart in her throat. She knew instinctively he wasn't going to want to hear the news any more than she wanted to tell him.

"What?" he said, sounding slightly annoyed.

"I'm pregnant again," she quickly said.

"Aww, no," he grunted. "Now what are we going to do? We're still deep in debt."

"Well it's not all my fault," she said defensively.

"I thought you said those condoms were supposed to work," he moaned.

"I don't know any more about birth-control than you do," she exclaimed.

"Well, nothing we can do about it now." He shrugged and walked away.

It was easy enough for him to say. She was less than pleased. In fact, she was frightened after the difficult delivery with Jimmy, and besides, she enjoyed her job in spite of having to leave her baby in the hands of a sitter. It gave her a newfound confidence. She felt more alive than she had in a long time and a new baby would end it all.

Winter melted into spring with warm sunny mornings, birds in song and blossoming trees dotting the roadways. Liz continued to work, but she was unsure how long she would be able to keep up the pace. Her stomach was bulging, and she was feeling haggard and drained as she trudged up the long staircase of the big apartment building where Jimmy was.

"Here's his diaper bag, and don't forget his little hat," said Mrs. MacDuff with her jolly round face. She plopped the hat lightly on his crown. Now, eight months old, Jimmy was a load to carry.

"Oh! and by the way, Brian dropped off this bag of groceries when he brought him today," she added.

"Oh, no!" Liz cried as she looked at the full, brown paper bag of groceries topped with loose oranges. *I could just kill him,* she thought to herself as she looked at her purse, the diaper bag, the eight-month old and the full bag of groceries.

She took a deep breath, tugged the strap of her purse up tight over one shoulder and the diaper bag strap securely over the other shoulder, threw Jimmy onto one hip, legs spread and threw the grocery bag on her other hip clutched in her left arm. Her belly protruded in the middle somewhere. She started gingerly down the long staircase. She'd come a long way from her Ronnie Hawkins evening of bliss.

As she reached the sidewalk outside, she spied her bus coming on the opposite side of the four-lane roadway.

*Oh, no! If I don't catch this bus I'll have to wait half an hour for the next.*

Adrenaline pumping, heart racing, juggling her cargo, she dashed out into the oncoming traffic. W-h-i-s-h, off went Jimmy's hat; she had forgotten to secure the chin elastic. She stooped to grab the hat; s-n-a-p! the strap of the over-stuffed diaper bag gave way and threw her off balance. R-r-r-i-p, the paper grocery bag tore, oranges rolled like bowling balls out onto the pavement. W-h-o-o-s-h, the traffic flashed past her on both sides as she tried to grab everything at once. This was the last straw. Certain that she had missed the bus by now, she could hardly believe her eyes. The bus had pulled over and a kind soul in a blue uniform was emerging. The big bus driver had seen her dilemma and was coming to her rescue.

Her heart swelled with gratitude as he took Jimmy from her arms while she picked everything up. Of all her trips on the bus, this was the first time she had seen so many smiling faces. They were sympathetic towards her. Liz was amazed. The cold, unfeeling, city automatons had come to life.

She held her tears all the way home, but as soon as she got off the bus they flowed like a river. She burst through the back door her face all puffy. Stacy had seen her through the upstairs window and raced down the stairs after her. Close on Liz's tail, she cried, "What's wrong? what's wrong?" Anxiety was stamped on her pretty "Dutch-girl" face.

"I'm okay," cried Liz.

Then the story poured out of her in vivid detail: juggling purse, diaper bag, grocery bag, and Jimmy; Oranges rolling down the street, traffic whizzing by, gawking cold faces, then kindly bus driver and smiling fellow passengers. Catching the underlying humour of the story, Stacy broke out in a fit of laughter. Soon Liz joined her; the pair of them rolled around on the wine-coloured Persian rug holding their sides. Jimmy sat on the rug and stared at them his mouth agape wondering what all the fuss was about. They roared all the more at the look on his face.

After telling Brian the events of the day, Liz boldly announced that she could no longer work. Unsympathetic to her ordeal, he was, to say the least, annoyed by her decision. The next day, she sadly gave her notice. She knew she had to quit, but the job had given her such confidence and made her feel alive again so she was somewhat unhappy to leave. Unhappy or not though she was relieved that the juggling was over. But now where was the money going to come from to make ends meet?

# Chapter 13
# Robbery With Violence

"What is all this stuff, Brian?" Liz asked as she opened the top cupboards in the bedroom closet and saw several cartons of cigarettes, ten packages of golf balls and other diversified sundries.

"Oh, it's nothing, just stuff I picked up downtown real cheap. A guy was selling it in one of the bars."

"Stolen goods?" she gasped.

"No, not stolen goods!" he snapped.

Because of his tone of voice, Liz didn't press the issue any further. She didn't want to rile him. She seldom saw him any more because he had gone back to day-shifts at the plant and acquired a part-time evening and weekend job driving cab to make up for the loss of her pay cheque. The little time she had with him she didn't care to spend fighting. If she had nothing else in the relationship, she wanted peace. She couldn't afford to lose him and leave herself victim to the carousel.

A week later on a hot August Sunday, she was feeding Jimmy in his high chair when a brisk knock came at the door.

Slowly she rose, with her hands clasped under her belly to help her to stand up. She sauntered to the door wondering who was there. The loud intrusion had startled her.

To her surprise and alarm, two men filled the door frame with their bulky figures. One waved a paper in front of her face and said, "Good day, ma'am. Sorry to intrude. We have a search warrant. If you'll just stand aside we'll get on with the task." He spoke as if he was bored, having probably repeated these words many times in the past.

"What? What's this all about?" she asked, fear rising in her throat as her mind flashed back to the items she had discovered in the bedroom closet.

"We'll explain later, now if you'll just move aside and let us get on with it," the other man said as he pushed past Liz into the apartment.

That they had performed this task before was obvious to her as they went about their business proficiently. Liz followed them from room to room forgetting about Jimmy for the moment, fearing what they might find. Her mind flashed back again to Brian's stash in the closet. It was only a matter of time until they found it, but she was too frightened to speak up.

Her face flushed scarlet with embarrassment and anger as they rifled through her dirty laundry hamper. Visions of soiled underwear danced through her mortified mind.

"Aha," the taller, younger man said with a grin as he fingered one of the cartons of cigarettes he had retrieved from the shelf in the bedroom closet. The cartons were numbered and the officer was checking a list.

"Bring him in," he continued, turning to the older man with the glasses and moustache. Then he headed for the couch as if he meant to stay awhile.

Liz thought fearfully, *I'll just keep quiet -- the less said the better until I find out what's going on.* She tried to remember from past TV shows or books what the penalty would be for buying stolen goods. Her flashing thoughts were interrupted as the older man returned from their patrol car, Brian in tow, cuffed at the wrists. *This doesn't seem right,* she thought, *handcuffed for purchasing some stolen goods?"*

"Now," said the younger man as he shifted positions on the couch and crossed his leg, which meant he was getting right down to business. "Tell us Brian, who was with you? Robbery with Violence is a very serious offense. Go easy on yourself. You help us, we'll help you."

"Robbery with Violence!" Liz gasped. "Just what is going on here?"

"Well, ma'am, a week ago there was a robbery at the Uxbridge Golf and Country Club. The culprits tied and gagged an old nightwatchman at knife point, a long Japanese dagger it was. He suffered a heart attack and was hospitalized."

Liz's mind raced back to their visit to the little second- hand shop on Wilson Avenue and replayed the scene.

*"Wow, look at that Japanese dagger from World War II. Would I love to have that,"* Brian said.

*Whatever would anyone want something like that for? Liz thought, reflecting on how she'd been taught to love her neighbour as herself.*

Liz hated war and violence and anything connected with it. But a few days later, she returned to that shop and purchased the dagger against her own better judgment, hoping Brian would be pleased with her.

Now, guilt flushed through her as she realized what he had done with it.

"I hope the old man will be okay," she stammered, snapping back to the scene at hand.

"Your husband and his accomplices better hope so too," the younger man answered. With those words the severity of the situation became clearly etched into her mind.

"Okay, Brian," he continued. "You left a wide trail behind you. We easily traced your car as being at the scene. We know you weren't alone, so if you'll just tell us who was with you, we can get on with it!"

Brian sat, head down, his face set in a stubborn pose, and refused to speak. The afternoon turned into early evening. Exasperated, the older man said "Well, I guess there's nothing else we can do. Alright, Mrs. O'Shea, you'll have to get a babysitter for your wee one there." He looked over the top of his glasses and pointed his finger in the direction of little Jimmy.

"You'll have to come downtown with us," he stated coldly. "Both you and your husband will be booked."

Panicking, she started to shake. "W-what? I-I didn't do anything," she stammered.

"You're an accessory," he stated coldly as he crossed his arms and glared at her.

Hot tears blurred her vision as she fumbled with the door knob and staggered up the stairs to the Vances. She heard the younger man's voice fading as the door closed, "What kind of a guy are you anyway, letting your wife go to jail for what you've done?"

"What's wrong, Liz?" Gord Vance asked, alarmed at her shaking body and swollen eyes.

"I'm going to jail," she sobbed. She cleared her throat and continued, "Could you please watch Jimmy? I don't want to leave him. I'm so worried about him."

Gord jumped up from his chair, his fatherly face livid with rage. "As long as I'm around you're not going anywhere" he spat out.

He raced ahead of her down the stairs, burst through the door and with great authority in his voice took command of the situation and roared, "What's going on here?"

The older detective took him by the arm and led him out of the room. Gord came back after a few moments, took Liz aside and gently whispered, "It's okay, it's just a ploy to get him to talk." He smiled down at her with a "father-look".

Stupendous relief flooded through her as she sank into a kitchen chair. She wouldn't have to leave Jimmy or go to jail.

Finally Brian agreed. "Alright, alright," he said. "There was one black guy and one white guy with me. They set it up," he continued, spilling the beans, and his voice faded as Liz realized with renewed fear that he was going to be taken away.

"Well, let's go downtown." The chilling voice shattered her fog.

"Where are you taking him? What will happen?" All anger aside now, she was worried about Brian, but even more concerned about what was to happen to Jimmy, and herself. She couldn't be alone.

"He'll be taken downtown to make a statement then transferred to Whitby Jail, pending court action," the older man said, compassion showing on his face as he glanced at Jimmy bouncing in his jolly jumper oblivious to the turmoil.

Brian was led out in handcuffs. Tears streamed down Liz's face as she watched his powder-blue shirt and blue jeans disappear through the screen door at the top of the stairs. She sobbed until she couldn't any more, then pulled herself together and picked up the cold black receiver of the telephone and dialled her parents' number.

The day was sunny and warm. A week had passed. Liz reflected angrily on how Brian's father had phoned her during the week and pleaded with her to stay in the City. He had promised to help her with anything she needed. She supposed he didn't want the community back home to know what happened. People would be asking questions. Liz felt sorry for his plight, but Jimmy needed some kind of stability.

"They're here!" Stacy blurted out, and Liz heard the tires crunch the gravel as her parents' white 1963 Chev pulled into the driveway.

The Vance family were gathered around to bid Liz and Jimmy farewell. She could see sadness in their faces.

Liz introduced John and Alicia to Florence and Gord Vance.

"You sure did something right when you raised this girl." said Florence. Alicia beamed.

A lone tear squeezed its way out and slowly rolled down Liz's cheek, encouraging others to follow.

"Oh by the way, I paid up Brian's medical at work for you," Gord said, his voice cracking. "So you'll be covered for the birth."

*What a dear man!* Liz thought.

"Oh! How much do we owe?" John asked.

"Nothing," Gord replied. "It was my pleasure. We love this girl, and little Jimmy," he said as he squeezed Liz with one arm.

Then Stacy and Liz clutched each other, tears flowing freely. "You've got to come and visit us sometime." Stacy burbled between sobs.

Liz nodded frantically, sniffing, unable to speak. Over her shoulder she saw Mrs. Vance's stern face melting. She hadn't wanted to rent the apartment out and was angry with Gord in the beginning but had soon succumbed to Liz's polite, eager-to-please manner.

After all goodbyes were voiced, they piled into the Chev, trailer in tow loaded with Liz's possessions and started the long trip home on highway 400.


"Mary, come here, Mary." Lois, Jane's girl, teased running around after Jimmy who was dressed in a frilly little apron of Grandma's. The girls would dress him up like a girl and tease him and call him Mary because he was the only boy in the house.

"Don't you girls call him that," hollered Alicia from the kitchen. Steam rose around her as she lifted the pot lid to test the stew.

Round and round they went, through the two arched doorways at each end between the living room and kitchen, Jimmy in the lead, Lois and Debra, now in their early teens, in hot pursuit. Jimmy squealed with delight. The girls giggled.

"You girls stop it!" Alicia yelled, annoyed. "If you've got so much energy, come and set the table for me."

"I'll do it," Liz yelled from the living room where she was watching The Fugitive on T.V.

"No!" Her mom said. "It'll keep the girls busy."

It had become a familiar daily scene as they waited for her dad and Jane to come home from work. At first Liz was delighted to be home. Then she started to miss Brian. At least, she thought she missed him, but actually it was just the old familiar emptiness coming back. Her addiction to the carousel was starting to gnaw at her. Even though there was no love between her and Brian, the compulsion for the carousel to turn was kept at bay when he was around.

Yes, she was terribly lonely even though the house was full. Jane was still there with her girls but she would soon be marrying Gord Bowman and leaving.

One sunny Saturday afternoon, while Jimmy was down for his nap, Liz watched Jane and Gord studying the plans for the construction of their new home. She felt a sad longing as she observed them, heads together in obvious unison and joy. They had together what she had always longed for...what she had with Edmund, and had not had since.

She quietly slipped out the back door, not wanting to disturb them. She wandered aimlessly up the eleventh line towards the highway deep in thought about how things could have been. She reflected on the day she had come upon Willy Morris and Bugsy Harlson on this very road. She smiled warmly as she recalled their words. "We know someone who likes you."

She gathered wild flowers here and there as she went. The late August sun offered her comfort through her soft cotton shift. At five and a half months pregnant her belly was swollen, but she didn't find the walk difficult because she was so engrossed in her daydreams.

Time and distance passed as she dreamed on and on about Edmund. Before she knew it, she had passed the mouth of the road and walked a mile down the highway. By this time she had a large bouquet of wild flowers and she was standing in front of the entrance to Mount Pleasant Cemetery.

The large black wrought iron gate was open. She wandered through the grounds looking for a certain tombstone. She searched and searched, but she couldn't find the one she sought. She started to panic running from head stone to head stone until finally, after checking every one she discovered an unmarked grave way at the back of the cemetery. She knew instinctively it was Edmund's. She could feel his presence. She laid down her bouquet. Then she knelt down and pressed her open hand against the ground. The earth was warm from the afternoon sun as she pressed her palm lovingly against it. Her tears welled up, spilled over and gushed down her cheeks. She brushed them away with the back of her hands as wisps of her hair blown by the warm breeze stuck to her cheeks.

"Oh, Edmund, what's going to happen to Jimmy and I? I wish you were still here to help us."

She sat there in solitude most of the afternoon, visualizing his twinkling eyes and half-smile/half-grin. She could see his face as clearly as if he was in front of her. She scanned her upper arm and his initials were still there.

"At least I will always have your memory," she said as she rested her palm on the grave again.

The sun crossed the sky to rest over the western horizon. It gave off a golden glow as she slowly rose to head for home with pain in her heart and emptiness in her soul.

# Chapter 14
## Two Years Less A Day

August leafed its way into October. The early morning sun sparkled through the hoar frost that covered everything, making the countryside look like a fairyland of rhinestone crystal. Liz enjoyed the scene even though she was very tense. She and Jane were on their way to Whitby for Brian's hearing. Wearing a navy blue heavy cotton skirt, a maternity vest and a white nylon blouse with navy blue polka dots, Liz felt businesslike and respectable.

Hanging from a hook in the back of the car was a grey pin-striped suit, white shirt, and black tie. Brian's lawyer had told Liz, "If he looks presentable it may go better for him."

As they travelled, Liz questioned Jane anxiously. "Do you think he'll get off?"

"I really don't know."

"Everyone I've talked to thinks he will," Liz said, trying to reassure herself.

"Well, we'll just have to wait and see."

"I'm sure he'll get off," Liz said. "It's his first offense. Besides he has a child and another on the way. Surely the judge will take all that into consideration." Her heart lightened as she convinced herself he would be making the long drive home with them. He had to come home with them. She needed him. He provided a home for her and Jimmy and not only that he kept the carousel at bay. With Edmund gone and things the way they were with Brian, she wondered if she would ever know the magic of being in love again. These thoughts occupied her mind as they travelled.

Liz was very tired when they arrived just before 9 a.m. As they walked through the front doors of the court building, Liz and Jane were greeted by a tall, thin man with horn-rimmed glasses, a sharp nose, and bright eyes.

"Good!" he exclaimed. "You've brought the suit. I'll take it downstairs to the cells so Brian can change. Just go ahead in through these doors and take a seat."

The court was the same as many Liz had seen in the movies with dark oak everywhere. There was a high judge's bench, and an oak railing between the spectators' seats, the witness's seat, the court reporter's seat, the lawyers table, and the prisoner's docket. Liz's hands nervously toyed with a crumpled Kleenex.

"All rise!" the shcrif called out and Liz and Jane slowly rose as the judge briskly entered. He was older, quite round and short in stature not unlike Tweedledum in the Tweeledum & Tweedledee nursery rhyme. Renewed hope ran through Liz. Surely a man who looked like a character from a nursery rhyme would be lenient.

Court opened with several mundane traffic violations and similar cases. Liz thought she would explode with anticipation when finally Brian and his two accomplices were called to the front. Brian was in the middle, towering over the two shorter men. After the facts of the case were read, pleadings heard, all said and done, the judge handed down the sentences. The guilty parties stood in a row, hands clasped in front of them. The fellow on Brian's left with the sandy hair and scarred face who looked somewhat like a weasel seemed not to be bothered by his twelve year sentence. He nonchalantly looked around the room shrugging and shifting from one foot to the other as though bored.

The shorter black man had hair that made Liz think of Buckwheat from the Little Rascals. It was twisted in little knots all over his head. He was just as hard-looking as his sandy-haired accomplice, though, and fidgeted nervously when the judge stated, "Five years".

The first man had received the twelve-year sentence because he had a long record. The same was true of the other man.

Liz, fidgety as the black man, anxiously awaited Brian's sentence. She thought the other sentences quite severe for a Tweedledum judge, but reassured herself with the fact that it was Brian's first offence, not to mention, that he looked like a lawyer himself in his smart, pin-striped suit and tie. A far cry from the appearance of the other two.

"Come forward, young man," demanded the judge.

Brian nervously moved forward and flashed a grin. Liz knew that meant he was nervous.

The judge said firmly, "This is no laughing matter, son," he continued, "As this is your first offence, I'm going to go easy on you."

Liz's heart leapt with hope only to be crushed in an instant. The suit had not helped.

"Two years less a day," the judge exclaimed as he banged his gavel down.

Tweedledum's voice dulled in Liz's ears. *What's wrong? I can't breathe. I think I'm going to pass out.* Blood rushed through her head to her ears, deafened her and then left a distinct buzzing in her ears. She let out a gasp, as she regained full awareness, just in time to see Brian being led away in handcuffs. Hot tears streamed down her face. Her big, round, helpless eyes looked to Jane for help.

"Come on!" Jane said, taking charge. "Let's go see if you can see him before he's taken away." They shuffled out into the hallway where a tall, husky guard stood. Jane cleared her throat and spoke up, "Excuse me, my sister would like to see her husband before he's taken back to prison. Would that be possible?"

"I'm sure something can be arranged," he said, sympathetically taking in Liz's swollen mid section with his clear blue, kind eyes.

In a matter of minutes they were being led down two flights of stairs to the holding cells. As they passed by the first cell, the Negro man shouted, "Hey, mama! Guess you all goin' to be doin' witout for a while," his eyes taking in Liz's distended belly. Feeling insulted and somewhat frightened, she moved along quickly past the second cell and the sandy-haired man who just glared.

Finally, she was at Brian's cell. As he reached through the bars to embrace her, she saw fear in his eyes. Her heart was touched in spite of all the hard times. She was loyal. She felt sad for him but at the same time her head was splitting as thoughts madly raced around -- *Where do I go from here? No job. No husband. No home. Two children. What is going to happen to them and me?*

When Liz and Jane left the courthouse that day a giant door slammed in Liz's heart. She would have to be strong, not feel, just think. She would have to fight the carousel on her own. She had two babes to care for.

After a long and sad ride home, Liz related the day's events to her parents. When she got to the part where she almost passed out her grandmother interrupted.

"What did the judge say then?" she questioned with her stiff British manner.

"I don't know," Liz sighed I don't remember because I thought I was going to pass out."

"Oh, silly girl, you should have listened," she stated. You could hear the disgust in her voice.

That was grandma! Liz loved her, but sometimes she could be exasperating. Anyway, what more needed to be said?

Two years less a day said it all.

# Chapter 15
# Who's Doing Time?

"Come this way, ma'am," directed a neatly clad prison guard.

"You sure you don't mind waiting here?" Liz asked Jane.

"No, you go ahead, I'm sure you want to see Brian alone.

Liz was led into a big room inside the Whitby jail. Heavy plate glass divided it in two. As she entered the room she saw Brian coming through a door on the other side of the cold impersonal glass. He was dressed in prison khaki. He sat down and gestured for her to pick up the black receiver of the phone. It was cold to the touch and fit in with the rest of the chilling atmosphere.

"Hi," she said shyly, feeling like a criminal herself.

"Hi," he replied sadly.

"How are you doing?" she questioned, knowing all the while how he felt by the look on his face.

"Not good. Listen, do you have any extra money?" he asked.

"No. I only get $86 a month from Mother's Allowance and I give most of that to Mom for our expenses."

Spitting out a curse, he continued."I'm not in a very good position in here. The two guys I ratted on are not very happy with me. They want me to get cigarettes for them."

"I can't help you," Liz cried feeling helpless. Pressure closed in on her as she imagined what they might do to him. She visualized them beating him to a pulp. She didn't want to see him hurt.

"Oh, never mind," he said discouraged. "I got myself into this mess, I'll have to get myself out."

She knew this was true, but it didn't help her feel any better as her mind began to dwell on his dilemma. He had hurt her plenty in the past, but she was not a vindictive person. She would have done anything to help him, but her hands were tied. There was nothing she could do. So after a short half-hour visit with him, all she was allowed, she left for home with a heavy heart.

Once home she started to worry about his safety. Then she started to miss him. She questioned her sanity. How could she miss such a man? Actually, it was just that old familiar emptiness haunting her again.

Two weeks went by and Brian was transferred to a minimum security prison in Brampton. Liz was eager to see him. She wanted to make sure he was alright so she asked Jane if Gord would take her to visit him. Gord agreed, so one brisk October morning, Jane, Gord, Lois, Debra, Jimmy and Liz all piled into Gord's new car and left for Brampton.

Even though Liz was anxious about Brian, the trip passed by quickly because she was entertained to the full by the hilarious antics of the two girls and Jimmy. Her heart swelled with joy every time she watched him at play.

"Look at him, Mom," cried Lois holding her sides shaking with laughter. Jimmy's pudgy little hands were stretched out, palms turned up, and his little chin jutted out. Both gestures were made in an attempt to help him hold up the big sunglasses Lois had plopped on his nose. He laughed as they fell off. "'Gain, 'gain," he cried, wanting her to put the glasses on and laugh again. He entertained them the whole distance to the prison.

Then when they arrived Debra said "Oh, look, there's no fences."

"I see that," Liz said as she surveyed the whole site. It was a large acreage containing several bunk houses and a few larger buildings. They were all built with clapboard siding and painted a dull yellow colour. Except for the fact that there were guards wandering about, it could have been a boy scout camp.

They were directed into one of the larger buildings which was empty except for the benches around three of the walls. An office of sorts dominated the fourth wall.

Brian was led in by one of the guards. Liz gasped as she looked up at him. He had the remnants of two black eyes and a jagged scar marred his left cheek. She didn't have to ask what happened. Obviously, his two cohorts had met up with him before he was transferred. Her heart instantly softened toward him, but she avoided the subject of the beating; she could tell by his body language he didn't want to discuss it. So to fill the silence Liz started to talk about how lax the atmosphere was in the prison. Brian was relieved and started to explain that the guys were on their honour and if they did try something stupid, they would just be transferred to a maximum security prison. Liz was thankful that he was there in Brampton. At least, he wasn't rubbing elbows with a harder criminal element, picking up worse habits, and more importantly, he was safer.

After talking for a while Jane, Gord, and the girls wandered off with Jimmy to have a closer look around and perhaps to leave Liz and Brian alone for a while.

"C'mere," Brian said. "You look real good." Liz's heart quickened and she blushed as he leaned closer. Their eyes locked and the room began to spin. Thoughts whirred around in her head, *Maybe this scare will change him. Maybe there's hope for us. Maybe I could love him.*

And Brian was having second thoughts of his own, *I've been a jerk for the way I've treated Liz. She's been so good to me through all this trouble. I better smarten up and take better care of her or I'll lose the one good thing in my life.*

He gathered her in his arms and kissed her, oh, so gently. The kiss was warm and enticing. But suddenly, Brian recoiled. His body stiffened, and he let her go. Liz looked up to see a guard gripping him by the shoulder.

"Sorry," he said coldly. "No bodily contact allowed.

Liz sat back obediently, feeling like a chastised child. *My husband! Two children! No bodily contact! How absurd!* Her heart did a twist. The kiss had caused the carousel to start to turn but the horses' faces were very sad.

Liz wrote to Brian consistently. He wrote her the one letter he was allowed, faithfully, every week. She had grown close to him and was finding it difficult to wait out the time even though she was being treated very well at home. Not only was she finding it difficult to wait out the time for Brian's return, she was finding it very wearisome waiting for the birth of their second child.

The weeks went by slowly. Then, finally, in the early morning of November 10, 1964, Liz sat blurry eyed on the toilet, thinking *Am*

*I ever going to stop peeing.* She had staggered to the bathroom in anguish, with a very full bladder. A full bladder was one thing, but this was ridiculous. She reached over from the uncomfortable seat and strained to push open the door.

"Mom, come here!" she yelled. Alicia came rushing up the long staircase to the hall leading to the bathroom.

"What's wrong?" she asked, deducing from Liz's tone of voice that something wasn't quite right.

"I can't stop going," Liz said, very concerned.

"Oh, I'll bet you're water has broken."

Liz had her water broken for her at Jimmy's birthing so she hadn't known what to expect. With her mother's words she felt relief, and excitement began to rise in her.

Finally, this long pregnancy would come to an end. She would soon carry this child on the outside instead of the inside. But the excitement soon faded and fear welled up in her as she recalled Jimmy's birth. Then her sister Joy's words echoed in her mind, *Like water off a duck's back, the second one,* giving her comfort.

"Here, stick this between your legs." Her mom's voice startled her back to reality. Alicia had fetched a huge tattered old bath towel. Liz stuffed it in her pyjamas and waddled to her room to get dressed.

Allen and his wife, Fran, were visiting so she accompanied Jane, Alicia and Liz to Newmarket Hospital. But Liz would deliver alone once again. As the doors closed on the elevator and shut out her mother and the others she fought back a tremendous urge to lunge through the cold steel doors and grab her mother's hand.

Having remembered the lonely time in the labour room before Jimmy was born, Liz brought an Alfred Hitchcock novel to the hospital with her in the hopes that it would help pass the time and keep her mind occupied. Now, she gripped the sides of the novel as though it was a lifeline in a tumultuous sea. The ink was blurring on the pages from her sweaty palms; she had no pain as yet, but plenty of fear.

Then an overwhelming pain gripped her mid-section. She buzzed the nurse. A tall, slender red-headed woman came through the door.

"Yes?" she said

"Can you call Dr. Blackman? I've had a severe pain."

"Dr. Blackman is a very busy man. It's midnight. I'm not going to call him out in the middle of the night for one pain," she stated bluntly. "You haven't even started serious labour yet."

"Well, then could I please have a sedative," Liz asked shyly, respecting the nurse's authority and wincing at the pain welling up in her again.

"Sure," she said and quickly left the room. She returned with the sedative and said, curtly, "Roll over."

Liz rolled. The nurse shrieked.

"Oh, my God," she yelled. "This baby is delivering."

She administered the shot and ran to get another nurse and a stretcher. Fully aware, Liz was rushed down the corridor, overhead lights flashing by.

"Did you call Dr. Blackman?" cried the red-headed nurse.

"Yes," said her assistant. "He's on his way but it's really foggy out."

Her words echoed through Liz's head. New fear gripped her. *Will he make it on time?* This baby was coming whether he did or not.

"Don't push! one nurse cried.

"Pant like a puppy," the other one said, "It will help the pain."

She was right, Liz realized, as she panted.

Fifteen minutes passed! Liz was in brutal pain! Where was that doctor?

Bang! Both doors of the delivery room flew open. Dr. Blackman's tall figure, bald head and moustached face catapulted through the opening.

"Let that baby go!" he yelled.

Realization dawned on Liz. The tall red-headed nurse had been holding the baby's head back with her hand. Startled she pulled her hand away and a little wet mucky head appeared lips, pursed in what seemed like disgust for her arrival being held up.

Stacy Ellen O'Shea was beautiful. A tiny tear squeezed out of the corner of one of Liz's eyes, then the other. She thought she would burst with pride. She longed to share the moment with Brian.

"Six pounds, thirteen ounces," the nurse said. Liz was wide awake this time as the sedative hadn't even had time to work. Only a half hour had passed since the first pain. Stacy was a smaller baby than Jimmy and looked nothing like Brian. She closely resembled an old family photograph Liz had seen of her father as a very small baby. All her anger at having become pregnant again totally dissipated as Liz gazed into her newborn child's face.

"What's the matter with her?" Liz heard a woman's voice say, sympathetically, from behind the curtains around her bed. Three days had gone by, and she had kept them closed. She sniffed and wiped away another tear that was slowly wending its way down her swollen red face. *After Baby Blues* the doctor had called it. She didn't know or care what it was. All she knew was she didn't want to see or talk to anyone.

She heard someone briskly enter the room. Through the slight opening in the curtain, she spied a delivery boy with yet another bouquet of flowers. *Don't these women have enough? The room is full.* she thought bitterly, regretting it as soon as she had thought it. *What's the matter with me anyway?* she moaned to herself. It was very out of character for Liz to react this way. She was always kind and caring never jealous or envious.

"Mrs. O'Shea!" the boy's voice called out, cheerfully.

*Me? No, he must be mistaken.* But she had heard right as he called again, "Mrs. O'Shea!"

"Over here," she said perking up.

"Where do you want them?" he said smiling broadly. Liz glanced up briefly and noticed he had a tooth missing in the front. Other than that he was quite handsome with his broad cheeks, dark brown hair and wide amber eyes.

"Just put them on the table there," she said as she pointed to the bedside table and then quickly bowed her head.

"Thanks," she murmured with her tear-stained face hidden as she looked down into her lap. She was embarrassed by her tears. Her fingers nervously played with the ribbon on her nightgown.

He was gone as quick as he'd come. She picked up the pink china baby boot that contained the tiny pink roses, pink bow and baby's breath. She breathed in the sweet rosy smell and reached for the card. It read "Love Brian". She was thrilled. *He does care after all.*

Though cheered by the beautiful bouquet, she continued to remain in her curtained prison until the day of release came, not wanting to reveal to the other women the whereabouts of her wayward husband.

As Liz walked through the door of her mother's big kitchen, Jimmy came running from the other side of the room and threw his pudgy little arms around her legs. He had missed her terribly. She had missed him too so she quickly handed her little bundle over to Jane and whisked him up in her arms. He had been the light of her life through all the dark times. Now, she had two lights brightly burning.

"Wow, she's a beauty. She's going to be very successful. You can just see it in her face," said Jane as she rocked the new babe back and forth. Liz puffed up with pride at her words.

A few weeks passed and Liz recovered swiftly from the childbirth. Thus, she felt she was ready for the long trip to see Brian. She longed to share Stacy with him. He had been so attentive since he had gone to prison and she had hope in her heart that he had changed so they could work out their marriage. After all, they had two children.

Hesitantly, she asked Jane, "Do you think Gord would drive me to Brampton to see Brian? I'd sure like to take Stacy for him to see."

"Gee, Liz, I really don't want to ask him now that the snow is flying and the roads are treacherous. He's really good to me, but I don't want to push it," she said.

Liz drooped with disappointment and felt envious over Jane's relationship. She was right, Gord was exceptional. He probably would have taken her, but Liz didn't want to come between them.

A few days passed, and overcome with loneliness and a swirling vision of Brian holding their new baby, Liz finally dug up enough courage to approach her mother, "Will you watch Jimmy if Stacy and I take the bus to Brampton to see Brian?"

"You're crazy," Alicia replied. "That's a long trip. You would have to bus to downtown Toronto and transfer to a westbound bus. It would probably be a three or four hour trip one way. Not to mention this terrible blizzardy weather."

Liz knew full well the blast of the frigid Ontario winters, but she was desperate. She longed to share her new offspring with Brian. Bringing the baby to show him was first on her mind, but underlying that was a very strong desire just to see him. The emptiness was taking over again, and she was beginning to have second thoughts about loving him. Brian had changed and the few visits and the letters she had received held out hope.

Then Jane piped up, "You can't take that baby in this weather and even if you decided to go by yourself what about breast-feeding? We can't feed her. What if she won't take a bottle? You better not even think about going"

Liz knew they were trying to discourage her. She was sure they didn't think Brian deserved her visits. Little did they know this visit was just as much for her.

So she came back with, "I'll just have to take her with me then," instantly making up her mind.

"Oh, no, you won't! That is totally insane, taking a two-month-old baby on such a long trip alone and in this weather," Alicia said firmly.

Liz was apprehensive, but youth knows no bounds. She was going. She still had a bit of a stubborn streak and an adventurous spirit and no one could stop her once she made up her mind. She phoned the bus depot in town and checked the schedules.

"What a day you picked to go. Can't you wait," said Jane as she played with the toast on her plate.

Liz peered out the one clean spot in the middle of the big picture window that wasn't frosted over with a thick white crust. The wind was swirling the snow in small funnel-like whirls rising and breaking, then starting again as they travelled their way across the front yard. The road already had small drifts forming. Liz shuddered as she thought about the long walk to the highway.

But bravery born of youth prodded her on as she packed the diaper bag with diapers, one change of clothes, powder, Kleenex and a wet cloth in a plastic container. She carried all she needed to feed Stacy on her person, always the right temperature.

Wrapped in a receiving blanket, a thick warm yellow blanket and a white lace shawl, merely for looks, Liz hoisted her small cargo into her arms and set out. With her scarf wrapped around her face, Liz had visions of the "Perils of Pauline" dancing through her head. She remembered the silent movie where poor "Pauline" and her baby were ousted from their home by the evil mortgage holder during a vicious blizzard. She could almost hear the piano accompanying the scene with its frantic tune.

The snow blew all around them, but it wasn't as cold as Liz had imagined. On board the bus, it was toasty warm. She felt more secure amidst the varied travellers. She was not alone should anything go wrong. She laid her head back for the long trip while Stacy slept peacefully on the seat beside her.

She dashed to the washroom on their arrival at the bus depot in Toronto to change Stacy and feed her. There was only a half-hour stop over so she was rushed. She needed to wash her hands after changing Stacy. She panicked. *How can I wash my hands and hold her at the same time?* She started to feel very alone. Reluctantly, she laid her on the counter beside the sink hoping that she wouldn't roll. She scrubbed her hands as fast as she could and never took her eyes off Stacy for a second.

The washroom door squeaked open. "Oh, what a sweetie. How old is she?" asked an elderly lady dressed in finery, every steel grey hair in place.

"She sure is." said another round, jolly lady with two cheeks painted red like a clown.

"She's two months."

"What a brave girl you are, travelling alone with such a young baby," declared the lady in finery. "Where are you off to?"

"Thank you," Liz said. She was very grateful for the encouragement, but she could feel her face redden with shame as she tried to explain where she was going.

"I, uh, have to meet my husband in Brampton," she muttered then quickly changed the subject. She sat alone for the rest of the trip not wanting to answer any more questions.

When she arrived in Brampton, she fumbled in her purse with one hand while trying to hold Stacy with the other arm. Finally, she found a dime and called a cab to travel the last leg of her journey.

Exasperated from juggling the baby and trying to do everything else with one hand, she was relieved to finally sit back in the cab and lay Stacy down for a moment.

Such a long trip for such a short visit. But Brian was so enthralled with Stacy that Liz felt it was worth it. She beamed with pride as he stared down with disbelief at his daughter's beauty. She had sparkling green eyes and a tuft of blond hair on top of her head that he touched almost reverently.

Liz felt renewed hope for their relationship as she started out on the long trip home, a tear trickled down her cheek as she stared out the bus window. She was missing him already.

Winter melted into the spring of 1965. Liz had only gone to see Brian the one time with Stacy. She no longer had bravery born of youth. Now, she knew how difficult it was to make the trip alone and chose not to go a second time. But the cold lonely winter nights had taken their toll on her, and now that spring was in the air she just had to go and see him. Feelings of love had started to develop for Brian and for better or worse she was determined to make their marriage work. So she contacted Stacy Vance and pleaded with her to come along and help with the baby.

Stacy was more than eager to help Liz out. She had missed her and was anxious to spend some time with her so plans were made for the girls to meet in Toronto to make the rest of the long trip together. Alicia tried to discourage Liz by refusing to babysit Jimmy so Liz took both the kids.

She arrived in Toronto, met up with Stacy and after hugs all around they boarded the Brampton bus in the Bay Avenue depot. They were laden down with kids and bags. Each girl carried a child, a purse and a diaper bag. Liz didn't understand why, but Stacy even brought an umbrella. There wasn't a cloud in the sky but that was Stacy, always prepared for the worst.

As she struggled on the bus with her cargo, umbrella sticking straight out in front of her, she tripped on the top step, surged forward and the cold steel shaft of the umbrella poked right up the skirt of a lady sitting in the front seat. The lady shrieked, Stacy blushed scarlet and Liz broke out in fits of nervous laughter. She couldn't help herself.

Then Stacy quickly got up removing the umbrella and straightening herself out. Liz didn't know how, but Stacy had managed to clutch Jimmy upright in her one arm the whole time. Stacy apologized profusely, and the girls moved on down the aisle giggling. The scene set the mood for the rest of the trip, and they had a delightful time visiting and reminiscing. The miles flew by and before they knew it they were in Brampton.

Brian was thrilled to see them and when the guard turned his back momentarily Brian grabbed for Liz and clutched her tightly to him. Letting her go she saw tears in his eyes as he whispered, "I love you."

How she had longed to hear those words. How she longed for him to come home. Brian was in the prison but they were both doing time.

# Chapter 16
# The Homecoming

Liz dove off her lawn chair and bolted to the silver mailbox perched on top of the fence post at the end of the lane. The little blue Volkswagen had stopped, and the mailman had deposited something in the box. It had been two weeks since she saw Brian, and she was hoping for a letter. It was there! She ripped open the envelope as she had done on so many occasions before, reading it en route to the house. An enormous smile formed on her lips, and her face just beamed as she read the words, *I'm getting released next week. I tried for parole for good behaviour. I was backed by the people from St. Vincent de Paul. They've offered to help me out when I'm released. All I need is a place to stay.* Then, tears of relief spilled all over the letter. It was May, 1965. It had been eight long months since Brian had gone away. Finally, he was coming home

"Mom, Jane!" Liz yelled, her feet and her words running simultaneously. "Brian's coming home. Brian's coming home." She burst through the back door. "Brian's coming home. He needs a place to stay. He can stay here. Right?"

"What? Well, I guess so," Alicia hesitantly replied.

Liz never noticed her hesitation as she chanted on,"I knew you'd agree." She was ecstatic.

The week dragged, but then finally the day came. Jane, Gord and Liz loaded into the car to take the long trip to Brampton for the last time. Liz was bouncing inside like a two-year-old jumping on a box spring. She hardly sat still for the whole trip.

When they arrived, she greeted Brian, her face beaming, smiling widely. She felt as if she had a coat hanger in her mouth. He looked the same way. They clutched each other as though they were afraid to let go for fear it was all just a dream. The carousel whirled, the horses smiled with delight.

Then he said "Let's go. "This is the last I want to see of this place."

The little family lived at Liz's parents' home for a month. Brian had truly changed. He was so grateful to be home that he was very congenial with everyone. He no longer verbally abused Liz or treated her as though she was less than him. His miserable, unhappy attitude had changed. He had returned to the fun-loving, caring person who had courted her. Liz was pleased. She grew to love him more and more.

"Well, I don't like all the stairs but the apartment is certainly big enough for all of us and within our price range," Liz stated as she and Brian left the old two-story wood frame house that had an upper and lower apartment. They had looked at the upper apartment and decided somewhat reluctantly to rent it.

As they walked away from the house, Liz glanced back over her shoulder and drank in the scene and a vision flashed through her mind. She saw herself and Edmund with Carol, Darlene, Sheryl and the gang heading downtown to Jack's laughing and joking and carefree as they passed this very house. She felt a slight twinge of guilt as she recalled her oath to Edmund. She hoped he would forgive her for falling in love with Brian. Then she smiled as her thoughts changed, *Funny how life evolves. Who would have ever thought at that time I would be living in this house with a different man and his two babies.*

They moved into the little upstairs apartment and the first month was like a honeymoon, the honeymoon they never had. Liz was ecstatic for a time. Brian was very loving. Then she had some news that she was reluctant to tell him for fear it would change things.

"Brian, you're not going to believe this," she said

"What?" he questioned.

"I've missed my monthly," she answered.

"What, again? I thought you said that foam stuff was foolproof," he said sounding alarmed.

"I thought it was."

"We should use those birth control pills," he said emphatically.

"I don't want to. They're just experimenting with them. You know what happened with those Thalidomide babies, born with no arms and no legs. I just don't like to take a chance. Besides, it's too late now."

Brian took the news reasonably well considering his past reactions to her pregnancies. The couple continued happy, in spite of the pressure of more responsibility coming, and Liz was relieved.

Spring blossomed into summer. It was the month of July. Liz was one month pregnant. She and Brian awoke one Saturday morning in their large bedroom. Sleepily, Liz opened one eye. At the foot of their bed were two very white faces, four dark eyes and four little white hands barely reaching the top of the oak foot board.

Liz's eyes scanned the whole room. Everything was covered with what seemed like a light skiff of snow. As she slowly sat up she blinked white powder from her lashes and looked at Brian. He blinked white powder and looked back at her, a grin forming on his white lips.

"What is this stuff?" she burbled through gales of laughter at the sight of him.

"I don't know," he said, "but you look hilarious."

And with that he just roared. The look on the kids' faces was priceless. Liz felt very warm inside as her mind recalled the words she had once seen on a plaque. *The closest distance between two hearts is laughter.* It was true. She melted as her and Brian's eyes met and the laughter joined their hearts together.

Jimmy, one and a half, and Stacy, not quite one year were out of their cribs. Stacy was not yet able to walk, but she could scramble up the side of her crib and just fall out. She had an adventurous personality just like Liz's.

"I think it's Polyfilla," Brian answered guiltily. "I was going to fix the cracks in the hallway walls," he said as Liz's eye caught sight of the crumpled bag on the floor. Jimmy and Stacy had shaken and shaken the bag until everything including Brian, Liz and themselves was coated in a thin, white film.

"I'll help you clean it up," he said cheerfully as they rose from the bed, little white clouds puffing up around them. Two grinning faces looked innocently up at them. Brian did help. It was a tedious job, but soon done, and Liz's heart was happy as they worked together.

Brian was so good-natured lately. Liz was grateful for what the prison term had done for him. They were finally a happy family. She was sure she had done the right thing in persevering. The only thing that bothered her at times was her oath to Edmund to remain faithful to his memory. They had been so close, but she convinced herself that Edmund would forgive her for trying to make her marriage work.

"Liz, I'm just not making enough money doing odd jobs. Manpower is offering a course in drafting, all expenses paid. I would have to travel to Toronto, but it would certainly put me in a better position to get a good job. With another baby coming we could sure use it," Brian said at the supper table.

Liz stopped feeding Stacy and looked around at the tiny cluttered kitchen with its faded white and black print linoleum The floors were slanted, the linoleum didn't even reach the walls properly, and she thought how nice it would be to have more money to rent a place with wall-to-wall-floors, so she agreed.

They had purchased an old grey '49 semi-automatic Dodge with money Liz's parents had loaned them to get on their feet. Brian commuted forty miles every day to the drafting course in Toronto.

"I just can't keep up this pace," Brian said after a few weeks of travelling back and forth. "I'm spending too much time on the road. I'm too tired to do all this homework. One of the guys in my class says I can stay with him during the week if I help out with the food. I would probably save as much on gas."

"What about the car? I'll be lost all week without it," Liz said.

"Well, you could drive me down on Sunday night and pick me up Friday after school," he offered.

Placated by the offer she reluctantly agreed. They had been apart for eight months and they were just getting their relationship on its feet. Not only that, she still entertained some fears about Brian because of his running around in the past. Her fears proved to be unfounded though, but she was getting lonely during his absences. So she was thrilled one Wednesday afternoon when a phone call came bringing relief.

"Hi, Liz, it's Carol!" the voice at the other end of the phone chimed.

"Hi! hi!" Liz exclaimed excitedly. "How did you find me?"

"I got your number from your mom."

"Where are you? Still in Toronto?"

"No," she said "I did go back to Toronto with Ben after the last time I saw you, but it didn't work. He drank too much and I couldn't stand it. I moved back home with Mom in the Holland Marsh. I've met a really nice guy named Derrick. He works steady at Superior Propane. He has two boys. He's the greatest. I got a small inheritance from an old maiden aunt, enough for a down-payment on a big house in Beeton. We're all going to move in. Derrick is going to make the mortgage payments."

"Wow, that's great! Who's going with you?"

"Mom, my sister Darlene, my two brothers, Derrick and I and little Tommy and Kerry to start with. Then, when we're settled, Derrick's two boys will join us."

"Wow, you're really going to have a house full. How is Darlene, by the way?"

"Oh, she's doing good. She has a baby now too. I forgot to include him in the list. His name is Devin. She's got a bit of a problem though -- she's working at Martingale Villa, you know, that old folk's home in town and she hasn't found a ride from Beeton yet. She works shift work, and it's been difficult for her to find someone on her schedule."

"Wow, I've got a great idea. Run this by Dar and see what she thinks. Brian is away all week at a drafting course in Toronto and I hate being alone. Dar could come and stay here. I could babysit for her, make a little extra money for myself and have companionship at the same time. Martingale Villa is just around the corner," Liz said, excitement rising in her.

"That sounds great. I'll bet she'll go for it," Carol replied. "I'll make sure she does," she added, sounding relieved.

Darlene did agree and moved in right away. Liz knew that the arrangement would work because she knew Darlene. She had a warmth and kindness that radiated from her. She was also very agreeable and easy to get along with. She was Liz's chum since her school days. Darlene, Carol, Sheryl and Liz had been kindred spirits in their teens and still were. Darlene looked as good as she did then with her golden blond hair and grey-green eyes.

The arrangement was working perfectly and one morning after a week of living together Darlene chatted on happily to Liz

"You've just got to come to the home," she said as she wriggled into her white nurse's uniform in preparation for another shift. "The old people are so cute."

"Cute?" Liz questioned and thought, *The girl is daft. They're all wrinkled and old.* Darlene was very kind. She made a great care-giver.

"Oh, yeah, I just love their little faces. They look like little wrinkled potato people. They're so lonely and fragile. They need people. I don't understand," Darlene continued, running a brush through her hair, "why some women get jobs there." Her face reddened with anger as she continued. "They are mean, some of them, I'd just like to slap them. If they don't care for the work, they just shouldn't be doing it."

"What do you mean?" Liz asked.

"They have no patience with the poor old folks. I've seen them be brusque and rude. I've even heard rumours that some of the workers get physically abusive, although I've never seen any of it. If I did you can be sure I would report it right away. I have seen lots of bruises though, but of course nobody knows anything."

"Wow! I guess it takes a special kind of person to do that job. I know I wouldn't have the stomach for it, so I wouldn't even try."

Darlene suited the job perfectly. She was kind, generous and extremely intelligent. If you ever wanted to know anything, you only had to ask Dar. If she didn't already know, she'd find out for you.

"Oh, by the way," she called back over her shoulder as she was leaving, "Arnie is going to come over after work tonight, is that okay?"

"Sure."

Arnie was Dar's beau and also her baby's father. He was married but separated from his wife. Liz thought that Dar deserved better, but Dar seemed to be happy with him.

Bang! Bang! Bang! An insistent knock came at the door. Liz looked sleepily at the clock -- 11:45 p.m. Dar wasn't due home for another 15 minutes. She sauntered lazily to the door yawning, unlocked it and opened it to a solid man of medium height. You could say he was good looking in spite of his flat owl-like face. He had sky blue eyes and a nose not unlike a small beak which added to his owl-look.

"Hi, I'm Arnie."

"Hi, I'm Liz."

"Is Dar here?"

"Not yet. She should be home in 15 minutes."

"Can I come in and wait for her?"

I'd rather you didn't. My husband is away. There's a restaurant on the corner. Come back in 15 minutes," Liz said firmly, hoping he wouldn't think her rude. She was always kind and hospitable. She tried to follow in Vera's footsteps, but she would have been very uncomfortable alone in her apartment with a man she didn't know. Darlene told her later that Arnie hadn't thought she was rude. He had been impressed with her.

That was Liz's introduction to Arnie. It marked the beginning of Arnie and Dar's lives interweaving in and out of hers for years to come.

Time seemed to fly after that and after six months of getting reacquainted, Darlene had to move out because Brian finished his course and was moving back home.

Brian's school term had lasted from September until March. Darlene had lived with Liz for the whole time. Her stay was just too short. Even though Liz was glad to have Brian back she missed Darlene terribly after she left. They were true soul mates. They shared the same sense of humour and the same kindness and caring.

Liz loved Brian, but they were not as compatible as she and Darlene. The girls had spent many evenings drinking tea and laughing until tears rolled down their cheeks. Brian didn't always share Liz's sense of humour or her kind spirit like Dar did. And with his being away for the fall and winter the couple had drifted apart somewhat.

So Liz wasn't as happy as she had been when Brian first came home from prison. Not only that, Dar had always watched the kids for her while she ran to the store or did the laundry. With Brian out looking for work most of the time she had to manage on her own again.

The three long staircases to the basement to do the mundane chore of dirty laundry and diapers was the worst. Washing clothes in the old wringer washer in a basement filled with spider webs was not fun. She was a good little mother and would never have considered leaving the kids alone in the apartment. With only one month to go in her pregnancy negotiating the stairs was becoming unbearable.

With Stacy on one hip, dirty laundry in a basket on the other, belly out in front, and Jimmy behind clutching her skirt with hands like a tiny pair of vice-grips, they made the trip.

Then she had to carry the wet laundry up a flight of stairs to hang it on the line outside with Stacy still on her hip and Jimmy in tow. It was more than she could face.

She was exhausted, so she started doing the laundry in the bathtub upstairs and wringing it out by hand. Two kids in diapers, clothes for four people, not to mention, bedding for all, how much more could she stand? In the back of her mind she wondered how women managed years ago when there were no washing machines. The honeymoon was over.

# Chapter 17
# Fragile Blocks

Then one blustery March day the landlady called at the door to collect the rent. Jimmy opened it wide to her, and at the end of the hallway through the open bathroom door she spied Liz on her knees scrubbing laundry.

"Whatsa matter for you? Thatsa terrible theeng you gonna wash all you clothes by hand," the middle-aged Italian landlady rattled on.

Liz struggled to get up. "Oh, hi, sorry I didn't hear the door." She blushed with embarrassment at the Landlady's words.

"I tella you what Ima gonna do."

Then she proceeded to tell Liz what she was "gonna do". She was "gonna" move Liz out of that third floor apartment, she was "gonna" move Liz into a one-story house just out of town next to one of the packing plants, and she was "gonna" move Brian and the kids too.

The three bedroom house was unfinished, and, crafty lady that she was, she had quickly figured out a way to solve Liz's problem and her own at the same time. She would get Brian to do the carpentry work in exchange for lower rent.

"I'ma gonna give it to you for the samea rent you apayin' for thisa small one bedroom," she calculated.

Brian and Liz agreed to take a look at the house, and a few days later they found themselves at the front door. Having all the rooms on one floor was definitely to Liz's liking, but little did they know what was in store for them there.

At one time the house had been a fruit and vegetable stand, but now the vending side of it had been closed and converted to two bedrooms, separated by a living room area. French doors opened to the older portion of the house which had a bedroom, bathroom and a large kitchen area.

Painted white cupboards and a new double stainless steel sink in the kitchen gave the impression of cleanliness which was appealing. However, the kitchen needed lots of repairs. Someone had rough-cut the holes for electrical sockets but had not installed them, leaving holes in the walls. They would have to be patched.

The bathroom was in bad need of dry walling as was the bedroom. The ten-test foundation walls were up but nothing was finished.

The front half of the enclosed fruit-stand area had been dry walled but needed painting. The place had real potential, but Brian had his work cut out for him.

Liz was sure though that with his expertise at construction work and the experience he had gained building summer cottages, he would soon make this into a comfortable little home for their ever-increasing family.

They made the move with renewed vigour and dreamed of a model home by early summer. Liz was much happier living on the ground floor but shortly after the move she became quite ill with the flu. Being drained from having three pregnancies so close together her body was just not able to fight it off. As a result, she got weaker and weaker so little Stacy, a year old, ended up staying with Alicia. Liz was not happy about being parted from her but was concerned for her well-being.

She couldn't look after her properly so she was relieved that her mom and Jane took over her care. Stacy thrived, cute as a button, and Liz was relieved. Jimmy stayed with Liz as "Mommy's little helper." Somehow, they managed.

Weeks after moving in Brian burst through the back door.

"Rats, great big ones! I've seen rats around this place," he said with an edge to his voice.

"W-h-a-t?" Liz blurted out, her hair standing up on the back of her neck. "They're not in the house are they?" she asked not wanting to hear the answer.

"I don't know. I haven't seen any in the house. I'll bet they're from the packing plant next door. They probably hang around there and eat the stored vegetables. It must be good food because they're huge," said Brian.

Hugging little Jimmy close to her, Liz shuddered.

"I don't think they can get into the house, but that crawl space under the house is open. I think to be safe I should put some rat poison down there," Brian continued.

"Good idea!" Liz responded, then quickly did an about face and changed her mind. "What about Jimmy?" Stacy was still away but Jimmy played in the sand at the back of the house with his little cars. "What if the rats carry the seed with the rat bait on it into the sand and somehow he swallows it?"

"Yeah, right, that could be dangerous. Rat bait cements the intestines of the rats, stopping up their bowels and eventually killing them."

Vivid pictures of this happening to Jimmy made Liz's stomach flip. Fear prickled up her spine as she said, "We just can't take a chance."

Brian agreed. The young, inexperienced couple didn't know what else to do, so they did nothing. But in spite of the rat scare, life continued smoothly in the little bungalow home. At first, Brian was thrilled with the opportunity to show off his skills. He became quite creative and worked hard renovating the little house. He truly tried to change and to love Liz, but with his abusive character being so ingrained in him, plus the fact that he was frustrated from being unemployed, the novelty of family-life began to wear off and one evening he came home drunk.

"Where have you been?" Liz demanded fear in her heart.

"What's it to ya?" he threw back at her as he staggered through the door.

"You're drunk."

"So!"

Reeking like an escapee from a brewery, he pushed past her to head to the bedroom.

"Why? You haven't been drunk since before you went away."

"Oh, leave me alone," he muttered as he flopped on the bed.

Feeling devastated by this first sign of his returning to his old life-style, Liz walked away with her head down, looking like she had the weight of the world on her shoulders. She started to wonder if she had been wise to let herself fall in love with him. It was too late now.

Her heart had been opened to him. It was in his hands to do with as he pleased. She was frightened.

She knew drinking would destroy the fragile blocks they had started to paste together. The cement of their relationship was new and could easily crumble. She had chosen some time ago to leave alcohol alone. She had hoped Brian would do the same. Since she'd started having babies, she had avoided it totally knowing its eroding effects. She hated the Jekyll and Hyde effect it had on her.

The next day Brian was hung over and feeling guilty for his actions. But try as hard as he might to change, his old nature seemed to break through with a will of its own. Trying to compensate he decided to do some work in the kitchen but he was feeling rough.

"I'm going to fix the leaky taps in the kitchen," he said grumpily. "I've turned the water off at the main valve in the bathroom. I'll show you where it is. When I holler, you go in there and turn it back on."

"Okay."

Liz went industriously about her business until she heard Brian yell something from the kitchen. Assuming that he wanted her to turn the water back on, she went into the bathroom and cranked the valve on abruptly. She acted quickly because he had been so grouchy and she wanted to keep him happy. She hoped his night out was just one little relapse. She wanted things to go back the way they were so she was willing to bend over backwards to make that happen.

The screeches from the kitchen sounded like the banshees from hell. Liz wrapped her arms around her big belly and ran. What a sight! Brian was soaked. The air was blue all around him. Obviously, he had had his head over the opening in the top of the pipe when she opened the valve. With the taps removed a pressurized geyser of water was gushing almost to the ceiling.

Liz waddled as fast as she could to turn off the valve, shaking with laughter all the way. She couldn't help herself. Her sense of humour was still in tact. It soon fizzled out though as Brian, grumbling, finished the job, turned the water back on and headed for the bar.

After that first night Brian continued to drink, and so he was gone a lot. Liz was huge with pregnancy and left feeling ugly, depressed with her lot in life, angry with Brian for drinking and miserable with the remnants of the flu.

After coming home from the bar one night Brian said,"Guess what?" He sounded optimistic.

"What?" Liz returned despondently.

Ignoring her tone, he continued, "I've heard about an excellent job."

"Where?" she asked, not knowing whether to believe it or not. She was very disillusioned with him.

"At Union Carbide," he said, his voice raising with excitement. "They're opening up a huge new plant near Richmond Hill. The guys at the bar were all talking about it. Quite a few will be hired. I'm going to the office tomorrow to apply."

As his enthusiasm increased, so did Liz's hopes. In fact the relief she felt when he was hired was enormous. She hoped that the results of his getting the job would relieve the misery at home and that life would take a turn for the better again. She hoped he would stop drinking.

After a few short weeks Brian proudly announced to Liz, "I'm up for a promotion."

"That's great," she said. "You always were pretty smart."

"Yeah, I'm going to be the foreman over the whole section manufacturing containers for honey," he said patting her playfully on the rump. Accomplishment made him happier, at least for a little while. Liz was optimistic, but at the same time, somewhat skeptical as he was still drinking on occasion.

Bonnie Ann O'Shea was born April 20, 1966 at Newmarket Hospital delivered by the invincible Dr. Blackman after 24 hours of arduous labour. Liz was exhausted from being ill for so long and from the stress of worrying about where her relationship was going to end up. She was very groggy during the whole process and barely remembered any of it. Stacy had delivered so fast making her totally unprepared for Bonnie's long journey to life on the outside. The personalities of the girls eventually reflected the style of their birthings. Stacy was quick and eager and Bonnie was slow and steady.

As Liz looked down into that little round face topped with copper hair she beamed and her fatigue vanished. What a beauty. She was a miniature female Brian.

"Where's Brian?" she inquired of June, Brian's mother, who had come to visit.

She shrugged her shoulders and said, "You know Brian, never around when you need him." Liz knew this was true. It was their third child and he had not been there for any of the birthings.

Embarrassed by her son's conduct, June added, "Yesterday, he went to an auction sale and purchased a bunch of chickens. Where he is today I have no idea."

"He did what?" Liz gasped "Why?"

Knowing full well that the chickens would end up in her charge, Liz could envision herself with a newborn, two little ones under two, and heaven knows how many chickens.

The hospital stay for new mothers in 1966 was seven days, but still the day for Liz's release from hospital came sooner than she wished. She was still exhausted from a long labour, punky from the flu, and she didn't know anything about looking after chickens. As it turned out though they were a delight. Jimmy and Stacy just loved them. They loved helping Liz collect the eggs.

With the bright April sun streaming in through the big kitchen window Liz was delighted with her task at hand. Jimmy and Stacy were down for their naps and she was giving Bonnie her bath. She placed the little baby bath on the kitchen table under the window. She was thoroughly enjoying the warm sunshine, and the view. She glanced periodically at the yellow green of the budding trees in the distance. She felt a rush of warmth as she basked in her time alone with Bonnie and the beautiful spring day.

She lifted Bonnie's dripping body from the bath and placed her gently on the fluffy white towel she had put beside it. As Liz patted her gently with the towel, she glanced through the window and shrieked in horror.

The neighbour's tri-coloured mutt was barrelling into the yard yapping and snarling. The chickens scurried as fast as they could but were no match for the ferocious attacker. Chickens squawking, dog snarling, the chickens were tossed into the air as Liz stood stunned, hot tears flooding down her cheeks. Jimmy and Stacy loved the chickens. She had to stop the dog before he killed them all.

Frantically, she wrapped Bonnie in the towel and put her in her bassinet. On her way back through the kitchen she grabbed the new yellow corn broom. She raced out through the door and stood her ground firmly between the dog and the chickens. The dog snarled, his lip curled and he bared his teeth. Liz was frightened, but her anger took over and she went in blindly wacking the big dog several times with the broom. He yelped and ran, tail between his legs, but it was too late! She turned around and saw blood and dead chickens everywhere. She was beside herself with grief. The kids would be heartbroken. All twelve chickens were dead.

She slumped down on a stump and wept uncontrollably wondering how much more she could take. She was furious with Brian for buying the chickens; exhausted from looking after the three babes; haggard from not having enough time for herself, and lonely -- for Brian was gone all the time now. When he wasn't working he was away drinking. Now Liz's sense of humour was at an all time low. Her fragile blocks were crumbling. The carousel was screeching to a halt, the horses faces full of sorrow.

# Chapter 18
# God Sees The Little Sparrow Fall

The death of the chickens, although traumatic, provided some relief to Liz's busy schedule and even though Jimmy and Stacy were sad they soon got over it. With the passing of time Liz started to feel stronger and was better able to care for her household responsibilities. This made her happier, but she was still lonely because Brian was seldom home. After working for a few months he was able to buy a Morris Oxford, a little English car. Having the car made it easier for him to escape his family responsibilities.

Having made lots of new friends at the plant, he became the proverbial party person,. He taught himself how to play the guitar and was quite an entertainer. Mr. Congeniality, he could be very fun-loving, but the fun didn't include Liz and the kids. It was quite ironic, as Liz's grandmother had dubbed her *the party girl*. Now she was the ultra-responsible one while Brian had become *the party boy*.

Up in the night to nurse Bonnie and rising early in the morning with Jimmy and Stacy was getting Liz down. She was feeling better, but she hated the fact that all the responsibility for the children fell on her shoulders so one Saturday morning before Brian had the chance to get out of bed she sidled up next to him and said, "I could sure use some help with the kids."

"Hey I work all the time and provide for all of you. What more do you want?"

"I'd like you to act like a father once in a while. You're never home anymore. The kids need you and so do I. I'm lonely."

"Yeah, maybe you're right. You need a break. Tell you what, there's a party tonight at Tom and Heather's place. Let's get a sitter and you come with me. The baby's two months old now. You can leave her for awhile."

It wasn't exactly what Liz was hoping for. She would rather he stayed home with them as a family, but it was better than nothing so she agreed.

She went to that party, but she never felt as if she fit in. She didn't drink so she didn't fit, and she really wasn't comfortable leaving the kids with a sitter. Before the evening was over she was exasperated. Everyone was feeling no pain, and she couldn't relate to anyone. Brian became annoyed with her. He was enthralled with his newfound friends, and Liz cramped his style so he never took her with him again.

They didn't do anything together as a family so in June when Brian came home with the news about a company picnic, Liz was thrilled. Finally, they would be doing something together.

When the morning of the picnic arrived Liz was busy giving instructions.

"Here, put the top of the carriage in the back seat and the wheels in the trunk," she said to Brian who was busy packing diaper bags and the picnic basket into the car.

"Just a minute!" he said, irritated at her excitement. She was so enthusiastic she was getting way ahead of herself, and he was feeling rushed.

"Okay, I think we're all in," Liz said as they settled into the wine-coloured leather seats of the Morris Oxford. Bonnie was in the carriage in the back seat, Stacy was on Liz's knee and Jimmy was standing on the floor in the back beside the carriage top.

The kids were all excited, and Liz was looking forward to the events of the day. There would be races, egg tosses, three-legged races together with all the usual company picnic activities. Liz had tried to train the kids to run for the races on her mom's big front lawn, but they were too young. Jimmy and Stacy had run one to the left, one to the right in a widening circle. Joining back together halfway across the yard they had whacked tummies together, knocking themselves off balance and had landed on their diapered rears. Because of the astonished looks on their faces, Alicia, Jane and Liz had held themselves in fits of laughter. It gave a whole new meaning to the phrase, "Let the games begin".

On recalling the scene, Liz had to smile thinking of the pre-race preparations. They would be winning no races that day at the company picnic but at least they were all together and could enjoy the family outing.

After the short drive to Woodbridge they rolled into the parking lot. Jimmy was jumping up and down in the back and Stacy was squirming to get free from Liz. They had no sooner unloaded the carriage, the diaper bags and the picnic basket when Brian disappeared with his friends, beer in hand -- so much for a family picnic.

Right away the kids wanted to go to the wading pool, so Liz obliged. The path to the pool was silvery sifted sand which felt great on her feet but bogged down the wheels of the carriage as she made the effort to push her way through the throngs of picnickers. The weather was perfect though and after her anger waned and in spite of Brian's absence, she decided to settle in and at least enjoy the day with the kids. She loved her little brood.

Arriving at the round cement wading pool that was sunk into the ground, Stacy and Jimmy ran straight into the water. Liz had a time! She splashed in after them afraid that they would drown. The water wasn't very deep, but they weren't very tall either. Like all kamikaze toddlers, they had no fear.

Getting into the spirit of things, Liz sat down in the pool with them and was actually enjoying herself. Bonnie was sleeping in her carriage, Jimmy and Stacy were having a good time, and Liz was getting over Brian's absence. She didn't much like it, but she decided to enjoy the day in spite of him.

The hot sun beat down, the cool water refreshed, she was enjoying her offspring and the scene. Her mind drifted as she gazed at hundreds of bathers in different coloured bathing suits dotting the sandy beach, together with multitudes of rainbow coloured umbrellas. She slipped into a daydream of Edmund. She couldn't help it. Every time Brian hurt her she couldn't help but think how different her life could have been with Edmund. She loved the kids but they were a lot of work at this point and her memories of him seemed to be the only personal pleasure she had left.

Then Bonnie started to whimper and before long worked herself into a full-blown crying scream jolting Liz back to the present. Dirty pants, Liz decided from the tone of the cry. She had learned, as all mothers do, how to distinguish between cries. A demanding hungry cry was different from a slow starting dirty pants cry and the shrill piercing of a pain cry. This was definitely a dirty pants cry.

She stood up water dripping off her. Her pink and black two-piece clung to her as she leaned over to speak to Jimmy and Stacy. Even after three kids she maintained a perfect hour-glass figure.

"We've got to go back to the picnic table so I can change Bonnie, then we'll come right back," she promised.

Jimmy took hold of her extended hand, but Stacy took off in the other direction. Liz grabbed for her, caught her around the middle and tucked her under her arm like a squealing pig. She was determined to get free and Liz was just as determined for her to stay put. Now she had two kids screaming their lungs out.

Jimmy rode on the fender of the carriage while Liz pushed with one hand and lugged Stacy with the other. Pushing the carriage down the hill had been a breeze compared to pushing it back up the hill in the deep hot sand. Beads of perspiration broke out on Liz's face. The cacophony of sound coming from the carriage and the very angry squealing pig under her arm rent the air. People stared.

She didn't think she could ever be more embarrassed when a man commented, "You would think that that husband of yours would give you a hand."

Liz flushed with anger and shame as he spoke. She felt totally humiliated. Out of the corner of her eye, she spotted Brian sitting on the hood of a sparkling, forest green Chevrolet. He had one thumb over the top of a bottle of beer and was spraying several very pretty bikini-clad girls. They giggled as they dodged the foamy spray.

Liz felt a hot surge rise in her -- a volatile mixture of anger and jealousy. She felt the sudden urge to take Stacy and plant her right in his lap. It would have made her trek easier and put some of the responsibility where it belonged, but she was afraid of his anger so she refrained from doing so.

As she came within earshot, she saw Brian's buddy, who stood beside him, point at her and say, "Gee, nothing wrong with the looks of your wife in her little two piece bathing suit. How would you like to have mine, the jelly roll?"

Brian shrugged. At the time the comment didn't make sense to Liz. She wondered what it meant. It roused her curiosity but she was too angry to ask. Much to her dismay, she would find out soon enough.

All this happened with Stacy screaming in anger and Bonnie with discomfort. After cleaning Bonnie up, Liz struggled with her anger. She tried to stifle it, but the day was already ruined. Brian's actions poisoned her heart, and his buddy's comment played on her mind. She was miserable. She tried to put up a good front, but she was seething underneath and was very impatient to go home. Finally Brian reluctantly gathered all their belongings and piled them and the kids into the car. They screamed at each other all the way home. Liz was livid with him for flirting with the young girls instead of helping her, and Brian was furious that his good time had been cut short. After that company picnic Brian only came home to sleep.

Then one day after going on a picnic with her siblings, Liz stood in her mom's kitchen visiting with the family when Allen's wife, Fran, asked, "So when does Brian go to court?"

"What do you mean?" Liz asked very puzzled.

"Oh, oh, you didn't know? I'm sorry. I guess I've let the cat out of the bag," Fran said looking guilty.

"No, I don't know anything, what's going on? You might as well tell me now."

"I'm really sorry. I didn't mean to interfere. I assumed you knew. A friend of mine told me that Brian was caught with her seventeen-year-old sister, drinking beer on a side road. He was charged with supplying liquor to a minor."

"I told you you shouldn't have taken him back," Alicia croaked.

"Oh, Mother, just shut up!" Liz stated firmly.

Liz was livid. All the years she forgave him, all the hope she put forth, for what? To have her heart crushed once again. Then overcome with the need to know more, she asked,

"How did he know your friend's sister?"

"He's her supervisor at Union Carbide. If it's any comfort she's in big trouble with her family."

"I wonder how she'd like to be cited as a co-respondent in a divorce case," Liz returned bitterly.

Her mind flashed back to the company picnic. Now she knew what Brian's companion was getting at when he had said *Gee, nothing wrong with the looks of your wife in her little two piece bathing suit.* He knew Brian was running around and didn't understand why.

Babes and belongings, all in tow, Liz left her mom's, feeling totally defeated and very angry. This would be the last time this big Irishman would rove around on her!

When she finally got home, she rushed to get all the kids in the house and in a towering rage went searching for Brian.

"Brian! Brian O'Shea!" She shrieked.

"I'm in here," he called from the bathroom sounding defensive.

She barged into the bathroom. The door swung wide hitting his knee. He shoved it back shouting, "What's your problem?"

"What are you up to now?" she demanded.

"I'm going to the bathroom," he exclaimed matching anger with anger. "Get out!"

"Why don't you just go to the bathroom somewhere else, like your girlfriend's place?" she screamed as she lost control totally and stomped out. He slammed the door behind her.

She ran to the bedroom, crushing tears on her cheeks with the backs of her fists and headed for the closet. She ripped his clothes from the hangers and gathered armloads dumping them where she felt they belonged, in the dirt of the driveway. She was enraged beyond reason and had four years of aggravation pulsing in her blood.

"You're insane!" he yelled stomping out the front door, stepping over his clothes and making his way to the car.

"Where are you going now?" she yelled. "To see your girlfriend?"

"Out! Anywhere away from you."

Completely spent, Liz sank down on the couch and sobbed into her hands, not knowing which way to turn. The Morris Oxford squealed out of the drive, spraying gravel. Liz turned and saw Jimmy looking up into her eyes. He put his little chubby hand on her leg and gently patted it in an attempt to comfort her. She went to bed that night her eyes puffy beyond recognition and had a restless sleep.

Sometime during the night Brian returned and slept on the couch. As she got up hungover from her emotional bender the night before, Liz noticed the empty blue sleeping bag on the sofa. She searched the house until she saw the note on the table. Tears welled up and she started to shake as she read, "Here's $20.00. When this runs out go to the welfare."

That was it, two years of courting, plus four miserable years of marriage, plus three kids two and under, plus one lonely woman, 21 years old. It all added up to one big zero.

It was a hot August day in 1966. It could have been Kansas. The emotional tornado that had spun into Liz's life at age 16, had picked her up for a wild ride and then dumped her out with a thud, leaving her bruised, confused and in a big mess. And there were no ruby shoes to soften the blow.

Liz ran to the living room window and saw that the car was still in the driveway. *At least he left me the car.* She put Bonnie in her crib and Stacy in the playpen and ran out. She got behind the wheel, turned the key and through eyes blurry with tears she saw the needle of the gas gauge below E. *No wonder he left it. A lot of good it does me now.*

Feeling lost and confused, she fetched Bonnie and put her in the carriage pushing her as far up as she could. She put Stacy at the bottom end and Jimmy on the fender to walk the quarter mile to the gas station to phone her parents for help. She had been very angry with Brian and had wanted him out, but now that he was gone she had become frightened. She was afraid of being alone with three babies, but more than that she was afraid of the carousel. What would it do to her now?

She leaned forward with all her might on the carriage handle as those thoughts ran through her head. The wheels kept getting stuck in the gravel on the side of the road. She would just get the carriage going and it would snag again ramming the handle right into her solar plexus almost knocking the breath out of her. With the struggle the dam of tears broke again.

Finally she made it to the gas station. Leaving Bonnie sleeping in her carriage, she lifted Stacy out and wearily trudged into the garage, one child on each side.

"C-Can I please use your phone," she stuttered.

An older man in wine-coloured mechanic's coveralls looked toward the other man in the office and raised his bushy, white eyebrows. Then he glanced back at Liz. She was a sight. Her hair was all askew. She was pale and her eyes were red and swollen. Then with a very kind look in his eyes he said, "Sure."

"Mom, Brian left," she cried into the phone receiver. "I feel sick and scared. Can you come down?"

"We'll be right there, hang on!" Alicia quickly replied.

As Liz thanked the kind gentleman and hung up the phone, she heard Bonnie screaming. She looked through the huge plate glass window just in time to see a big German Shepherd dog moving away from the up-turned carriage. Her body stiff with alarm, she raced through the door her plight forgotten in the heat of the moment.

Her wee babe lay face down on the pavement. She threw the carriage to the side and reached down swiftly for her. Liz rocked Bonnie back and forth and wet spots from her tears spattered on Bonnie's tiny hand while Bonnie's tears made silver tracks down her cheeks. Bonnie's tiny forehead was all scraped from the asphalt.

In the midst of her turmoil, Liz had forgotten to put the brake on. The big dog had merely brushed past the carriage on the narrow sidewalk and started it rolling. Guilt was added to desperation and fear as Liz neared collapse. She made the trudge home hanging on knowing her mother would soon be there.

"What are you going to do now?" her father questioned nervously. "You can't come home with all these kids. Your mother's too old and besides she has just raised six plus Jane's two."

Liz knew her father's words were really her mother's, but she didn't mind deep down. She needed help, true, but she couldn't see herself living at home again feeling the restrictions of Alicia's rule. She was a fighter and she knew she would overcome this once she got on her feet.

"I know, Dad," she said agreeing, "I don't want to move back home again anyway, but I sure could use a couple of weeks there to get my bearings. I will have to make arrangements to get a job or get mother's allowance or something. I will need help with the kids while I figure it all out."

"Your mother and I were just about to take off on a holiday," he continued, "But Allen and Fran are coming to look after Grandma for us. You can check with them. I'm sure they won't mind helping you out. But just for a couple of weeks."

"That's good I don't want you to miss your holiday," she said sadly, wishing she was going on a holiday too.

Once at her mom's, she called Darlene and Carol and told them the news. She needed all the moral support she could get and she knew her old friends would be more than willing to give it to her and they did.

A few days later Liz sat on the wooden bench just outside her mom's porch door. Her tears poured freely down her cheeks. She was grieving the death of her marriage. She was aware of the warm sunshine offering her comfort, but her breaking heart refused to accept it.

Suddenly, she heard a frantic chirping! The sound penetrated her mental fog. Getting up, she followed the squawks which led her to a rusty 45-gallon drum filled with rainwater. She peered in and through eyes blurred with tears, she caught sight of a little sparrow flailing wildly. Blinking to clear her vision, she saw panic in its eyes as it was about to drown. She reached in slowly so as not to frighten it further and gently folded her warm fingers around its quivering body. Liz and the sparrow became invisibly linked by their fear and pain and as Liz's body was wracked with sobs, fellow-feeling flushed through her comforting her heart.

The words, *God sees the little sparrow fall,* kept echoing in her mind. She felt just like the little sparrow. She was flailing just like he was. She had broken her vow to Edmund. She had taken a chance and given her heart to Brian. He had crushed it. How she longed for someone to pick her up. How she wanted someone to hold her until she stopped quivering. She held on desperately, but gently to that little bird shaking with him until he dried. Saved, he flew away. If only she could fly away with him to a land of fluffy cotton clouds, rainbows and golden sunbeams. If only she could fly away to Edmund. But the future for Liz would be nothing like that.

# Part III
# FROLICKING FREE

## Chapter 19
## Circle Of Steel

A piercing, shrieking scream rent the still night air. Liz jolted straight up in her bed. Dar came running into the bedroom in a fit of hysterics.

"Liz, Liz, they're there, in the kitchen I heard them," she cried.

Liz rubbed the sleep from her eyes and said, "Heard what? What's the matter?"

Dar was white as a sheet as she rattled on.

"I heard scratching noises in the kitchen. Come to the bathroom with me just in case Brian was telling the truth."

Liz's mind raced back to Brian's story about seeing big rats outside the house. The words of Gordon Lightfoot's song, Circle of Steel, came to her mind, *A child is born to a welfare case, where the rats run around like they own the place.* When Liz had married Brian O'Shea, she never dreamed she'd be a welfare case, but with three babies all still in diapers she'd been left with no other choice.

Just as she had promised Liz had left her mom's and returned home after two weeks. Her best friend, Dar, had moved in to help her with her babies. She had brought her two year old son, Devin, so between them, the girls had four little ones to take care of. In spite of Alicia's words, "Two women with kids in a house together, it'll never work," the girls were determined to make it work.

"Are you coming?" Dar squeaked.

"Yes," Liz replied anxiously. On her way, she picked up the cornbroom that was standing in the corner by the French doors. She slowly turned the knob on the doors and flicked the kitchen light on at the same time. Dar screamed again! Liz jumped nervously as several huge brown rats with snake-like tails scurried across the length of the kitchen. They disappeared through one of the electrical wall plug holes that Brian never did fix. Liz wondered how they could slither through such a small opening.

"Damn! I really have to go, but I'm scared," Dar said clinging to the back of Liz's flannel night gown.

Armed with the broom, she said bravely, "Go ahead, I'll watch."

With eyes as big as saucers, she gripped that corn broom for all she was worth and stood guard until Dar finally came out.

"This is awful," Dar said. "The landlady has a nerve charging rent for this place."

A new terror suddenly filled Liz's mind. "They might get in with the baby," she gasped. She reflected on stories she had heard about rats chewing babies' ears or fingers off. The thought chilled her blood.

"Let's put lots of food out," Dar said, trying to find a solution.

"Yeah, maybe that will keep them in the kitchen and I'll put Bonnie's basket on top of the desk in our room."

"We'll have to keep those French doors closed all the time," Dar said.

"Yeah, I don't think they can get through them."

The girls put cookies and bananas on the counter. They weren't sure if it was a good idea to feed the rats, but they thought that if they did, the rats would leave their babies alone. They were afraid to put rat poison down for fear of the children getting into it. So the rat feeding became a nightly routine. Through the tiniest slit the rats could suck a whole banana right out of the peel. Liz wondered how many nights they had slept peacefully unaware of the rats? She shuddered as she wondered how many times they might have been in the very room with them.

The girls planned to give notice and move out as soon as possible, but before they had a chance to do so their landlady showed up at their door. The deal was *Brian was to do repairs on the place for cheaper rent,* and he was long gone so she was upset to say the least.

"I'ma sorry but you girls are gonna hafta move out. There'sa no way I want two girlsa livin' alone ina my house. Next theeng you gonna be havin' men around and wild parties," she said coldly, her Roman nose twitching nervously.

"No problem," Liz said.

"We can't wait," added Dar. "This place is infested with rats."

The landlady moaned a big sigh and left. Liz wondered if she knew about the rats all along. The cozy 3-bedroom bungalow was clean enough, but it was located next to a huge vegetable packing plant which Liz assumed was where the rats were coming from.

After she left the girls grabbed the newspaper to browse the rental ads, in search of a new home.

Then after a week of searching they were totally exasperated when at one place after another they faced the same problem, "No kids! No pets!" Where were they supposed to go? They packed as much as they could do without and piled the boxes neatly in the living room. The landlady was anxious to have them out, and they were just as anxious to get out of the rat house, but they couldn't find a place to go.

Two more weeks went by and the landlady informed them she had already rented the house to people who were ready to move in right away. The new tenants' place had also been rented, so they had to move in immediately. With winter coming on, it became harder and harder to find places to rent.

"The new tenants will be in for a big surprise," Dar said, after a day of searching.

"You mean the rats?" Liz asked.

"Yeah, rats and all of us living in with them too, if we don't get a place."

Liz laughed as she painted a picture of it in her mind, four adults, eight kids, and goodness knows how many rats all lined up in the kitchen waiting for something to eat. Then her mood changed as she started to feel bad for the new tenants because of the rat situation. She wasn't sure the landlady would tell them, and she and Dar hadn't met them yet. The new people had rented the place sight unseen. They were as anxious as the girls were to find a place to live.

Then two days before move-out day, the landlady showed up again. Liz and Dar had searched a thirty-mile radius for a place.

"Whatsa matta for you? No house yet?" asked the anxious landlady.

"No!" They blurted in unison.

"I hava solution. I got a bigga house right ona Main Street."

The house had been condemned and was slated to be torn down in the spring. There were Portuguese people living upstairs and they had until spring to get out. The landlady talked to town council and they agreed to let Liz and Dar move in until then also.

Desperate by now the girls agreed.

Jane and her husband, Gord, moved Liz and Dar in with his half-ton truck.

"What a dump," declared Dar.

"Oh, this is terrible," said Jane.

"Well, what can we do?" Liz said, discouraged. "We have no choice. At least there are no rats, I hope," she added on second thought. The place was grey clapboard and reminded her of the nursery rhyme -- *There was a crooked man, who had a crooked house.*

Stepping right off the sidewalk of Main Street, through the front door, they entered a huge foyer with a curving, oak staircase that ran up to the second floor. The house must have been a mansion in its day, but its day was long past. Liz's eyes travelled down the hall past the staircase to a grey kitchen. She wasn't sure if it was supposed to be grey or if aging had made it that way. If that house could have talked, it would have told quite a tale. There was a walk-in closet that had a secret passageway to the kitchen, and the kitchen had a back set of stairs that led who knew where. As they were peering at the back stairs, the back door of the kitchen flew open and several dark and very good looking men came through. The men smiled, flashing bright white teeth, nodded and pointed to the stairs. They muttered indistinguishable greetings.

"Wow! These must be the Portuguese," said Dar out of the corner of her mouth. She grinned and nodded in their direction. Her grey/green eyes were dancing with mischief.

"Looks like they have to come through our kitchen to get upstairs," she continued. "This could turn out to be quite an adventure."

An adventure, indeed, it turned out to be, as Liz and Dar looked for a bathroom.

"There isn't one." Dar yelled from the other room.

"There must be. Maybe it's upstairs." Liz called as she started up. To her surprise, she walked right in on a big family eating a meal. There were several men, one woman and a couple of kids. The room smelled tantalizingly delicious.

"Uh, I'm looking for the bathroom," she muttered, feeling embarrassed about interrupting their meal. They smiled and nodded. She realized then that they didn't understand a word of English but as she turned, she spotted the washroom down the hall.

"There it is," she said, pointing her finger self-consciously and backing out. They all nodded and smiled.

So, the two-storey house was actually a single-dwelling place. There was no division between the two apartments which meant Liz and Dar had to go through their neighbour's place to go to the bathroom, and their neighbours had to go through Liz and Dar's place to get upstairs. They shared such close quarters, but the two families never did get to know each other because of the language barrier.

Rats? -- No. Holes in the walls? -- Yes. There was nothing they could do about the holes in the walls in their combination livingroom/bedroom, nor could they fix the tiny holes in the floors because they didn't know how. They did, however, acquire some bright yellow wallpaper and some white paint. They brightened up the kitchen with the paint and wallpapered a portion of the large foyer to serve as a dining area where they ate with some privacy. There wasn't much point in doing more as it would be torn down anyway, but they did insist on cleanliness where they had to prepare food and eat.

At dinner one evening, Jimmy, Stacy and Devin couldn't sit still. They kept looking upstairs and giggling.

"What's your problem, you guys? Eat your supper." Liz chided.

Dar grinned and pointed upwards to the stairs with her fork and said, "Looks like we've got company."

There, wedged between the rails of the bannister, were two sets of mischievous eyes peering down at them. The eyes were accompanied by two shy little smiles.

Jimmy, Stacy and Devin squealed with delight.

"Hi", Liz said and immediately the Portuguese kids took off giggling.

"Cute, eh?"

"Yeah."

The rat house and the condemned house were just the beginning of Liz's problems. Thank goodness for Dar. She was as quick as a whip with a great sense of humour and a deep warmth that Liz adored. Liz was so grateful for her. She helped to dispel the emptiness that had haunted her since childhood plus she helped Liz to feel braver.

A few days after they moved in a brisk knock came at the door. Liz opened it to a very British-looking woman, staunch in her demeanor, with a pointy nose, wild eyes under thick glasses and bushy brown hair.

"Hello, my name is Miss Nutworthy. I'm your social worker. "May I come in for a moment?"

The girls had both acquired mother's allowance to live on. Dar had given up her job at Martingale Villa when she had to move back to Carol's in Beeton. With shift work it was just too difficult to get a ride. This was the girls' first home visit from their worker, and they were nervous about what she would have to say about them living together.

Liz slowly opened the door for her to enter. She came in, talking all the way to the kitchen chrome set and sat down.

"Now, what do we have here? Two girls living together on Mother's Allowance and four children. Do you girls intend to stay together?"

"Yes we do!" they both piped up, fearing that she might want to separate them.

"Well, why doesn't one of you go to work while the other one babysits, alleviating one Mother's Allowance cheque and babysitting charges."

"That's a great idea," Liz said wanting desperately to be off welfare. She entertained a dream for her children. She would put them all through college and help them to become something, so they didn't have to struggle the way she did. "I could start looking for a job right away."

"Not you, you've got three children. It would be better for Darlene to go to work. Then you could be home with your babies."

Darlene's face flushed red. She almost looked guilty.

"Well, I'm not going to be on welfare very long anyway," Liz said with a wide smile, "I'm going to meet a good man who will take care of us." She was determined to find someone to love her and help her care properly for her offspring. She was optimistic.

Miss Nutworthy laughed. "Oh, my dear, you have high hopes. What man would take on a woman with three children?"

Her words ripped through Liz's heart like a knife. Her voice caught in her throat. Nothing came out. How dare she? Miss Nutworthy indeed. *She is a nut,* Liz thought, trying not to be discouraged by her words. She never thought for a moment that she wouldn't be able to get another man. It was all important that she do so. She had to keep the carousel under control. And three kids or not, she was confident she would get one eventually, but in the meantime, Dar would work and she would be housemother.

Now, back in Bradford and not needing a ride Darlene applied at Martingale Villa. It was no surprise to Liz that Dar immediately got her old job back.

Then one blustery winter day Dar came home from work and said, "What a nerve that Betty had today. You know what she said?"

Dar screwed her face up into a sour expression and squeaked her voice in imitation of Betty Smith, one of her co-workers.

"I guess Liz will be out running around now that her husband's gone. Her being used to having a man around and all. You know what I mean?"

Liz laughed at Dar's impression and then on the serious side said, "What a witch. It's hard enough to look after three kids by myself and rough it on welfare without people talking behind my back to boot."

Liz's mind flashed back to Dar's mom's plight. How the "nice girls" at high school had talked about her being left by an alcoholic husband. Betty Smith had been one of the "nice girls". It was like history repeating itself.

"Well, I set her straight," Dar said emphatically, knuckles on her hips, "I told her, not Liz, she's a good Christian."

Liz didn't attend a place of worship, but she had been taught good Christian morals. In spite of her strong need for male attention and affection, she tried to stick by those morals, so there was often a war waging within her between her strong moral self and her powerful need. She had experienced a couple of close encounters with Olly and David, but she still considered herself morally clean and was proud of that fact. She wanted a man, true, but she certainly wasn't going to be a sleazy run-around. She would wait for Mr. Right. Betty Smith's words made her even more determined to stick to her guns. She had already broken her vow to Edmund. She wasn't about to do worse.

So Liz stuck close to home and continued to be the proverbial house mother -- baking pies, cleaning house, making supper, doing laundry, and tending to four children. Jimmy, Stacy, Bonnie and Devin were a joy to her, that is most of the time. She could have abandoned them all, though, the day they dumped her freshly baked graham cracker pies upside down on the floor.

And while Liz stayed home Dar continued to go out to work. Months went by and everything was working out just fine. Then one evening while they were having tea Dar said, "I've got something to tell you."

She was sitting straight and stiff. She fiddled with a button on her blouse with her head down as though she was hiding something.

"I haven't been totally honest with you and I feel just sick about it. I can't live with myself any more."

Searching her mind for clues, Liz couldn't imagine what Dar was keeping from her.

"What is it? There isn't anything you can't tell me."

"I'm pregnant. I was pregnant when I moved in with you at the rat house. I was embarrassed to tell you," Dar said.

"Why? We're good friends."

"Well, you've got such strong morals, and I didn't know if you'd want me around with another child to care for. I just about died when Mrs. Nutworthy said *I* should be the one to go to work."

"Hey, my morals are for me. *Judge not lest ye be judged*," Liz quoted. "And as for another child, what's one more?" She laughed, then Dar joined her, feeling very relieved. "How far along are you?" Liz asked.

"Six months."

"Six months! Where is it? There's nothing there. How can that be possible. How could I not tell when we sleep in the same bed?" Liz was flabbergasted. At six months pregnant she had to waddle. Dar didn't even show yet.

Dar was tall and willowy and hid her pregnancy extremely well. With her long torso and billowy flannel nightgown, she had completely concealed it.

Liz hugged her and they spent the rest of the evening chattering about having a new baby in their family. Dar's pregnancy was a hurdle for the girls but they had jumped it gracefully and their friendship grew even stronger.

Winter froze its way into February, 1967. Icicles three feet long dangled from the roof of the crooked house, and the problems just kept coming.

"Boy, it sure is cold in here!" Dar shivered.

"I know," Liz quivered in sympathy.

The plaster was gone from the inside walls, boards were gone from the outside in various spots, so between the exposed slats on the living room wall, they could see the snow falling. They had piled all the blankets from their bed onto the kids. They wondered how their Portugese neighbours were faring. The house had been toasty warm until mid-afternoon, and then it started to cool off rapidly. Now, they could see their breath.

Just then, Arnie, the father of Dar's children, dropped in for a visit.

"Arnie, there must be something wrong with the furnace. Will you check it for us?" Dar asked, shivering to keep warm.

"First I'll check the oil tank."

Back in a few minutes, Arnie came in stomping the snow off his big work boots and brushing off the shoulders of his thick denim jacket.

"You're out of oil," he called from the front door.

"Oh, shoot, it's three days 'til payday. I hoped the oil would hold out until then. I guess with all these holes in the walls it takes a lot more. It's like we're trying to heat all of Bradford. I'll call the oil man." Liz said.

"Hi, this is Liz O'Shea calling. We've run out of oil. Will you deliver at this time of night?"

"Sure," he said,"As long as you have cash."

"Well, that's the problem. My friend and I get paid in three days and for sure we'll pay you on the first."

"No cash, no oil!"

"But we have four little kids, and it's getting really cold in here."

"Sorry ma'am, no cash, no oil!" he repeated callously.

Liz hung up the phone feeling totally discouraged.

"Arnie, do you have any money?" Dar asked.

"Not a cent to my name; I'm between paydays. I've got an idea though. I'm going to the job site. I'll be back soon."

Arnie worked with heavy machinery. He drove bulldozers and steam-shovels and the like. He was what you would call a man's man, rugged and tough.

In a jiffy, Arnie was back with his pick-up loaded with several five gallon pails of diesel fuel.

"Will it work?" Liz asked, nervously.

"I don't know, but if we blow up, we'll know it didn't," chuckled Arnie.

He carefully poured the pails of fuel into the oil tank one at a time. Then he lit the furnace. Lo and behold, it worked.

Dar and Liz hugged each other, dancing around, laughing, as the room warmed up.

They burned that fuel for three days until their cheques came in. In spite of Arnie's exterior ruggedness, he turned out to be a knight in shining armour for two damsels in distress.

The set up initiated by Mrs. Nutworthy had been perfect, but as Dar got farther along in her pregnancy, she got tired out and had to stay home more. Eventually she would have to quit her job completely. Her staying home gave Liz a nice break. Liz was getting bored with being the housemother. Not only that, the old emptiness was eating away at her and the carousel was tugging, persistently trying to turn.

At first Dar's company had helped tremendously, but with the passing of time the hollow feeling began to work on her again. She never dreamed that she would miss Brian as much as she did. If she hadn't let herself fall in love with him perhaps the overwhelming feeling of loss wouldn't have been so severe. She would look for him in the crowds at the mall. She would see a man in the street from the back and think *Aha! There he is!* She would feel excitement rising in her and then the man would turn around, not Brian, a stranger and despair would set in.

Carol and Darlene could see Liz deteriorating so together they came up with a plan. Carol's favourite saying was *Look good! Feel good! Do good*!. She recited it to Liz and then said, "Come on, we're going to Newmarket Plaza. You need a new look. Derrick made a real good bonus at work this week and he shared it with me. I know you've been putting every extra cent away in your college fund for the kids and I'm going to treat you. You can pay me back someday when you get rich."

The girls shopped all afternoon while Dar watched the kids. Liz came home with brown stirrup pants, a brown simulated suede coat, knee high brown leather boots and several sweaters of varying colours that she could mix and match with the rest of the outfit. She had tried to dissuade Carol from spending so much money on her, but Carol wouldn't hear of it.

"Now, get changed, put on your makeup and fix your hair because Derrick and I are taking you out on the town. Enough of this grieving. Time to come alive again," Carol said as she gave her dear friend a big hug. She was worried about Liz being so despondent.

Derrick and Carol took Liz to the Village Inn in Bradford while Dar babysat. Liz had followed Carol's instructions and gazing at herself in the full length mirror in the ladies room, she was amazed at the transformation. After four years of pregnancies and problems she had become somewhat haggard looking. But now, she looked fantastic. She hadn't looked as good since the time she went out with the girls at Gold Bond Company to see Ronnie Hawkins. Her new look gave her a tremendous lift. Carol was right. Look good! Feel good! She was feeling better already.

The bar was new territory for Liz. She had only been to a night club once before. She was nervous. She didn't drink. She didn't like the effect alcohol had on her in the past, but she certainly did enjoy the live band, the gay atmosphere and the happy people.

Going out with Carol and Derrick became a weekly event. Several young men showed interest in her, but she didn't return their advances. She found she wasn't quite ready to get into another relationship, but their attention certainly gave her confidence a boost.

With this newfound confidence, she felt pretty. She started to long for the carousel to turn but she feared the results. She wanted a man, but after Edmund dying and Brian leaving, she was afraid. The losses had been terribly painful, but at the same time, she was battling the emptiness inside her again. She tried to soothe it by dwelling on Edmund's memory. It helped to some degree. Her friends Dar and Carol helped too, but the cursed emptiness just wouldn't go away. Betty Smith's words *"being used to having a man around"* plagued her as the carousel tugged relentlessly.

# Chapter 20
# Bee Town

Beeton -    Originally named Bee Town because the settlers were
Beekeepers

The long icicles on the eaves of the crooked house were dripping
in the warm afternoon sun. The mere beginnings of torrid rivers
trickled down the gutters. They could smell it in the air, spring
was just around the corner. Liz and Dar had to start thinking about
moving.

Carol informed them about an apartment in Beeton that had
been empty for some time. Rumours had it that the reason this
particular apartment was empty for so long was because it was full
of cockroaches. That in itself wouldn't have deterred Liz and Dar
from checking it out; after all, they had lived through the rat house
and the condemned house, but Liz was somewhat reluctant to move to
Beeton where Carol and Derrick had settled. Bradford was home, and
she had lived there a long time. She had met and fallen in love with
Edmund there, had her babies there. But in the end, she did agree to
at least look at the place.

Viewing the apartment clinched the deal. Liz and Dar were very
impressed. Each room was tastefully decorated, and it was sparkling
clean. They came through the large windowed porch into the kitchen
which was huge. Complementing the shiny grey tiles on the floor was
white wainscotting with lime-green trim. The top half of the walls
were covered in a quaint teapot wallpaper in tones of yellow, orange,
and lime green on a white background. They were delighted with the
big, bright, clean kitchen.

Off the kitchen was a hallway leading to a nice baby pink bathroom,
just right for two girls. Walking into the living room was like walking
into an atrium of willowy trees in a serene landscape. The wallpaper
created an atmosphere of cozy dreamy comfort complemented by the
soft cream colour of the wainscotting. After the condemned house

with its holes in the floors and walls, walking through the rooms of this place was a delight. Down the hallway were two bedrooms. One was papered with tiny pink roses, perfect for ladies. The other was a carnival of clowns, perfect for kids. It was exactly what they were looking for.

They could put Bonnie, Stacy and Devin in the clown room. With the hallway for Jimmy's little bed, they would have the rose room for themselves. Now the only dilemma was, would he rent to them with so many kids?

Before the kindly old gentleman with the white hair and soft blue eyes could say anything, Liz blurted out, "We'll take it!"

"When can you move in?" he asked in a flash.

Liz looked at Dar and saw the same astonished look on her face that she was sure was on her own.

"Right away," Liz said just as quickly before he could change his mind.

They were beside themselves with joy. As they were getting into the Morris Oxford Dar said, "He actually rented to us. I can't believe it. It's a miracle. He didn't even ask about the kids. Pinch me! Is it real? What a great place. It's the nicest we've seen. There can't be any cockroaches, it's too clean. It's a good job we didn't listen to the gossip, we might have lost out."

All the way home, they chattered about where they would put things and how they would get moved in. It seemed too good to be true. It was. Shortly after moving into the apartment, they discovered that the cockroach rumours were true. They never saw any cockroaches, but what they did see was very hard to believe.

The first Saturday morning after they moved in the kids were quiet as mice so Dar and Liz, exhausted from the move, slept in. Simultaneously, the two young women, stirred by a sixth sense, felt the presence of someone strange in the room. Liz blinked awake and could hardly believe her eyes. There at the end of the bed was a man.

In the clarity of astonishment, her mind registered that he was in a blue grey uniform, had sandy brown hair and a non-descript face. With a puzzled look on her face she turned to Dar for an explanation. Dar was looking at Liz with exactly the same expression.

On the man's back was a small tank of some sort and in his hand was a nozzle. He was spraying who knows what around the baseboards. In the slow motion of profound amazement they sat up. Glancing towards them with a curt nod of his head he said, cheerily, "Good morning, girls," clicked his heels together, saluted and went out the door!

"Who was that?" Dar said, as she stared at Liz in bewilderment.

"*What* was that is more like it?" Liz sputtered through fits of laughter.

"Never mind that -- how did he get in here?"

"I don't know," Liz said, "The kids must have let him in somehow. What the heck was he doing?"

"He was the exterminator, I suppose," Dar said as she got up.

"How strange. Sure is a friendly place, this Beeton," Liz said as she crawled out of bed and went in search of the kids.

"How did that man get in here?" she asked as she walked through the archway to the kitchen, with her hands on her hips.

Six little innocent eyes stared up at her then turned simultaneously to gaze at the corn broom in the corner. When the exterminator had come to the door, the kids had used the broom to push up the hook that the girls had installed at the top of the door to prevent them from getting outside on their own.

So the rumours about the cockroaches were true and the landlord knew it. Liz and Dar weren't the only ones eager to rent the apartment. The landlord was just as anxious to rent it out. It had been empty for months because of the rumours and when Liz and Dar were so enthusiastic, he jumped at the chance, but he had very kindly hired the exterminator. The exterminator was supposed to arrive *before* they moved in. But nonetheless, they never did see a cockroach.

Weeks flew by in their clean, comfortable apartment and spring was in full bloom. The girls were sitting at the kitchen table drinking tea and basking in each others company. They had grown to love each other like sisters. The front door was wide open and a warm breeze was blowing through the screen door. From Dar's position she could see right out onto the street.

"Liz, you'll never guess who's here," she said, grinning and rolling her eyes as she got up and went to the front door.

"Who?"

"Your mom. That's no big surprise; she probably came to see our place. But guess who brought her?" she teased.

"I don't know, who?" Liz said, coming to join Dar at the front door. "Oh, it's Fred! I haven't seen him since I was a teenager. I have often wondered what happened to him. Oh, Dar, look; he's missing an arm."

"Yeah, I see that. Hey, what about him? He's a really nice guy and he did have a crush on you at one time?"

As a teenage boy Fred had adopted Liz's family as his own. He was a drifter who worked on a farm up the road from Liz's. He had had a crush on Liz, but she had just met Edmund at the time. He hung around anyway and won Alicia's approval. Alicia had been kind to Fred, and he had just loved her. For some reason the two had hit it off. It always amazed Liz. It seemed out of character for her mother. Now, here he was coming up the walk to Liz's place. Liz toyed with the idea that Dar had suggested as she watched his muscular male body saunter up the walk.

"Hi Fred, you're a sight for sore eyes," Liz said as she sidled up to him smiling widely.

He threw his one thick muscled arm around her and playfully squeezed.

"It's good to see you. Come on in. What happened to your arm?" she asked, sympathetically.

After introductions all around, Fred began his story.

"When I was about seventeen, I spent the summer hopping freights to see the country. I misjudged the distance and fell while jumping off a train. I landed on my back and my arm flew up over my head and was severed completely by steel on steel." He held his jaw tight and the girls screwed up their faces, squeamishly.

He told them that it happened outside a small town. Totally in shock, he had carried the severed arm with him into town to get help in the hopes that they could somehow stitch it back on.

"Besides," he said finishing up the tale, "my good ring was on the third finger. Soon as I got there I passed right out. Don't remember a thing after that."

Liz was amazed. He didn't seem to be affected by the loss of his arm. He still had the same sense of humour. She had complete admiration for his obvious strong constitution. She started to get hopeful. Then he continued, telling her that he was happily married. Her hopes were dashed. She was happy for him, but she couldn't help feeling a little envious. She wondered, *Why is happiness so elusive in my life?*

With the move, Liz's problems started to settle down and not only that, she was growing to love Beeton with its small population of 962. It was no longer Bee Town. It had become kids' town. Some places are retirement towns, some are industrial towns, others are business towns, Beeton was kids' town. Families thrived there. It was safe, as safe as it had been in the 1800s. It was perfect for Liz's little family and the kids loved it there.

Main Street was short with store fronts that could have been featured in a western movie. The business section was made up of a small I.G.A. store, run by a very friendly Italian couple; a small hardware store; A five cent to a dollar store that had a snack bar where the local gentry met to socialize; a family restaurant run by two sisters who prepared all the home-cooked meals on a wood stove; and a beauty salon with the best hairdresser in the county. In addition to that there was a community pub where the words "everybody knows your name" were invisibly written on the marquee. Of course, Otto's, the corner store, was where all the kids went to spend their quarters. This unique little shop with all its gadgets and sundries was a frequent haunt for Liz and Dar's family. Otto was a German gentleman with thick glasses and a bald head. His Swedish wife Eva was almost twice his height. As she welcomed Liz and Dar to the community Eva called to her husband, "Dadee, dadee, cum ant see our nuuu nabors." Liz and Dar felt welcome.

But the best of Beeton was Centre Street which ran off Main Street. Growing on both sides as far as the eye could see were giant maple trees, towering over the street and touching leafy finger tips, forming a living green canopy which in the fall was transformed into a blaze of crimson.

It was easy to love Beeton with its fall fair and its lush green park. Morning greetings were abundant as Liz and Dar walked to the post office for their mail every morning. The warm, friendly atmosphere slowly nursed Liz back to life. She began to feel whole again, coming out of the grief over the death of her marriage.

She was eased out of her depression. Instrumental in this transformation were the many happy hours that Dar and Liz spent in Carol's kitchen and also the Sunday dinners around Vera's old oak table. In the grain of the oak wood you could find the lines of their lives, the times the girls had shared in their teens, the love, laughter and the tears. Now, at Carol's, the grain of the wood absorbed even more of the same. Liz, Carol and Dar's kids played together, being within the same age ranges. Shortly after their move to Beeton, Dar gave birth to her second baby, Sherri, so with Dar's two, Liz's three and Carol's three there were eight kids in all. The combination of the families was like a melody, different notes, well orchestrated and in harmony, a delightful tune.

Yes, Liz was healing and with the healing came a better disposition. One unusually hot May afternoon, after a torrential-like downpour she got a gleam in her eye and eagerly exclaimed to Jimmy and Stacy, "I've got an idea. Come on, let's get our bathing suits on."

Jimmy and Stacy, now three and two, started to jump up and down and squeal with delight at Liz's excitement. Bonnie, now one, was down for her nap. After changing into their suits the three of them ran out the front door.

"Come on look at the water running down the road. Let's run through the puddles." Rivers of accumulated crystal clear raindrops were gurgling down the sides of the road.

Grabbing Jimmy and Stacy by the hand Liz ran with them back and forth through the little lakes that had formed on the side of the road. The water sprayed up all around them and the kids giggled with glee. Liz laughed along with them. She was like a big kid herself. She was having just as much fun as the kids were.

She reflected on how she had done the same thing as a child. She had run through the puddles in the school yard and loved the feel of the water spraying up on her. She had laughed and laughed, but the joy had soon been taken out of it as she had trudged home soaking wet, picturing what Alicia would do. Fear had plagued her all the way home. Her mother was going to be mad, and she had known it. The turtle had taken off her shell to romp and play. She had known what the results would be, but the temptation had been too great as she had watched all the other kids having fun.

Now, she was allowing her children to have the fun without the fear. She would not follow in Alicia's footsteps. Her kids would never be afraid of her.

The atmosphere in Beeton was perfect for her to enjoy bringing up her brood. Where else could you run down the Main Street in your bathing suit without being noticed? So in spite of her reluctance in moving to Bee Town it turned out to be the best move she ever made. At least in the beginning.

# Chapter 21
# Seriously Altered

It was another hot day in May, 90 degrees. The temperatures broke records all that week. Liz, Dar and Arnie sat around the kitchen table nursing frosty glasses of iced tea. Liz was looking terrific. She was thriving in Beeton. She had loyal friends. She had three beautiful kids. Jimmy measured three feet high on the door post. He was developing into quite a little man. He was protective over his little sisters and was quite a cautious, well behaved boy. Stacy on the other hand turned out to be a handful for Liz. She was constantly getting into trouble. She had Liz's adventurous spirit, and Liz almost felt empathy for Alicia. Bonnie, on the other hand, was following in Jimmy's footsteps. She was quiet and somewhat aloof.

Liz felt very much alive again and with the renewed physical and emotional health, came the first stirrings of physical craving, yearnings for male companionship. The move to Beeton and the family atmosphere there had taken her mind off the loneliness and the emptiness that always plagued her, but now she was surging with energy like a teenager, perky and sassy. Brian had been gone for nine months, she had grieved, and now she had bounced back to her old self.

True, she had been lavished with attention in the warm family atmosphere at Carol's, her relationship with Darlene in their small home was beyond compare, and her children brought joy to her heart. They all lit up her life. But something was missing. The carousel! It never turned anymore. It seemed forever. As long as she'd been with Brian the need for it to turn was kept at bay, but now the need was eating her up.

She was still young and it was normal to want male companionship at her age, but she had a full-blown addiction to the carousel. She didn't know it. She only knew something was not quite right. She should have been content with her surroundings but she wasn't. She started to think that maybe Betty Smith was right.

Common sense said to stay within her cocoon of safety, but the craving for a man to hold her was becoming increasingly more difficult to handle. It was as if she was half of a whole with the other half missing. The desire for the other half was becoming a constant nagging in her soul.

While sipping her iced tea, her mind drifted to something she had seen in the park a few days before. An old couple sitting on a bench. The shrivelled white-haired lady sat demurely with her hands folded in her lap. The withered old man in the overcoat reached out with his gnarled hand shaking and placed it over hers. She looked up into his eyes with all the trust in the world radiating from hers. His eyes gleamed back at her as though she were a precious gem. Liz's eyes began to water. Would she ever have that closeness with a man again. She quickly sniffed, gathered her composure and came back to the scene at hand. But it didn't help. Arnie was bent over giving Dar a big kiss. Liz stared off into space and tried not to notice. She squirmed in her chair. She felt that hollow feeling inside her. She wanted to run. They stopped kissing and turned to face Liz. Dar looked a little embarrassed. Liz weakly tried to smile. The ache inside wouldn't allow warmth to reach her taut lips. She tried hard, but her face was etched with pain.

"You know what you need?" Arnie asked, grinning as he got up and leaned against the counter.

"No, what's that? The grin on your face tells me you think you have all the answers."

"Yeah, I know human nature," he said still grinning, teasing her. "You need a man."

Liz was repulsed by his words. She knew what he meant. She needed someone alright, but not in the way he was thinking. Sex was the farthest thing from her mind. She never had sex with Edmund and sex with Brian was less than desirable. What she needed was someone like Edmund to hold her close, to care for her, to love her. Like the old man in the park with his lady. She needed to be loved by a man. She never truly had been since Edmund had died. Brian had tried, but it didn't last.

Taking a deep breath, Arnie said, "Tell you what. I've got to pick up my brother Ryan over at Grant's. Why don't I just bring him back here and we'll all go out?"

"I don't know," Liz said cautiously, "What's he like? Is he single?"

"Ryan's an okay guy, you'll like him and yes he is single." Arnie yelled over his shoulder as he went out the door to go and pick up Ryan.

The thought of having a date made Liz's pulse quicken. Excitement flushed through her. Brian seemed to have disappeared into thin air. She hadn't heard a thing about him or his family for a full nine months. She was a good mother and her days were full, but once the kids were in bed her life seemed to stop. Thoughts whirled around in her head, *Why shouldn't I go out and have some fun? It isn't as though I'd be "running around".* She convinced herself to go so Dar phoned Carol and she said she'd watch the kids for them.

Arnie returned in a jiffy with Ryan. After Liz hugged and kissed the kids, Carol gathered them all around her so the girls could get out the door. Liz was content with Carol watching them. She knew they were safe.

The foursome headed to the Tottenham Hotel. The Tottenham Hotel was Dar and Arnie's favourite stomping ground. It featured country and western music which was right up Liz's alley. She loved country music. On this particular night, the entertainment was performed by Roy and Donna Kelly, local Beetonians. They were excellent singers, but the seductive tone of their music added to Liz's loneliness.

She glanced over at Ryan. He was not as tall as Brian, only about five foot nine. He had very dark hair, not quite black and dark brown eyes. He had a certain animal appeal. He was like Arnie, rugged and tough. Liz was very nervous. Her nervousness reminded her of how she had felt with Ben. Ryan, like Ben, was very cocksure of himself. She was extremely uncomfortable. She felt as though she had swallowed a live pigeon. She wanted to have a good time, but she was afraid of Ryan. Not only that, the side of her that needed the carousel to turn was battling with her fear of it and her very strict moral side. Ryan put up his muscular arm to signal the waiter and made a circular motion with his forefinger indicating a round for the table.

The waiter returned with eight glasses of draught beer. Liz stared at the beer sitting in front of her. Tiny bubbles in amber were rapidly floating to the surface where they broke against the snowy white head. She didn't want to drink it. She was afraid to drink it. She hadn't had a drink since before her babies were born. She had accompanied Derrick and Carol many times to the Village Inn, but she had always resisted the alcohol.

"Come on, it won't bite you!" Ryan said as he winked at her. He seemed so full of confidence; it unnerved her.

She fought with herself, but before she could stop it her hand reached for the glass, took it to her lips and she drank. A warm glow spread through her immediately and she began to relax. It worked! So she guzzled several more, to further drown the uncomfortable feeling she had.

"Would you like to dance?" Ryan asked.

She took his extended hand. As her fingers touched the warmth of his, she instantly became filled with a yearning to be held close. A smile lit up her face as she followed him to the dance floor. As his body pressed close to hers, she became short of breath. They danced several dances. With each one, he became more familiar.

His hand slowly caressed down the curve of her back, then lower and with one swift movement he drew her closer to him. She could feel the warmth from his body right through their clothing. As they stood stationary and rocked back and forth to the rhythm of the music she curled one of her legs around one of his and rubbed seductively. He sucked in his breath and kissed her neck. She pushed her hand inside his open shirt and teasingly rubbed her fingers through the hair on his chest.

As the evening wore on, Liz got drunker and drunker. She had to. With the strong moral side she had developed she couldn't have acted in such a way without getting intoxicated. The alcohol enticed her and coupled with her lonely spirit the stage was set for danger. She failed to see the warning signs. Her yearning for the carousel to turn was steering her into trouble. It was taking her farther than she intended to go.

By the time the evening was over she was hardly able to walk. Her rubber legs couldn't carry her up the stairs and out of the bar. With ease Ryan's muscular arms swooped her one hundred pounds to chest level, and carried her out.

He drove back to Beeton with Liz tucked snugly under his arm. Arnie and Dar were seated comfortably in the back seat. When they got home Dar and Arnie went in to stay with the kids while Ryan and Liz drove Carol home.

Carol's face was hazy and distorted to Liz as her head spun from the dizzying effects of the beer. Once at her place, Carol made a valiant attempt to get Liz to stay with her.

"You don't really want to go with Ryan now, do you?" she asked. She rolled her eyes at Ryan in the hopes that he would help her talk Liz out of going with him. He didn't.

And Liz was too far gone. She had slipped down into a vortex. Its suction had a grip on her, and she could no more have climbed out than she could have sprouted wings and flown away. It was too late. Liz was not able to listen to Carol. Short of being bodily carried into the house, she was beyond all aid.

Ryan drove out of town. He turned off the highway onto a back road and then turned off onto a wagon trail that led into an empty field. He put the car in park and turned to Liz. He kissed her warmly. She returned his kiss with eagerness. She was surprised at her brazenness. She had never been this bold with a man before, at least not with one she didn't really know. The alcohol enabled her to walk a path that she had never dared to tread before. They became entangled in each others bodies. Nothing could stop her now. It was too late to turn back; she had gone too far. Her power of reasoning was gone. In a torrid moment Liz broke the strong cord that linked her to her moral self. The carousel had finally had its way. It had turned, but now, the horses were sneering.

Ryan took her home and dropped her off on the street in front of her apartment. She was woozy as she staggered to the front door on her own.

The next day, sober, she was filled with shame. Her heart broke as she thought of Edmund. She had really betrayed his memory this time. She was repulsed by her actions. She stood in front of the bathroom sink and glanced at her image in the mirror. Angrily, she flipped the mirrored door on the medicine cabinet open. She couldn't stand to look at herself. Something had snapped inside her. Something had changed. She felt a hardness seeping into her soul. She lost her determination to be moral. She thought, *It's too late now anyway.*

She never dated Ryan again, but it was the beginning of Liz's "frolicking free". Betty Smith's words came back to haunt her, "I guess Liz will be running around now that her husband is gone, her being used to having a man around and all, you know what I mean?" What haunted her even more was Dar's words, "Not Liz, she's a good Christian."

Betty's words were branded on her soul like a scarlet letter. Was Betty right? Was she sleazy? Was she damaged goods? She was still the same person in the same body but something had been seriously altered.

# Chapter 22
## Jamie Beaton from Beeton

A week after the mishap with Ryan, Liz was sitting at the kitchen table staring out the windowed porch where she could see the main street. The hot sun was just setting in a blaze of red and people were pouring into the Beetonia Hotel next door for tall frosty ales to cool them down. The unusual May heat wave had lasted over a week. Liz wished she could join the throng heading to the bar. The humidity was very high, and she was sweating without even moving. It was Saturday night and the haunting sound of the band playing "Please Release Me Let Me Go" drifted in through the open window. Dar was away with Arnie and their kids, Liz's mom had her kids; she was all alone and the loneliness was playing on her mind. She was toying with the idea of going to the hotel.

In the past she would never have dreamed of going to a bar on her own. She had often accompanied Dar and Arnie, or Carol and Derrick, but to go alone would have been out of the question, definitely not proper for a woman in 1967. It just wasn't done. Then again, wasn't she different now? *Perhaps the "old me" couldn't have done it, but what about the "new me"?* she thought.

Driven by loneliness, she did something totally out of character. She went into the Beetonia by herself in the hopes that she would meet up with someone she knew. She didn't. She didn't know a soul. Everyone stared at her. She felt very uncomfortable. She drank a Coke and left. She would *never* drink alcohol alone. However the ice was broken and new territory had been charted.

New territory had had to be charted because circumstances had changed and Liz was going mad. Since the birth of their second child, Dar was spending a lot more time with Arnie. If Liz was in her boots, she would have done the same, so she didn't blame Dar, but it left her feeling like the fifth wheel on the wagon. Not only that, the girls had so many children between them that it was hard to find a sitter so they could go out together. It ended up that the girls had to babysit for each other on weekends just so they could have a break. Dar would go out Friday night with Arnie while Liz sat, and Dar would sit for Liz on Saturday. In the beginning, Liz didn't always go because a lot of the time she didn't have anyone to go with. But staying home every weekend started to drive her crazy.

Not knowing many people in Beeton and determined not to drink alone, she eventually decided to venture out on her own to the Village Inn in Bradford. It was a scary undertaking for her, but having spent many enjoyable evenings there with Carol and Derrick, she was convinced that she would meet up with somebody that she knew.

So the next Saturday after her venture into the Beetonia, she bathed the kids, got them all into their pyjamas, played with them for awhile and then read them a story. After they fell asleep, she hesitated a few minutes and stared down at them. Her eyes misted over. They looked like little angels, hair like spun silk, Jimmy chestnut, Stacy flaxen blond, and copper fire glinting on the top of Bonnie's wee head. She felt torn. Alicia would have been appalled at her going to a bar alone, let alone leaving her babies with someone else. It just wasn't done in her family. She felt guilty. She loved the kids and somehow felt her mother was right, but the cursed carousel was twisting her around. She knew she was a good mother to the kids, but inside she felt like a scarlet woman. She was driven by her own empty longing.

She quickly dismissed her thoughts, rushed around and got ready. With Darlene and Arnie babysitting for her she went off to Bradford. She didn't feel right about going, but the loneliness was driving her mad.

She didn't know which was worse, the emptiness at home or the sick stomach she was experiencing because of what she was going to do. As she drove she talked to herself. *It kills me to watch Dar and Arnie together with their kids. It was better before Arnie started coming around so much. I can't blame them for wanting to be together. I probably make them uncomfortable with my sad face. It's better if I go out and let them be alone. It'll be alright. I'll meet up with somebody I know. I won't do anything wrong. I won't drink, for sure.* By the time the drive was over, she had convinced herself that she was doing the right thing.

Standing in the doorway of the Village Inn, she nervously surveyed her surroundings until her eyes spied an older couple that she knew. They were decent people so she knew she would feel safe with them. This was a new experience for her. She had always been under her parent's wing and then Brian's. She had never really ventured out on her own. She just wanted some socializing and music. At least that's what she convinced herself to believe, but subconcsiously she wanted the carousel to turn again.

She took a deep breath and crossed the room. She felt comfortable in her new olive-green, slim leg pants that she had tailored herself. She was feeling confident about her looks. Her off-white, low cut, v-necked blouse with the antique lace trim made her feel very feminine and classy.

As she got closer, she realized that someone was sitting at the table with Bill and Dorothy. They introduced her to a young man who caught her attention right away. It was not so much because of his looks that she noticed him -- as a matter of fact, he was not good-looking at all. In complete contrast with the other men in her life this man was very small with brown wavy hair combed straight back. His mouth was too wide and *his eyes*! His eyes were huge and bugged out giving the overall impression of a frog. She later learned he was dubbed "bug eye" by his friends. No, it sure was not his looks that drew Liz to him, but there was something special about him. His manner was very appealing, he had a kindness that just oozed out of his pores and a friendliness and warmth that was mirrored in his eyes. It was an instant friendship. He put Liz right at ease with his warm smile and kind eyes.

Bill's voice penetrated her thoughts, "Liz, this is Jamie Beaton."

"Are you from Beeton?" she asked jokingly.

"I used to be," he answered smiling warmly.

Jamie Beaton from Beeton! How are you?" she said flippantly, extending her hand.

"Just fine, thanks. Waiter, bring the lovely lady a beer."

"Oh, no thanks. I'll just have a Coke," she said holding up her hand in a gesture meant to stop the waiter.

"Oh, come on, have a beer," Jamie coaxed, "It'll help you relax, you seem a little tense."

She sucked in her breath, a moving picture of the night with Ryan flashed through her mind. She quickly dismissed it and said "Oh, alright then." She was afraid of the alcohol, but she thought that perhaps if she drank slowly instead of guzzling, it might help. She certainly did need something to relax her.

She had a wonderful time that evening. Jamie was a real gentleman and a great conversationalist. She drank very little and very slowly. After her experience with Ryan, she was very cautious.

Alcohol is a marvellous social lubricant. It did help her relax and have fun. She thought that perhaps if she was really careful, she could get away with its use on such occasions.

Thus was the beginning of a summer filled with fun and adventure. Jamie was a "party guy" for Liz, the "party girl".

Saturday nights at the Village Inn became a weekly event for Liz. Jamie Beaton became her friend and lover. He was fun, he was kind, he was loyal. A strange thing was happening though the carousel wasn't turning. Jamie did, however, like Brian, keep it at bay so she wasn't desperate for the carousel to spin. She was in control. She thought she was cured.

After leaving Jamie's apartment in Bradford one Saturday night, Liz was pulled over by a police officer. Her muffler had fallen off. He gave Liz a fix-it ticket and she was on her way.

The next Saturday night, the same officer pulled her over again. She had the muffler fixed so she politely asked him what the problem was this time. He refused to tell her. He just ordered her into the front seat of his cruiser. He told Liz he was taking her to the station. He was an authority figure so she obeyed.

Instead of driving from the town limits to the station, he headed north from town, finally pulling off on the first side road leading to a desolate dead end.

"W-What are you doing?" she stammered, fear rising in her throat. "This is *not* the way to the station."

He remained silent in the dark. Liz couldn't make out his face in the dim light from the dash. She could barely distinguish his form as the ominous black of the night enveloped them. There were no street lights on the deserted side road.

He finally pulled the car to a stop and shut off the ignition. Smothered in total darkness, Liz couldn't see him as he lunged for her. Groping hands reached for her rigid body. Her mind was racing in panic, but she couldn't speak. *What can I do to save myself?* The thought rushed through her mind as he tore at her blouse. She scratched down his face. They became entangled in a fierce struggle.

C-r-a-c-k-l-e. The static of the two-way radio shattered the menacing silence.

"Come in, Earl. What's your position?" a disembodied voice said.

Earl switched on the light and picked up the hand mike and spoke into it. "I'm just coming into town," he lied.

"Well, come into the station immediately, there's a B & E in progress on John Street," the dispatcher ordered. Never had Liz heard a more welcome voice.

Earl quickly turned on the ignition. Liz breathed a sigh of relief as she pulled her blouse together. Saying nothing whatsoever, he returned Liz to her car. As she jumped out of his car, her feet pounded to the staccato of her heart beat as she raced to her own car. She got in, slammed the door and set the locks with such force that she bruised her hand. Forcing herself to breathe more slowly, she pressed her backbone into the seat and tried to think. After regaining her composure, she drove home all the while trying to make sense of what had just happened to her.

Taking total blame, she wondered if her altered state showed on the outside. Did she have "easy" stamped on her forehead? Who should she tell? Could she tell? Fear of not being believed stopped her. Circumstances had prevented him from raping her, but her self-blame, fear that it was her fault prevented her from going to his superiors. The incident made her start to question her behaviour, but she quickly dismissed the thoughts. The ever-present emptiness inside took over every time. If she didn't feel loved by a man she felt worthless. So she continued seeking out male companionship at all cost.

But the full horror of the incident impacted on her later as she related it to Dar, Carol and Derrick.

"He has no right! He has no right! Ordering you into the front seat of his car should have been your first clue," Derrick exclaimed emphatically as he thumped his fist on the table.

"But he's the law."

"No way!" Derrick responded. "A woman alone never has to accompany an officer, if she hasn't broken the law."

Liz felt vindicated. Her friends took her side. It reassured her that her behaviour was okay. With renewed determination, she decided to continue her weekend fun.

Then a few weeks later, the same officer pulled her over again. She was appalled that he would have the gall to try again. This time she was very angry, told him to go to hell and flatly refused to get out of her car. He just shrugged and walked away from her.

Her weekly excursions continued; she kept the alcohol in check. Jamie was fun to be with. Liz felt very independent. It was the first time in her life that she had been her own boss. She felt exhilarated. Her veins flowed with effervescence like bubbly champagne. Her inner joie-de-vive was showing on the outside. The party had begun. Liz was the "party girl". She was frolicking free without a turtle shell. The sun was shining down on her and all was well.

She even kept up the college fund account. She now had $500.00 put away. Her evening outings never cost her anything. The men at the table would always pay for the rounds, even if she offered. She deprived herself of many female indulgences in order to keep the account going. She sewed her own clothes and sometimes she would even go without a meal to scrimp.

Her days were spent tending to her children. She loved them dearly. She was confident in her mothering capabilities. She never spanked them like her mother had done to her. She broke the chain of abuse that had passed from generation to generation. She just didn't feel right about spanking. She remembered how it had frightened her and made her feel. Her children would never experience that! Indeed, her days belonged to the kids.

But her nights were hers. She spent them with Jamie when she could. When her mother would take the kids to give her a break, Liz would even spend the weekends with him.

"Your mom's got the kids for the weekend, so why don't we take off to Wasaga Beach?" Jamie suggested over the phone one Friday afternoon. "Listen I know a few people who'd like to come along. It'll be a hoot. Bill's car is broke down so can we take yours?"

"That sounds great," Liz answered. "Only one problem though, my car won't start unless someone pushes and jump starts it. The starter's gone, I guess. If you guys don't mind pushing it every time we park it, it's alright with me. Carol and I take it shopping all the time. As long as we park it on a hill we can roll to a start anytime."

"Not a problem. We can go early tomorrow morning. Bill and his wife and their friend Michael want to come too. Michael just recently separated from his wife, so Bill doesn't want to leave him home alone. With three guys to push, we'll do just fine."

They were full of adventure. Nothing could tie them down, not even a defunct starter. Fun was the order of the day, the crazier the better. Liz was living life to the full. She was living the free and easy life that she had missed in her teens while she was chained to Brian.

The next morning Arnie gave Liz a push start, and she drove to Bradford to pick them up. There they were, Jamie, Bill, Bill's wife and Michael.

*Michael*! Michael was tall and muscular -- body beautiful. His blond hair tumbled in curls onto his forehead. His healthy tan made his eyes stand out like turquoise jewels of Carribean sea blue. His face was handsome, so handsome. His features were smooth. He looked like Troy Donahue. Looking at him took Liz's breath away. She wondered why his wife had left him. It didn't make sense to her.

Suddenly, something strange happened. The carousel jump started of its own accord and against her wishes. All the time she had been with Brian it had remained entombed within her. She thought being in Jamie's company she was safe from it. It hadn't turned in the whole time she was with him. It seemed one man was not enough any more.

Jamie was her friend and lover so she fought to get off the carousel during the whole drive to Wasaga. But at the same time she surreptitiously snatched glimpses in the rear view mirror at Michael's beautiful face. She fought to get off alright, but not very hard. The carousel was winning. Electricity sparked from his eyes to hers and then back again through mirrored messages. Currents of warmth coursed through her. *What's wrong with me*, she thought but quickly dismissed it.

Finally they arrived. They turned off the highway onto the beach road which followed the course of the lake for miles. The traffic was bumper to bumper and the day was scorching hot. The little car started to heat up and as Liz pulled to a stop behind the braking traffic the Morris Oxford sputtered, coughed, then died!

"Oh, no!" Liz cried. She giggled nervously as her eyes flashed with mischief. Horns started honking! Headlights flashed as the angry drivers lined up behind her.

"We'll just have to push," Jamie said as he let out a big sigh.

The three guys pushed that Morris Oxford the entire length of Wasaga Beach road in bumper to bumper traffic. There were no hills in sight, and not even a stretch long enough to get the little car started.

Through the rearview mirror Liz, watched Michael as beads of perspiration broke out on his forehead. She could tell he was not otherwise affected by the severe heat as she caught a glimpse of his warm smile.

They finally found a hill to leave the car on, and set out for the amusement park. The day was filled with excitement and frivolous pleasure. Liz hadn't been to Wasaga Beach since the time that Brian had held her over the bridge. This time was different. This time she was her own person, filled with confidence and a passion for life that she had never experienced before. Jamie held her hand and the two of them laughed as they went from the swings, to the scrambler, to the Ferris Wheel. He kept pulling her on the next ride, like a big kid, but even so Liz was acutely aware of Michael, and Michael was acutely aware of her. He watched her closely. She was torn between loyalty to Jamie and the cursed carousel, her addiction, pulling her inch by inch closer to Michael. Her heart longed to go where her conscience feared to tread. The whole day was a push/pull of Jamie, Michael, Michael, Jamie, as Liz struggled to avoid the inevitable.

Weeks went by and Michael was in Liz and Jamie's company as often as he could be. Unbeknownst or perhaps unacknowledged by Jamie, the chemistry was flowing freely between Michael and Liz and the pressure was building to a fever pitch. Liz was not sure how long she could keep things in check.

She cared for Jamie. He was kind, a good friend, a lot of fun, but the carousel just never turned for him. Her strong moral side had been nullified somewhat by the incident with Ryan so being immoral no longer presented a problem, but she had always been a loyal person, and she liked to think she still could be. It was her loyalty to Jamie that was the strong deterrent. What did it matter any more if she was immoral? But could she be disloyal as well? Not while she was in her right mind, she couldn't. Feeling double-hearted, she wished Michael would go away, and yet she was afraid that he might.

It was another usual Saturday night of fun and frolic, but things had reached a boiling point between Liz and Michael. Her loyalty to Jamie needed to be drowned to enable the carousel to make its turn. Liz started to guzzle her beer. She was not aware of how quickly she was consuming it until it was too late.

"Hey, Liz, don't you think you better slow down a little bit?" Jamie asked. "Come on maybe you should head for home while you can still drive."

"Don't worry about it! I'm fine!" Liz said as she danced around the floor. She was in a world all her own.

Michael was sitting at their table. She came up behind him and threw her arms around his neck. "Come and dance with me?" she asked, a saucy look on her face. She felt confident, on top of the world. Nothing could touch her now. Her timid shy side had totally disappeared in the last few weeks and the alcohol was making her very bold.

Michael turned around and put one arm around her. "Sure," he said as he got up from his seat and shrugged at Jamie. Jamie's face reddened as the pair wrapped themselves around each other on the dance floor. Once again Liz was out of control.

She staggered back to the table. "Come on, Liz. I'm driving you home. There is no way you can drive." Jamie snarled.

"I don't want to leave!" she yelled.

"Come on." Michael said, "Bill and I will come too."

Reassured that Michael was coming she said, "Let's get a case of beer to bring home with us."

Jamie complied with her wishes just to get her out of there, but he was beginning to get angry with her.

The foursome left the bar and Jamie drove Liz's car home. She insisted that Michael come with them. Bill followed in his car to drive the others back.

Bursting through the door, three men and a case of beer in tow, Liz ran to her bedroom. "Dar! Dar! Sh sh sh! I better be quiet. I might wake the kids. Just whisper. Okay, *Dar! Dar! Hey Dar, wake up please."*

"Huuh, Liz whatsa matter. Sh sh you'll wake the kids."

"Come on Dar, Bill, Michael and Jamie are here, come party with us. We've got a case of beer. Whoops I forgot. I gotta whisper, sh sh sh!"

"Liz are you mad? It's two in the morning. Arnie would kill me if he knew I was partying with three men. You better get them out of here or I'll have to leave."

Beyond reason Liz just shrugged her shoulders and walked out of the room.

Dar got up from the bed, pulled on her jeans and sweater. "I'm going to Carol's. You better get these guys out of here and don't wake the kids."

"Don't go. Stay and party," Liz slurred.

Dar pushed past the guys and went right out the front door.

Liz turned the portable stereo on and grabbed four glasses. "We'll have to stay in the kitchen so we don't wake up the kids. Oh, I just love this song. Michael come dance with me. Jamie you don't mind do you?"

Jamie shrugged and Liz grabbed Michael by the hands and looked up into his eyes, hers were filled with passion. Jamie gave them a sideways glance, hurt showing in his eyes. Bill just drank his beer.

Liz put her arms up around Michael's neck and moved closer and they started to sway to the rhythm of the music. Jamie's face got redder and redder. Liz never noticed. She was too busy in her own little world. As a matter of fact, she was totally oblivious to all around her as her total attention was focussed on Michael. She was sure she was in love with Michael, but the alcohol was blurring her ability to reason clearly.

Michael was a nice man and he was very lonely after the break-up with his wife. He had fallen for Liz after watching her playful ways at the carnival. He wasn't thinking clearly either. Had the two left the alcohol alone, reasoned out their situation and talked to Jamie, perhaps they could have come up with a solution, but it never occurred to either one of them to do that. Liz started to kiss Michael on the side of his neck. He was overcome by her advances. He grabbed her and kissed her soundly on the lips. The two were overcome with passion and locked in a fiery embrace.

Jamie jumped up from the table knocking his chair over. He grabbed Bill by the arm and hauled him out of his chair. He was mad! "Come on let's get out of here and leave the lovers alone!"

Bill, drunk by this time, merely complied with Jamie's wishes. The two went out the door leaving Michael and Liz wrapped around each other, totally oblivious to their departure.

Liz and Michael were carried away with ecstasy. The two remained in a clinch all the way to her bedroom. Once again, Liz gave in to the carousel. It had turned, but the horses faces were very sad. Weeks of struggle had gone into trying to maintain her loyalty to Jamie. She had failed.

Once Liz and Michael had given vent to their passion the pressure was off, but the two lay wrapped around each other feeling like a pair of snakes.

Sobered somewhat Michael said, "Maybe I should go." He was feeling his neck for seducing his friend's woman.

Liz, more sober now, felt sick. Somewhere in the back of her mind she got a glimpse of a flickering scene. She could see Jamie's hurt face. The picture of it had registered there, but she had been too drunk to see it. Now, it came back to haunt her. What had she done? What had they done?

Michael's words finally sunk in. *Maybe I should go.* She was too ashamed to look at him. "Maybe that would be best," she muttered.

Michael got up and put his clothes on while Liz cried quietly into her pillow. The dream had turned into a nightmare. The free frolicking, shell-less turtle had run into the tumultuous storm and was left huddling and crying.

When Liz awoke, the first dawn of realization through her sober splitting head was the memory of the previous night.

Michael, beautiful Michael was gone. She rolled over to an empty bed. She was alone! Jamie was gone probably never to return. Her sweet, kind, funny Jamie was gone. Worse than that her soul-mate, Dar, was gone too. *What have I done? How can I make it right?* How many times had alcohol got her into trouble? How many times had needing to be loved got her into trouble? To this point her children had not been affected by it, but something had to be done and fast or they could be.

The alcohol had hurt them all: Jamie, Darlene, herself and even Michael. She had deceived herself with the carousel and the liquid sin that facilitated it's turning. She had been immoral. Worse than that, she had been disloyal. Her heart was broken. She had desperately wanted to be a good person.

She got up, head splitting and staggered to the kitchen where the happy sounds of children at play were coming from. She walked through the archway to the kitchen with her chin resting on her chest. She glanced up to see Dar feeding Sherri in the high chair. Jimmy, Stacy, Bonnie and Devin were sitting around the table eating cereal.

Darlene looked towards her with a warm smile. "How's the head? Sorry I had to leave last night, but Arnie would have killed me."

"Oh, no, that's okay. I'm sorry! I never should have brought them all home. I feel just sick. Forgive me?"

"Oh sure. You know I love you, Liz, but I think you should do something about your drinking before you really hurt yourself. It seems to have a bad effect on you."

"I know. I don't know what happened to me. I was just so taken in with Michael. It seemed like I couldn't help myself. I didn't want to do anything wrong. I didn't want to hurt Jamie or you. I was right out of control."

"I know. Don't worry about me though, it's you that's in the pickle. Oh, by the way I read something in the paper yesterday that might cheer you up. It seems some police officer named Earl was charged with attempting to rape a young girl at the city dump. He's been dismissed from the force."

"Yes! There is justice after all. That is good news," Liz said as she put her arms around Jimmy's neck and kissed the top of his head. He turned and looked up at her with excitement in his eyes.

"Look Mom, look what I got out of the cereal."

Liz's heart warmed as she took the little toy and inspected it with him. All the kids giggled as Liz took the plastic top and spun it across the table.

"C'mere!" she said as she held her arms wide open. The kids all ran into her arms and she hugged them tightly. They were all looking up at her, Jimmy's dark brown eyes were warm, Stacy's snapping green eyes were full of mischief and Bonnie's were sky-blue innocence. She smiled down at them, determined she would do what was right.

That was it! She'd had her last drink. She never saw Michael or Jamie again. They never called, and she never returned to the Village Inn. Her weekly escapades with her friend, Jamie Beaton from Beeton, were over. She was starting a new life, no alcohol, no carousel. She was determined, but could she keep it up? Would the carousel let her rest?

# Part IV
# THE TURTLE SHELL

## Chapter 23
# Norman James Carter

With the back of her hand, Liz brushed away the piece of chestnut hair that had fallen down on her forehead. Her forehead was wet with sweat.

"Eww, this damn piece of hair keeps getting in my way."

She was on her hands and knees scrubbing the white tiles on the bathroom floor. The room was all steamy because she had just bathed all the kids, Dar's included. She hadn't been out for two months, and she kept working day and night in the apartment to keep herself occupied. The place was gleaming. She cleaned even when it didn't need it.

And when she wasn't cleaning, she spent her time with the kids, taking them to the park, reading to them and playing with them. But try as hard as she might, the all-consuming emptiness in the middle of her soul just would not go away. She tried to work it away. Tried to fill it with the kids, with her friends. Nothing worked. The loss of male companionship in her life seemed almost too big a price to pay for a soothed conscience.

There was nothing wrong with having a man in her life. Brian had been gone for a year. But after the experiences with Ryan, Jamie and Michael she wasn't sure she could trust herself. She figured abstinence was the best policy, but after two months the gnawing inside her was becoming unbearable. She was physically craving a male. Her need was showing on the outside.

Her face was beet red from exertion as she just kept on scrubbing the bathroom floor. The floor was spotless, but she just kept on. She was trying to scrub her feelings away.

"Whoa! You better take it easy. You're going to blow a gasket. What's the matter with you anyway? Don't you know all work and no play makes Jack a dull boy? You haven't been out for ages," Arnie said as he leaned against the bathroom door jamb.

"No and I don't intend to go out either. I only get myself into trouble when I do."

"You know what you need," said Arnie.

Liz had heard Arnie tell her what he thought she needed before. She wasn't even sure she should grace his statement with a reaction, but before she could say anything he proceeded to tell her anyway.

Seriousness written on his face and sincerity in his eyes, he said, "You need a good, hard working guy who will look after you and the kids."

Arnie making sense? That was a switch.

The laugh lines around his eyes started to crinkle, and his eyes shone with anticipation as he said with a grin, "And I know just the guy for you."

*Oh boy, here we go again.* Liz thought.

"C'mere," Arnie said as he headed across the kitchen. He crooked his finger and motioned her to come and stand beside him at the screen door. Peering out through the window past the porch her eyes followed the invisible line to where his finger was pointing. She spied a bright red, brand new 1967 Plymouth Fury II parked on the other side of the street. Leaning against the front driver's door, deep in conversation with another man, was a man with bronze coloured skin, black hair, thick eyebrows, nice nose, and a wide smile which revealed a missing tooth in the front. In spite of his thick eyebrows and missing tooth he was not at all unattractive. His native Indian look reminded Liz of Edmund. He wore work boots and a dark green workman's uniform. The sleeves of the shirt were rolled up revealing very thick, muscular, obviously well-worked forearms.

The two men continued in conversation as Liz turned to Arnie and said, "So?"

"That's him," he said, pointing again. "The one leaning on the Plymouth. He owns that car. He's 28. He works for Parker's Coal & Grain. He's worked there for 10 years. He's single, never been married. He's just the guy for you."

"Quite an impressive resume, so what's the catch. If he's all that good, how come nobody's nabbed him yet."

"He's been going with the same girl for quite a few years. He's a real family man, and he wanted to settle down. She didn't want to get married so he split up with her. Well! Are you the least bit interested? It doesn't matter to me. Just trying to help you out."

"Thanks, Arnie, I think you've helped me enough already."

"Yeah, sorry about that. Things didn't work out too good with Ryan. Well, if you want to give it a try, let me know."

"Do you know him?" she asked with cautious interest.

"No, but Grant does and I know Grant."

Grant was the local grease monkey who owned the sole garage and gas pumps in town. The guys always hung around there working on cars and shooting the breeze and Arnie was one of the guys.

"I guess it wouldn't hurt to give it a try. But how do you know he'll want to go out with me?"

"I don't, but I can always ask."

Liz didn't want to get into the dating game again, but Arnie was right. A good, hard-working, family-type man might be the answer to her problem. If he turned out to be Mr. Right, he would certainly dispel the emptiness she was feeling, and if he was a decent guy, he might make the kids a good father, and they sure needed one.

The date was set! Liz was to accompany Norman James Carter to Musselman's Beach where there was a large dance pavilion.

She was in a panic, what to wear? The air in Carol's bedroom was ignited with excitement as Dar and Carol fussed over her. They all chattered incessantly. They were enthusiastic about the date in the hopes that Liz could finally settle down and be happy.

After trying on all of Dar's and Carol's best dresses, Liz decided upon Carol's turquoise, satin, Chinese dress. Completed with slit up the side, high collar and buttons down the front, left, side, it was a beauty. Derrick had it especially tailored in Chinatown for Carol. It was her favourite dress, and as Carol and Liz were the same size it fit Liz perfectly. Liz felt like Cinderella going to the ball. She hoped he would be her Prince Charming.

The big night arrived. Norm brought his 15 year old brother Donny to babysit so that Dar and Arnie could go with Liz, Carol and Derrick. Liz was too nervous to go out with Norm alone after her past experiences. She'd had enough of picking up with men in bars. This was a proper date with proper chaperones. She was determined to do everything above board from here on in.

Norm grinned, and Liz felt very flattered as Donny told the tale of how he always babysat for Mandy, his sister, on Saturday nights, but Norm offered him double what Mandy usually paid and he couldn't refuse. It seemed Norm was very eager to date her. She felt hopeful he would be the right man for her.

The party of six arrived at the front door of the dance pavilion at 9:00 p.m. It was a big wooden building not unlike a barn. At the entrance the doorman took their money and stamped the back of their hands with a rubber stamp. As they walked through the big opening Liz drank in the scene. The room was huge. Splashes of different coloured lights reflected off the polished hardwood floors. Down each side of the room were huge window openings that let in the cool evening air. It was refreshing after a hot August day. Patio lanterns were hung everywhere giving the room a luminous glow. Through the windows on the left Musselman's lake was shimmering in the moonlight.

Liz looked like a princess in the satin dress with her chestnut hair piled high and ringlets coiling down around her face. Norm's snapping black eyes and bronze skin were complemented by his pink shirt, black pants and sports jacket.

A live band played "Crystal Chandeliers" as Liz slid into her seat. She glanced over at Norm. She was feeling shy. He seemed to be too. He was nothing like the men she had dated before. They all seemed so confident and cock-sure of themselves. Norm sat with his head down. He rubbed his sweaty palms together then rubbed them on his pant legs, trying to muster up the courage to ask Liz to dance. With his head still slightly bowed, he glanced up at her and said, "Uh would you like to dance?"

"Sure."

He pulled out her chair as she stood, took her hand and walked beside her to the dance floor. He was a perfect gentleman. He was a good dancer, but Liz could tell he was a little nervous because his hands were clammy and he didn't lead with the confidence that Ryan or Michael had.

Liz was very nervous too so when they returned to the table, and Norm asked her if she'd like a drink she didn't refuse. As always the alcohol helped her relax, but she was very careful. She didn't want to spoil the date by getting drunk.

It was a different type of evening than she had spent with Ryan or Jamie. It was not exactly exciting, but Liz was content. They danced some, but mostly they spent the evening getting acquainted. Through the course of the conversation, Liz learned that Norm came from a large family. He had two brothers, Donny and Ray; three sisters, Mandy, Anna and Becky. His parents John and Lorraine lived in a big house on Patterson Street in Beeton. The kids came home every Sunday with the grand kids. They were a very close knit family. He seemed the perfect man for her to settle down with.

So Norm and Liz became an item. Lots of nights were spent at the bar in the Tottenham Hotel with Arnie and Dar, listening to country music. The couple drank some, but Norm didn't seem to drink like the other men she had been with and Liz slowed right down with her drinking as well. Somehow she was able to keep the demon-alcohol under control so she thought that perhaps she had outgrown its adverse effects. Norm was well-known and seemed to be well-liked, so things were working out perfectly.

Not only did they have lots of evenings out, but they spent a lot of time together with the kids, at the beach, the drive-in theatre, the park, and on picnics. They became a happy little family

Norm was a family man by nature. He did dishes, helped with the housework, played with the kids, and was not even averse to rinsing out dirty diapers. He was the kind of man every woman dreamed of.

Norm came and spent his lunch hours with Liz, then she drove him back to work and took his car for the afternoon. He trusted her with his brand new car, and Liz never let him down. She and Dar loaded up the car with the kids and food and headed for the beach on those days. It was fun for them, fun for the kids and Liz was grateful for Norm's generosity. After refreshing days at the beach, they got Becky or Donny to babysit and the four of them, Arnie, Dar, Norm and Liz went out for evenings of fun. The rest of that summer continued in this delightful way.

True, the summer was delightful but a strange thing was happening, the carousel was not turning. Liz was somewhat perplexed, but she was beginning to think that the whirring of the carousel only got her into trouble anyway. Every time it turned she ended up in distress; with Edmund she suffered a severe beating; with Brian she got her heart broken; with Ryan she lost her morality; and with Michael she lost her loyalty. What could happen next? Better to have a nice, quiet, reliable relationship. Anyway, she felt it was time she grew up. After all she was twenty-two.

Having been chastened by her conscience, she was now deliberately choosing a more narrow road. Did that mean no more excitement? Did that mean that she would have to accept the turtle shell and safety, instead of the carousel and rapture? Life with Norm was like life with Alicia, normal, not exciting or ecstatic, but reliable and steadfast.

Norm was strong and she felt protected. He was also a steadfast worker. He drove truck for Parker's Coal & Grain and he and Liz often went on long trips in the big truck. Dar would watch the kids for them so they could go.

"So, this is the big weekend," Dar said as the iron in her hand easily glided over the crisp white blouse.

"Yeah. We're heading to Toronto with a load of grain for Monarch. There we'll pick up 100 lb. bags of cocoa powder to be delivered to World's Finest Chocolate in Campbellford. Norm is so strong. You should see him throw those bags around. Then we'll spend the weekend in Campbellford. Oh, I guess I've told you all this before."

"Only ten times."

Sorry, I'm just so excited. It seems like a long time since I've been away. I really need this break. I owe you one for watching the kids. Next time you and Arnie want to go away I'll watch Devin and Sherri."

"Don't worry about it. Your kids are easy to watch. They're not a problem. But I'll take you up on your offer sometime."

Friday morning arrived and Liz got up early. She was like a young thoroughbred at the post, straining, ready to go! She looked in on the kids to see if they were awake.

"Come on guys, I'll get your breakfast before I go."

"Mommy, my head hurts," said Stacy.

Liz clicked the light on. "Ow, that hurts my eyes," Jimmy yelled.

"Oh my God!" Liz exclaimed as she looked into four little faces full of red spots. Bonnie, being red haired and Devin being platinum blond, were the worst. Their little faces looked as if they were covered in a hundred swollen bee stings.

The measles!

Dar came running to see what was wrong.

"Oh Liz, your trip. Listen you go anyway. I can handle this."

"No! No way. I won't go away while the kids are sick. They need me. Norm will just have to go alone."

Liz felt disappointed, but there was no way she could go and enjoy herself knowing her little ones were sick at home and needing their mom. She knew instinctively that when you're sick nobody but nobody can take the place of your mom. She and Dar spent the whole weekend soothing crying kids, applying calamine lotion, holding little heads while they threw up and applying damp cloths to burning foreheads. The two women were exhausted. But eventually the kids got over the measles nicely.

Not only that, Liz's life was coming together nicely too. She was staying home most of the time and being a good mother, and she had a man to dispel the emptiness. With Norm the carousel was still. It was everything she needed. She pressed herself into the mould that her mother wanted her to be in. She was pleased with herself. She would get used to the weight of the turtle shell. Or would she?

# Chapter 24
# The Family Circle

A warm spring breeze blew in the front door of the Main Street apartment. Dar and Liz sat at the kitchen table, not speaking. Norm had just left in a huff. He had insulted Dar by making derogatory remarks about her housekeeping, and Liz didn't know what to say to her. Finally, Liz apologized.

"It's not your fault," Dar said. "He's a jerk!" Liz felt a knife twist through her at Dar's words. She was torn. She cared for Norm and she loved Dar. Why couldn't they get along? The last summer had been great, but over the winter the situation had deteriorated.

The girls were still together in the apartment and Norm and Arnie visited often, but the perfect set-up the girls had for themselves had begun to disintegrate. It had never bothered Arnie that the girls lived together with all the kids, so Liz had been quite surprised with Norm's reaction. He resented Dar and her kids being in the apartment. He resented it when Liz babysat for Dar. Actually, he was jealous of their friendship. This should have been a warning signal for Liz, but wanting a father for her children and a man to dispel the loneliness became as strong a pull as her friendship with Dar. After all, Norm was a steady, dependable family man. He would be a good provider. He was what Liz felt she needed. Alicia was happy with him. For the first time mother and daughter agreed.

But because of Norm and Dar's differences, a rift started to develop between Dar and Liz. Dar became uncomfortable with the situation and opted to move out before the circumstances got any worse. She loved Liz and didn't want anything to happen to their friendship, so when the upstairs apartment became available Dar grabbed it. Same landlord, same building -- the girls could still continue their friendship but without the static from Norm. Liz was very relieved because she loved Dar too, but she needed Norm. She didn't want to give up either one. She stayed alone in the apartment though because Norm's pay cheque didn't provide enough to support her and the kids.

But even though Norm didn't move in with Liz and the kids, life with him became a circle of family activity. The young couple rented a cottage at Wasaga Beach for a week, not unlike the one Liz's parents had rented when she and Allen were young. They spent Sundays at Norm's parents' place with all his siblings and their kids. When they didn't go to his parents, Liz cooked a roast for their own Sunday dinner. They even started attending a place of worship. Liz was feeling happy that she was doing all the family things. All the family things, indeed. During the "family vacation" she got pregnant again. Alicia was thrilled that Liz had finally settled down, but she got on Liz's back about getting legally married before the baby was born. To complete the circle though, Norm needed a better paying job and Liz needed a divorce. But it seemed as though Brian had disappeared off the face of the earth. She hadn't heard a word about him in almost three years. No one knew where he was, not even his family.

Alone in the apartment, one month pregnant, Liz was mulling over her situation. Norm had gone home and the kids were all in bed so melancholy descended around her like a cloak. She really missed Dar living with her. She only visited with her when Norm wasn't around which wasn't very often. Her relationship with Norm seemed to be perfect on the outside, but on the inside Liz had some doubts. It troubled her that she had to meet with her friend on the sly.

Then a loud knock startled her back to reality. Midnight. Who would be calling at this time? She opened the front door of the big kitchen and there standing large as life was the missing Brian. He was thin and white-faced with a prison pallor.

"Hi!" he said as though he had just returned from going out to get an evening paper. "Can I come in?"

Liz slowly moved aside in shock. How did she feel? She wasn't sure. Then suddenly that old familiar feeling crept in. The carousel slowly started to spin.

There was a slight touch of excitement, a slight flame still burning waiting to be refuelled in the centre of her somewhere. But remembering the trouble her disloyalty to Jamie had brought, she quickly extinguished the ember. She would be loyal to Norm.

"Where have you been?" She asked with an edge to her voice.

"Well, first of all, I went out west to Winnipeg for a while. Then I came back here and got into a little trouble." He chuckled as though embarrassed, then carried on, "I just spent a year in Kingston Pen."

"So what do you want from me?" she asked sourly.

"I missed you and the kids."

Liz laughed bitterly.

"I did!" he emphasized. "C'mere." He made steps towards her, arms out, trying to grab her. She ducked from under his reach determined to be loyal to Norm in spite of the warm flush that was pulsing through her blood stream.

Liz had had enough of Brian's shenanigans and she wasn't about to let her heart rule her head. She would get a grip on this carousel thing if it killed her.

But he was persistent. Liz moved from the kitchen into the living room. She realized her mistake as he stood in the archway with his arm stretched out blocking her way. The next step was toward the bedroom. She pushed against him and ducked under his arm. He smiled down at her with a warm, teasing smile that made her pulse quicken. Feeling herself weaken, she finally dashed into the bathroom and locked the door.

"Go away!" Liz yelled from her safe corner. Her head was whirring. The insistent carousel was spinning inside it, confusing her. She cupped her hands over her ears.

"Aw, c'mon, c'mon out, I'm not going to hurt you."

She leaned against the bathroom door; its firm barrier gave her strength. She placed her hand on her stomach. Remembering her condition gave her courage.

"Just get out of here!" she yelled.

"Okay if that's the way you want it."

A lone tear made its way down her cheek as she heard the front door slam forever behind the father of her children. She had done the right thing, hadn't she? He was her legal husband but she carried Norm's child. The carousel turned for Brian. It didn't for Norm, but Norm was solid, a family man, not an unreliable run-around like

Brian. Surely she made the r[...]
bad?

Months passed qu[...]
Jimmy was five, Stac[...]

"Stand back, let's h[...]

Jimmy took a step ba[...]
together in front of him like[...]
pants, white shirt and a blac[...]
in shyly. The shoes were glean[...]
with Vaseline. They didn't have [...]
the Vaseline did just fine. Not only [...]
well. The little cow-lick was slicked [...]
face warmed Liz's heart.

Jimmy was a quiet, shy boy and very [...]
a little nervous but Liz's excitement carried [...]

They walked down the street hand in hand[...]
want to be late."

They hurried the last block together. As they got[...]
was aching with each step. The lump in her throat was[...]
her. There was pain in her chest as she fought back the o[...]
urge to cry.

*Damn, what's the matter with me. This is a special day fo[...]*
*Why am I feeling so sad. What is this ache in my heart and h[...]*
*my throat all about. I can't cry. It's his special day. God, please [...]*
*me to be strong.*

She took him through the front door and got him seated. Then
she slowly backed out the door, smiling and waving at him the whole
time.

Just as soon as she was out of his sight, she ran with her head
down, tears flooding down her cheeks restricting her vision. She
stumbled all the way home her heart breaking. She had to leave her
baby at school.

Months passed by quickly after Jimmy started school. Liz was
bulging with pregnancy. Dar was pregnant again as well. They
certainly were soul-mates.

Miss Nutworthy paid them the usual six-month home visit.

"What is it wit[...]
shrugging her sho[...]
Liz's mind re[...]
one who challe[...]
three children?[...]
All the sa[...]
longed to be [...]
convinced a[...]
job at Supe[...]
had been [...]
the job a[...]
the matt[...]
sent Br[...]
N[...]
job p[...]
abou[...]
H[...]
w[...]

h you girls always getting pregnant?" she asked
ulders in bewilderment.

*lected, Why should she be surprised, she was the*
*ged me saying "What man would want you with*
*" "What man?" Norm is what man.*

he her words stung. Liz felt like a criminal. She so
ree from the scrutinizing eyes of mother welfare so she
very reluctant Norm to speak to Derrick about getting a
ior Propane. Norm was a very good truck driver and he
t Parker's for years but it just didn't pay enough. He got
Superior Propane without a problem. But there was still
r of the divorce to complete the circle. Liz regretted having
an away without finding out his whereabouts.

divorce in sight but Norm moved in with Liz anyway. The new
ovided enough money to keep the family, and Liz was nervous
t living alone with little children so far along in her pregnancy.
Norma Jane Carter was born on February 10, 1969 in Alliston
spital. Norm was the epitome of the word father. Unlike Brian, he
as there holding Liz's hand through the whole process.

New medical information had been released by the Surgeon
General about the dangers of smoking while pregnant, so Liz had
quit during her pregnancy. As a result Norma Jane was the biggest
baby she had. She was 8 pounds 6 1/2 ounces. Quite a size for tiny
Liz. The birth had been a struggle, but Norma Jane was worth it.
She was a beauty, a miniature of Norm. She had his Native Indian
features. He was as proud as any father could be.

Now that their family had increased, the apartment that Dar and
Liz had so loved was becoming too cramped. Norm and Liz talked
it over with the landlord. Liz had been such a good tenant that the
landlord didn't want them to leave so it was decided that Norm would
build another room on to the back of the building, and they would
stay there.

Norm was very handy. He built a new living room and they
transformed the old living room into a big bedroom for themselves.
They put the girls in the rose room, and Jimmy was transferred from
the hallway to the clown room.

When summer came, Norm got sod from the sod fields and laid a lush new lawn in the backyard. He built a fence and a sandbox, They got a swing set and a BBQ. Family life was in full bloom. But the circle was still not complete. There was still no divorce for Liz because Brian had totally disappeared again.

The hot August sun beat down on the asphalt roof of the Main Street apartment. The heat rose in liquid waves and inside the brick structure Liz wiped the sweat from her brow and wondered why on earth she had started the job of painting the big kitchen in such sweltering heat. Not only that, she was having a time keeping three youngsters from touching the wet paint. She was exasperated and then to top it all off the phone started to ring off the wall. "Oh damn, who can that be now?"

Picking up the phone, juggling paint brush and paint can in the other hand, Liz heard a stranger's voice say, "Hi, you don't know me. My name is Gloria and I'm calling from Winnipeg. I got your number from your mother-in-law. I just had a son with your husband Brian, and we want to get married. Would you file for a divorce? You have grounds now."

With great effort, Liz suppressed a hearty cheer. She was elated. The last step needed to complete the family circle was at her finger tips. Not only that, she discovered she was over Brian. What he did with Gloria didn't even bother her. She had stood her ground with him, and now she didn't need him anymore. She had beaten the carousel! She had the carousel under control and the strong moral side of herself was content. Now they could be a happy, clean-living family.

Summer bloomed away, fall leafed away and winter froze into the year 1970 and tell-tale signs of discontent were starting to gnaw at Liz. She was beginning to squirm inside as though her life was too tight. But things were perfect, weren't they? Norm was a wonderful provider and a good family man. They had a beautiful baby, a cozy family, a perfect apartment and a yard special for kids. The divorce was final. The wedding date set for March 14, but something was missing. Intuition told her that something wasn't quite right, but she couldn't put her finger on it.

Then just as though a bright light switched on, realization dawned on her. It was the damn carousel! The carousel *never* turned anymore. What was this carousel anyway, this whirring thing that made her feel so good? She had it under control, didn't she? She didn't need it anymore, did she? Did it matter that the carousel didn't turn for Norm? What did the carousel mean? Why did it turn for Edmund, Brian and Michael but not for Jamie and Norm. Liz couldn't make sense of it all so she just turned her back on all her questions and her uncomfortable feelings and decided to marry Norm anyway. After all, it was the right thing to do, wasn't it?

March 14, 1970, Norm's sister Mandy and her husband Luther's large living room was transformed into a wedding chapel. The room was decorated with pink and white flowers and streamers. Sunbeams danced across the polished hardwood floor. The air buzzed with gaiety.

Liz wore a beautiful full-length, off-white, lace wedding gown. Jimmy was a darling in his little suit. He was a perfect ring bearer. Stacy and Bonnie made lovely wee flower girls in their powder blue gowns. One-year-old Janie was dressed in a tiny pink pleated nylon dress with pink leotards. Norm was handsome in his black tuxedo with the royal blue cumberbund. They were a handsome family. Dar, of course, was the maid of honour and Carol and Mandy the bridesmaids in matching royal blue floor-length gowns.

Norm was grinning like a Cheshire cat, and Liz was pleased with the day's events. The vows were said. The circle was complete. Alicia breathed a big sigh of relief. The wedding party moved to the hall above the arena where they feasted and partied all evening long. Most of Beeton was there to share in the festivities.

A month later Liz sat at the kitchen table staring out the front door. Water drained off the eaves in a solid sheet. Jimmy and Stacy were at school, Bonnie and Janie were down for their nap and Norm was at work. The April showers had continued for weeks. Liz was fed up with the constant rain. She was fed up with more than the rain.

She twirled the remnants of her coffee around in the mug. She glanced in at the warm liquid as if it was magic, as if it had some answers for her. As the coffee settled she saw Edmund's face reflected there. Then it was Brian's, then it was Michael's. She got a warm whirring feeling in the pit of her stomach.

She shook her head. She felt like she was going crazy. She didn't know what was wrong with her. Norm had seemed wonderful, but now he was smothering her. After they married, he didn't want her to go for coffee with the girls or have them over. If the housework wasn't done just so, he was mad. She also discovered that he had a habit of fabricating stories. Liz never questioned him about the stories because she was afraid she would embarrass him. These lies were breaking the fragile cords that bound them together. Why hadn't she noticed before? It wasn't until after the wedding that Norm's faults became glaring.

Liz discovered Norm was not her intellectual equal as well so there was no meeting of the minds, no melding of hearts. The turtle shell was weighing heavy, but Liz just kept plodding along trying to keep up the family atmosphere she felt she and the kids desperately needed. Norm provided a good home and a good income. The college fund was growing in leaps and bounds which pleased her so she would just have to put her feelings on the back burner.

But putting her feelings on the back burner became more and more difficult. Just a few years before she had stood on Carol's porch, alive and full of a passion for life. Now, her free spirit was slowly dying like a black hole that implodes into itself, leaving a vacuum.

Damn, that haunting emptiness was back in full force!

# Chapter 25
# The Dark Side

The summer of 1970 advanced into fall. Centre Street was ablaze with crimson. Norm and Liz had been together only two years, but Liz had come to know Norm's family better than her own. She was very fond of them all. Anna lived in Hamilton with her husband Fred so she didn't often see them, but Mandy and her husband Luther lived in Beeton so Norm and Liz spent a lot of time with them. Luther was German and very handsome. Not outdone by Luther's good looks, Mandy was very sensual and very beautiful, all the way to the inside. Even though she was a sister-in-law, she came to be more like a sister to Liz. Norm's brother Ray was married to Maria and they lived in Newmarket, but often came to Beeton to be with the family.

Norm's whole family were fun-loving and very social. They all loved music, and they loved to dance. Every weekend the clan would gather together and head to the Beetonia for an evening of fun, including Norm's parents John and Lorraine. Liz loved these gatherings. They were the highlight of her life. They almost made up for the emptiness she felt living with Norm. But going out every weekend got to be quite an expense for the young families. Not wanting to give up their social life, they all talked it over and decided that it was better to hold house parties and rotate between their various homes. Of course Carol and Derrick and Dar and Arnie were included as well. Each wife brought a pot-luck dish for a midnight meal and each couple brought their own favourite drinks.

The rotation game was fun for a while. Then on one of these occasions, at Norm's parents' house, Liz learned there was a dark side to Norm. Her life was filled with all kinds of stable family-type events, so Norm's dark side came as a shock to her.

On this particular night, Norm had a little more to drink than usual.

"Aw, c'mon Norm, cut it out," Donny said shyly, red-faced with embarrassment, as Liz and Norm danced around him in Carter's big living room. Donny was dancing with his sister, Becky. Norm was shadow boxing around Donny and occasionally poking him harder than he realized. Liz had grown very fond of Donny. He was a real good kid and so she said brusquely,"Norm, leave the kid alone!"

Norm took offense at her interference and an argument broke out between them.

"Let's go outside," Liz said, feeling embarrassed about arguing in front of Norm's family.

They slipped out through the back screen door, down the two steps and into the dimly lit yard to continue their discussion.

"What are you doing interfering between Donny and I?"

"I like him. I don't like the way you're treating him."

"I like him too. He's my brother. I always treat him that way. He doesn't care."

"How do you know? He didn't look happy to me."

"What do you know? You haven't been around this family all your life!" Norm said his voice raising.

"I know plenty about human nature. He doesn't like it!"

"Are you saying I don't know what I'm talking about?" Norm yelled.

"If the shoe fits wear it!" Liz yelled back.

"You're stupid! Just like a woman! Don't know anything!"

"Oh shut up!" Liz screamed back at him.

All of a sudden -- thud! Liz saw stars. She found herself in a prone position on the dew-soaked lawn. Head whirring from the punch and from the initial shock, Liz stumbled slowly to her feet. Norm looked as stunned as she felt. Terrified, she started to run wildly in the direction of their apartment, about a mile from Norm's parents' place.

As she ran she twisted her head around and saw headlights following her. Norm's car, it had to be. Headlights sliced through the night. She picked up speed but was quickly overtaken and was knocked over the deep embankment to the right. She flew! She landed with a jarring thud in the deep ditch and immediately felt a searing pain shoot through her. Her whole body was on fire as she slipped into unconsciousness.

Coming to, after what seemed like only seconds, Liz became acutely aware of her surroundings. Fear shot through her. The grass was long and wet with dew. She shivered as sensations of pain and cold permeated her body. She could hear water trickling and through a fog of pain she realized that she was lying in the bottom of a deep drainage ditch. She realized that if she lost consciousness again, no one would ever find her there.

She moaned, aware that she would need to initiate extreme effort to climb out of the ditch. A new fear, a fear of dying shot through her. With the dread of dying there undiscovered by passing motorists motivating her, she redoubled her efforts to get to the road.

A lifetime lived in a second of thought spurred her on -- a vision of her children left alone! Clutching handfuls of tufted grass, she pulled her pain-wracked body slowly towards the road. She clung to her purse as though it were a lifeline, but it was hindering her progress. She tried to keep a level head, but the pain didn't allow her to think clearly. All she could think of was, *My purse, I've got to bring my purse.* Then gripping it in her hand, she gave it a heave that sent it over the top of the ditch onto the road. The jerk of the toss almost rendered her senseless again.

But now she was able to use two hands. *Don't give up, don't give up,* she thought wildly using the pain as a spur to go the next few increments to the top. She pulled herself, inch by tormented inch, as the pain pierced through her with every tiny movement. An eternity passed, but finally she was at the side of the road. She laid her head on her arms, breathing deeply.

No sooner had she reached her goal than a pair of headlights cut through the night. Their welcoming incandescence pierced the darkness, encouraging her to hang on. Then a new fear struck her. *What if it's Norm? What if he's come back? What if he runs over me?* She struggled to see the shape of the car in the dark. She couldn't. She didn't know whether to try to wave or to hide. She did neither. She couldn't move.

Whoosh! The car passed by so closely, she could have almost touched it. It wasn't Norm's! She felt instant relief and then total despair as the car continued down the road. *They didn't see me!* The words screamed in her consciousness as her head dropped.

Then, suddenly, she saw a bright red flash as brake lights illuminated the night with a rosy glow. Renewed hope flushed through her.

Crunch, crunch, crunch, she heard footsteps on gravel come closer, strong arms encircled her and lifted her into oblivion.

*I can't breathe*! Liz's mind raced in panic as she struggled to consciousness. *Why can't I breathe?* Then through the fog of her semi-conscious mind, she realized hot wet lips were pressing tightly and demandingly on hers. She felt groping hands touching her body as awareness flooded through her. She became vaguely aware that she had been moved but before she could collect her thoughts she was being kissed again. The strong pungent odour of alcohol enveloped her. Her rescuer was obviously very drunk.

"W-What are you doing?" Liz finally managed to squeak out. "Aw-w-w, please, don't. Look at my leg!" she moaned as she fought to pull away.

The startled eyes of the young man peered down at Liz's leg at the same time as her own eyes took in the sight. From her sitting position in the front seat of his car, her stomach turned, the bile rose in her throat as she viewed the twisted hanging foot, turning black, at the end of her limb and the jagged shin bone sticking out through her torn pants.

"Oh wow, sorry," he slurred. "I thought you were just drunk and passed out." Realizing the extent of her injury and in spite of the haze of his own drunkenness, he mumbled, "I can't take you to the hospital. I only have first gear in my car."

"Take me home then," she begged as she gave him the directions to her apartment. On the drive home, Liz bounced in and out of consciousness as the car slowly rumbled along.

"There he is!" Liz moaned as she spotted Norm standing firmly on the sidewalk in front of their apartment, legs spread and arms crossed eyes peering first to the left and then to the right as if looking for someone, who just wasn't there.

"Get him!" she demanded of her drunk companion as she pointed to Norm. The door of the old car squeaked open as Norm's face screwed up at the sight of her limb.

"Oh no, did I do that?" he cried, sober remorse written all over his face. Norm and his buddy Wally transferred Liz from the drunk's car to Norm's. Then Norm rushed her to the hospital in Alliston.

The damage to Liz's leg was very extensive and corrective surgery was necessary. The bones on both sides of her ankle were broken and it was dislocated. Her shin bone was shattered and had pierced through the skin. The pain was excruciating. She was never sure if Norm had deliberately hit her with the car or just hadn't seen her. She was afraid to ask and Norm never said.

Filled with regret and constant apologies though, Norm visited faithfully during her lengthy convalescence. At first Liz was very angry with him, but with time, his persistent visits, and his repentance, she began to soften.

Norm and Liz talked a lot and Norm decided that perhaps alcohol was creating the havoc in their relationship. Liz had sworn in the past that no man would ever hit her and get away with it. But she was afraid of being on her own again. She was afraid of being immoral. She couldn't stand the guilt that plagued her when she was.

Not only that, but somewhere deep inside she had the feeling that underneath it all, their troubles were her fault. The carousel didn't turn for Norm so she wasn't able to give him the same warmth and affection that she had given Edmund and Brian. Theirs was a marriage of convenience, and she knew it. She thought that perhaps Norm could sense that fact and she felt guilty.

Besides Norm was a family man and steady worker. Plus he showed sincere remorse about what he had done. She made the decision to stick with him. *They* made the decision to stop drinking.

After several weeks, Liz was finally sent home from the hospital with a cast from her toes to the top of her leg, but that didn't slow her down. She continued her duties as housewife and even struggled to hang clothes on the line using crutches. With four kids there was lots of laundry. She was young, strong and a real fighter. She wouldn't give in. Her babies needed her.

Jimmy had just turned seven, and Liz planned to get him enrolled into hockey that winter. He loved to skate, and he was very good at it. He was a strong boy and loved sports, but he hated school.

Stacy, six-years-old, on the other hand was brilliant beyond her years. She was already reading at a grade three level. She was a spitfire too with lots of determination. Liz had taken the time to read to all the kids and teach them a b c's from books before they even went to school. She was determined that they would all amount to something.

Bonnie, now four, was a little Florence Nightingale. She was always bandaging her dolls or the family cat. She was opposite to Stacy. She was a quiet cautious, responsible girl.

Janie, almost in the terrible two's, was a trucker. She was one year and nine months old and she could really move. Liz had a time keeping up to her. Janie was constantly on the go mowing her way through everything with a big grin and no fear!

Liz was doing her best with her family life in spite of the fact that she was feeling the emptiness all the time. Norm never filled her senses. She felt as though she was plastic, just going through the motions, never warm and alive. And ever since Norm had hit her she was even more withdrawn. She started asking herself, *Is this it? Is this all there is to life?* She recalled Arnie's words, *All work and no play makes Jack a dull boy.* Her life certainly was dull. She didn't even have the pleasure of the family parties anymore since she and Norm had quit drinking. And it wasn't that she didn't love or appreciate her children. She did, but she was still a person in her own right with her own needs and desires. Her wild adventurous spirit kept screaming out for excitement of some form. Did she have to sacrifice the fun-loving side of herself because Norm drank too much? Little did she know relief was just around the corner.

# Chapter 26
# Cocktails Anyone?

Once again, spring was in full bloom in the little town of Beeton. Purple and yellow crocuses, bright yellow daffodils and scarlet tulips danced in the warm breezes in the front garden Norm had made. Liz's leg had long since healed and she was busy preparing lunch for the kids when a brisk insistent knock came at the door. She opened the door to a very round man, not unlike a penguin, with dark hair and glasses, thick like the bottoms of coke bottles. He wore black pants and a white shirt with a gravy stain that seemed to be the badge of his profession, chief cook and bottle washer. She judged by his anxious state that he was very upset about something.

Talking in circles he blurted out, "I need help! Can you help me?"

Liz shrugged and gestured for him to go on.

"Oh, sorry, My name is Dave. My dining room waitress quit on me just this minute. I'm expecting a crowd from Borden Metal for the lunch hour and my wife is alone in the kitchen. I can't help her because I'm alone in the bar. I don't know anyone," he rattled in staccato fashion.

Liz knew the hotel business next door had just been sold and that the new owners were from out of town. Obviously, this was the new owner.

"I don't know," she said, turning and gesturing to show her brood anxiously awaiting their lunch.

He looked as though he was about to burst into tears. Liz softened with sympathy and said, "Just hold on a minute, I'll run upstairs to see if my friend will watch the kids. I have to warn you though, I've never worked in a restaurant before."

"Don't worry, my wife will show you exactly what to do," he said, sighing, visibly relieved.

While Darlene watched the kids, Liz quickly changed her clothes and headed to the hotel, eager to help.

She kept the job. At first, she waited tables in the dining room and cleaned rooms upstairs. Not exactly glamorous, it did, however, put her in close proximity to the excitement of the bar life which gave her dull existence a bit of a spark.

A good food waitress Liz was not. She had been trained to do office work and was good at it. Food service, however, was definitely not her line. Juggling soup bowls and dinner plates was fraught with danger, for both herself and the customer. Even with perseverance, she never did become adept at it. So when the bartender, Gord, extended an offer to work for him in the lounge she jumped at the chance. She knew the waiters made plenty in tips, and she was thinking about her college fund.

Gord was a little man with a big personality. Loaded with charm he knew just how to woo the ladies. Liz wasn't immune to his charm and eagerly agreed to join his little corner of the hotel business. During the day, She cleaned rooms, but when she finished she went down to the bar for lessons from Gord. He showed her exactly how to balance a tray full of drinks. Gord was extremely good at what he did and showed Liz all his tricks.

A job in the party atmosphere was just the thing for her. She was a "party girl" and she thoroughly enjoyed the gaiety of the bar. Liz learned her lessons from Gord quickly and well. She was eager to start. Now, there was only one obstacle to overcome -- Norm.

"You want to do what? I don't think so. I didn't like you going to work there in the first place. Working in the dining room and cleaning rooms is bad enough, but working in the bar at night is out of the question. Men grabbing at you and drooling all over you! Forget it! The answer is no and that's final!"

Liz didn't argue with Norm because she knew it wouldn't do any good. He would only get angrier. She was feisty, but she didn't want to upset the family thing. She had vowed to do right after her dating game episode.

Then, one early evening, Norm came to meet her after work.

"Hey, Norm, c'mon, sit down have a beer. Take a load off," Gord, the bartender, called out.

"I don't know, I haven't had a drink in almost a year. We've got a bunch of kids waiting at home."

"Aw c'mon, just one won't hurt."

Liz gave Norm a sideways glance. He had promised to quit after the incident with her broken leg. Her look screamed out no! With a flick of his hand he ignored her look and said, "Oh, what the heck, a beer would go good right about now."

One led to many and before the night was out, Gord had convinced Norm to let Liz work with him on the condition that Norm be given a part-time job in the men's room serving draft beer. That way he could keep an eye on her. They were to launch their new careers the next weekend.

On Friday night Norm was dressed to the nines, handsome in white jeans and a white sweater trimmed with burgundy. The outfit accentuated his dark features. Liz was dressed in a short navy blue dress, fitted at the waist and complemented with white design and trim. She looked good. They were quite a team. They set out to conquer.

But this particular lounge had never had a female waitress before. Beeton was an old fashioned town, and the hotel kept up a standard from another era. To date it employed men only and still maintained a men's room that to Liz's knowledge had never been graced by the presence of a female. Clem, the usual lounge waiter, refused to work with a woman so at the last minute Gord was left high and dry. It was Clem or Liz, and she was new. Gord picked Liz. He had gone out on a limb to hire her, and she was not about to let him down. She was ready!

She began her shift feeling nervous, but in a very short period of time she felt right at ease. She felt like a performer on a stage. The band played on and she danced through the crowd, tray over her head the way Gord had taught her. The atmosphere was gay and bubbly. Her veins pulsed with electric excitement. Her personality easily adapted to whoever she served. She was very courteous and polite with older folks, witty and frivolous with the young ones, and friendly but firm with single men. Liz excelled. She had found her niche. Her veins pulsed, the plastic woman had come to life!

The night was too soon over. The time flew easily on the wings of frivolity. Clem was watching, like the nervous director of a play. He wanted to see Liz fall on her face. But at the end of the evening, he was the first to extend his hand in congratulations. Liz had won approval from her hardest critic. Clem told her he would work with her any time.

From behind the bar, Gord looked smug. He was a terrific judge of character. He had Liz pegged, and she didn't let him down. For Liz's part, she was beaming with success. Norm was not immune to the gaiety of the evening either as Gord lit a big cigar for him. He had done well as a draft waiter. Norm was not unhappy with his decision for he and Liz to become hotel employees.

Liz loved her job. It gave her the excitement she needed to thrive and allowed her to be home with her children during the day. After a very short time, she gained a reputation as the best and most honest bar maid in the county. People she didn't even know asked for her by name to wait on them. She was flying high. Enthusiastic about her job, Liz purchased some perky little cocktail outfits so she could look the part. The one she liked the best was a long sleeved white peasant blouse, embroidered with pink flowers around the scooped neck and a matching pink linen skort, shorts with a little skirt attached. With it she wore knee high white patent leather go-go boots. She felt young and alive for the first time in years. She was young, only 26. Who would have guessed she had four kids at home?

Pretty soon though, it became evident that there was trouble in paradise. Norm could no longer keep up the pace with his day job truck driving and his weekend job pulling draft. Working two jobs became too much for him. He was tired out so he was forced to quit. He was unhappy that Liz continued to work but it was too late for him to stop her. Once bitten with the "party" bug, she wasn't about to go back to cleaning rooms. She knew her kids were safe. Norm had his day job. She enjoyed her weekend job.

She was nervous that Norm might try to make her quit, but she wasn't about to stop now. She was feeling independent again and nothing could deter her. She had a turtle shell of protection with the family life and a carousel of sorts at work, it seemed the best of both worlds. But was it?

Norm, being jealous, possessive, and insecure, didn't trust Liz so he continued to come to the bar to keep an eye on her. He insisted on being at the bar as long as she insisted on working. Liz was reluctant to have him there. While Norm had worked at the bar he had stayed sober and occupied. Now, he stayed neither sober nor occupied. He became obsessed with watching Liz. In order to perform her job satisfactorily, it was necessary for her to be congenial with everyone. Norm had a hard time accepting that and with his dark brooding eyes, he would sit glaring at Liz as she worked. Soon his silent war escalated from glaring eyes to derogatory remarks and lewd comments, all directed at Liz. This upset the customers and finally Dave, the owner, asked him not to come to the bar while she was working. But Norm, being so jealous, didn't pay any attention to him. He came anyway.

Norm and Liz began to fight at home. It was a stalemate. Norm wanted her to quit, and Liz refused to give up the job that gave her renewed self-esteem without getting into trouble. Working at the bar gave her the same lift the dating game had without her being immoral or feeling guilty. Norm continued to be verbally abusive until Liz could tolerate it no longer and after an evening of work, Liz followed a staggering Norm out the door of the Hotel. She was fighting mad.

She stomped across the lawn between the hotel and their apartment. Norm, super drunk, went ahead of her into the quiet apartment. Liz, close on his tail, came through the door and slammed it hard behind her.

"That was smart. You'll wake the kids," Norm slurred.

"Oh, shut up, Norm. The kids are spending the night with Dar." Then she screamed, "How dare you!"

"What?"

"How dare you call me a slut in front of all those people.

I've had it, Norm! I'm not giving up this job. It makes me feel alive. I'm not doing anything wrong and I'm making lots of money for the college fund. If you can't stop drinking then don't come to the bar."

"You are a slut. Any woman who works in a bar is a slut."

"Don't you say that! I'm not a slut. I've always been faithful to you and it's not that easy when I feel so lonely all the time."

"What are you talking about?"

"Never mind," she snapped quickly as she realized she had let the cat out of the bag.

With that, Norm grabbed hold of her by her upper arms and started to shake her. "What do you mean lonely?" he screamed.

"Let me go!" She twisted free and he slapped her hard in the face with his open hand.

Liz ran to the front door and held it open. "Get out of here!" she screamed. "I've had enough of your jealous insecurity."

"Gladly!" Norm grabbed his coat from the back of the chair and stormed out the door.

Norm went home to live with his parents and Liz stayed at her apartment with her friend Dar upstairs. With Norm gone and no longer contributing to their support, Liz was forced to start working full-time. She hated to leave the kids but with Dar so close and available to watch them, it was a little easier.

Months went by and Liz was busy juggling her time between work, kids, housework, grocery shopping, laundry and school functions; not to mention Jimmy's hockey on top of it all. He had spent the past winter playing forward and he was really good at it. Now the new season had started up. Liz hoped someday he would play professionally. It was what he wanted, and if she had anything to do with it, he would succeed.

Not only was she busy with her life-style but Norm kept calling and hassling her. He kept begging her to forgive him and promised faithfully he would never give her a hard time again.

He always offered to help with the kids. He took Jimmy to hockey on occasion, and, over the summer, he had taken the kids camping several times. Liz was grateful for his help, and he was slowly breaking her down. She was burdened with a heavy load, and she began to think he might make it a little lighter. If only he would keep his word not to give her a hard time anymore. She was confused. It was as though Norm had a dual personality. On the one hand he was a caring family man and on the other he was violent, jealous and insecure.

Not only was Liz feeling confused, haggard and tired, but the ever-plaguing emptiness kept gnawing away at her. She was starting to fear that she would start running around again. Norm didn't fill the emptiness or keep the loneliness away from the door, but as long as she had a man she would be moral. Her loyalty to Norm was a strong deterrent. Loyalty came to be a very strong part of her character.

Six months flew by. Old man winter was in full force. The cold north wind howled outside the living room window. The panes were encrusted with thick white frost. Liz shivered. She sat on the couch staring at the TV without really seeing it. She pulled her quilt snugly up under her chin. She was exhausted. Her mind wandered. *If only he'd promise not to drink and to stay away from the bar while I work. I'm so afraid of running around again. I hate the way I feel when I do. Maybe I should just quit the job to keep him happy. But then it makes me feel so alive and it really helps the fund. Those kids are going to go to college if it kills me. Oh, I just don't know which way to go.*

Arguing with herself she finally drifted off to sleep on the couch with all her clothes on. After she dozed, she started to feel a whirring sensation. Then she was sitting on a beautiful carousel of painted white steeds garlanded with pink ribbons and roses. It was twirling slowly and warm wind was caressing her face and gently flowing through her long chestnut hair. Pleasant music drifted from the centre of the carousel. She felt wonderful. She smiled warmly.

Then as she turned and glanced over her shoulder she saw Edmund riding one of the horses behind her. His beautiful mouth formed a warm smile and his eyes twinkled with delight. He was beckoning her to join him. She tried to dismount and go to him but she was stuck. She twisted and struggled as he motioned for her to join him on his horse. Then finally she broke free and moving swiftly from pole to pole she made her way back towards him. But every time she got closer, he drifted farther away. Then finally she reached his horse. He was looking behind him. He turned. It wasn't Edmund! It was Arnie's brother, Ryan! His face was horribly distorted as he laughed mockingly at her. All the horses turned towards her sneering. She woke up in a cold sweat.

# Chapter 27
# The High Cost of Loving

Norm won. Afraid of the carousel, Liz decided to take him back. He asked two things of her, that she give up her job and that they move into the country. Liz reluctantly agreed. The kids cared for him. He was good to them. They needed a father figure. She needed protection from the carousel.

Her job was like a breath of springtime to her, it made her feel alive. Nonetheless, she knew she would have to give it up if her marriage to Norm was to have a fighting chance. So it was with a great deal of sadness that she handed in her resignation. It seemed to Liz that when she became so alive she only got into trouble anyway. She had that old feeling that she was bad, and she longed to be good. She was determined to make every effort to be good and to fit into what she thought was a normal life setting, a life setting similar to her parents. Norm convinced her he was right. He was the good family man and she, in contrast, was the "party girl".

After giving up her job, Liz also gave her notice to move out of the little "cockroach" apartment she and Dar had so loved when they first saw it five years before.

With sad heart, Liz left the apartment and the job that she dearly loved and moved to a large country home to please Norm. She was twenty-seven years old, so young and yet part of her felt as though her life was over. But she was doing the right thing wasn't she?

The house they rented in the country was huge with three large bedrooms and a large bath upstairs. The kitchen took up one whole side of the downstairs and the living room the other. Built out from the back of the house were two more very large rooms. The house was tastefully decorated, but it just wasn't home so at first Liz became very despondent. But then she got an idea! In a desperate attempt to keep a small part of the old Liz alive, she undertook the huge task of painting and wallpapering the country house in the same fashion as the apartment in town. It worked, at least for a little while. It kept her busy and the house felt more like home.

Before Liz knew it the pages on her calendar had turned from February to July, 1972. During that time, she had struggled to make sure Jimmy made it to all his hockey games. She worked hard to help the girls with their schooling. She became "the perfect wife". She performed her duties of housecleaning, laundry, cooking and sewing as a good wife should. She sacrificed everything for Norm and her marriage. He was happy. She was trying to be. She did try but "To try" is a left brain activity, the logic brain. Spontaneity, music, joie de vive are right brain activities. Could Liz suppress her right brain, the part of her that was so alive? She did try, but that part was screaming inside her, "Let me out. I want out."

Every evening was the same, day after monotonous day -- kids around the TV watching "Get Smart", Liz waiting for Norm, setting the table and pulling her hair out with boredom. *Shoe phones indeed, how absurd.* She thought she would go insane. Something was definitely missing. How long could she go on like this?

*What's wrong with me*? She asked herself. *I have a good home, a hard working husband, four healthy, wonderful children.* But she was desperately unhappy. What made her unhappiness more unbearable was that Norm was as happy as a clam. Liz hated him for that. How could he be so happy when she was so miserable? Did she have to sacrifice her happiness for his? Something was really wrong and Liz just didn't know what. The truth of it all was Norm was choking the life out of her. He wanted the country home to keep her away from her friends, but she didn't realize that. She thought the way she felt was all her fault. She wanted so bad to do the right thing but every time she tried she was so unhappy. She began to question her sanity.

Then half way through the summer, Liz received a phone call that would alter her entire life. On the other end of the line was a desperate voice. "Hello Liz, this is Dave, at the Beetonia, listen, I've got a real dilemma. Linda had to go out of town for her grandmother's funeral and Maria just quit on me. I don't have any cocktail waitresses for the bar tonight. So could you come to work just for two nights until Linda comes back?"

"Ah, Dave, I'd love to but I don't know what Norm will say. I don't want to upset him. He'll be home in half an hour so let me call you back then, okay?"

"Okay, but call as soon as you can because if you can't do it, I've got to try and get somebody else."

Liz hung up the phone and felt like jumping for joy. What an opportunity. She could feel alive again, if only for two nights. How could Norm deny her? Just two nights.

"No, I don't want you to work even for two nights. Next thing you know it'll be more," Norm insisted firmly.

"Aw, c'mon Norm, just two nights, I promise," Liz pleaded. She wanted it so bad she could taste it. She didn't just want to work, she needed to. So she begged.

Norm looked at Liz through dark brooding eyes, "Alright, just two nights but I come with you," he conceded unwillingly.

Liz knew he didn't really want her to go, so she jumped up and kissed him and hugged him. She had given up so much for him and now he was giving some back to her. She put his supper out and flew upstairs to get out her cocktail outfits to iron. Excitement percolated in her, making her feel like a kid going to the circus. She was getting back on the carousel, if only for a little while.

The night was wonderful. It took but a moment to get back into the swing. In addition to that, Dave had a new younger bartender named Peter. Peter was tall, blond, and looked like a clean-cut college student. Fresh out of bartender school, he was good at his job. As for Liz, she was in her prime. As the band played "Proud Mary" Liz danced through the crowd, tray held high over her head. She loved the job. She was good at it, and it made her feel good.

Liz could serve six tables with four people per table, take all their orders by rote. Then at the bar, from memory, she could rhyme off the orders to the bartender as he punched them into the cash register. As fast as the cash register was making the tally, Liz was making the total in her head and had the money from her float ready to the cent for him when he turned around. He was fast, she was faster.

Time flew! The evening went by too quickly, and it was all over too soon. According to custom, after the bar was closed the staff relaxed over a few drinks. Peter, eyes sparkling with excitement, praised Liz, "You're a class A waitress. There aren't very many like you around. You've just got to come back and work with us. You can work circles around the other two."

Peter was on a high because they obviously worked so well together as a team. The vibes between them were very good.

Liz thought she would burst with pride as she said "Thanks. I love my job, that's why it comes so easy to me. But I just can't work full time. My husband doesn't care for me working in a bar."

"I can't say as I blame him. I wouldn't want my fiancee working in here myself," he empathized.

After working the second night, Liz so longed to go back to the job that she was not averse to the attempts by Peter and Dave to change Norm's mind. They plied him with drinks, cigars and compliments until he agreed. She was to work weekends only and Norm would have to be there. That was the deal. Liz agreed as long as Norm agreed to behave. He did. Liz's career was launched once more. Liz was not happy with Norm drinking again, but she was ecstatic to have her job back, and she was happy he had agreed to keep his jealousy in check.

She continued to work weekends and, as usual, working built her confidence back up and made her feel classy, intelligent, accepted and successful. Something she never felt at home. There never seemed to be any rewards for the difficult job of housewife and mother.

But with the bar job came the drinking again. At first the alcohol made her feel confident, classy, and cool. But then it intensified her feelings of loneliness and her longing for the carousel to turn. Because of the loneliness she started going out with Carol, Mandy and Dar on Wednesday nights. They had started a girls night out for relief from the mid-week doldrums. They would go to the theatre or they would just go and listen to country music at a bar. They had invited Liz to go along before but she had refused in order to keep peace with Norm.

But now with her newfound independence and with alcohol egging her on, she stood up to Norm and informed him she was going out with the girls. Taken off guard by her firm stand, Norm grudgingly agreed and watched the kids for her just as Luther, Derrick and Arnie babysat for Mandy, Carol and Dar. The other men didn't mind, but Norm's jealousy was eating away at him.

Norm hated the girls night out. At first he didn't say anything but as his resentment festered he started to balk about it. His drinking accelerated, and he became moody and morose. He was jealous of the time Liz spent with her friends.

Then one cold blustery night as she was getting ready to go out Norm blew up. "If you're going out again, get a babysitter. I'm not staying home this time," he shouted in anger.

Liz was stunned. He had never reacted this way about her night out before. She had thought things were getting better between them. She was feeling happier, and she thought he was still happy too. The nights out had become precious to her. She was a good housewife. She did all the things she needed to do with the kids and this was her special time. She was faithful and loyal to Norm and felt she deserved some time with her friends. Not only that, she needed some time to herself. So she defended her need.

"Alright, I will," Liz answered returning anger for anger. She reached for the phone, "Hi, Carol, can Ronnie babysit tonight? Norm is mad, and he won't watch the kids."

"Sure, I'll bring him down when I come to pick you up."

Ronnie was Carol's step-son and he often babysat for Norm and Liz when she worked. The kids now nine, eight, six and three didn't mind Liz going out. They loved her and she gave them plenty of attention when she was at home.

As they went out that evening, the freezing cold winter night chilled Liz and Carol to the bone. They shivered uncontrollably as they got into Carol's brown 1972 Ford. At the same time Norm climbed into his big yellow propane truck which was parked in front of the wagon shed. Having to work in his own area the next day, he brought the truck home instead of his car. Carol's car was running with the heater blasting warm air. They waited for Norm to back up because the propane truck was blocking the only spot they could turn the car around. Norm wouldn't move, so instead of turning around as she planned, Carol had to start backing slowly down the long lane to the highway. The lane was frozen, ice coated and treacherous.

As Carol and Liz were looking out the rear window, backing slowly down the lane, they became aware of the bright lights of the propane truck bouncing in front of them. Norm had started up the truck and was speeding towards them.

"What is that maniac doing?" Carol screamed in panic as the big yellow truck's menacing bulk advanced ever closer to them.

"He isn't going to slow down." Carol cried as she pushed her foot harder on the gas pedal. "I'm going to spin out of control if he keeps up this speed. I don't think I can control the car on this ice going backwards," she yelled.

Liz's finger nails bit into the leather dash as she squinted at the bright lights of the truck cutting through the darkness. Seconds turned into an eternity as they raced backwards down the lane, and beads of perspiration broke out on Liz's face. With the big truck bearing down on them, the car careened backwards right across the highway and down into the ditch. They made it out of the way just in time. Norm's truck barrelled out onto the highway and he turned towards town. Liz shuddered to think of what could have happened had the highway been busy.

Carol, shaking uncontrollably, gripped the steering wheel with white-knuckled hands. It was a moment before she could talk, but when she did she gasped out, "He could have killed us. He's absolutely crazy!"

Liz agreed with her, but she was shaking so badly that she couldn't speak. After catching their breath, they drove out of the ditch and straight to the Village Inn in Bradford. They both needed a drink.

Norm, was angry all the time after that and being in his company was almost unbearable. On one occasion he put his fist through the window in a rage. Liz tried to stay away from him as much as possible.

The more Norm tried to prevent her from seeing her friends, the more he pushed her away. His jealousy toward her friends was insane, but she continued to go out on Wednesday nights in spite of it. Besides the love of her kids and her job it was the only bright spot in her life. She loved and enjoyed her friends. She had since childhood and she was *not* going to give them up.

One evening after bar closing time Carol and Liz were on their way home from Barrie and stopped at the Chatter Box restaurant on Highway 400 for a burger.

"Oh, look, Carol, there's Peter's cousin, Lenny. He works in the men's room at the hotel. I'm going to go and say hello to him."

Lenny was not good-looking like Peter. In fact, he was the total opposite. In contrast to Peter's fair, well-groomed college-man look, Lenny was very dark and rugged looking. He had shoulder-length, coarse black hair, and a nose that looked as if it had been broken several times. His mouth was too small for his large face and nose, so his face had a sort of unbalanced look. He was over six feet tall.

Liz didn't know Lenny. She only knew that he was Peter's cousin. "He seems really nice, but really shy," Liz said as she returned to Carol.

After that night Liz became very aware that Peter's cousin, Lenny, had taken notice of her. He was bending over backwards to be nice, but he really didn't appeal to her. Besides, she was married.

Then one cold but sunny winter afternoon Carol and Liz were busy wallpapering Carol's kitchen. Liz had just had a long piece fold sideways on her when a knock came at the door. As she struggled to get the wallpaper straightened out, Carol came back from the door shivering and said, "It's for you, Liz. It's Lenny." Carol rolled her eyes teasing.

"Lenny, for me? What could he possibly want?" Liz asked baffled.

Grabbing a towel to dry her hands, Liz went to the door.

"Hi!" greeted Lenny shyly. Clouds of breath puffed around him as he lifted her patent leather boots up before her eyes. Liz had broken the heel off one of the boots at work one night and had just left them there.

"I took your boots into the shoemaker and had a heel put on for you."

"Oh thanks," she said, very surprised. "How much do I owe you?"

"Nothing. I just wanted to do it for you."

She thanked him, took the boots, said goodbye and closed the door quickly to shut out the cold. She turned to Carol and rolled her eyes and grinned.

"Watch out, I think somebody likes you," Carol teased.

"Aw, forget it!" Liz said screwing up her face. She wasn't attracted to him and besides she was married.

Carol, continuing to tease, said, "Watch out you don't end up with him."

"I don't think so!"

"Be careful, Liz, the seed has been planted."

Liz laughed, shrugged it off and went back to the wallpapering.

Liz continued living a double life emotionally. At home she was a dutiful wife and mother but with a very empty feeling inside that was gnawing away at her. At work she was the classy, successful career woman feeling fulfilled by her job.

Norm continued to accompany Liz to the bar. He was drinking more and more, and it made her very uncomfortable. One night after closing time, Dave, the owner, Peter, Lenny, Norm and Liz were having a pick-me-up drink in the back kitchen. It had been a particularly busy night and Liz's feet were killing her. Although the staff were sober, Norm was drunk beyond reason. Usually he kept his jealously in check as he had agreed, but on this occasion he was totally out of control.

"Hey, slut," Norm sneered. "How much did they pay you tonight? Huh, slut."

Liz ignored his comments and just continued her conversation with her boss. They were discussing the liquor order.

"I'm talkin' to you, bitch. You answer me when I talk to you."

Liz's face went scarlet. She was ashamed to call him her husband. She had worked very hard that night and was just about at her wits end. Not knowing how to deal with the situation, she remained silent, head down, her body pulsing with anger.

When Norm got no reaction from her, he reached across the table and grabbed her. He shook her like a rag doll and her head flopped back and forth as he spat out, "I said answer me when I talk to you."

She felt totally humiliated. Dave and Peter grabbed Norm. Liz ran out of the kitchen into the darkness and privacy of the bar to hide her embarrassment. Tears streamed down her cheeks. She turned around and there was Lenny. She hadn't heard him follow her. In one encircling embrace, his long arms gathered her in. With shame and humiliation she buried her tear-stained face in his chest and sobbed her heart out. For the first time in a long time she felt safe as his arms tightened around her. He was big and solid. There was a very distinct gentleness about him that Liz had never noticed before. He leaned back, looked down and with two fingers lifted her chin, then two large thumbs gently wiped away her tears. Blurry-eyed, she saw him come even closer as he very tenderly bent to kiss her lips. The kiss deepened and became passionate and demanding. Her inner core came instantly to life. The room began to swim as the carousel started to turn. *How can this be possible?* Her heart quickly dismissed the thought as the kiss continued to carry her along oblivious to her surroundings.

After that night, Norm's abusiveness became worse and worse. Liz had tried to ignore it before, but now that he had made it so public she could no longer pass it off. She had been trying so hard to be the good wife, but Norm was always berating her. It seemed he had a vendetta against women. He was not only jealous of her friends, he was envious of her intelligence, her success and her kind manner. He had seemed like the perfect family man, but he had hidden his insane jealousy and envy beneath a mask of deceit.

Lenny was being very kind to Liz at work, but when he said he wanted to see her, she turned him down. He wasn't about to give up though. He had fallen hook, line and sinker for her. It was hard for her to keep saying no, considering the abuse and loneliness she endured at home, so eventually she gave in.

Wednesday night, girls night out, was the perfect set up for meeting Lenny. Liz's friends stood by her. They helped her set up rendezvous with him and they never said a word about it even to their own husbands. Alicia once said of the girls' friendship, "If one of you committed a crime, all would hang for it." She was right. They were close. Their friendship was unconditional. Even Norm's sister Mandy went along with it. Although Norm was her brother Mandy loved Liz, and she didn't like the way Norm was treating her. Norm's whole family were very nice people, but Norm seemed to be a misfit.

Without realizing it Norm was pushing Liz more and more towards Lenny. Liz knew that Norm was unaware of the affair. She shuddered to think of what he would do if he found out. Now she was guilty of having the affair that he had accused her of having for the previous two years. The old adage, get the name, play the game, eased her conscience somewhat. But by the time winter blossomed into the spring of 1973, Liz's conscience was tearing her apart. Not only that, she was afraid of Norm's anger. Compounding the fear and the guilt was her concern for her children. Where did they fit in all this? Without peace she was becoming a basket case. Her nerves were so bad that she started drinking a little more to try to drown her woes.

Liz knew she had to do something before she lost her mind. She had to choose. Either she had to tell Norm and leave, or stop seeing Lenny. She just couldn't go on and stay sane.

What she really wanted was to continue seeing Lenny. Their relationship was so powerful. It was bigger than both of them. Lenny was her prince. He called her Princess. He plied her with romantic cards which she kept hidden. They talked on the phone to each other for hours. Unlike Norm, Lenny was her intellectual equal with a romantic nature the same as hers. He was her cavalier. Not since Edmund had anyone filled her emptiness so completely. She couldn't thrive without love and with Lenny she was loved. They were one in the universe. So she knew what her choice had to be.

She decided to approach Lenny with the idea of her leaving Norm. Because of her guilt, she didn't want Norm to be the one to have to move out again. She was the one who was cheating so the proper thing was for Lenny to take the kids and her in. Presenting her decision to Lenny, she said, "I can't continue to see you while I'm still with Norm. You'll have to find us a place to live. If not, I'll have to split up with you. I can't go on the way things are."

Lenny misunderstood her words. He thought that Liz meant she didn't want to see him anymore. He knew the situation was driving her mad, and he didn't make enough money to provide for a family of six. So to ease her plight, he quit his job at the hotel and moved 90 miles away. He knew if he couldn't have her, he couldn't stand to be around her. He didn't even tell her he was leaving. It was too hard for him to say goodbye. She went in to work the next day and he was gone.

Her heart was broken. It was as if something inside her had died. The carousel turned for Lenny and now he was gone. Weeks went by and she went through the motions without really being alive. Even her job didn't seem to give her the same lift any more. Then at work one evening, Peter called her aside to talk privately to her.

"Lenny called today. It's none of my business what you do, but I think you're playing with fire here. You're already in enough trouble with Norm. Anyway, think this over carefully before you decide. Lenny asked me to get you to come and see him. He said he can't live without you. I'm to call him tomorrow and let him know. He'll be waiting for you on Tuesday at the little corner cafe on the main street in Mount Forest.

Liz felt elated by his words. "I don't know." she said feeling herself blossom with new life but at the same time feeling apprehensive, "It's a long way to travel alone and there's the kids to think about." Then without any further ado, she quickly made her mind up to do it. She would work out the details later. Liz told Peter to call Lenny.

When Tuesday finally came, Liz was as nervous as a mare with a newborn colt. With the excuse that she needed to go to the school for a parent/teacher interview, she had convinced Norm to get a ride to work with Derrick so she could have the car.

She made arrangements for Dar to stay at the house. All the kids were in school except Janie. As soon as Norm was gone Liz hugged and kissed Janie tenderly then left. Janie giggled. She didn't mind because Angie was there to play with her. Angie was Dar's youngest. Dar and Liz had carried the girls at the same time and it seemed as though they were friends before they were even born. The two were as inseparable as their mothers, and as much as their mothers were alike so were the girls, truckers both.

Liz drove out of the lane like a woman with a dual personality. On the one hand she was ecstatic. She was going to see Lenny. But on the other hand she was plagued with guilt. She was torn by what she was doing. She was drawn to Lenny as much as she had been to Edmund, but she didn't want her children marred in any way by what she was doing.

The miles dragged by as she anticipated their meeting. Time seemed an eternity until she finally pulled up in front of the cafe. There, in the window watching for her, was Lenny. Her whole being lit up as she saw his face peering out from behind the checkered curtains. The old bell attached above the door tinkled as she walked in. Their eyes locked in an electric stare and she moved towards him like iron filings drawn to a magnet. He grabbed both her hands and squeezed them. In his eyes she read the truth of how much he'd missed her.

They ate burgers and fries and then left the restaurant and headed for a place where they could be alone. The radio in the car played the words "My, my, my beautiful Sunday. This is my, my, my beautiful day" and Liz's heart sang along with it. It was *her* beautiful day. She drove out of town and Lenny directed her to a wooded area that he had discovered while hiking. In the middle of the woods was a meadow full of wild flowers. It was totally secluded.

"Do you know how many times I dreamed of being here with you?" he asked smiling and drinking her in with his eyes. He grabbed her around the waist and spun her in circles, round and round they went. Then they laughed as they dizzily keeled over in the long grass. For the longest time they didn't speak. They just watched the passing clouds and held each other quietly and gently. The whole day was a dream come true. They didn't make love. They just loved each other and then it was over.

Too soon the time came for Liz to have to leave. Lenny kissed her tenderly. He clung to her, then slowly, reluctantly he let her go. They said their goodbyes, not knowing when they would see each other again. With the image of the man she loved in the rear view mirror looking after her longingly, Liz sadly drove away. A solitary tear squeezed its way out of the corner of her eye and slowly trickled down her cheek. She swallowed hard to remove the lump in her throat so she could concentrate on the long drive home. Then it was as though a curtain came down and she crossed over into another world. She left a dream world of clouds, rainbows and golden sunbeams and passed into a world of guilt, deceit and intense loneliness.

The day had been wonderful, but the next day the cost proved to be very high.

"Where were you yesterday?" Norm said angrily.

"J-Just around," Liz lied, shaking inside. Lying was not a thing she did well.

"How come you went so many miles?" he continued getting angrier. "There's 200 more miles on the speedometer of the car."

Liz felt as if she was in front of the Spanish Inquisition and was on the rack. She shook like a leaf as Norm smashed his fist down on the table.

"I checked the mileage before you got the car," he shouted red faced. She found out later that not only did he always check the mileage on the car, but he checked ash trays for different kinds of cigarette butts and the driveway for different kinds of tire tracks. He was paranoid in his jealousy.

"I-I don't know," she stammered feeling like a rat in a trap.

He slapped her hard across her cheek knocking her off the chair. Then he slammed the door shaking the house, as he left her alone with her conscience. Liz didn't know which was worse, Norm's anger or her guilt.

Torn between what she desperately needed and the most severe guilt she had ever felt, she was relieved that Lenny lived so far away. Liz made a decision that day that she couldn't go and see him again. She loved him dearly, but the cost was just too high. She was a nervous wreck. She was just not the type who could cheat and lie and Lenny couldn't afford to support a wife and four children. So she sadly decided she would have to give him up for the sake of her children. They needed a full-time mother and she couldn't be one as long as she was torn in two.

# Chapter 28
## "Paying the Piper"

"Stand back. Now, let's have a look at you." Liz examined Bonnie's costume with her head cocked to the side. Then a warm smile of approval formed on her lips. She sighed and as the breath swelled into her lungs a warmth spread through her whole being. Love for her daughter tingled in every fibre of her.

Bonnie was a little teapot for the spring pageant at school. Liz had worked for days on the outfit. A big round pot of cream coloured cotton held rigid by coat hangers went from Bonnie's knees to her neck. She wore a cream coloured sweater underneath. Around her neck was a large starched collar representing a lid. Bonnie's head was the knob on top of the lid. One arm bent at the elbow, knuckles on hips made the handle. The other arm stretched out and crooked at the elbow, hand bent down, was the spout.

Liz wanted to laugh. Bonnie looked so cute and so funny. It was all she could do to fight back the urge. She didn't dare laugh though. Bonnie was the kind of kid who hated to be in the lime light. She was very shy and timid. Liz had worked very hard to convince her to play the part. When Bonnie had come home from school with the note from the teacher about the pageant, she had cried her little heart out. She was terrified about getting on the stage in front of all the people. If Liz laughed, it would embarrass her, and there would be no way she would perform.

Had it been Stacy, there wouldn't have been a problem. Stacy loved to be the centre of attention. She would even fight for it. She was tough not thin-skinned like Bonnie. Sometimes she exasperated Liz with her adventurous spirit.

"Okay, perfect. Now, Mommy's going to go and sit in the audience. You'll be alright."

Bonnie, looking frightened to death, gave a quick nod. Liz wanted to gather her up, cuddle her and say forget it, but she knew it wouldn't be good for her so she fought the urge, kissed the top of Bonnie's head and left the stage.

The lights were dimmed for the performance. Liz was glad because she felt like she was naked. She couldn't help the emotion she was feeling. She had always worn her heart on her sleeve, and she didn't want anybody to see her face glowing with pride at her daughter's performance.

"I'm a little tea pot, short and stout. Here is my handle, here is my spout. When I blow my whistle, hear me shout. Tip me over, pour me out," Bonnie sang, but as she tipped her spout she leaned too far and the weight of her costume put her off balance. She crashed to the floor!

"Oh, no!" Liz cried.

Bonnie's face was scarlet; she laid there looking at the audience, sheer terror reflected on her face. Liz wanted to run to her. She had an overwhelming ache in the pit of her stomach. A tear trickled down her face in sympathy for her offspring. Bonnie finally got up and ran back stage. Liz bounded from her seat at the same time.

"Oh, baby," she crooned as she rocked Bonnie back and forth. She could feel the warmth of the tiny body as it shook with sobs. Liz wanted to protect her children from all of life's little embarrassments and pains but she knew it wasn't possible and it wouldn't be good for them either. But the pain of standing back and watching them struggle was excruciating.

That spring bloomed into the summer of 1973. Liz hadn't seen Lenny for months. By keeping busy with her children, her job and her house duties, she hoped she would eventually get over him. She was glad at least that he was 90 miles away.

She resigned herself to staying with Norm. She was too scared to go and see Lenny again after Norm's inquisition and the pangs of her own conscience. She had no romantic love in her life, but it was easier on her nerves even if she was lonely. At least it was easier for a while. Then Norm's suspicious nature got the best of him and caused his temper to skyrocket to an all-time high. He didn't know about the affair, but he never got over the 200 miles on the speedometer. It ate away at him. Living with Norm was like living with nitro-glycerine, never knowing when it would go off. Because of her guilt

Liz constantly tried to placate him so her nerves were shot most of the time.

Then one warm June day while working in the ladies' room at the Beetonia, Liz took a break. The Ladies' room was deserted except for one old couple drinking draft beer and Liz had just served them two each so she went and stood at the front door to get some fresh air. She blinked once, then again, to clear her eyes and focus better. In an instant her pulse rate became very rapid. *I can't be seeing straight. Is my heart deceiving me?* There he was! He was back! In a deserted building across the street stood Lenny, naked to the waist with crowbar in hand. He touched his forefinger to his forehead in greeting as Liz devoured him with her eyes. A slight smile touched his lips. Lenny was not handsome, he was far from it, but he was rugged-looking, well built and very big. The tanned skin on his chest and arms gleamed with sweat from his labour. He looked like a modern-day Hercules. He tore at the building that was being renovated and the mere sight of him tore at Liz's heart. Nothing had changed. All the passion was still there as her whole being flushed with awakening.

Liz knew she had to see him again and so she did. Their relationship picked up where it had left off. In spite of Norm's anger and in spite of her conscience, Liz was driven by an insatiable hunger. She had to feed it at all cost. She was willing to pay the piper whatever the cost, the high cost of being loved. Norm was angry all the time anyway, no matter what she did.

Liz continued to work and Norm continued to accompany her. He kept himself composed during the early evenings but as the evenings wore on and the drinks tallied up he lost his self-control many times. After hours with the staff stopped being pleasurable for Liz. Not only had the situation become untenable for Liz, but Norm had alienated most of the staff at the hotel.

Eventually, Dave sold the hotel business and everyone was invited to a big party in celebration of the sale. Dar and Arnie came to stay overnight with the kids so Norm and Liz were free to go. The whole staff and their spouses were invited to Dave's big beautiful home outside of town for dinner and drinks. As an ex-employee Lenny came with Peter. Liz was nervous about him being there so she totally ignored him, being very careful not to let anything show in front of Norm.

Nonetheless, Norm got very drunk and after several unsuccessful attempts to make conversation with the other guests, he became very restless and angry. Meanwhile Liz was engrossed in deep conversation with Peter's fiancee. Then the nitro blew. Norm demanded that they leave. Being embarrassed, angry and slightly inebriated, Liz wasn't able to move quite fast enough for him.

With amazing speed for someone so drunk, Norm grabbed her by the arms and whipped her up from the lawn chair she was sitting in. He dragged her behind him with such a force that her buckled shoes were ripped right off her feet. Then he brutally pushed her into the front seat of the Plymouth.

"What's the matter with you? Are you crazy? Have you no shame, making such a scene in front of everyone?" Liz yelled in anger and fear. She didn't understand Norm's outburst. She had avoided Lenny like the plague. She had given him no cause to act the way he did. All eyes had been on them, as though they were players in some perverse play. She was totally humiliated.

Gravel sprayed up behind the car as he squealed the tires out of the yard. As they turned onto the sideroad from the long lane and started to speed up, he gritted his teeth and said, "I'm sick of this life. I'm going to kill us both."

Sheer terror froze Liz's blood as she screamed out the words, "Not me, you're not!" Without thinking, she opened the car door and bailed out.

She hit the ground, her body rolling and thumping, and sobriety whacked her like a ton of bricks. Realization dawned on her through her alcohol haze that jumping from the car hadn't been such a good idea. In the eternity of seconds, she finally came to a stop dust flying all around her. She felt sore all over, and as she began to take stock, she became aware that Norm had slammed on the brakes and was out of the car in a flash. Without pausing for a breath, he loaded Liz back into the car and sped off again. Out of the corner of her eye she could see Lenny bolting down the lane after them, but he was too late.

Norm was driving wildly, holding one hand tightly onto the steering wheel while grasping Liz just as tightly with the other to prevent her from jumping again. Oblivious now to any pain, and in shock, Liz shook with terror at Norm's rage and the speed they were going. Alcohol was the fuel and rage was the spark that set him ablaze. Norm was an excellent driver but this was insane. He was hitting speeds of over 100 mph. The car careened into the air as they flew over railroad tracks. Liz squeezed her eyes shut in total fear, as she was lifted out of her seat and then smashed back into it as the car hit the road. She was relieved that there was no other traffic.

About a mile from home Norm suddenly slammed on the brakes in the middle of the road and rammed the gear shift into park causing Liz to slide forward and land on the floor. He jumped out of the car, pulled down the zipper in the front of his pants and urinated in the middle of the road. As soon as he got out, Liz quickly slammed down the buttons on all the doors. Then she moved into the driver's seat, whipped the gear shift into drive and squealed the tires leaving Norm standing in the middle of the road. She didn't even look in the rear view mirror to see his reaction. She was too afraid. Terrified, she drove the rest of the way home and ran into the house.

"Get up, please get up!" she cried, yanking on the covers trying to wake up Dar and Arnie.

"Whatsa matter?" Arnie muttered, rubbing the sleep from his eyes.

"Norm's going to kill me!" she gasped, trying to catch her breath.

"Calm down, calm down, Liz," Arnie soothed, getting out of bed and pulling on his pants. Dar sat up instantly awake, aware and ready for action. "He's not going to touch you as long as I'm here," Arnie said, grinning, and Dar was nodding her head. Arnie was tough and loved any opportunity to prove it. He was confident Norm would never take him on, but Liz was petrified.

Dar pointed to Liz's foot and said with concern, "What happened?"

Liz looked at her foot and gasped. Her panty hose were full of blood. The end off her big toe was almost completely severed.

"Ewww, that's going to need stitches," she said wincing in pain. Her fear had buried the pain, but on seeing the damage to her toe, the pain spread through her like a hot poker.

Arnie, naked to the waist, was casually leaning against the kitchen counter and Dar was dressing Liz's wound when suddenly the back door flew wide open hitting the wall with a bang. An enraged Norm filled the door frame. His hands were formed into tight fists at his sides and a very dark cloud loomed over his countenance. He literally shook with rage.

"Enjoy your early morning constitutional?" Dar questioned jovially trying to break the ice.

You could almost see steam coming out of Norm's ears. Then he caught sight of Arnie leaning against the counter, arms crossed with a challenging look on his face. Norm's head dropped, and he stomped through the living room into the kitchen, threw open the fridge door, popped the cap off a bottle of beer and headed upstairs to the bedroom without saying a word. Arnie grinned.

Dawn was in full bloom when Liz curled up with a blanket on the couch. She knew she had to do something about her situation, but what?

By the next day Norm was in a sober state and feeling his neck, especially with Arnie there. Arnie made him a little edgy. Norm didn't mind picking on Liz, but he was a coward where another man was concerned.

Liz, feeling very frightened and very angry, demanded that they move back into town as soon as possible. Being afraid of Norm's anger, she wanted the comfort of knowing other people were around to help her should he explode like that again. Fortunately for Liz, Dar and Arnie had been there to protect her. What could have happened to her if they hadn't been, made Liz shudder. Norm took a sideways glance at Arnie and reluctantly agreed he would move to town. Liz won that round.

Within a months time they rented a large apartment over the five cent to a dollar store. The store had closed down and the snack bar was no longer frequented by the local gentry like it had been when Liz first moved to Beeton. It saddened her that the store was closed. She had been so happy when she first arrived in town and all the townsfolk gathered gayly around the snack bar's counter and chatted incessantly. It seemed like a hundred years ago. She felt old and tired. The little town that had been a haven of joy and safety for Liz had changed drastically and so had she.

Liz felt a little safer after they moved, but the situation with Norm didn't change any. So she continued to seek solace and comfort in Lenny's arms. She didn't care how Norm felt. She detested him. He made her skin crawl when he touched her. Not only had the carousel never turned for Norm, but now the turtle shell was shattered by his violence, and Liz was completely naked and vulnerable.

Because of Norm's abusiveness, she did feel within her rights about seeing Lenny. But at the same time she had a strong moral side to contend with. That side had been ingrained in her since childhood. It was not easy to shake. And then in the middle of the whole situation were her children. She felt like a squirrel trapped in a cage treading the mill round and round. So her drinking started to escalate. She was nearly crazy and drank more to drown her troubles. The solution would have been to leave Norm, but Liz was very afraid of him, afraid to tell him she wanted out.

She continued to work, but the job no longer held the same excitement for her because of Norm's presence. She just went through the motions, being as congenial as she could with the customers and, at the same time, trying to keep Norm appeased.

Then one evening after the bar closed as they stepped down the first step at the front doors, Norm, being drunk and cantankerous, gave Liz a shove. She went flying down the five stairs landing in a heap at the bottom. Any normal person with self-respect would have been furious by this treatment, but Liz merely got up, dusted herself off, displayed a weak smile, and flushed with embarrassment.

Lenny, just leaving the bar behind them with Peter, saw it all. At the end of his rope and no longer able to tolerate the way Norm treated Liz, he blurted out through clenched teeth, "Norm, don't *ever* touch her again."

Norm stopped in his tracks, turned and sneered, "Oh, and what business is it of yours?"

"It's very much my business, I love her," Lenny growled.

*Has he lost his mind?* Liz thought feeling intense fear. Her body rigid, she backed slowly away from Norm whose face exhibited total shock at Lenny's words.

The two men stood, fists clenched, glaring daggers at each other.

"Go home, Liz!" Norm spat through clenched teeth.

Liz walked slowly across the street with her head down feeling as though she had a scarlet letter "A" embroidered on her chest.

Glancing back, she caught sight of Lenny and Norm heading around the corner of the grocery store toward the back alley. She assumed that they were going to fight it out. She was just sick. She hated Norm and part of her wanted Lenny to kill him, but she felt, somehow, as though the whole mess was her fault because she couldn't be the wife Norm wanted. It was because of her they were fighting and she didn't want either of them to get hurt on her account. She wanted to run to them and scream at them to stop. She just wanted to walk away with Lenny, but she couldn't walk away and leave four others behind. Never before had her heart been so torn. She crept away feeling as if she should have her head shaved in penance.

Shortly after going into their apartment, Liz heard Norm's heavy boots stomping up the wooden staircase. Her body twitched involuntarily as she lay on the double bed waiting.

"W-What happened?" she stuttered trying to break the ice.

"Nuthin'," he blurted out. "I didn't want to fight him." He stood head down looking totally defeated. "Liz, how could you do this to me?" he said as though he was perfectly innocent. A slap in the face would have hurt her less. He looked astounded. Liz was amazed by his astonishment. He was playing the martyr, and it made her feel even more guilty. She was puzzled. Hadn't he constantly accused her of having an affair; hadn't he called her all the dirty names in the book. Didn't he mean it?

The severity of the truth seemed to sober him, and he walked around looking like a lost soul. Liz's guilt made her feel bad for him in spite of all the things he had done to her. He got the desired results. He wanted her to pay.

"What are you going to do?" he asked with a calmness that disturbed her.

"I don't know," she answered, because she really didn't.

Liz wasn't ready to move in with Lenny. At one time she had thought she was, but after thinking it over, she realized the kids didn't even know him. It wouldn't be fair to them.

And she knew she couldn't live with Norm with only sympathy as a bond. The only emotion she felt for him was pity. That was certainly not enough. She found it impossible to ask Norm to leave, and she had nowhere to go. Liz just shrugged, head down, too ashamed to look him in the face.

"Let me make it easy for you," he said looking forlorn, "I'll just go." He was playing the part of the poor jilted husband to the hilt. He wanted Liz to suffer some more. All through their relationship he had controlled her to the point of almost killing her spirit. Now, he knew he couldn't anymore, but he took one last shot at hurting her. He didn't want her to enjoy her freedom with Lenny. It worked. Liz felt awful.

That was it. That was all there was to it. It was over. There was no big explosion. Simply, "I'll just go." But his long-faced, martyr act took its toll on Liz.

When he finally walked out of the door and out of her life, tears of relief flowed freely down her cheeks. She had paid the piper with a pound of flesh.

# Chapter 29
# Left in the Lurch

"Hello."

"Hello, is Lenny there please?" Liz asked apprehensively. Lenny was staying at his mother's until he could find a place of his own, and Liz was nervous about calling him there. She wasn't sure how his mother would feel about a married woman chasing after her son.

"Just a minute," the voice on the other end chimed.

"Hello."

"Hi, Lenny, why don't you come over and see me?"

"Come over and see you? What about Norm?"

"He's gone."

"Really! You mean it. You mean I can just come over to your place anytime? Wow, this means I can take you out to dinner or dancing or even walk down the street with you. How about if I come over, and we just walk down the street together holding hands? I've wanted to do that ever since I met you. We've always had to sneak around and hide. It will be so wonderful to be free to see each other whenever we want. Oh, Liz, I love you so much," he rattled on and on excitedly.

It was a wild fun-filled summer. She was Lenny's girl. She never saw Norm. He didn't come around, and she was relieved he didn't frequent the same places that she and Lenny did. Lenny was very adept at wooing her. He brought roses, romantic cards, gifts even a gold lighter with "Princess" inscribed on the side. Liz was his princess and he was her prince. All was well. Liz's life was an ever turning carousel of romance. Not only was Lenny a hopeless romantic like Liz, but he was also her intellectual equal. There was definitely a meeting of the minds and a melding of the hearts. They spent hours talking about books they had read, famous authors, the stock market, you name it they discussed it.

Lenny introduced her to all his friends. He was proud to show her off. She liked them right away. Hippies all, Lenny and his friends were a few years younger than Liz. She was impressed that some of them had even been to Woodstock. Liz was taken in by their laid-back life style. She thoroughly enjoyed their gentle manner. She knew that they smoked marijuana and hashish, but she wasn't alarmed. It wasn't for her, but to each his own. After all, she liked to drink and drink they did. They celebrated their life together with fine wines and champagne.

But that summer was filled with more than fun and romance. Alone again with four kids to support, Liz needed to work as well so her time was juggled between Lenny, kids, home chores, and a job. Bob, the new owner of the hotel, hired her full-time.

Norm's sister Mandy was in a similar situation to Liz. Luther had run off with his secretary, and Mandy was now living alone with her three kids. At Liz's suggestion she applied for a full-time job at the hotel as well. Bob split the shifts between them. The pay wasn't great but the tips were stupendous. Liz earned enough to keep herself and four kids comfortably, plus she was still able to save for their education. She now had $5,000.00 in a savings account at the Royal bank for her college fund. She was pleased with herself.

Liz enjoyed her job much more now that Norm was not hounding her. Between Lenny's appreciation of her and her success at work, she was feeling on top of the world. Bob had her working in all three rooms, the cocktail lounge, the Ladies' room and even the men's room. With some pride, she became the first woman in the history of the Beetonia Hotel to set foot in the men's room. It was a great challenge as she wasn't sure how the male patrons would take to having a female in their domain. As it turned out, they loved it. It worked very well until one Tuesday evening.

"Liz, Lorraine and I have to go to Toronto to pick up a liquor order. I think you'll be alright on your own. Tuesdays are really dead anyway," Bob said as he put on his suit jacket.

"Sure, not a problem," Liz answered, feeling confident, "There's only two couples in the ladies room, one salesman in the bar and half a dozen or so of the railroad gang from upstairs in the men's room."

"Great, you know Liz, if you were a little tougher I'd retire and have you running this place," he said with a big smile and a teasing twinkle in his eye. He always bugged her about being too soft and easy going, but Liz also knew he had a lot of confidence in her ability. She worked in all areas of the hotel now and knew the business as well as he did.

Waving his arm as he looked back over his shoulder he yelled, "Wally's always around anyway, if you run into trouble."

Wally was a part-time waiter in the bar. On the weekends he worked the ladies' and men's rooms, where only draft beer was served, while Mandy and Liz worked the bar, where mixed drinks were served. This particular night, a Tuesday, Liz was alone and covering all three rooms which she didn't expect would be difficult because week nights were always slow. The lone salesman would probably be the only customer in the bar. A few might come into the ladies' room. Aside from a few of the local yokels, the railroad gang would probably be her only customers in the men's room. she didn't anticipate any problems and was feeling proud and confident that Bob had left her in charge of the whole hotel.

"How's it goin'?" Wally asked as he stood in front of the stainless steel bar that housed the draft taps.

"Okay, Wally," she said from her stool behind the bar. "I'm glad you're here though, just in case. I don't think there's anything I can't handle with this crowd though."

She no sooner spoke the words than the far door of the men's room flew open. In spewed half a dozen young men. They sauntered in with their hands in the front pockets of their jeans, chests puffed out and shoulders held high. The chips on their shoulders were calling out "knock me off". Their faces were set with defiance.

"This could be trouble," Wally said surveying the surly looking crew as they filed through the door. "Better check for ID."

"Good idea," Liz said as she picked up her tray to make her rounds. In an instant her eyes swept the room as she moved confidently towards their table. In the middle of the room sat the half dozen burly railroad men who roomed upstairs. They were big and solid but not boisterous. Liz had been serving them for a week or so, and they had caused her no problem.

Over on the bench along the wall sat Tubby, a family man who came in regularly for a few beers, then went home to his family of nine. No problem there either. Frank, the eighty year old janitor, sat next to Tubby -- definitely not a problem. Otherwise there was just a few boys from Borden Metal.

Liz made her way to the table on the far wall where the six young men were sitting. She asked for ID hoping to get rid of them, but was trumped because they were all of age. Liz was somewhat uneasy by their presence but served them anyway as she had no valid reason not to.

The evening progressed, and Liz was beginning to get a little edgy because the young punks from Tottenham were getting obnoxious. One in particular was very small and was likely suffering severely from small man syndrome. He kept baiting the big guys from the railroad crew, who were trying their best to ignore him.

"I think you better cut those guys off," Wally said as he viewed them from his vantage point in front of the bar.

"I think you're right Wally," Liz said, wishing it was him and not her. The only area she was uncomfortable with in the job was being a four foot eleven inch bouncer playing tough. But not wanting to let on to Wally how she really felt, Liz marched into the room taking full control.

"Sorry boys," she said as she picked up the half-full glasses of beer from their table. "You're starting to get out of hand. I'm afraid you're going to have to leave."

"Aw c'mon. We'll behave."

"No way!" Liz said as she turned to walk away.

But as she turned her back, the little guy with the big ego took a poke at one of the railway crew. The railway worker came off his chair like a tornado. The little guy backed off and his big friend came to his defence. Before Liz knew it a donnybrook was in full swing and she was in the middle of it.

"Call the police!" Liz hollered to Wally who was already reaching for the phone. She had no sooner hollered out than she was flying through the air. She landed with a thud. The tray, the glasses and the beer all went flying too. The sound of glass shattering rung in her ears as a very heavy bar table fell with her and landed sideways across her wrist. She felt a seering pain as though branded with a hot iron, then she blacked out.

The next thing she knew she was being lifted to her feet. Tears were gushing from her eyes, and her hand hung abnormally loose at the wrist. Frank, the janitor, had picked her up from the floor and was taking her back to safety behind the bar. Out of the corner of her eye she could see Tubby standing up and whipping off his coat. This was unusual. Tubby usually sat through all kinds of skirmishes, unconcerned, drinking his beer. But they had gone too far this time. Liz was hurt, and he was mad. He grabbed one of the punks by the scruff of the neck and the seat of the pants and ran him to the door. The punk's feet were dangling barely touching the floor, and his arms were clawing at the air. Tubby swung him back and forth like a pendulum and then threw him half-way across the parking lot where he landed in a heap on the pavement. The rest of the men in the bar followed Tubby's lead and all six young men were disposed of in the same fashion. They never touched the ground. They just flew out the door and landed in a heap in the parking lot, then scrambled to their feet and took off running. Tubby grinned, dusted off his hands and sauntered back to his spot by the wall. By the time the police got there everything was over. The only thing they had to do was take Liz to the hospital. Wally kindly volunteered to take over for her until closing time.

Liz continued to work broken arm and all. Nothing could deter her. She had four kids to support. She would balance the tray on the arm with the cast and serve with her good hand.

Her juggling act with the tray went well until one very hot day when a paving crew came into the men's room to enjoy nice frosty cold beers. There must have been twenty of them. They were all teasing Liz and pulling on her apron strings. She was set off balance and before she knew it she had dumped twenty frosty cold glasses of draft beer down the bare back of one very handsome, dark skinned young man. He jumped up as though scalded and yelled as the ice cold beer hit his hot back. There was a lot of knee smacking, foot stomping and raucous laughter around the table. Liz made an attempt to wipe off his back apologizing profusely all the while. Getting into the spirit of things he recovered from the initial shock, grabbed her around the waist, swung her around, laughed, and said "It's okay. At least you cooled me down." The paving crew all chipped in with a big tip to help pay for the spilled beer and Liz was grateful.

Yes, Liz was kept very busy juggling her time between Lenny, housework, four kids and working, all with a broken arm, but it was still better than living with Norm. She felt free and easy. She was working at a job she loved with no interference, there was peace at home, and she was dating Lenny with no guilt. The tension was gone, but the funny thing was her drinking didn't decrease any. It was too late. Alcoholism had gripped her.

The insidious thing about alcohol is that first it giveth, then it taketh away. The intoxicant was still giving to her and had not yet asked anything in return. That is until one Sunday afternoon.

"Boy, I'm feeling rough," Liz said laying her head on Lenny's knee. She had worked a tough shift and then gone out afterwards with him to celebrate his birthday. Raising four kids, dating Lenny and working full-time was taking its toll.

"Yeah, me too. I think we must have gotten into a bad batch of beer last night," he said playing with her hair.

"I'm going to have to get up and get something for the kids for supper. They'll be home soon."

"Where are they anyway?" Lenny asked.

"Where they always are. Down at Carol's with her and Dar's kids," she answered as she got up and went to the fridge. "Wow, there's nothing in the fridge to eat. I work so much I hardly get time to shop. My head feels like it's going to pound right off my shoulders," she complained rubbing her forehead. She squeezed her temples and closed her eyes tightly trying to make the pain go away.

She grabbed her purse and opened it. "I must have spent all my tips last night. I had to buy all the kid's school pictures this week I don't get paid until next Friday. I'll get tips at work tomorrow, but that's no good now. Do you have any money left?"

"Yeah, I've only got ten bucks though."

"Can you get something for the kids to eat?"

Just as he answered, "Sure." a rap came at the door and Lenny's friends walked right in.

"Hey man, what's up?" Rob asked.

"Nuthin' much, it's my birthday today," Lenny beamed proudly.

"Hey, wow, what better for a man's birthday than a concert. We're just heading to Toronto now. Why don't you and Liz come along?"

"Liz?" Lenny posed a question with her name and shrugged waiting for her consent.

"I don't know Lenny. We've been out a lot lately. I don't really want to leave the kids again. I've got to get them something for supper. I just can't leave it all for a sitter to worry about. Besides, it's Sunday and I have to work tomorrow."

"Hey Lenny, you come then," Dillon piped up.

"Yeah, man, it's your birthday," Rob repeated.

Lenny looked at Liz, pleading with his eyes.

Liz shot back, "No!" with hers. She was slightly possessive of Lenny. He meant so much to her.

He looked back at her, shrugged, picked up his jacket and headed for the door. Lenny had his own mind and being a younger bachelor he was not accustomed to a family life style. He really loved Liz, but he was used to coming and going as he pleased.

"You mean you're really going to go out and leave us?" Liz barked sharply.

"Well I don't want to miss a concert with my friends, after all, it is my birthday. I'll come back later when it's over." He blew her a kiss as he disappeared around the corner.

She couldn't believe it. How could he just walk out on them and leave them in the lurch. It was their first disagreement. Liz was finding out Lenny wasn't perfect after all.

She was feeling so hung over that she didn't want to be alone; she was so angry, she wanted someone to yell at; she was so tired from working and juggling her schedule and so perplexed as to what to do about dinner that before she could think straight, she reached for the phone and made a quick call.

Lenny was an intellectual, a romantic, a fun-loving dreamer and he made the carousel turn for her, but he would need to learn some responsibility. In the mean time, she would have to resort to something else.

"Is Norm there?"

"Just a minute."

"Norm, it's me."

"I know. What do you want, Liz?"

"I have nothing to give the kids for supper, and I have no money. You haven't paid support yet this month. Can you please bring it over."

She had plenty of money in her college fund, but the bank was closed, and besides, she would never, never, touch that. It was her dream.

"Where's Lenny?"

"He took off with his friends to Toronto for a concert."

It seemed Liz had no sooner hung up the phone than Norm was at the door. The kids had come home, in the meantime, hungry. Norm walked right in with two large grocery bags full and a forty-pounder of whiskey. He knew her weaknesses.

"Want a drink?" Norm asked.

"No! Thanks for the groceries, but you could have just brought the money."

"Not a problem. You know I always like to take good care of the kids."

That was true. No matter how badly he treated Liz he had always taken care of the kids. It was just too bad he was so bad-tempered and so insanely jealous. It was like he had a dual personality.

"Come on, Liz. Just one drink. I'll help you get the kids supper."

Liz was hung over, exhausted and angry at Lenny, so she finally broke down and said, "Well, just one!"

Liz got drunk. The alcohol had given to her, made her feel classy, confident and cool, now it was collecting its dues. Now it was the master. She was its slave.

Because she was so exhausted, the whiskey worked fast. She passed out on the couch and Norm carried her to her bed. Norm was in control again, and a very startled Lenny stood on the other side of the door later that night when Norm opened it to his knock.

# Chapter 30
# Looking for Lenny

"Uh, what are you doing here?" Lenny asked.

"I've moved back in. Liz was mad at you for leaving her in a mess so she called me to take care of it. I'll give you a little bit of advice Lenny, if you want to live with a family, you've got to be a family man, like me."

"Oh, yeah! Let me talk to her. Where is she?"

"She's already in bed. She doesn't want to be disturbed. I'm just heading there myself so I'd appreciate it if you'd just go."

Norm started to shut the door, but Lenny placed his palm firmly against it and tried to push it open. Norm, being the stronger of the two, slammed it shut on him and locked it solidly. Lenny punched the door, then slowly turned, and went down the stairs.

The next morning Liz woke up to the alarm with her head pounding like a locomotive was chugging through it. Her mouth felt as though it was packed with dry cotton. She slapped her hand on the alarm button without moving any of the rest of her body for fear of it shattering. She felt as if she was made of glass. She could have sworn that she could feel her hair growing. She lifted her head and immediately felt as though the back of it had been walloped with the broadside of an axe. But the worst was yet to come. She opened one eye and let out a groan. There in the bed beside her was her worst nightmare. Norm grinned back at her.

*Oh, my god. What's he doing here? Where's Lenny? What have I done to myself?* Liz had needed help. The whiskey had dulled her senses, and Norm took advantage of her. The alcohol was doing a very good job of collecting its dues.

*I wonder what happened after I passed out. I wonder if Lenny came. Oh, no! He would have. Norm must have opened the door to him. Aww, no! What must Lenny think. I'll bet he was so hurt. I'll bet he's gone now for sure. I know Lenny he'll take right off because he'll think I'm back with Norm. Damn Norm! Oh, my head hurts so bad. Now what am I supposed to do. There's only one thing I can do. Norm's here I guess I better try to make the best of it. What am I thinking? Norm is a jerk. He treats me like a piece of crap. He is good to the kids though, and he is a hard worker. Am I losing my mind? I can't go back with Norm. But maybe he sensed the thing between Lenny and I. Maybe that's why he got so mad all the time. Lenny probably won't be back today and I just can't be alone, I've got the shakes so bad. Maybe I can put up with Norm, just for the day. I feel so alone and frightened. I need someone with me. I wonder if a marriage counsellor would help. Maybe with some help this marriage could work out. Oh, who knows?* Liz went on and on until she was nearly crazy.

Once in the door Norm refused to move out. Every day for a week Lenny stood on the street across from Liz's apartment, hoping for a chance to see her. In fear of Norm's threat to have her kids taken away from her, Liz didn't go out. She hid behind the curtain in the front room and watched him day after day. It broke her heart, but Norm refused to leave and Liz just couldn't get into the triangle thing again. After that Lenny moved right out of town. He cursed himself for going to that concert.

Norm hired the services of a marriage counsellor. Reluctantly Liz agreed to go. Obviously, they didn't have any answers, maybe a counsellor would.

"Well, Norm," the middle-aged counsellor with greying hair and sharp nose said as he peered over the top of his thick glasses, "What do you have to say about the problem in your marriage?"

As if his question were a key to open Pandora's box, Norm gave him a long list of grievances. The complaints about Liz would have made Jezebel look innocent.

As Norm rambled on, the counsellor peered over his glasses now and then, sending accusing and shocked looks in Liz's direction. His close scrutiny made her squirm in her seat. She felt as though she was on trial, pronounced guilty, and sentenced by these two men before she even had a chance to speak.

If she could have liquified, she would have slid off her seat and oozed out under the door in shame. *It sure is a man's world. Look at the two of them heads together enjoying every minute of chopping the evil woman to bits. If they think I'm ever coming back here again to be at their mercy, they're nuts.* Brave thoughts but the following week she was sitting in the orange leather chair in the counsellor's office again.

"Well, Liz Norm had plenty to say last week. How about telling me your opinion of it all this week?" asked the counsellor.

Liz was taken aback. She hadn't expected this. She had her back up thinking the counsellor had judged her badly and that he and Norm were going to have a field day running her down again, and she was not prepared to say anything.

"I don't know what to say," she uttered, sheepishly. She felt embarrassed that Norm had painted such a black picture of her the week before. She had plenty to say alright, but that inner part of her that harboured loyalty refused to let her reveal Norm's shortcomings. She clammed up and wouldn't speak.

"Alright then, Liz," the counsellor continued, talking to the top of her head because it was bowed in shame. "I'd like you to come next week by yourself. I need to hear your side and if it's too uncomfortable in front of Norm, then I'll see you alone."

She lifted her head, her eyes brightened with renewed hope. *Maybe this guy isn't judge and jury after all.*

The next week Liz poured out her side of the story to the counsellor. She told him about Norm's severe jealousy, his bad temper, his abuse, her disrespect for him and how he fabricated stories that irritated her no end.

The counsellor sat silently staring over the top of his thick glasses, the finger tips of one hand pulsing against the finger tips of the other hand like two giant spiders.

All the poisons of the last three years poured out of Liz in rhythm with the spiders. The counsellor remained mute, to her great relief. When she was finished he said, "Fine then, Liz, I think we can work on this. Will you tell Norm I want to see both of you next Wednesday night at 8 o'clock?"

Wednesday night came in a flash. Liz was eager to see what the counsellor would have to say.

"How are you folks tonight?"

They unanimously answered, "Fine!"

"Now," he sucked in a deep breath expanding his chest and let the breath out slowly before he spoke, "Liz, working in a bar environment is not exactly healthy for a marriage. It might work well for a single person but not for married folks."

Liz stared at him mouth agape. *Did he hear nothing of my side of the story? What a traitor.* She shook her head in anger.

"And Norm, Liz is never going to quit a job where she gets her self-esteem built up as long as you continue to run her down."

*Wow,* thought Liz, anger receding. *He's right. Norm is always running me down. I never thought about it before.*

"And another thing, Norm, Liz has mentioned that you have a habit of fabricating stories. Is this true?"

*Oh, no!* She thought as she looked at Norm's face. She was afraid of seeing extreme anger there, but instead she saw child-like embarrassment and guilt.

"Ever since I was a kid," Norm began, "I found it really hard to talk to people. I discovered that if I made up exciting stories, people would listen to me. I guess it's just become a bad habit."

Liz felt sorry for him. she even warmed up to him a bit after his disclosure. They left the counsellor's that night and headed to the bar.

Had they continued with the counselling sessions, they might have been able to get somewhere. But Norm decided after a few more sessions that all was well because he had Liz back. That was all he really wanted so he refused to go anymore. She was his wife, she was back where she belonged and he would take control again.

Norm, thinking it would help to bring the marriage together, insisted on buying a new house. He thought a nice new home would make Liz happy. He just didn't understand that she needed to be loved, material things didn't mean anything to her. Besides, it never made any sense to Liz because in order to keep up the mortgage payments, she needed to keep working at the bar. As the counsellor had said, working at the bar was definitely detrimental to their marriage. It was a no-win situation. She tried to reason with Norm and got nowhere. Against Liz's better judgment, they bought and moved into a new house on Queen Street in Beeton.

So Liz continued to work and her drinking increased even more. Like a slippery serpent her addiction to alcohol was wrapping itself around her. Norm continued to drink excessively as well. Along with the drink went the abuse so the couple made no headway in improving their marriage.

Gradually Liz started spending more and more nights away from home. Once she had the kids in bed, she was gone. It was too late to love or even respect Norm, and try as hard as she might, she just couldn't stomach him and the longing for Lenny was killing her.

It was all too much for Liz -- Norm's abuse, no love in her life, the emotional turmoil and the increased alcohol abuse. She didn't care any more if she lived or died. As she sat on a bar stool stirring her fifth drink of rye whiskey and ginger ale, a man named Wayne sat next to her. She was familiar with everyone who drank in the bar. Wayne was a regular and she knew him as well as anybody. He was a boring kind of guy. Nobody special. He had no pizzaz. He was like a blank TV screen, if he went away, nobody would ever miss him.

She was crying into her drink, and in his know nothing kind of way, he was trying to comfort her. She told him all her troubles, and when he said he knew where Lenny was, she perked right up. He smiled, pleased with himself for cheering her up. He no more knew where Lenny was than he could fly to the moon, but he was basking in her attention. Needing Lenny's romantic comforting, Liz asked Wayne to take her to him. She missed Lenny terribly, and with her inhibitions lowered by the alcohol, she made a bad choice.

Lenny had moved to Caledon East that much she knew, but she had no idea where. Wayne swore up and down he knew where. Liz wasn't sure she could trust him, but the emptiness inside her was driving her mad. Lenny filled that emptiness. She longed to see him. She was driven by an insatiable hunger. Wayne had a bottle of whiskey in his car, and after stopping at a pop machine to get mix, he poured them both a drink in white plastic cups.

By the time they arrived at Caledon East Liz's mind was absolutely saturated with whiskey. Her head was spinning. She almost forgot why they were there. Wayne drove round and round Caledon East with the excuse that he had forgotten exactly what street Lenny was on.

He had no idea where Lenny lived, but he had other ideas in his mind, he would keep driving around until the whiskey rendered Liz helpless.

After an hour or so, Wayne was pleased to look over and see Liz slumped over in the front seat. Finally, she had passed out. He tried to wake her up. *No response. Good.* He drove immediately to a motel he had seen while driving around. He rented a room, deposited the empty whiskey bottle in a garbage can. Then he licked his lips lavisciously as he struggled to carry Liz's unconscious body into the motel room.

He laid her on the bed and laid down beside her, but his plans backfired. He had drunk as much whiskey as Liz, and he promptly passed out too.

Wayne came to before Liz. Spotting her still passed out beside him and remembering his intentions, he tried to slip her clothes off without waking her, but Liz slowly came to. Her head was splitting.

"Get away from me, you creep!" she yelled slapping at him.

"Sorry, sorry." he backed off as she struggled to get up off the bed.

Catching sight of herself in the big mirror across the room, she shuddered. Her hair was all askew, her eyes were red and swollen shut from crying the night before, her clothes were all dishevelled. She wreaked of stale alcohol, body sweat and stale perfume. Her stomach pitched with nausea at the sight of herself. It turned again at the thought of what could have happened. She was sick to the very pith of her soul as she dragged herself to the bathroom in shame.

"What time is it?" she called over her shoulder.

"Uh, it's four o'clock," he said. It was dim in the room with the heavy drapes pulled.

"What? Four o'clock in the morning or the afternoon?" she cried, fear prickling its way through her body. Norm was already abusive to her, now she was making it worse.

"In the afternoon," Wayne called out.

"Oh, no you've got to get me home right away. I've been missing for almost twenty-four hours -- the kids -- Norm."

Her thoughts raced as she envisioned the scene at home. She wasn't worried about the kids. She knew they would be alright. Norm always cared for them. His vendetta was against her not them. Now, he had good cause. Cold sober her head was clear. *What have I done? How far down have I sunk? I just don't know what I'm going to do. What's the matter with me?* It never occurred to her that alcohol was the problem.

By the time they got back to Beeton, dusk was working it's way slowly from east to west blanketing the little town in darkness. How she longed for the years when this cozy town had brought her so much joy. What had happened to the dark-haired, confident, lively, young woman who felt so blessed with good friends and good times.

Liz turned the knob slowly on the back door of their new home on Queen Street. The whole house was in darkness. She shuddered as she climbed the three steps to the kitchen. She felt like a criminal. She had no idea what was awaiting her. The house was deadly quiet. The floor creaked under her stealthy footsteps. Norm's car was in the garage, but where was he? Where were the kids? Guilt crept up her spine like a disease and spread rapidly through her whole being and the heat of fear burned through her veins.

She crept silently through the living room towards the kids' rooms without turning on the light. She felt better in the dark, safer, somehow cleaner.

"They're in bed!" an angry voice rattled from the darkness sending flushes of sheer panic through her whole system. She stopped dead in her tracks, saturated with terror and guilt.

"Where have you been?" the voice from the darkness shattered the still silence.

She was relieved that the lights were out, so her face could not reveal her guilt and shame. She was afraid of a beating. The only thing on her side was that Norm was sober.

She was about to make up a lie as to her whereabouts, but the words never had time to leave her lips before a very welcome knock came at the door.

"Will you get that?" She asked, not wanting to be seen.

Norm gave her a shove and sneered as he passed by. He clicked on the kitchen light while Liz stayed hidden in the darkness of the living room. She could hear a voice with a distinct southern drawl say, "Hi, does Liz O'Shea live here?"

"Liz Carter does," she heard Norm answer.

"I've got the right place then," the southern drawl continued. "I'm Brian O'Shea. I used to be married to Liz. Can I see her? As a matter of fact, I'd like to take you both out for a drink on me," Brian said firmly, almost demanding.

"Just a minute." Norm's voice softened at the prospect of free drinks. He loved his booze and he had always been cheap. "Your ex-husband's here," he barked at Liz.

"Just a sec," she hollered from the living room. "I need to change and freshen up." She was very relieved for the interruption, but at the same time she was shocked. What was Brian doing there?

She rushed to her bedroom as the voices faded in the distance. Norm and Brian were leaving to pick up Donny to babysit. She quickly grabbed fresh clothes, rushed to the bathroom, sponge bathed briefly, applied fresh makeup and fixed her hair. "Not bad!" she said as she looked in the mirror at her fresh appearance. Despite her red eyes, she looked presentable.

She was eager to see Brian. She hadn't seen or heard from him for years. He was the father of her children. Grateful for his timely arrival she squashed her guilt and shame deep down in the middle of her somewhere. Norm and Brian returned with Donny, and Liz avoided Norm's piercing gaze as she extended her hand to shake Brian's.

He had gained quite a bit of weight. He wore a big black cowboy hat that matched the big white Cadillac parked outside. The southern drawl was adopted as was his new home, Texas. He had married a red-haired beauty. He showed Liz a photo of himself with her and a young boy and girl. It was a photograph of the perfect family. Liz wondered if he had truly settled down. She almost felt a little jealous. They all looked so happy in the picture. She wondered why her marriage to Brian hadn't worked? She felt a very slight twinge of excitement at seeing him, but quickly dismissed it. She wondered why he was in Beeton.

Norm and Liz spent the evening at the Beetonia with Brian, Carol, Derrick, Dar and Arnie. It was like old home week as all of them caught up on each other's news. As they talked, Liz learned Brian had some business in Canada and decided to look her up while he was there. She was glad he did. The timing couldn't have been any better. He had saved her bacon.

Her escapade with Wayne had been temporarily forgotten by Norm, but obviously, not forgiven as he continued to grow more abusive in the months to follow. Norm and Liz attended lots of parties. It made Liz's life more bearable, or so it seemed. Norm was always getting into trouble though. On one occasion they were invited to a BBQ party at Carol's. Norm got putrid drunk in a short period of time, and in an angry outburst, he picked up the lit BBQ and threw it across the lawn. Liz was so ashamed in front of all the guests. Fortunately no one was hurt, but Derrick was livid. In all the years that Liz had known him she'd never seen him so angry. He had helped get Norm the job at Superior Propane, and now, Norm had made a fool of himself in front of his workmates. Derrick never invited Norm and Liz to his house again after that incident.

So as Norm and Liz's drinking escalated they spent less and less time with Liz's friends. Her friends didn't drink like they did so Liz avoided them. Buried alive in a life of drunken escapades and unhappiness, Liz plodded along like a robot displaying very little emotion. She had given up. She hated where she was and didn't know a way out. Her nights were spent drinking while her days were spent tending to her children. Even sick and hung over, she tried to make sure they were well taken care of.

That was how it went until one evening the lost couple found themselves at the Village Inn in Bradford. Fifteen years had gone by since Liz was part of the gang hanging out at Jack's with Carol, Darlene, Edmund, Sheryl Morris and all her brothers. She had lost track of Sheryl and her husband Brad. They had moved to Peterboro, but here at the Village Inn that night were Sheryl's brothers Willy, Darcy and Dan with their wives. Liz smiled as she gazed at Willy. He still sported the Durante nose and he hadn't grown any taller. As for the twins they were pretty much the same as they had been fifteen years ago.

"Liz, how are you?" Willy said as he pumped her arm in greeting. "It's so good to see you. Come and sit at our table."

Norm and Liz joined them and the evening sped by as they laughed and joked about the old days, Clancy's Elvis impersonation, Edmund's horse, the hide and seek games in the wheat field, Clayton's old car, and on and on. Liz started to come alive again. The boys were like family to Liz and when the bar closed Norm invited her friends to follow them home for a few more drinks.

Then after an hour or so of entertaining Liz's old friends at home, Norm became very moody and morose. Liz was accustomed to it and just ignored him most of the time. But this time he insulted her friends and ordered them out of the house. That was the proverbial last straw. Liz was furious. For months she had felt nothing. Meeting some of the old gang had brought her to life again and now they were leaving in a huff because of Norm.

"You son-of-a-bitch. How dare you order my friends out of my house?" Liz screamed as she tossed a full carton of cigarettes at Norm. He ducked and came after her. She ran and locked herself in the bathroom. He tried to break the door but he couldn't.

"Get away from here or I'll call the police. I've had enough of you Norm."

Finally, exasperated and afraid she might call the police on him, he slammed out the back door and headed for his mother's house.

Liz hadn't fought with Norm for some time. It hadn't been worth the effort. She had just died inside and let him do whatever he wanted. But running into her old friends stirred Edmund's memory inside her heart. The memory of her love for him, how wonderful it was, and as though a bright light was turned on, she realized what the carousel was all about. It only spun when she was in love. It wasn't just male attention. That's why it spun for Edmund and eventually for Brian and then for Michael. She had been in love with them. She hadn't been in love with Jamie and she wasn't in love with Norm. The carousel hadn't turned for Norm so she had tried to push it and it just didn't work.

She was elated! She had discovered the secret of the carousel. She had to be in love for it to spin. She felt so alive when she was in love.

She loved Lenny. She needed Lenny and he needed her. Most of all she needed the carousel to turn again.

Her life with Norm was absolutely no good to either one of them. It would never work. She had to get out before she died completely. In the morning she got the kids up, told them to gather up some clothes, and called a cab. The cab took them all the way to Angus where Dar was living with Arnie. The kids were relieved. Even though Norm was good to them they hated the hostility between him and their mother. Liz had tried to care for them the best she could, but the environment was certainly not good. There was no joy in their household, the kids were unhappy and that had to change.

She didn't know what the future would hold, but she knew one thing for sure, Norm could not be part of it and Lenny had to be, if she was to stay alive. She was finally free. But where was Lenny and would he still want her?

# Part V
# BLACK GLASS MARBLES

## Chapter 31
## Vagabond Lovers

Liz wiped her brow with a Kleenex. The day was sticky and humid. The temperature had hit an all time high of 104 degrees Fahrenheit, and there wasn't a stir in the air. But it was more than the heat that had Liz sweating.

"Just call him!" Dar chided.

"I can't. He probably hates me now."

"I doubt it. If he cared for you as much as you said, his feelings wouldn't change overnight. Anyway, you'll never know if you don't try."

"Okay, but let me have a drink first, I need some courage."

Dar poured Liz a shot of rye, and topped it off with ginger ale.

Liz had been at Dar's for a week. Arnie was away with a paving crew. He had been on the road for weeks and Dar was ecstatic to have Liz stay because she was terribly lonely living way out in Angus with Arnie away. The fact that Liz had four children with her was not a problem for Dar. The women had often stayed at each other's homes or at Carol's with all their kids. They were more like family than friends, and they all had the same attitude, the more the merrier.

Liz didn't have to worry about the kids being out of school because they were on summer vacation. And as for her job, she had called Bob as soon as she arrived at Dar's and explained her situation. He was sorry to see her quit. Not only was she an incredible worker, but he liked her so he wished her well and accepted her resignation graciously.

She did need to get back to Beeton and get established as soon as possible though because fall was just around the corner and Jimmy's hockey would be starting up. But for the time being he was happy to be hanging out with Devin. The boys spent the long hot summer days at the swimming hole.

Janie and Angie, both five, were thrilled to see each other again. As they were only a month apart in age, they were already like soulmates. And of course Stacy and Bonnie were kept busy meeting all Sherri's new friends.

When Liz had first arrived at Dar's she longed to locate Lenny. She desperately needed to see him again. She had missed his touch. But she was afraid Lenny wouldn't want her anymore so she had held off. Then longing turned into resolve so she contacted Peter to help track Lenny down. Peter gave Liz Lenny's number, but she was still afraid of being rejected. After all, he had been jilted pretty severely. How much would he take?

After she finished her first drink, she poured another to sip on while she called Lenny. She sat on the chrome chair with her knees up under her chin and one arm wrapped around her legs. She played her tongue back and forth along her inner cheek as the phone rang several times. She cupped her hand over the receiver, looked at Dar and mouthed the words, "I don't think he's home."

"Hang on a minute," Dar encouraged.

"Hel-lo!" Lenny gasped as though he had been running.

"Hi, Lenny," Liz said shyly.

"Liz? Is it really you? Oh, Princess it's so good to hear your voice. I was out. I heard the phone ringing from the sidewalk and I ran. I'm so glad I caught your call." He was ecstatic. But then as though he was slapped in the face with a wet mackerel, he changed his tone. "Where are you? Where's Norm?" he asked cooly.

"Lenny I'm so sorry. I called Norm to bring the maintenance money so I could get supper for the kids. He came right away with groceries and a bottle of whiskey and talked me into having a drink the next thing I knew it was morning and Norm was there and you weren't. I guess I was still partly lit from the night before. Anyway, the whiskey sure worked fast and knocked me out cold."

"You mean you didn't call him to move back in with you?"

"No, what gave you that idea?"

"Norm, he said you called him to move back in."

"That liar!" Liz hissed.

"I stood outside every day for a week waiting to see you."

"I know. I saw you. I felt just sick about it, but Norm threatened that he would have the kids taken away from me, if I saw you again and I was afraid he might just try it."

"That son-of-a-bitch. I should have thumped him before when I had the chance."

After he hung up the phone, Lenny dropped everything and in spite of the sweltering heat hitchhiked the sixty miles from Caledon East to Angus just to see Liz. Lenny filled the emptiness in Liz in a way that nobody had since she had loved Edmund. Obviously, she did the same for him. Neither could thrive without the other.

A couple of weeks after Liz moved to Dar's, she called Norm and they made arrangements to divide their assets. Norm didn't want to stay alone in their new house so he moved out and went to his parents. Liz moved back in, and Lenny moved in with her; she wasn't taking a chance on losing him this time. But eventually the house would have to be sold because Norm refused to make payments on it when he wasn't living there, and Liz couldn't make the payments because she had quit her job.

Norm wanted the car and the new colour TV in exchange for the new bedroom, dining room and living room suites, the kids beds and dressers, all the appliances, household utensils and a portable stereo. Liz would miss the car, no doubt, but it had been Norm's to start with so she accepted that without a problem and as for the TV she didn't care in the least. She'd rather listen to music than watch TV any day, so she was more than happy to trade off the TV for the little stereo. She could do without TV but she could never survive without music in her life so she figured she got the best of the deal all around. Not only that, she had Lenny to boot.

Life became a carousel of romantic adventure again. Liz was fully and truly in love. Finally, she got what she needed. Lenny filled all her senses. She felt on top of the world. The emptiness that she had felt since childhood, the emptiness that only Edmund had filled, was finally gone.

But Lenny and Liz couldn't live on love alone so Carol got them jobs at Homeware Industries in Tottenham where she worked. Their life became a whirlwind of work, fun, frolic and romance. Liz no longer needed the hotel job to build her esteem. Lenny did that for her. He constantly praised her telling her how beautiful she was and his intense need for her made her feel important and worthwhile. She found the key to happiness -- true love.

But it was too late. Alcoholism had wrapped itself around her like an eerie mist on a cold dreary morning. Not only that, it was working its way around Lenny as well.

Nevertheless, for the time being, the couple were basking in their newly established life of romance. Not only that, with peace in the house the kids were a lot happier. Jimmy was ten, Stacy nine, Bonnie eight and Janie five, and they had grown considerably. They were capable of looking after themselves to some degree by this time, but Liz had a sitter come in while she and Lenny worked because they were not quite old enough to be left alone. Even so, they helped out all they could. The girls tried to keep the house tidy, and Stacy made the lunches. Jimmy would start supper and Stacy even insisted on doing the family laundry to help out. She was determined, headstrong and smart.

But before long Lenny became fed up with the job at Homeware. It was a terrible place to work Liz had to admit. They spent their days inside a huge concrete building with giant presses and machinery banging and clanging all day long spitting out metal ironing boards, clothes dryers and hose reels. Liz didn't mind the job so much, but it was taking its toll on Lenny because he was more of an outdoors person.

Lenny complained to his cousin Peter about his plight. So eventually Peter got him a job at Toronto International Airport. Peter had given up the job as bartender at the Beetonia and joined the ground crew at the airport because it paid more money. Lenny was much happier working outside, and the higher wages put him more at ease. He had been a little nervous about making ends meet with a woman and four kids to support.

But nonetheless, he was deliriously happy and so was Liz.

They burned sandalwood incense, listened to soft jazz music and made love in the flickering glow of candle light night after wonderful night. Lenny took Liz to heights she had never been before, and she did the same for him. They lived on love for months and then came the news that the house was sold.

Ironically Norm's brother Donny, who was now married, bought the house and was moving in right away. Lenny figured Norm put him up to it, but Liz didn't agree. Donny wasn't like Norm. In any event, with nowhere to go and not much money to speak of, the vagabond lovers had to move and fast. Unable to find a house right away, arrangements were made for Lenny and Liz to temporarily move in with Lee, her foreman from Homeware Industries. There wasn't enough room for all of them at Lee's so they had to send the kids to Liz's family while they kept looking for another place. Half of Liz's furnishings were stored in Donny's garage, the other half at the home of a waiter she and Lenny had met at the Beetonia.

So Lenny and Liz ended up leaving the house on Queen Street with only a matching set of luggage, two green garbage bags, which contained all their worldly belongings. They didn't care. They walked down the street, the new house fading in the distance, holding hands and gazing starry-eyed at each other. The love nest with romance by candle light shifted from Queen Street, Beeton to Second Street in Tottenham.

Lee was alone in a large three bedroom apartment and had plenty of room. But when his wife had moved out she had taken most of their furnishings with her so Liz and Lenny slept on an old mattress in an empty bedroom. Liz didn't mind as long as Lenny was there. Being loved was more important to her than material things and she was definitely loved.

The next two weeks went by in a blur. Lenny and Liz were both working during the day, drinking fine wines at the Tottenham Inn in the evenings and enjoying sensational sessions of lovemaking well into the night.

At first it was a treat to be alone with Lenny. It was like a honeymoon. Then she started to miss the kids. She had never been away from them for so long. She missed Jimmy's little man attitude, Stacy's adventurous spirit, Bonnie's innocence and Janie's busy beaver ways. Being with Lenny was very gratifying, but she loved her kids dearly. She realized they were just as important to her as he was. Besides, school would be starting soon and so would Jimmy's hockey so Liz got in a bit of a panic.

"Lenny, we've just got to find a place so we can get the kids back."

"I know, don't worry, Princess we'll find one."

They searched high and low for a place to rent in Beeton but found nothing there. Liz was at her wits end.

Then Dar called to tell her she had moved to London, Ontario with her kids. She explained how things just hadn't been going too well between her and Arnie. After talking for awhile Liz learned that Arnie was living alone in a large three bedroom house in Cookstown. Dar suggested that Liz get in touch with him about sharing accommodations. Dar was sure that Arnie would help Liz out. After all Liz and Norm had taken Dar and Arnie in one time when they had given notice and hadn't been able to find another place. Dar and Arnie and all their kids had stayed with Norm and Liz for two months at the country house outside of Beeton.

After talking to Dar for awhile, Liz hung up and called Arnie. She didn't particularly like the idea of moving in with Arnie, but she was desperate to get her kids back. He didn't sound ecstatic about the idea, but he did agree to let them move in temporarily. She would have preferred to move back to Beeton but there just weren't any places to rent.

Reluctantly Liz and Lenny moved in with Arnie in Cookstown. Once established they picked up all the kids from Bradford where they were staying with Liz's nieces, Debra and Lois.

"Mom, Mom, I've got a job!" Stacy cried as she came flying through the back screen door.

"What do you mean? Where?" Liz questioned.

"Next door. Mr. Lemon hired me to help him in the bakery. I cut the cookies, sprinkle sugar on them, help clean up, and lots of other things. Look he gave me a box of cookies for helping him."

"Wow, can we have some?" Jimmy asked.

"Sure." Stacy said as she passed the box around. She always liked to be the centre of attention. She grinned like a Cheshire cat and puffed her chest out like a big shot as all the kids gathered around her.

She had Liz's adventurous spirit. Sometimes it scared Liz because she knew first hand how much trouble an adventurous spirit could get a person into. Stacy had probably gone right over to the bakery and asked for the job. She was not afraid to talk to strangers. Unlike Bonnie and Jimmy who were shy and cautious, she was very outgoing and too trusting.

"Hey, you guys, you want to see something funny?" Stacy asked.

"What?"

"C'mere, look at Lemon's clothes line."

All the kids roared with laughter and Liz came to the back door to see what the commotion was all about. There, on the line, was Mrs. Lemon's bloomers. They were white cotton and they took up half the clothesline and hung almost to the ground.

"Hey, you guys, you shouldn't make fun of people." Liz said as she turned away trying to stifle her own laughter. Stacy was right they did look hilarious. They were huge. Liz and the kids had a common sense of humour. Their sense of humour bonded them together like thick glue.

Liz was glad to have the kids back but living at Arnie's presented its own problems. Arnie was drinking heavily since Dar had left him, and in order to tolerate it, Lenny and Liz just joined him. It wasn't difficult as they were already more than halfway down the slippery slope to alcoholism. An effervescent party atmosphere prevailed until the drinking took its toll and the bubbles went flat.

"Mommy, mommy, please wake up!" Janie's five-year-old voice barely penetrated Liz's wooly brain. Her voice sounded a long way off as if it was being funnelled down a long tunnel.

Groggily, Liz struggled to consciousness. "A-a-a-h my head. Would somebody p-l-e-a-s-e stop the rubber mallet that's pounding inside it," she said more to herself than anybody else. Her throat was so dry that she couldn't swallow. She placed her hands on either side of her head in an effort to hold its disintegrating segments together as each pound of the mallet cleaved it apart. When she closed her eyes she could see the veins in her eyelids. They looked like hairline cracks. With great effort she heaved herself up on one elbow and squeaked out to Janie who was standing by her bed, "Get Stacy!"

"Stacy, Stacy, mommy wants you," Janie screamed into Liz's ear, rattling her whole nervous system.

Stacy came in dragging her feet. She had torn herself away from the TV and didn't really want to come.

"What Mom?" Stacy groaned anxious to get back to the TV.

"Please get me a drink of cold water," Liz managed to whisper. Her tongue was thick and stuck to the sides of her mouth. She was sprawled across the bed on her stomach, not having the strength to move. She felt as if she had been poisoned and was about to die.

"Here Mom," Stacy said, as she held out a dripping glass.

Liz drank and felt the cold liquid making its slow descent down her throat. It hit her stomach with a splash. She retched, then swallowed hard trying to hold the water down.

"Oh, I'm so sick," Liz muttered. "Stacy, could you please get Janie ready for school for me?"

Lenny and Liz had enrolled the kids in school in September, shortly after they had moved to Arnie's. It looked as though they would be there for awhile.

"Aw, Mom, do I have to?" Stacy whined. Her face was all screwed up in a frown. The novelty of helping out had long since worn off.

"Yes!" Liz said emphatically, feeling a flush of guilt. She knew it was wrong to shirk her responsibility, but her body was too racked with pain to move.

Stacy stomped off with Janie in tow as Liz held her arm tight around her head to try to stave off the pounding for just a moment's relief. She dozed intermittently aware of pounding, nausea and kid sounds.

"Mom, wake up!" Stacy demanded. "I can't find anything good for Janie to wear."

"Well, if you can't find anything, give her breakfast, leave the TV on for her and just leave her home. It won't matter if she misses a half a day of kindergarten."

Stacy left and Liz drifted into a deep unconscious state, holding onto her head lest it should explode from the pressure building inside.

Sometime later, she awoke in a cold sweat, feeling nauseated and paranoid. The house was quiet. Obviously, Lenny and Arnie had gone to work. Liz wondered how they could manage to drink like that and still get up.

As she became more aware, she thought, *It's too quiet.* "Janie, Janie!" she called shrilly, beginning to panic. *Where is she?* Holding her stomach with one hand and her head with the other, Liz ran through the big house looking for Janie. There was no TV on. The breakfast table was littered with bowls, spoons, messy knives, toast crusts, and juice glasses, all of which indicated that life had gone on in her absence. Waves of guilt washed over her. No Janie in sight. Liz gasped as she looked at the clock. It was ll:15.

"They must have got her ready and taken her anyway," she muttered to herself.

Janie got out of school at eleven thirty and it was a five minute walk down the very busy Highway 27 that ran through the middle of Cookstown. Then she would come to the lights and have to cross the highway. Liz had to get there before Janie. She had twenty minutes to get ready and be at the crosswalk. Could she make it? Seized with panic, she raced around and got dressed with adrenaline pumping through her veins and nausea pitching in her stomach.

Liz's mind flashed back to the summer when they had first arrived at Arnie's. She remembered the accident at that very crossing and renewed panic set in as she relived the scene.

*She was cooking a big pot of stew for the working men and the kids. Stacy was at the Lemons' Bakery next door. Jimmy was away playing so Liz called Bonnie in. "Go to the store for me and get some carrots please. Here's the money. There'll be some change, you can have it."*

*"Okay, I'll bring Joey with me."*

*"Who's Joey?" Liz asked.*

*"He lives down around the corner. I've been playing with him."*

*Liz watched as they walked down the street to the highway hand in hand. The little boy with Bonnie wore a little yellow bathing suit.*

*He had a tuft of very blond hair on the top of his head. He was quite a bit younger than Bonnie and Liz wondered why he was allowed to be so far from home. Janie stayed home not wanting to make the trek to the store.*

*A few moments after they left, Bonnie was back screaming at the front door.*

*"What's the matter? Calm down Bonnie, I can't understand you,"* Liz rattled out as Bonnie screamed and sobbed.*

*"J-Joey's been hit by a car!" she cried between sobs. "It's all my fault. He pulled away from my hand and ran after his ball. It's all my fault. I shouldn't have let him go," she sobbed on and on.*

*Liz cuddled her close as she reassured her, "No way is it your fault. Come on show me where." Bonnie was a very responsible child even at eight years old. Liz's heart went out to her as she tried to comfort her.*

*Liz called Janie and they all raced hand in hand to the busy highway where a crowd had gathered around. There on the road Liz spotted a little twisted body, hair red with blood. Only the little yellow bathing suit identified him as Joey.*

The picture of Joey lying in the road covered in blood was vivid in Liz's mind as she rushed around, frightened half to death, thinking of what could happen to Janie. Joey had lived but suffered severe injuries that kept him hospitalized for months. Now Liz's little Janie was coming up to that very same crossing on that very same busy highway. Liz met her there every day. The guilt for sleeping in and being late plagued her and left her feeling weak.

She raced down the street and crossed the highway. A great wave of relief washed over her as she saw Janie coming. But it was immediately followed by another wave. A wave of shame. Janie was wearing nothing but a smile and a lime-green bathing suit -- no shoes, no coat. She was skipping down the street hand in hand with a cute little black boy dressed in jeans and a suede jacket with tassels on the sleeves.

*How could the kids have let her go like that? Why didn't the teacher send her home? Why didn't anyone phone me? Why didn't I get up? Why did I drink like that? What's happening to my life.* The thoughts whirred around in Liz's tortured mind. It was a perfect opportunity to pay attention to the danger signs of alcoholism. But instead of thinking about the alcohol being a problem, she dwelt on the humiliation. She quickly whisked Janie home out of sight of the neighbours.

Liz found out later that Janie had got herself ready. She had Stacy's determination and true to her trucker personality she was going to school come hell or highwater. She didn't care. It didn't bother her to be in class dressed that way. She was as happy as a clam.

Liz phoned Carol, sobbing as she told her the tale. Carol reassured her that she was not the worst person in the world and suggested that she and Lenny try to find a place as soon as possible to get away from Arnie and the drinking.

Liz felt ashamed to show her face outside the door. She wondered what the townspeople were saying. That night she begged Lenny to find them a house so they could move away.

"Tell you what, I'll get my friend Kurt to drive me around tomorrow and look for vacant houses. There's nothing in the paper and I don't know what else to do," Lenny said as he cuddled her close and nibbled on her ear.

Liz was taken in with him. She couldn't live without him. Lenny had control of her heart, mind, and soul. She idolized him. He became her carousel of delight and her turtle shell of protection. He was her prince. He would take care of everything properly, wouldn't he?

# Chapter 32
# "Wuthering Heights"

Liz got up from the table and shut the back door. The kids had left it open when they rushed out to go to school. A cool, fall breeze chilled her to the bone as she stared out at the miles of barren farmland surrounding Cookstown. *I've just got to get away from this place. The neighbours must think I'm the worst mother in the world. Even the land looks cold and uncaring.* She shivered and quickly shut the door.

A week had passed since Janie's bathing suit escapade and Liz was getting desperate. She and Lenny had checked all the papers and all the surrounding area for a place and found nothing. At daybreak Lenny had gone with his friend, Kurt, to look one more time. She sat reflecting on the whole mess while she sipped her tea. Then the back door flew open again.

"I found the perfect house," Lenny cried as he came through the door. He hugged Liz and twirled her around. "You've just got to come and see it. It's way out in the country, and it's huge. It's out in the middle of a large acreage surrounded by a cow pasture with rolling hills of green grass. Not far behind the house there's a large ravine with a wood lot for hunting and a river for fishing. Liz it's perfect. It's empty and available right now."

"It sounds, uh, interesting," she said feeling reluctant. She had always been a town girl and her one experience of living in the country with Norm had been a disaster. She really wanted to get back to Beeton so Jimmy could play hockey, but she was sensitive to how excited Lenny was so she kept quiet. She didn't want to burst his bubble. Lenny's dream had always been to get back to "mother earth". He just wanted to make love, live off nature, and enjoy a gentle existence. Liz liked the love part but wasn't so sure she could live off nature.

Her parents were middle-class, and she had been raised with the security of a steady income. They always knew where the next meal was coming from. Even though she was a romantic dreamer, she was torn between the practical stability of her parents' life-style and the love of her life, dirt poor, but romantic Lenny. But having failed miserably in the stable environment with Norm and being so attached to Lenny, she became willing to give his life-style a try.

"But how will we get to town and get groceries and stuff?" she asked. "I've got good news about that too. Kurt is buying a new car, and he's giving us the old Volkswagen. I have it here right now. We just have to transfer it over into our names."

"Great", she said with her tongue in her cheek. I couldn't stand to be stuck way out in the country with no way to get around."

"Tomorrow we'll go and see the house together." Lenny chimed.

Next day while the kids were in school, Lenny and Liz drove out to view the house. They met the landlord in the little town of Everett which consisted of a few homes, a general store and one gas station. They drove about a mile and a half east of Everett and there it was, their new home. Liz's first thought on seeing the place was "Wuthering Heights".

Located at the end of a very long lane was a three-story dwelling set in the middle of nowhere. It sat on a flat plateau, with the land dropping off at the back of the house.

The blustery wind whistled all around the old farm house as the landlord proudly showed Liz and Lenny through, room by room, exclaiming all the while, "They sure don't make 'em like this anymore."

Liz thought to herself, "They sure don't, thank goodness."

The house was a huge empty shell. The ground floor consisted of two large bedrooms, a large living room and a tiny kitchen. Off the kitchen there was a pantry with an old enamel sink which had one cold water tap. Built on as an addition was a huge summer kitchen with doors and windows on either side to let the breezes blow through which made cooking on a wood stove more bearable in the summer months.

All the rooms were wallpapered in big, old fashioned flower or fern patterns. The condition of the wallpaper wasn't too bad, but the pattern on the linoleum floors had long since worn off on all the heavy traffic spots and the black backing showed through.

The upstairs was divided into four very large bedrooms with a stairway leading to a very dusty attic full of spider webs. The upstairs rooms were floored with tongue and groove painted gray.

"Where's the furnace and the bathroom?" Liz asked naively.

The landlord smiled. Obviously, he was thinking of an earlier age. "Oh, there's no furnace. We heated with wood and coal in the wood stove. You'll have to get yourselves a wood stove." With a knowing wink and a nod towards the back door, he chuckled. "There's a little old shanty out back, but the hole's getting pretty full. You'll have to dig a new one." He shrugged.

Liz grabbed Lenny's arm and held him back as the landlord rambled on, hurrying to the next room. "This has got to be a joke," Liz whispered to Lenny when they were out of earshot. "We can't possibly live here. There's no hot water, no furnace, no toilet. Surely you can't seriously think of moving here." Ten years earlier Brian had asked her to move into a place with no indoor bathroom to save money, and Liz had flatly refused. She couldn't imagine living without a bathroom.

"You don't like it?" Lenny asked, disappointed. He made pretty good money at the airport, but Liz wasn't working any more and with four kids to support, the money was tight. They couldn't afford much better, and he hoped Liz would ease his burden a bit by moving there. Besides, he loved the idea of a back to the basics life-style. But Liz was not happy about the idea of moving into a house with no amenities so she refused to do so.

Meanwhile Liz and Lenny's drinking continued to get worse with Arnie buying all the booze and wanting them to join him. It was easier to join him than fight about it. Besides they felt it eased the tension of them all living in the same house. But actually the opposite was true, the drinking made it worse. Lenny and Liz didn't realize how much the demon alcohol had its hooks into them.

Lenny was getting really frustrated. He and Arnie just didn't get along. Lenny was drinking too much, too often and hating Arnie more every minute. Being a hippie, Lenny felt out of place with Arnie's red-neck friends who constantly teased him about his long hair. But it was Arnie's house so Lenny had no choice but to put up with whatever happened there. And he did, until he just couldn't take any more and a fight broke out between Arnie and his friends and Lenny and his friends. It didn't last long and no one was hurt, but it scared Liz. So against her better judgment she finally gave in and agreed to move into the house in the country. It was the lesser of two evils and would be safer for the kids. The house had no amenities but it would be peaceful compared to living at Arnie's

So the next Saturday they borrowed a truck and picked up some of Liz's furniture from Donny's, then they went to Wayne's to get the rest. Apologizing profusely, Wayne explained to them that someone had broken into his house while he was at work and stolen some of Liz's stuff. Her new electric stove with the window in the oven was missing as was the home-made bar that Norm had built. She needed the stove to cook on. She had never cooked on a wood stove before and the thought of it scared her. That was bad enough, but the worst was her portable stereo was gone too. No music! Liz had always loved music. Her life wouldn't be the same without Simon & Garfunkel and John Denver.

Liz didn't believe Wayne and neither did Lenny. There was something in the tone of his voice that didn't ring true. They went immediately to report it to the police.

"Sorry, we can't do anything about it. It's a civil matter," the officer stated flatly.

"Civil my foot!" said Lenny as they left the station. "I don't believe Wayne. I think he sold the stuff to get money for booze. But I've got a plan. Just wait until one night while Wayne's at work, we're going to check out his house. And if there's any of your stuff still there, I'll get it back for you, don't you worry, princess."

After they got the furniture moved in Lenny and his friend, Kurt, had to dig a new hole for the outhouse. They started right in. The two men took turns digging and taking a break. It wasn't difficult for them because Lenny was very big and strong. Kurt wasn't as tall as Lenny but he was muscular and solid. He eagerly jumped in the hole when Lenny climbed out to take a break. Lenny hollered over his shoulder as he headed to the house, "We gotta dig it deep, Kurt. Make sure you dig it deep."

As Liz and Lenny sat drinking coffee they heard a loud splat.

"What the heck was that? It scared the heck out of me." Liz cried.

"I don't know. But there it is again" Lenny said as a louder splat filled their ears. Baffling them, the splatting kept up at regular intervals.

Then Jimmy pulled back the kitchen curtain and said, "Look, here it is!" Huge clods of mud were stuck all over the outside of the kitchen window.

"What the hell's he doing?" Lenny yelled. "He's gonna break a window.

Lenny and Liz raced outside. Kurt was nowhere to be seen. They went over to the rim of the hole. They looked at each other and grinned. Then they started to chuckle and finally, burst into uproarious laughter. Kurt looked up at them with a silly grin on his face. The top of his golden head was three feet below the surface of the ground and he couldn't climb out.

Between fits of laughter Lenny croaked, "I said deep Kurt, not to China."

Lenny lowered a rope and once on the surface, Kurt grabbed Liz around the waist and swung her around playfully as he joined them in their mirth.

After they got a grip on themselves Lenny and Kurt moved the shanty by tying a rope to it and to the Volkswagen. They slowly pulled it into position, then filled the old hole with the dirt from the new one. Their country adventure had begun.

Liz's brother Jack had provided them with an old wood stove, but it had a hole in the front of it, so Lenny patched it that night with a suggestion from his Mother Earth book. He used salt, ashes from the fire, and water to make a thick paste. Once the paste was applied to the front of the stove the heat from the fire baked it on, sealing the hole. Lenny was very proud of himself and his first project from his new Mother Earth almanac. On Monday they ordered a truckload of slab wood from the mill in town which nicely filled up the wood shed. It cost them $50.00.

They decided when it got colder they would close off all the rooms in the big house except for the small kitchen, the pantry, the living room where they had set up the wood stove and the one bedroom upstairs where the kids all slept. The stove pipes ran from the living room up through the kid's bedroom to the chimney. The rising heat in the pipes would keep the kids toasty warm and Lenny and Liz would be just as cozy sleeping on a hide-a-bed in the living room.

They bought a square galvanized tub for bathing in and a chemical toilet so the kids wouldn't have to run outside in the winter. Liz and Lenny kept it in one of the closed bedrooms downstairs. It would be chilly in there but not as cold as outside.

The last thing on the agenda, and probably the most difficult for Liz, was getting the kids enrolled in a new school. They had started their school years in Beeton and had always attended there until they moved to Cookstown. They had good friends in Beeton. At the Tossorontio school, they wouldn't know a soul, and they'd have to ride a school bus which they weren't used to. Liz was worried about them adjusting.

The only other thing left to do was to get Jimmy back into hockey. Liz planned to get him on the team in Alliston, just ten miles away, as soon as possible. Other than that, they were all settled in nicely.

The next weekend Lenny and Liz returned to Wayne's farm house on Highway 27.

"Lenny I'm really nervous. This just doesn't feel right. Are you sure that Wayne is working?" Liz asked as they parked the Volkswagen in the long lane and headed to Wayne's front door.

"Yeah, I'm sure, I saw him serving beer in the ladies room. He'll be there until at least 3:00 am. It's safe."

"Well, maybe so, but it just doesn't seem right," she said as they crept through the front door of the big, dark, deserted old farm house.

"I can't see anything. Don't go too far ahead," she said as she reached out to hold onto his denim shirt. The darkness inside the house enveloped them like a bad dream.

S-c-r-a-t-c-h. Liz heard the sound as soft golden light from the match Lenny lit dimly illuminated their way.

"Ouch!" Lenny cried as the match burned his finger tips. He shook it fiercely. Then the darkness swallowed them again.

"Darn. I can't see a thing," Lenny said as he struck another match. The two of them crept along together from room to room and up an old wooden stair case.

As they entered Wayne's bedroom, Liz surveyed the room in the dim light of a match. There was a big double bed with a mass of dirty, tangled bedding in the middle of it, and the pervasive smell of unwashed male filled the air. Then what Liz spotted next to the bed made her blood boil. Just before the match burned out, she spied the proof of Wayne's deception. On the night stand beside the bed was her portable stereo.

"Lenny, hit the light switch!"

He pivoted and groped for the switch, then quickly caught himself.

"No the neighbours might see the light and wonder what's going on."

"Light another match then."

With the light of a new match Lenny saw the stereo too. "I told you!" he said triumphantly. "I knew Wayne was lying. We'll probably never see the other things again, but at least you have your music back."

Liz smiled and hugged him around the waist and said, "Thank you, thank you, thank you, I'd be lost without my music.

Lenny felt pleased with himself that he had made her a little bit happier. He unplugged the stereo from the socket and reached to pick it up.

"Come on, Liz, let's get out of here."

Then suddenly, Liz's mood changed to fear as she thought of the possibility of getting caught.

"Lenny, Wayne will know we've been here if we take it. He'll see all the matches burnt and the stereo gone."

"That's right!" Lenny said with just a hint of humour in his voice. "What's he gonna do, go to the police and tell them that he stole it, and we stole it back?"

"Well, maybe he could report us for breaking and entering."

"Let him go ahead and try to prove it. What did we do except take our own stereo back? He doesn't have a leg to stand on and as soon as he figures it all out, he'll know it."

It still didn't seem right, but Lenny did make sense. With Liz's stereo tucked safely underneath his arm, they stealthily retraced their route. Liz had to admit that she was happy to have her stereo back even though she felt guilty for sneaking around in someone else's house. Justice was done and Lenny was her hero.

Then just two weeks later the cold north wind howled like an express train through the upstairs rooms as Liz climbed the stairs to put the kids to bed. White clouds of breath puffed around them. "Quick get into your room where its warm," Liz cried, laughing and hugging Janie to her as they ran down the hallway together. She tugged the big quilts up over each child and kissed them all goodnight. Then after getting the kids all snugly tucked in for the night, she raced back down the hallway and the stairs, opened the living room door, rushed through it, and shut it quickly to keep the cold out. "Burrr!" she said to Lenny and his friends, Kurt and Dillon, who were relaxing around the wood stove. Then she settled in beside Lenny on the couch where it was cozy and warm.

"This is wonderful," she said as she smoothed out the skirt of her full-length, floral-print dress. She felt like a princess. She was a princess, Lenny's princess. Lenny poured her a drink of the Blue Nun wine that Kurt had brought to celebrate their move.

"I just love the sound of the fire crackling in the wood stove. It's so cozy warm and smells so good. It's the first time I've ever lived with wood heat and I think I could get very used to it," she said and took a sip of the sharp-tasting wine.

"Yeah, it's great," Kurt agreed, his voice coming from the depths of the big old easy chair. He looked thoroughly content slumped there enjoying the warmth.

"Hey, Lenny, there's a play on CKEY tonight at 10 o'clock. Want to listen to it?" Dillon asked.

"Sure," Lenny said, grinning and winking at Liz as he reached over, turned on her stereo and dialled in CKEY.

Kurt, Dillon, Lenny and Liz nestled in to listen to the play. All the kids were cozy and warm in their beds upstairs. Liz snuggled in under Lenny's arm and let out a deep sigh of contentment, convinced that they had made the right decision to move there. They were all set for their first winter at their "Wuthering Heights".

It came with a blast! Winter proved to be a lot harder than they had anticipated. By the time January rolled around, all the slab wood that they had so carefully piled in the wood shed was almost gone. Never having heated with wood before, they had no idea how much they would need. It had seemed to be so much when they had piled it. They never considered that it wouldn't be enough.

"Lenny, what are we going to do? The wood is down to the last row. It's not going to last the winter," Liz said as she looked out the small opening in the frost-covered window. She could see the snow whipping in mini-twisters -- snow devils they called them. They were twisting all around the front yard. Liz shuddered as she thought of how cold it was and what it would be like without the fire burning to keep them warm.

"We'll just have to haul wood from the ravine. We can't afford to buy another load."

During the winter, Lenny was laid off at the airport. Now unemployed, he worked on the landlord's farm shovelling out the cattle stalls in exchange for the rent. His small bi-weekly unemployment cheque of $66.00 could not cover a load of wood as well as their living expenses.

"How can we get wood in the ravine?" Liz questioned. "We don't have a truck or a chain saw."

"We'll just have to be like the pioneers," he said with a teasing smile. "There's a swede saw in the wood shed. I'll cut down the trees. There's a lot of dead elm trees with the bark all stripped off. They're good and dry. And there's some birch and some dead cherry and apple trees. I can carry long limbs if I balance them properly on my shoulders. Then we can block and split them out behind the wood shed."

So began the daily routine of bringing in the wood. Lenny would cut down a tree, then he and Liz would make the long trek from the ravine to the wood shed with the limbs of the tree balanced on their shoulders. Lenny, Liz and Jimmy took turns sawing the limbs,

Lenny split the blocks and the girls piled the wood. They all worked together as a family. It became a daily chore as they could only bring in enough in one run to last a day. It was a lot of hard work, but they had a pioneer spirit that helped them to get it done. Afterward they would throw snowballs at each other and the kids would make snow angels. Then Liz would make hot chocolate for everyone from the big kettle that sat at the back of the stove, always full of hot water. Not only was the kettle always on, Liz always had a pot of homemade soup simmering on the stove as well.

"That soup sure smells good," Lenny said as he came through the back door brushing the snow off his mackinaw jacket. He smiled down at Liz contented with his new mother-earth life, and his mother-earth wife.

The wood stove was her only means of cooking since her new electric stove disappeared from Wayne's, but she had mastered it and overcome her fear. She had learned to make something out of nothing with the aid of the Kate Aitken's cook book that Lenny's mother had given her.

"It *all* smells so good," Liz said back to him as she breathed in deeply. There was a potpourri of wonderful aromas: chicken vegetable soup simmering, bread baking, cherry wood burning and the fresh smell of bleached clothes, drying on the line that Liz had strung near the wood stove.

Her senses were alive with the smells, the sounds and the sights. The wood was crackling, and the girls were giggling and playing ring around the rosy while Lenny settled in for a long game of chess with Jimmy. The steam was rising from the laundry making eloquent carvings of crystal leafy designs forming glittering gardens on the windows.

"I never knew that burning different woods produced different smells," Liz said to Lenny.

"Oh, yeah," he said. "Every wood smells different."

"I know, apple is neat, so are birch and cedar but my favourite is cherry. It smells so sweet. She went and stood behind him and curled her arms around his neck. He lifted one muscular arm, placed his hand on the back of her head and gently pulled her to him, then he turned towards her, and they kissed, completely content.

The frigid winter lost the battle against the returning sun and sadly retreated to an early spring. Lenny, Liz and the kids had survived their first mother-earth winter and were proud of themselves. They had survived, but Liz was so relieved that it was spring. She was also very happy that she had been able to get Jimmy on the team in Alliston. He was becoming quite a good little hockey player.

With the warmer weather, they were able to open up the whole house and stretch themselves out. Each child had one large bedroom, and so did Lenny and Liz. Opening the house up let the warm sunshine in. Liz's mood became lively and excited. Lenny and Kurt moved the wood stove to the big summer kitchen and opened the doors and windows on either side to let the spring breezes blow through while Liz worked away at the mountain of laundry.

As she hung the washing outside on the clothes line for the first time after the long harsh winter, she daydreamed about crawling into bed with sheets dried in the bright sunlight, smelling of fresh air. It was one of life's simple pleasures that she thoroughly enjoyed. She watched for a moment as the warm wind whipped the blue-white sheets into the air.

Then she turned to look all around her. Standing on the stoop, she could see for miles. Trees were blossoming with new buds of yellow green. Shoots of brilliant emerald green that come only with new spring grass, blanketed the countryside. Lilacs were blooming everywhere. Flocks of metallic green barn swallows were swooping and soaring all around her, singing their merry song. She sucked in a long deep breath, gathered all the fresh country smells of spring into her nostrils, and breathed out satisfaction. Then her dreamy mood was abruptly interrupted by Lenny's shouting.

"Liz, Liz, come and see the fish. They're huge. I've never seen such big rainbow trout," he hollered, excitement gushing out of his pores as he ran up the hill towards her.

Caught up in his enthusiasm, Liz dropped the blue denim shirt she was about to hang and ran towards him. They ran together to the river.

"There, lie on the log jam and look down between the logs."

Liz crept out onto the log jam on her hands and knees then laid face down.

Her face glowed as she looked up and mouthed the words, "I see them! I see them!"

The fish were spawning, and the river was full of them.

There were hundreds of them and they were huge, some three feet long. The sun beat down on her back warming her whole being as she gazed into the pool formed by the natural dam. Sunbeams streamed through the murky water. The huge rainbow beauties twisted and turned lazily stirring up the mud on the bottom of the river. Then with sudden speed, they darted in and out around each other in their spawning dance. Flashes of silver reflected through the water as they swam. Liz looked at the fish, then at Lenny. He beamed with satisfaction at the child-like pleasure that he saw reflected on her face. Love for her pulsed through his whole being.

Lenny and Liz spent the spring basking in the pleasures of their new country home. Then with summer came the heat. That's when the river proved to be a real blessing.

The sweltering hot sun beat down on Liz as she watched the kids playing in the cool water with the raft Lenny had built for them. *Okay for them, but I'm not going into a river that might have crawfish in it and get my toes pinched,* she thought as she took a drink of her ice-cold Coke.

She watched them for an hour. She was afraid to leave them alone, but the hot sun was taking its toll on her. Beads of perspiration formed on her upper lip. Then all of a sudden, she jumped up and ran headlong into the river with her canvas running shoes, shorts and peasant blouse on. Lenny was just coming down the hill and spotted her daring feat. He laughed as he watched the cool water spray up in crystal beads all around her. Then he thought, *looks good to me,* and ran in with his moccasins and jeans on. He dove under the water and surged up right in front of her. She splashed water in his face, then she swam for the shore. He swam after her and when she stood up, he grabbed her around the waist and they fell into the water together laughing.

All fun aside though it was a harder, simpler life than Liz was used to. But in spite of their hardships, she had never been happier. Their life together was good. She had Lenny's love, which was all she ever really wanted. Finally, the love of a male to fill the emptiness. Not only that, they had even cut down on their drinking considerably.

Lenny had mother-earth, and she had Lenny and the carousel. They were very much in love. So much in love that Liz failed to notice just how much she was changing. She never saw her old friends anymore. She had begun to dress like a hippie. She wore long skirts, laced up sandals, halter tops, lots of beads, a band around her forehead and sometimes when the kids were at school, she even wandered around outside in the vegetable garden topless. The changes were slow and subtle. She was so happy with Lenny, she hardly noticed her change to the hippie life-style and with that change came some serious problems for Liz.

# Chapter 33
# Lizzie in the Sky
# With Diamonds

Liz didn't want to smoke marijuana, but it was all around her. Until living with Lenny, she hadn't realized how much a part of his life it was. Finally, to please him, she joined him and his friends. When she started smoking it, she found she enjoyed it. Under its influence everything became more alive, more colourful, more vivid and more beautiful. Not only that, *everything* seemed funny. Lenny, his friends and Liz would giggle contagiously at the silliest things. Of course, they didn't smoke it when the kids were around which made Liz a little more at ease. And the horror stories she had heard about it didn't seem to be true. At first, she saw nothing wrong with it. The marijuana was very relaxing and made her feel on top of the world.

Lenny and Liz had thoroughly enjoyed the isolation at "Wuthering Heights" for the first year. It was like a honeymoon, but after a while the novelty wore off so they hired a sitter and went to town with Kurt and Dillon where they met up with more of Lenny's friends. On the way home from their night on the town, Liz discovered the danger of toking marijuana. One thing leads to another.

"What's that they're passing around?" Liz asked Lenny from the back seat of Kurt's new Gremlin.

"It's called purple micro-dot. It's acid dropped on a blotter. One minute drop of that and life just soars," Lenny slurred. He was three sheets to the wind.

"Exactly what is it?" she asked.

"LSD," he answered.

"Oh, that stuff is dangerous," she said, remembering things she had heard and read about it.

"No, no, Liz, it's great stuff. You don't know what you're missing. Trust me! It's the best thing that can happen to you. It's the most fun you'll ever have."

"Alright, if you're sure it won't hurt me," she said, game for anything while she was drinking and under Lenny's influence.

"Aw, it won't hurt you. Besides I'll be with you the whole time. Would I let you do anything that would hurt you?" he coaxed. He loved Liz, and he wanted to take her to the same heights that he enjoyed with drugs. He never meant her any harm. After all, he enjoyed the drugs and thought she would too.

So trusting Lenny, She took a tiny piece of blotter and stuck it on her tongue. By the time they arrived at home, Liz was feeling the effects.

"Oh, man, will you look at those snowflakes falling!" she said as she tipped her head back. They were starting into their second winter at "Wuthering Heights". "They're huge and they're all different colours, oh, look at that one, it's blue, really blue, far out. Can you guys see them too?"

"Sure," Lenny said, pleased with himself. "I told you acid is a gas."

"Oh, wow, the place looks like a palace," she said as she pushed open the door to their big, rambling, antiquated farm house. "No wonder you guys do this stuff." Liz had never seen the pictures on the walls look the way they did. They were magnificent works of art. Everything was brighter, bigger, sharper.

But then she looked at one of Lenny's friends, and right before her eyes his face began to melt. His skin seemed to hang like drooping stretched pieces of taffy. She blinked hard, but his face stayed the same. In a horror filled voice, she cried, "Your face is melting!"

Lenny's friends all giggled. "Neat, eh? I told you it was great stuff," Lenny said as he took a big gulp out of the beer he had smuggled out of the bar under his baggy shirt.

Liz was beginning to wonder if it was all that great. She was unsure about this latest manifestation. People's faces melting seemed a little grotesque to her.

She left the room and went into the large empty bedroom with the chemical toilet. She shivered as she shut the door behind her. Her breath puffed out in little clouds all around her face. It was as though she had walked into a giant refrigerator.

She sat on the toilet and as she glanced across the empty room, the linoleum on the far side of the floor started to ripple. A wave travelled across the floor right under her and then back again. It was as though a giant had grabbed it by two corners and was shaking it like a blanket.

"Whoa," she said, "That was strange."

As the night passed and the hallucinations continued she became very weary. "Lenny, I need to sleep. Why can't I sleep?"

All Lenny's friends had left and she was lying on the couch trying to doze off.

He told her, "When you take acid, you can't sleep until it wears off."

"How long will that take?" she whined, feeling trapped and wishing she could pull the chemical right back out of her system.

"It varies, usually about fifteen hours. Just relax and go with it. You'll be alright. I'm right here if you need me, Princess."

She tried closing her eyes again.

"What the hell!" she cried as she blinked her eyes open.

"What?" Lenny asked.

"When I closed my eyes, a huge army of soldiers dressed in World War I uniforms seemed to be marching into my head through my eye sockets. It's gross. I can't stand this," she said as she started to cry, feeling frightened and frustrated.

Lenny patted her head gently and held her close. "It's just an hallucination. It's not real. Just relax. It'll pass."

"No, it's not going away!" she cried as her eyes closed briefly, then flashed open again. "It's so real! I see soldiers by the thousands." She cupped her hands over her ears as she was deafened by the marching of their boots.

She cried and cried, afraid to close her eyes, and Lenny rocked her back and forth for the rest of the night. Shortly after dawn she finally slipped into slumber. Her "good time" had turned into a "bad trip" and Liz never did LSD again.

Drugs started to become a big part of Lenny's life. He was hooked, but Liz knew she couldn't let them become a big part of hers. They frightened her. She had four children to think of and she needed to keep some balance. She already had enough trouble struggling to keep her drinking under control.

She loved Lenny, and she knew Lenny loved her but a wedge was coming between them because of their difference of opinion about drugs. So they started to drift apart.

There were other pressures too. With the onslaught of winter Lenny was laid off from the airport again and money was sparse. With a family of six to care for, he was really feeling stressed. He slowly started to change. He spent a lot more time away from home and was restless and cranky. It was as though he had the weight of the world on his shoulders. Liz was getting panicky. She was afraid of losing him. She started to wonder if he was having an affair.

Not only that, the winter of 1975 proved to be especially severe. The snow was over four feet deep. Huge icicles dangled from the eaves of the old farm house almost reaching the deep snow piled around it. Ferocious blizzards attacked the barren countryside, almost on a daily basis, giving very little reprieve. Gale force winds whipped the white powder in twisters. The family was encased within the walls of their giant cocoon. The cocoon was like an island in the midst of a frozen white sea. And to top it all off wood gathering was still a daily chore that couldn't be ignored. The original plan had been to fill the wood shed in the summer time. Lenny's friends had offered to come over with chain saws and a big trailer to haul the dry wood up from the ravine. With so many young men, it wouldn't have taken very long to fill the shed. They came with good intentions but didn't follow through because they always brought beer and marijuana. Once they got mellowed out they couldn't move so the wood-gathering capers were always left for the next time. The next time eventually became winter and then it was too late.

So when Liz saw Lenny putting on his Mackinaw jacket she moaned,"You're not going to town *again*, are you?"

"Yeah, I gotta meet with some guys at the Windsor House Hotel."

"What for? You know I hate being left way out here with no car and no phone."

"Never mind, what for." he snapped. Then his tone softened as he continued, "Besides, I gotta get us some groceries. We're just about out of everything. There's a break in the storms so I better go now. You'll be alright, Liz. Stop reading that Helter Skelter book. You're just scaring yourself to death. No one is going to bother you," he said as he gathered her into his arms.

"You go with him, Mom." Jimmy, now twelve, said, "We'll be alright by ourselves."

"No, you know I won't leave you in the winter with that wood stove. Lenny, please don't go again," she whined as she twisted out of his arms. The idea of his having an affair crept through her mind like poison so in a last ditch effort to keep him home, she cried, "We have no wood for tonight and tomorrow."

"Get off my back. I gotta do this," he grumbled as he went out the door. "I'll be back before tonight to get some wood in."

Liz was upset about Lenny hanging around the Windsor House Hotel so much. It wasn't just the fear of him having an affair. Sometimes, he would bring some of the guys from the bar home with him and Liz didn't care much for his new-found friends. They were nothing like Kurt, Dillon and Rob, his childhood friends. He seemed to have pulled away from them and replaced them with a new breed of biker-types, at least, by the way they dressed, they looked like bikers and they frightened her.

Shortly after Lenny left for town another fierce storm with gale force winds blew up out of nowhere and continued until late afternoon and Lenny, frantic about his family at home, was stuck in town. Liz was just as frantic.

"I don't know what we're going to do for tonight and tomorrow's wood. Lenny said he'd be back as soon as he could, but it's getting late and it doesn't look like he's going to make it before dark. We'll freeze if we don't get some wood in. But we need him to cut down the tree and carry the big pieces," Liz said despondently.

"Come on, Mom, we can do it. There's a lull in the storm. Let's go now before it's too late," Jimmy said trying to bolster her. He was very mature for his twelve years.

"I don't know how to cut down a tree," she said feeling broken and discouraged.

"I can," Jimmy said. "I've watched Lenny do it a hundred times. I'm sure I can do it."

"Yeah, Mom, c'mon, we can do it," Stacy encouraged. All the kids nodded enthusiastically. Liz's eyes watered as they all gathered around her jumping up and down with eagerness to help.

"Okay, but next time we go to town there are four kids who are going to get great big gooey hot fudge sundaes topped with whipped cream and maraschino cherries," Liz said as she quickly blinked her tears away before they could see them.

They all dressed warmly with scarves, mitts, boots and heavy coats and headed for the ravine.

C-r-a-c-k! The sound of the big tree splitting at the base where Jimmy had cut it with the swede saw, echoed through the ravine.

"You did it! You did it!" Liz cheered and clapped as the dead tree smashed to the ground splintering hundreds of twigs into thousands of pieces. Snow and dust blew up and filled the air as it landed. The girls grabbed Liz by the hand, pulling her along as they danced in a circle and cheered. Jimmy grinned, his chest puffed out, proud as a peacock.

Jimmy used the swede saw to cut the tree into lengths that Liz could carry. The girls carried the lighter branches for kindling. Six-year-old Janie smiled proudly as she carried her share. They all made their way back up the ravine to the house leaving a meandering trail in the deep snow behind them. They cut, split and piled the wood together and then they celebrated their success over steaming hot chocolate with marshmallows melting on top.

Liz stayed up late, trying to keep the house warm. She put the last log on the fire and hoped Lenny would be home before morning. The house was toasty warm when she went to bed, but by the middle of the night the fire went out.

"Mommy, Mommy, wake up," Janie cried as she shook Liz awake the next morning.

Liz's nose felt frozen as she turned under the heavy trucker's quilts. Her movements were restricted as she tried to turn over, and in a semi-conscious state, she realized that she was wearing a heavy wool coat and all her clothes. And she was *cold.*

She looked at Janie and the other kids dressed in their winter coats, mitts and scarves and saw clouds of white billowing from their mouths as they breathed.

Through half-closed eyes, Liz looked at the foot of the hide-a-bed and saw that a little snow drift had formed there from the spot in the door where the jamb was missing.

"Is Lenny home yet?" she questioned, shivering as she got out from under the quilts.

"No, the roads are still blocked," Jimmy said.

"Ewww, I've got to start a fire," Liz said as her arms encircled the girls. She hugged them all close and rubbed them briskly. She looked at the thermometer nailed to the wall. It read thirty degrees below zero, Fahrenheit. And that was inside the house.

"But, Mom, there's no wood," Jimmy said.

"Oh, damn that's right," she said as she rubbed the sleep from her eyes,"I used it all up last night." She stared desperately into the empty wood box then she glanced outside at the snow whipping around in the chilling wind.

Bonnie's voice pierced her fog as she shivered. "Mom, what are we going to do?"

"I don't know. But don't worry I'll take care of it. I've got to find something to burn right away. We can't go to the ravine today; it's too stormy."

Liz walked through the kitchen her breath puffing out into frigid clouds around her. On the table, left out from the night before, was a glass of water frozen solid. The tap in the pantry which they always left dripping to prevent the pipes from freezing, was trickling water down the icicle that had formed from its mouth to the drain in the sink.

She opened the door to the summer kitchen. The old dresser that her uncle had made in high school was made of wood! Without giving it a second thought, she grabbed the axe that was leaning against the wall and swung it down on the dresser. Wood splintered in every direction as she wacked away at the dresser her uncle had spent months carefully fashioning. In a short time, she had a little bundle of kindling and some larger pieces of firewood. She started a fire in the wood stove while the kids stood around the stove trying to get warm.

"This wood is really dry so it's going to burn fast. I've got to come up with something else we can use."

What about all those bags of clothes we were given?" Stacy asked.

"Yes, get them. Anything that will burn is good," Liz said remembering the several garbage bags full of clothes the neighbours had given them. She didn't know if it would work but they were desperate. "I'll run to the basement in the meantime and see if there's anything else down there that we can use."

"I'll come too," said Jimmy.

"Janie, you and Bonnie stay put on those chairs in front of the stove to keep warm," Liz ordered as she went down to the basement with Jimmy.

Between them Jimmy and Liz pulled down all the shelving from the stone walls in the basement. The wood was old and Liz assumed the shelves had held preserves in the past. Now they would serve a different purpose.

"I have another idea, Mom," Jimmy said. "We could take the top row of railings from that old cedar fence out beside the lane."

"Good idea," she said, not worrying about the fence. They needed to stay warm to stay alive.

Between the dresser, the clothes, and the fence railings, they were able to bring the inside temperature up enough to take their coats off.

An hour later the back door of their frozen white cocoon flew open and white powder swirled in, carried by the blustery cold wind. Lenny and another man rushed in, loaded down with groceries.

"Quick shut the door!" Lenny hollered over the howling wind as he brushed snow off the shoulders of his thick jacket.

Liz had never seen such a welcome face. When the storm died down Lenny and his friend went to the ravine with his friend's skidoo and brought in a large supply of wood.

Liz told Lenny about burning the clothes in the stove, he told her she shouldn't have done it.

A week later she found out why.

Kaboom!

"What the hell was that?" Lenny yelled from the depths of the easy chair where he sat reading The Lord of The Rings.

He jumped up, ran to the stove, lifted the lid and looked inside. "There's nothing in there but some glowing ashes. I better check upstairs."

Lenny flew up the stairs in the freezing cold, and ripped open the bedroom door. "Get up! Get up!" he yelled at the four sleeping kids. The pipes running across the room by the ceiling were cherry red. The ceiling was blistering and ready to burst into flames.

"Jimmy Get dressed warm and run to the neighbours and call the fire department! And Liz run downstairs and get water, lots of water, all you can carry! You girls help her!" Lenny ordered as he grabbed the red hot pipes and pulled them down.

Jimmy threw on boots, coat, hat, mitts and wrapped in a scarf as fast as he could and flew out the front door. Liz ran up the stairs with two buckets of water and the girls followed her with pots full. Lenny threw the water up as best he could to cool down the ceiling. He looked up the chimney hole and could see flames burning inside the chimney. He threw water up the opening of the chimney and it immediately sloshed back down carrying ashes and soot with it which landed all over him. He cursed. Then he ran with Liz to get more water to throw on the sloped ceiling in the attic where the chimney went up through the roof. Within a short but frightening period of time everything was under control. Then Liz went after Jimmy to bring him back before he disturbed the neighbours so late at night. She caught up with him at the end of the lane and they ran back to the house.

"Phew, that was a close call," Lenny said to Liz and Jimmy as they came through the door. He wiped the sweat from his forehead with a sooty hand.

"You got that right, Supershorts," Jimmy said as he looked at Lenny who was wearing nothing but white jockey shorts and lots of soot.

"Yeah, Liz said, grinning at Lenny. "How did it happen?"

"I told you, you shouldn't have burned those clothes in the stove. The artificial fibres left a residue on the inside of the pipes and started the fire. Anyway I'm glad it's over and there's not much damage."

"Me too." Liz sighed.

She fell exhausted into the big easy chair and recalled the fire she had survived when Brian and she were superintending the apartments. That one was scary, but this one was worse. Liz had been terrified that the house would burn down all around them. She was so grateful that Lenny had been at home when it happened. She hated to think of what would have happened if he hadn't been. Because he was away so much, lately, it was a distinct possibility. She hated that he was away so often and that he was so touchy most of the time.

In the weeks to follow she became even more sensitive about Lenny having an affair. She started looking for signs, lipstick on his collars, perfume on his clothes, strange phone numbers.

Liz was under a lot of pressure. She was worrying about getting wood in every day, Lenny possibly having an affair and their financial situation. Then to make matters worse, the Volkswagen broke down. They couldn't afford to get it fixed so she wasn't able to get Jimmy to his games and he had to quit hockey at least for that season. Not only that, but she hadn't contributed anything to her college fund in over a year. She never told Lenny about the account. The college fund was her dream and she wouldn't touch it or let anyone else, not even Lenny. Liz and Lenny's relationship was under a lot of strain, but she still loved him. The carousel still turned intermittently, but the horses' faces were sad. As Lenny and Liz drifted farther and farther apart Edmund's memory started coming into her mind. Even after all the years that had gone by she could still see his dark twinkling eyes and his half smile/half grin. The memory almost made her feel guilty, somehow, as though she had cheated on him with Lenny. And now, she wasn't even sure of Lenny anymore. Was he cheating on her?

Winter melted its way to spring -- a cold, rainy, bleak spring. Liz slept soundly unaware that Lenny had already left for town. A knock at the door roused her. Blurry-eyed, she staggered to the door.

"Is Lenny here?" a young blond-haired man questioned.

His companion looked anxiously past her peering into the room as though trying to see if he could see Lenny.

"No," she said. "He must have hitchhiked to town already this morning. He was gone before I got up."

"Oh, no, now what are we going to do?" the blond haired man said, obviously alarmed.

"Can I help?" Liz asked.

"Uh, uh, no, I don't think so," The other piped up. "Do you have any idea where he might have gone?"

"I don't know where he might be right now, but I'm sure, by this afternoon, he will end up at the Windsor House Hotel. He always hangs out there."

"Thanks," they said in unison and turned on their heels and left.

Liz studied them closely as they walked away. They were clean cut, dressed in decent casual clothes. They were neither like Lenny's hippie-type friends nor like his biker-type friends. Liz rubbed her chin trying to figure out what they wanted with Lenny.

Then she noticed that the sun had peeked out from behind the clouds so she made coffee, got dressed and went outside to bask in the warm sunshine. The kids had gone off to school, and she was alone. The sun was warm and comforting as she sat on the porch gazing down the long lane. She smiled to herself as she noticed the cedar fence. Since the snow had melted, she could see it was at least a foot shorter. She didn't realize they had burned that much of it in the wood stove.

Then after a short time she spied a heavy set man and a young boy walking up the lane. The man was dressed in black, and the boy had red hair and a million freckles.

"We were just passing by and saw your old Volkswagen there," the man said as he tipped his fedora back off his forehead. "Would you be willing to sell it?"

"It doesn't work."

"That doesn't matter. I just want it for parts."

"How much?" Liz asked, figuring Lenny wouldn't care and feeling good about making the deal.

"Fifty bucks," he said.

"Done deal!"

They shook hands as he said, "I'm on my way home. I'll be back in an hour or so with a tow bar to pick it up, and I'll pay you then.

He was back within the hour, put fifty dollars in Liz's hand and towed the old car away.

Liz went in the house to make breakfast and clean house. After finishing her chores and feeling bored, she decided to go for a walk. She was alone a lot at their "Wuthering Heights", but the countryside was beautiful, with the wild fruit trees in bloom, and finally, a sunny day. So it was a pleasure to walk around the grounds.

Feeling pleased with the fifty dollars she just made, Liz set out across the large cow pasture. Her mind skipped from one thought to another; how rough her life had become; she envisioned the pertly dressed cocktail waitress she used to be, then the long-skirted earth mother she had become. What a difference. She had loved her job. It had given her confidence and self esteem. But even with the loss of her job and old life-style she would rather have Lenny than Norm. She didn't always agree with Lenny's ways but she understood him. He had been brought up by an alcoholic father who beat him and had never taught him proper life skills.

All these thoughts filtered through her head as she walked along, deep in thought. It was as though she was sorting her life out like a filing system in a mental library. In the spring sunshine, smelling the freshness of the grass and the trees after all the rain, her mind cleared for the first time in months. She had her first lucid moments in a long time; she was trying to make sense of it all. She thought about the kids, and how hard their new life must be on them isolated in the country with no bathroom, and cold mornings before the fire was started. Then she thought about Lenny. She was torn because she loved them equally. Should she move for the kids' sake or stay for Lenny's? Did Lenny still love her? Then she started thinking about him cheating again. She just couldn't get that notion out of her head. She started to feel afraid when she thought of him not being in her life anymore. She couldn't imagine life without the carousel that Lenny caused to whir with delight.

Then the words "Volkswagen! Volkswagen!" penetrated her thoughts and stole her away from her deep concerns.

Lenny and the two men who had been searching for him earlier were racing towards her and shouting excitedly at her.

As they came closer Lenny was repeating, "Where's the Volkswagen? Where's the Volkswagen?"

"I sold it," she stated proudly, pulling the fifty dollars from her pocket.

"You what?" Lenny asked, incredulously.

"I thought you'd be pleased," she said, noticing the mouths of the other two men agape, eyes bugging out. "What's the big deal?"

"Who bought it?" Lenny asked frantically running his hands through his hair in frustration but striving for calm.

"I don't know," she said, fear rising in her throat and went on to describe the man and the boy.

"I know them," Lenny sighed. "It must be John Gardner who lives two lines over."

"What's wrong?" she repeated impatiently. "I thought I did good making fifty bucks."

"Fifty bucks is nothing compared to thirty pounds of marijuana!"

"Thirty pounds of marijuana, in the Volkswagen? Lenny what's this all about."

Lenny slapped his hand to his forehead. In his state of anxiety he had slipped up and now the truth was out. He tried to explain. "These guys were making a drop, thirty bricks of marijuana. When I wasn't here this morning, they hid it in the Volkswagen. They didn't want to take a chance taking it back to town. Yeah, you might as well know the whole story. It's out now. I'm dealing drugs. I'm a middle man. The drugs are delivered to me and I distribute to pushers on the street. That's why I'm away from home so much. That's why I'm so uptight all the time."

Lenny hung his head as he spoke, afraid to look her in the eye. He was afraid of what he'd see on her face. Would there be disappointment, anger, loathing? He didn't want to lose her love and respect, but he had been desperate. In order to support his drug habit and to ease the pressure of providing for a family of six, he had become part of the drug syndicate. He was not well-educated and had not been taught any skills so he had taken the easiest route he knew to try to cope with caring for the family because he was afraid of losing Liz if he couldn't provide for her.

The next thing he heard was uproarious laughter. He lifted his head slowly and looked towards Liz. She was shaking so hard with laughter that she was bent over. She couldn't stop. She was gasping, laughing almost hysterically.

"What's the matter?" Lenny asked a puzzled look on his face.

Ha, ha, ha, I can't stop laughing, just a sec," she squeaked out.

"It's not funny," The blond said, scowling.

"It is funny," she said between gasps. "You don't understand. Lenny, I thought you were having an affair. All these months I've been just sick. I thought you didn't love me anymore. Oh, man this is too funny, marijuana in the Volkswagen, and I sold it. You should see your faces," She started to laugh again.

Lenny's face broke into a wide grin, then he started to snicker and finally he broke into fits of laughter along with her. After months and months of tension, the barrier between them was finally broken down. One of Lenny's buddies was scratching his head and gaping at Lenny and Liz while the other one stood with his mouth wide open wondering what was wrong with them. Lenny had lost thirty pounds of marijuana. That was serious! They could all get shot or dropped in the river with cement boots on!

After Lenny finally got a grip on himself he turned to his two companions and said, "Come on, we better go and see John Gardner."

Liz had laughed so hard because she was relieved Lenny wasn't having an affair and because of the looks on the guys faces when they heard the news that their marijuana had been sold right out from under their noses. But underneath it all, she certainly wasn't happy to learn that Lenny was dealing in drugs. After calming down, she thought about the seriousness of the situation. There was a possibility that she could lose her kids if the authorities found out. She was caught in a web of deception, loving Lenny and hating what he was doing.

Lenny certainly did have the weight of the world on his shoulders, and now, Liz had a heavy weight on her shoulders too. She needed to do some serious thinking. Had she been plopped down into this situation in the early years, she would have bolted. She would have balked about the whole set-up, but the subtle deception of drink and marijuana and her changed life-style had numbed her sensitivities. She didn't care for Lenny dealing drugs, and she didn't like the way the drug trafficking had changed him. He was more determined somehow and more intense, but he was a big part of her now. She couldn't walk away. She would have to take her chances. She fooled herself into thinking it would be alright. Lenny would be careful. They wouldn't get caught. Nobody would ever know. The kids would be fine. Anyway, she would fight tooth and nail, if anyone tried to take them away. She would just up and run away with them if anybody tried.

Lenny and his dealers rushed over to John Gardner's farm and told him a cock and bull story about leaving some hunting equipment in the trunk of the Volkswagen. Fortunately for Lenny's companions, the farmer hadn't gone through the car. He was only going to use it for parts and never bothered to clean it out. One of the dealers kept the old man busy talking about his farm while Lenny and the other young man loaded the bricks into garbage bags and quickly transferred them into their van.

Liz was so relieved they got it back. It could have meant serious trouble for Lenny. They had the marijuana back, but it wasn't in very good shape. It was damp and moulding because of all the rain that spring. Lenny and his friends rushed to dry it out before the kids got home from school. Liz was as nervous as a thoroughbred race horse at the post, prancing back and forth to the door to make sure no one was driving up the lane. She didn't like what was going on in her summer kitchen, but she felt there was nothing she could do about it. The men separated each of the bricks, placed them on pie plates and put them in the oven of the wood stove to dry. Once dried, one of the guys sprayed the marijuana with Raid.

"What are they doing?" Liz asked appalled, "Why Raid?"

"It's probably lost it's oomph from being wet and then dried out in the oven. We don't want any disappointed customers. The Raid will give it an extra kick," Lenny explained.

"What about the harm it could do to people who smoke it?"

"It won't hurt them."

"It's poison!" she cried.

"What do you think alcohol and drugs are," he said as he pulled her closer to him. He looked down into her eyes and gave her "the look", the one that made her melt, the one she was so defenceless against.

She wasn't sure if he was right or not, but to keep peace, she let it go. She was torn between knowing that the whole set-up was criminal, and loving Lenny.

Lenny's drug dealing days continued with Liz's nerves constantly on edge until one day in the early summer of 1976. Since Liz knew about his drug dealing, Lenny felt easier about bringing his cronies home. So a lot of dubious looking characters had begun to hang around Lenny and Liz's place. In addition to their tough appearance and ways, they all had guns as well. Lenny took quite an interest in their guns. He had his own because he liked to hunt.

Worse than hunting guns, however, were the sawed-off shot guns and hand guns. Some of Lenny's cohorts from Toronto had started to use their "Wuthering Heights" as a weapons cache. Lenny and Liz's beautiful romantic spot in the country had become a drug depot and a bunker with an arsenal of weapons.

Then one warm day in June, Lenny invited his suppliers from Toronto to come to "Wuthering Heights" for a hunting expedition. Lenny and his cohorts were sitting around the living room, drinking beer, making deals and fooling with guns.

Suddenly, the whole place shook on its foundation as a ferocious sound rent the air and reverberated off the walls. Liz's hair stood on end. She was deafened at first, then Janie's screams pierced her ears. Pandemonium broke loose. Ears ringing, Liz shrieked, "What the hell happened?"

"I dunno," Lenny said, dumbfounded, holding the gun that had just misfired at arm's length as though he expected it to go off again. He stared in shock at where the bullet had gone through the wall by the staircase. Then he heard the scuffle of several footsteps at the bottom of the stairs.

The door to the stairwell opened and three pairs of bug eyes peered into the living room. "Mom, what happened? You should see the hole in the wall."

Liz's heart skipped a beat as she realized the kids had just come down the stairs ahead of the blast. Beads of perspiration broke out on her forehead. Running up to check the damage, she saw the small hole where the bullet had entered the wall on the right side of the stairs. Her eyes bugged out in horror as she surveyed the damage on the left wall. There was a hole two feet wide. She grabbed the kids and hugged them to her shaking with fear at what could have happened. "This is craziness," Liz screamed. "I've had enough! You could have killed one of my kids." She sobbed and shook. "That's it! I'm outa here!"

The whole scene jolted Liz into reality. It was as though a bright light was turned on, and she was disgusted by what she saw. She packed up her four kids, walked out the door and headed to the neighbour's to phone a cab. She went directly to her sister Jane's new home.

Liz and the kids stayed at Jane's for about a week in a small travel trailer in her yard. It was an unbearable situation with five of them crammed in a little trailer, and Liz going through withdrawal from alcohol. She was forced to quit, cold turkey. Liz had worked hard on slowing down her drinking, but never having quit completely before, and not realizing she was addicted to alcohol, she had a difficult time understanding her irritability and tenseness. She equated it with missing Lenny and the carousel.

So when Lenny came to call with promises to give up the drug business and get a job she was eager to return to him. Lenny had missed her terribly and needed her back. He was willing to do anything. The strong determination in his voice convinced Liz and made it easy for her to believe him. Still being deeply in love and discouraged by staying in the trailer with four kids, his promises sounded pretty good. They returned to their "Wuthering Heights" in a cab that very day. But would Lenny be able to keep his word?

# Chapter 34
# Kurt and Meggie and Me

Lenny, faithful to his word, quit dealing drugs immediately, severed all connections with the syndicate and started looking for work.

As soon as Liz got back home she went directly to the bank and put all her college funds into a term deposit account because she knew times were going to be rough, and she didn't want either one of them touching her dream.

By July, 1976 life at "Wuthering Heights" had reverted back to the way that it had been before Lenny started dealing. She was reasonably happy with Lenny, but she was right about their finances, things got very tough. There was however one good thing, Lenny lost touch with his drug-involved friends so his old friends started to hang around the way they used to, especially Kurt. He was a constant at the country house and Liz was very fond of him. He had a handsome face framed by medium-length dark curly hair that was tipped with sun gold. He had a brown moustache, and he reminded her of a golden Tom Selleck. When he came into a room it came alive. He loved to tease. He had laugh lines at the corners of his eyes that had been etched there from years of laughter.

Kurt and Lenny had been chums since kindergarten. He was fun to be with and because he was Lenny's best friend Liz and Lenny were often in his company. He came every weekend to take Lenny out to the Windsor House Hotel in Alliston to have a few beers and listen to the band. He was very sensitive to Liz's feelings so he always insisted that she come along too. Because he wanted their company he would always foot the bill.

"Wow, she sure is a looker!" Kurt whispered to Liz with a big grin on his face.

Liz had to admit he was right as she watched the waitress approach their table to take their order. She was beautiful, sensual and had a very feminine way about her. While Liz was trying to play the hippie-type, this girl by her very nature was one, born and bred so to speak. Liz almost felt jealous of her.

She had straight, long, blond hair, full lips painted a pale pink and wide blue eyes that reflected a simple innocence. She wore a black cotton skirt with a floral pattern of bright colours that clung to her hips and then flared around her calves. Her sandals were laced up her legs and accentuated their length. Her black halter top left her long back bare. Liz could see why Kurt was smitten, the woman positively oozed mother earth.

"Find out her name for me," Kurt requested.

"Sure," Liz said, sensing his fascination. Knowing that Kurt had been single for some time, she wanted to help him out.

"Uh, excuse me could we have another round and please tell me your name so we don't have to keep calling you waitress. I used to be a cocktail waitress, and I always appreciated it when customers called me by my name." "Oh, sure, it's Meggie."

"Man, I just gotta get to know her," Kurt said as he watched her walk away from the table.

"Tell you what," Liz said, "I'll invite a few people over for drinks after the bar closes, and I'll include her."

"Thank you, thank you, thank you. I'll buy a couple of cases of beer and I've got a bottle of whiskey in the car. That should be enough, eh?" Kurt said smiling warmly at her and squeezing her hand. They were good friends. She was always willing to accommodate him.

A few people from the bar did come to their "Wuthering Heights" after closing time for a few drinks, and Meggie did accompany them. The only problem was the plan backfired. The evening turned out to be a fiasco.

"Would you like another drink?" Kurt said as he sidled up to Meggie.

"No thank you," she replied cooly. Then she turned to Lenny, who was talking to Dillon.

"This is quite a place you have here, Lenny. I just love it. I wish I had a place like this," she said in a sugary sweet voice as she demurely fluttered her long black lashes and rolled her big blue eyes at him.

A smirk touched Liz's lips as she watched from the other side of the room. *What a fool! Lenny will blow her off right away. At least, he better*, she thought.

"Oh thanks," Lenny said with an astonished look on his face. He stopped talking to Dillon and turned his full attention on Meggie. "I loved it the first time I set eyes on it. I had to do some tall talking to get Liz to move in though."

Liz fumed.

"Why don't you show me around," she said as she slipped her arm through his and snuggled up to him.

"Sure," Lenny said as he wrapped his arm around hers and took her hand in his hand.

"What does he think he's doing," Kurt barked at Liz. "I should be showing her around."

"I don't know, but he better watch himself; he's already treading on thin ice with me," Liz replied.

Kurt playfully grabbed Liz around her mid-section and tickled her as he said, "Never mind if Lenny runs off with Meggie, I'll just grab you."

"Stop it Kurt! I'm serious he better just watch himself.

For the rest of the evening Meggie was all over Lenny. He acted like a silly school boy, Kurt sat around with a long face, and Liz just boiled. Now, she was definitely jealous. She wanted to kick Meggie out of their house. Meggie didn't care, she just kept coming on to Lenny.

After everyone finally left that night, Lenny crawled into bed with Liz, and she promptly turned her back to him. Even though she was hot with anger, he got the cold shoulder. But by the time half the week had gone by all was forgiven and forgotten.

Then, a week later, Lenny burst through the summer kitchen door at noon.

"I need you to wash and iron my good black pants and my good orange shirt," he said sounding excited.

"Why?"

"I've got a job interview. I've got to meet a guy in Alliston at five o'clock. Can you have them ready by then?"

"Five o'clock, that's an odd time to meet for an interview, isn't it?"

"Seems like it, but that's what he said. So do you think you can have them ready?"

"Yeah, but what about supper. We have nothing to eat at all. I've used up that five pounds of rice and all the apples we had." she said, reflecting on their struggle in the last month since Lenny had quit dealing drugs and was not working. She was pleased with herself that she had thought to put her college fund in the term deposit so it was safe, even though times were really tough. Surely, they would have spent some of it if she hadn't.

"I'll hitchhike to town and borrow some money to get something for you and the kids, but don't worry about me 'cause I'll be in town at supper time."

When he returned with food he washed his hair, changed and left again, not returning until four in the morning.

"Where have you been?" Liz moaned as she wiped the sleep from her eyes.

"After the interview, I met up with some of the guys and we went to the Windsor House for a few beers. After that we ended up at a house party at Rob's," Lenny explained as he slipped out of his shirt and pants.

"Sure, I'll believe you where thousands wouldn't. You're not dealing drugs again are you?" she whined.

Lenny gathered her into his arms as he crawled in beside her. "C'mon, Princess you trust me don't you?"

She thought she detected a little flash of guilt in his eyes but soon passed it over as he wrapped his large sinewy leg around her and pressed her close to him. The warmth of his muscular naked body enveloped her and she became totally lost.

A week went by, and as regular as clock work, Kurt came in his red Gremlin to take Liz and Lenny out to the Windsor House for their usual evening of entertainment.

As they sat at their table waiting for service Liz cried, "Oh, no, not her again!"

Meggie sauntered up to their table, stood beside Lenny and pressed her leg against his. Lenny glanced at Liz, cringed and quickly pulled his leg away. Kurt's face reddened with anger. Liz's face flushed as she wished Meggie would drop dead somewhere.

Lenny, nervous and fidgety, drank excessively, and by eleven o'clock he was totally inebriated. Hardly able to hold his head up, he muttered something about taking a cab home.

"I don't want to leave yet," Liz said. She was enjoying the band and Kurt's company. Kurt had been plying her with an unusual amount of attention during the evening, and Liz was not immune to his attention as Lenny was so preoccupied and drunk. She didn't care to accompany him home just to watch him pass out.

Kurt and Liz were having fun, and Lenny didn't seem to care as he took off leaving her in Kurt's hands. He trusted Kurt. After all they were best friends.

"Phew! This booze sure is working fast tonight. I feel really woozy. Hey, what's Lenny's problem?" Liz asked

"I don't know," Kurt lied.

"Oh, I'll bet you don't." She could sense a tension between Lenny and Kurt. She knew something was wrong.

Liz kept bugging him and then as the evening progressed and Kurt's tongue was further loosened by alcohol he blatted out, "That Lenny just kills me. I thought we were supposed to be friends."

"What do you mean?"

"Oh nuthin'. I can't tell you."

"Oh, you can't tell me! Well, you better tell me now you've started," Liz stated firmly.

They bantered back and forth for awhile and finally Kurt revealed his secret.

"Lenny took Meggie out last Saturday night. He wined and dined her and then took her to see the movie Tommy. What happened after that I don't know. He said he was taken in by her, but he felt really bad afterwards. Said he needed to confess to somebody. I don't know why it had to be me. He knew I wanted to take her out."

"I don't believe you!" Liz gasped. Then her mind drifted back to the previous week when Lenny had come in at four in the morning. The little glint of guilt in his eyes shone like a beacon in her brain and she knew deep inside it was true. Besides, Kurt would never lie to her. She didn't want to believe him though so she tried to fight the truth. It was a losing battle. She slapped her hand over her mouth as a sob ripped from her throat. Her heart was rent in two. Her carousel screeched to a halt.

"Get me outa here!" she moaned as tears gushed forth. She felt disoriented as the pain enveloped her and sucked the life out of her.

Ever sensitive to her feelings, Kurt wrapped his strong arm around her and comforted her as they walked together to the front door of the hotel.

In spite of all the hardships, drugs, and problems, she loved Lenny with all her heart, and she thought he felt the same way about her. He had, she was sure. She couldn't believe that he cheated on her. True, she had been suspicious in the past, but in her heart of hearts she never really believed it could happen. Brian had cheated on her. She had cheated on Norm. But Lenny and her were different. They were so much in love that she had thought they were above fooling around on each other. No matter what happened, they stuck together through thick and thin. She was right about Lenny, of course. He did love her, but never having been so blatantly pursued by such a beautiful woman, he was overcome. But he was just sick about it afterward.

As Kurt and Liz climbed into his Gremlin, Liz pivoted in the bucket seat to face him and said, "I don't want to go home."

"Where do you want to go?" he asked

"I don't know. Anywhere but home. Lenny will be passed out and I don't want to be alone right now. Let's just drive around for awhile, okay?" she said between sobs. She dabbed at her cheeks with a wet Kleenex.

Kurt said, "Sure," as he squeezed her hand. "Look I'm sorry. I shouldn't have told you. I didn't mean to hurt you like this. I was just so mad at Lenny. I didn't think. I sure didn't mean to hurt you. You know I've always liked you. Lenny's a bastard for what he did to you."

Liz wiped more tears from her cheeks and moved over to snuggle under his extended arm for comfort.

They drove around for awhile and finally parked on a side road.

Sniff. "I can't believe Lenny did that. It must have been the night he was out 'til four in the morning. If they went to a movie, what did they do after, until four?" Another sob burst forth from the depths of her soul.

Kurt wiped away her tears with his thumbs, and then rubbed her back, oh so gently. She buried her face into his powerful shoulder. She could smell his musky cologne. It filled her nostrils and spread through her leaving a pleasant feeling. She could feel the warmth of his body through his tee shirt as he stroked her hair. She leaned back and looked up into his eyes. They were so blue and so full of compassion that it touched her heart. Their eyes locked, and he realized at that precise moment that he loved her too, always had. But she was Lenny's girl, and Lenny was his best friend. Then, overcome by seeing her grief, he put his forefinger under her chin, lifted it, and kissed her very gently as though she was a fragile flower. The carousel spun with delight; the horses were drunk with passion. Liz returned his kiss with a fiery hunger. Their bodies melded together in the heat of the moment, and they eventually slithered between the bucket seats into the back driven by their overwhelming desire. Hours passed quickly, the windows of the Gremlin were smeared with the steam of their passion and the sun was rising in a blaze of red.

"What have we done?" Liz moaned as she straightened herself out. "I don't know what to say."

"How about I love you? Leave Lenny, come with me. I love you Liz. I guess I always have, I just never knew it until now."

For years to come, Liz would find herself wishing she had taken him up on his offer, but for the time being she just muttered, "Oh, Kurt please don't. I'm so mixed up right now." Her head was pounding partly from the onslaught of a hangover, partly from crying so much, and mostly from what she had just done.

Lenny's disloyalty had hurt them both and himself as well. To make matters worse now Liz had cheated on him. *Tit for Tat,* she thought making herself feel better for a brief second but then she realized two wrongs don't make a right and she started to feel sick, sober, and sorry.

"What am I going to tell Lenny?" Liz asked of Kurt, nervously.

"Tell him we went to a party in Alliston after the Hotel closed."

That sounded reasonable to Liz as they often did that. She hadn't intentionally set out to get revenge. She only sought comfort in Kurt's arms. The rest seemed to come naturally. The unintentional revenge was not in the least bit sweet. It was very bitter. Now, she had to lie as well. She wondered if Lenny had felt the same way after going out with Meggie.

She was really fond of Kurt. She had always found him attractive, but she didn't love him the way she did Lenny. She slumped down in the seat as she realized her latest escapade was not going to make things any better.

Kurt and Liz pulled in the long lane and drove up to the porch where Lenny sat with his rifle aimed at the car.

Kurt jumped out of the car arms up yelling, "Hold on, Lenny! What's you're problem? We were at a party."

"Where?" Lenny sneered.

Kurt came up with some lame excuse that Lenny just didn't buy.

"Get out of here before I blow your head off!" Lenny shouted gesturing with the rifle.

"No way, man! I'm not leaving her here with you. You're crazy," Kurt shouted back matching anger for anger.

"Just go, Kurt. I'll be alright. He won't hurt me. I'm not afraid. He'll calm down after you leave," Liz shrieked. She had never seen Lenny so angry, and she was afraid he might just shoot Kurt. She had to get him out of there for all their sakes.

Kurt finally walked to his car with his head down, accepting that Liz knew Lenny better than he did. He couldn't make her come if she didn't want to, and he knew it.

Liz admired him greatly for wanting to defend her. She hung her head in sadness for him as she watched him sink into the front seat of the Gremlin.

Lenny started to prod her about where she and Kurt had been. Liz matched his anger with hers, "Never mind me. How about Meggie?" That was her ace in the hole, and it worked.

Lenny crumpled.

"Kurt told you didn't he? I'm sorry Liz. I feel just sick about it. I was just so taken in. I never had a woman come on to me like that before. I didn't know how to handle it. She made me feel so good, but she's just a witch. She screws around and entices married men all the time. It's just a big game with her. I found out too late. I love you, Liz and only you, and I'm so sorry."

Liz felt furious, then guilty, then furious, then guilty. What a mess their lives had become. Lenny apologized over and over and said it would never happen again. They struggled back and forth over their infidelities for some time, each lying to the other about having sex with someone else, until Lenny had to leave for work at the army base where he had acquired a job the week after he had taken Meggie out.

He was a maintenance man for the base and was making very good money. It was a good move on his part, but was it too late? Had too much damage been done?

# Chapter 35
# Merry-Go-Round of Denial

After the Meggie and Kurt episode Liz and Lenny were both on edge. Lenny never did fully believe that Kurt and Liz had gone to a party and Liz never fully believed Lenny didn't sleep with Meggie either. After all, he didn't get home until four in the morning. They were both really sorry about the incident, but it left a bad taste in their mouths. The whole thing was like a sliver buried under the surface of the skin, not visible but festering underneath. So Lenny started staying away from home more and more drinking at the clubs on the base and sometimes spending all of his pay check on booze. And just as upset as Lenny, Liz started drinking heavier at home. They had lost something essential to their love relationship -- trust.

A few weeks later Liz was sitting on the couch in the living room contemplating all these things when she glanced out through the front window of their country home. She became very nervous as she watched a police cruiser drive in the yard. She put down her bottle of beer and went out onto the porch.

"Liz Carter?"

"Yes. Is there something wrong?"

"We have a warrant for your arrest. Please come with us."

"What? You must be mistaken. I've done nothing wrong," she said as her mind flashed back to the drug dealing days. *Had they found out?*

"It seems you failed to appear for a small claims court hearing."

"Oh, that," Liz said relieved. "Has that passed?" she asked. Her mind was fuzzy from a three day binge.

"Yes ma'am and you missed it. So if you'll just get in the car peacefully."

"You mean I get arrested because I failed to go to court over a phone bill. I thought debtor's prison went out with the dark ages."

After Lenny got his job at the camp, they installed a phone. Unfortunately they drank most of their money away, so they neglected to pay the bill. The phone was in Liz's name so she was the one called to small claims court.

"Yes ma'am, failure to appear constitutes a warrant for your arrest."

"Well I just cant' go. I've got four kids coming home from school in about fifteen minutes, and they won't know where I am."

"That's not our problem. We just have to bring you in. Do you want to leave them a note?"

Tears started to fill Liz's eyes as she became panicked at their insistence. She was so angry with Lenny for not paying the bill.

Questions plagued her as she wrote a note for the kids. *Why am I drinking so much? Why is my life such a mess? When did it all start?* When she thought back she realized that she always drank at the parties and gatherings. But when had it become habitual. When had it gotten out of hand. *I really need to get out of all this mess. I've just gotta try somehow, but I don't even know where to begin.* What Liz didn't realize was that escaping the grips of alcoholism was going to be a lot tougher than she ever could imagine.

As she heard the clink of the handcuffs closing around her wrists, she wondered what had become of her. She had always been bright, conscientious, hard-working, kind, and honest. Her beautiful carousel had turned into a carousel of horror. More thoughts plagued her as she rode in the back of the cruiser, the plexiglass window closing in on her. Edmund's face flashed in her memory. She quickly dismissed it. It was as though she was even ashamed to face his image.

Liz was taken to the station in Alliston where she signed a paper stating that she was being released on her own recognizance. Her hand shook as she penned her name.

She appeared in small claims court the next time she was summoned. Her arrest indelibly etched on her mind the need to appear no matter what, drunk or sober.

In a private chamber off the court room, she stood between two tall average looking lawyers, one for Bell Canada and the other one court appointed for her defence. The judge sat at a large desk in front of them.

Lenny had to go to work so Liz was there all by herself, and she was very nervous. She had never been in court before for something she did wrong. The only other time she'd been in court was when she had gone for Brian's hearing and for her divorce from him and that was different, very different.

She shuddered as she remembered the divorce case. The judge had been cold and callous, asking her very personal questions like when was the last time she had intercourse with her husband. She was so young and innocent then. The questions had totally embarrassed her.

Her memory flickered like frames in a home movie. She saw a young, innocent girl quivering in fear, afraid of authority figures. The scene was a courtroom in black and white, the only colour was a young dark-haired, naive girl clad in a straight, long turquoise wool dress with white vertical stripes and a little white pill box hat. Hats were required in court then. She recognized the girl as herself.

Liz's heart grieved her as she longed to be that innocent, young girl again. Now, here she was, a drunk most of the time, feeling like a criminal and feeling very defensive in front of this skinny long-nosed, arrogant looking snip of a judge.

But she was no longer innocent so she decided she would no longer quiver. She drew in a deep breath and was ready to do battle as he cleared his throat and sternly spoke the words, "Well, young lady, can you tell me why you didn't appear in court the last time?"

"I was sick with the flu, and it slipped my mind," she lied, gritting her teeth. No way was she going to admit she had been drinking or had a problem. She was just too ashamed.

"Sickness is no excuse for missing her majesty's court. Can you tell me any good reason why I shouldn't sentence you to a week in jail for contempt?" he said, as he smirked.

Feeling very squeamish about this idea, Liz took in another deep breath, regained her composure, flipped her head back, held it high and stated, "Yes, I do have a good reason, four of them as a matter of fact. I've got four children at home who need me."

Fear of being parted from her children chilled her blood. Fear of prison bars chilled it even more, but she was damned if she'd let Mr. Arrogance see it.

"Well, I've got four children at home, too," he said very flippantly.

So just as flippantly, Liz exclaimed, "Well, would you want to go to jail for a week and leave them home alone?"

The man on her right shuffled nervously as did the man on her left. She glanced to the right first, then to the left, without moving a muscle. Both men were just about bursting trying to stifle their laughter. They had to maintain their dignity in front of that snippet of a man, but Liz didn't.

"Hmmph," the judge muttered. Then to save face, he quickly changed the subject and very firmly stated that Liz had to make monthly payments of $5.00 to Bell Canada. The payments were to be made through the court.

Liz rode home with a very nice cab driver who empathized with her close call. He was a very attentive listener so she poured out all her troubles to him and he suggested she accompany him to an A.A. meeting that night, which she did.

The meeting took place in a very small room of a church basement. Bare light bulbs glared from their ugly fixtures in the ceiling. Cigarette smoke filled the room. The group consisted of about eight men and two women of which Liz was one. She listened attentively to horror stories of alcoholism. The last one scared her half to death. A dark haired man with horn-rimmed glasses and large pouches under his eyes told the story of how he had started to drink on a Friday evening and had no recollection of anything until Monday morning when he woke up in jail to find out his wife and his three children were all in hospital. He had beaten them so badly that they all had to be hospitalized. Never having had a blackout, she decided then and there, alcoholism didn't apply to her. She never returned to any of those meetings.

But the court case and the meeting she did attend were the beginning of a wild spiralling ride down a vortex of misery and mayhem.

# Chapter 36
# Anguish of a "Family" Secret

A month passed quickly and Liz was one very sick woman. All the days after the court hearing found her either drunk or so badly hung over that she couldn't function properly. Alcohol had full control of her now. Not only did it have control of her, it had wrapped itself tightly around Lenny as well. He drank non-stop when he wasn't working on the base. As a matter of fact, he never came home sober, and Liz was furious because she didn't trust him anymore. He was still drugging as well and the alcohol and drugs were damaging his mind and spirit beyond repair.

Not only was Liz heavily addicted, but she found it easier to face Lenny when she was drunk. She was uncomfortable with him most of the time now and the alcohol gave her false courage. He was a big man and he had become unpredictable when he drank. She could never tell what kind of mood he would be in when he came home. The alcohol tended to make him violent. Ever since they had cheated on each other, Liz and Lenny's life wasn't the same and neither one knew what to do to make it right so they just kept drinking.

Lenny came home very drunk as usual one night and crawled in bed beside Liz. She had been drinking all evening and was in no mood to be amorous, and Lenny wasn't exactly appealing in his condition. He had two days growth of beard, and he smelled of stale beer and body sweat, but he insisted on having sex. He handled her roughly in his drunken state.

"Lenny, stop it!" Liz cried. She didn't like his forced advances. She moved away from him in an attempt to get out of bed. With his fingers entangled in her hair he grabbed and yanked. She pushed at him and he slapped her forcing her back down on the bed.

"Lenny, stop it! What's got into you? I don't want to make love this way."

"Whassa matter? I'm not good enough for you since Kurt?"

"Stop it! You have no room to talk. I said I was sorry about that. Let's just leave it alone."

"No I want sex tonight, and I'll have it."

"No! Please don't! Not like this."

His anger escalated with Liz's struggling. She caught a glimpse of his eyes as he held her down on the bed. They were empty, like black glass marbles. He just wasn't there anymore. His body was still functioning but he wasn't there. She wondered, fearfully, just who was in control because it sure wasn't Lenny.

He gripped Liz by her arm with one big hand and tried to take his clothes off with the other hand. He was so drunk and clumsy he couldn't strip with one hand so he let go of his grip on her arm. She took advantage of the opportunity and jumped up off the bed and lunged for the door. She ran to the kitchen. He was hot on her tail. This strange man she no longer knew grabbed her arm forcefully. Drunk, angry and out of control, he slapped her hard across the face.

She started throwing dishes at him. They were crashing and breaking all over the place. Fighting back only seemed to aggravate him more. The stray dachshund that they had adopted went after Lenny. The dog snarled and tried to bite him. Lenny ducked the flying dishes and tried to kick at the dog. He missed and his steel-toed boot connected with Liz's left calf as she turned to dodge him. The blow brought her to her knees.

She got up and grabbed a cast iron frying pan half full of scrambled hamburger left over from supper, raised it over her head and tried to swing it down. He put his arm up and broke her aim. The hamburger went flying all over the room. Liz saw his big fist come full in her face, and then she saw stars and blackness. She felt nothing. She came to after an unknown length of time. She was lying on the couch. Through slits in her swollen eyes she spotted two police officers, standing tall in their uniforms looking down at her. One had a pen and a note pad in his hand and was questioning Lenny. She touched her chin. A stream of blood had jelled there from a split at the corner of her mouth.

Noticing that Liz was coming around, the fair-haired officer with the note pad turned to her and asked, "Have you two been fighting?"

"Uh, no!" Liz stated emphatically, wanting to protect Lenny. It wasn't her Lenny who had done this ugly thing. It was the stranger who had taken over his body. She was sure Lenny loved her. He was just upset over everything and drinking too much.

"It's obvious to me that you have been fighting," the police officer said as he turned and took in the whole scene with his eyes. As he surveyed the room, Liz's eyes followed his lead. The floor of the living room was covered in smashed dishes and hamburger and in the middle of it all was one heavy black frying pan.

"What happened to your hand?" the dark-haired policeman asked Lenny.

Lenny tried to hide his left hand with the other one. The hand was puffed up and turning black. He just looked away and said nothing.

"Well we know he's hit you, but there's nothing we can do if you won't lay charges."

"No, no everything is okay," Liz lied partly in fear and partly because she didn't want to hurt Lenny. She was a victim of her own guilt. She thought that if she hadn't gone with Kurt none of this would have happened. She knew she really hurt Lenny. Out of the deal, he not only lost their close relationship, but his best friend to boot. Then feeling uncomfortable with taking all the blame she thought, *that cursed Meggie it's all her fault. She started the whole thing.* In actual fact, alcohol was to blame for the whole mess. But they all failed to see that. Her beloved carousel had turned into a miserable merry-go-round of denial.

The police left. Lenny got a cold cloth for Liz's face. He had sobered considerably. He stroked her hair and apologized profusely.

"Oh, my little princess. What has happened to us? I'm so sorry. I just get so mad sometimes." He rocked her back and forth. Tears streamed down his face. The ugly stranger had disappeared and her romantic Lenny was back.

Tears ran down Liz's cheeks too. She cried for the loss of their beautiful carousel.

"How did the police get here?"

"I don't know. I think Jimmy went to the neighbour's and phoned them. What are we going to do, Liz?"

"I don't know. I don't know how to fix it," she said as they cuddled together and drifted off to sleep.

"I think I broke my hand," Lenny said the next morning. "I'm going to hitchhike to town and go to the hospital and get it checked. Are you okay?"

"Yeah. I'll be alright," Liz said, as she glanced at herself in the mirror. Her face was swollen beyond recognition. Both eyes were black and a one inch split marred the left corner of her mouth. She also had a very large bruise on her left calf that made her limp. She winced as she gently rubbed her finger tips over her head and felt several lumps. She felt sick to her stomach as she glanced quickly, one more time, at the image in the mirror that wasn't her. She turned away.

"Oh, man, you look terrible. I can't believe I did that to you." He hugged her and gently caressed her back. "Come with me. Get yourself checked out," he said.

"No you go get your hand looked at. I feel too embarrassed. I'll be okay. Nothing is broken. Besides, I've got to stay with the kids and somehow try to make them understand. I'm sure they must be really upset about this."

Lenny and Liz had sunk into a mire of misery that neither one of them wanted to be in, but neither one of them knew how to get out of. The simple solution would have been to quit drinking, but that notion somehow seemed beyond them. The demon alcohol was in full charge now.

Battered, bruised and guilt-ridden, Liz stayed home and tried to comfort the kids. Jimmy explained to her how he had tied bed sheets together and climbed out the second story window to go to the neighbour's and phone the police. Liz shuddered at the thought of him climbing out the window. She imagined him falling and felt terrible guilt and promised herself and the kids nothing like this would ever happen again.

Lenny had broken his hand and had to have surgery. He came home with one hand in a cast and the other one clutching a dozen red roses. He tried to treat Liz better after that, but their teeth were on edge. Neither one trusted the other and when not in each other's company suspicions and tempers would flare, especially when fuelled with alcohol. They both hated what was going on and yet they were bound together in their misery.

Liz's mind was so foggy from alcohol abuse that she couldn't think straight. She was numb. She didn't know what to do to make her situation better so she just stayed in her predicament.

Liz didn't want Brian to leave and he did. She wanted Norm to leave and he wouldn't. Neither Lenny nor Liz wanted to leave. It was an untenable stalemate, so the pair stayed together and continued to drink, but Lenny tried very hard not to fight with Liz.

Then one Friday night while Lenny was drinking at the base, Dar, who had been away in London for over a year, showed up on Liz's doorstep. She had missed Arnie so much that she had given in and returned to him, but their life together wasn't much better than Lenny and Liz's.

Liz was ecstatic to see her. Not only because she had missed her so much, but because she was so tense and angry at Lenny for staying at the base and drinking without her. Her mind had been busy concocting all sorts of visions of Lenny fooling around with bar maids and it was driving her crazy. So when Dar suggested they take off and head to the Beetonia where Liz hadn't been for years, she was more than grateful for the distraction. She hired an eighteen year old girl to watch the kids, and she and Dar took off for Beeton. They had a wonderful evening renewing their friendship, but the next day all hell broke loose.

Lenny had left for town, and Liz was checking the house to see what damage had been done by the kids the night before. When she went into Stacy's room she kicked at Stacy's shorts and underwear that had just been dropped on the floor. "Darn kids never ever pick up after themselves."

Then she was sickened by what she saw next. On the floor beside Stacy's bed were several empty beer bottles and an ash tray full of butts. "That son of a bitch. He must have been making out with the babysitter in Stacy's room. That's why Stacy was sleeping in with Bonnie this morning. He must have fed the sitter beer and got her drunk before he sent her home in a cab." She was crazy with visions of Lenny seducing the sitter.

When Lenny came home she tore into him. He fought tooth and nail with Liz denying that he had done anything wrong. He said the beer bottles and the cigarette butts were all his. He said he had come home, found her gone, paid the sitter, sent her home in a cab, and in his drunken state crawled into the wrong bed, drank a few beers and passed out.

Liz accepted his explanation mainly because she couldn't stand to believe otherwise, but her inner core didn't fully buy it so things got even more tense between them. A week or so went by with the tension building and by the weekend Lenny was drinking again. He staggered through the living room door. Liz was lying on the couch in the dark. She had been trying to sleep, but couldn't drift off because she never knew what shape Lenny would come home in. She could smell the alcohol from across the room. Lenny clicked on the light switch and stark bright light surrounded him. Liz rubbed her eyes. Then the festering sliver came to a very explosive head. "I've done the worst thing that you could possibly think of," he muttered as he weaved back and forth.

Liz, sitting up instantly, raised one eyebrow and cautiously looked toward him, "Did you kill someone?" she asked her voice shaking.

"No, worse than that."

Now her mind was racing. *What could possibly be worse?* The full realization hit her like a cannonball. A vision of the shorts and the underwear on the floor in Stacy's room flashed on and off like a strobe light in her brain. "No! Oh, no! Not that!" she screamed. She grabbed fistfuls of hair on either side of her head and tugged trying to rip the thought out of her mind.

"I never hurt her!" Lenny slurred.

Liz's soul was rent in two. The man she thought replaced Edmund had abused one of her precious babies. Her heart split. She had always loved to walk on the razors edge and now it had cut her to the core. In that one instant a blackness that would follow her for the rest of her life enveloped her soul.

Then, in spite of her fear, she got real mad. "You bastard, I'll kill you!" She grabbed a lamp by its base and hurled it at him with all the strength she could muster. He ducked.

Her head started to buzz and her mind whirred. She thought she was going insane. In an attempt to avoid the horrible truth that her mind couldn't fathom she desperately thought, *he's punishing me. That's it, he's lying. He wants to hurt me. He's just made up the worst thing that he can think of to get even with me for going with his best friend. Surely, I would have known if he was that "kind of guy". Just what does that "kind of guy look like? Somebody's uncle, somebody's brother, somebody's step-father?*

Liz sank down in the easy chair silently stricken and started to cry.

Not getting the reaction he expected, and in defence of himself Lenny stated again, "I never hurt her."

Liz's mind was spinning. The words were muffled in her head as though they were being funnelled down a long tunnel and were not quite real. "You never hurt her?" she whispered. The words were hardly audible. She was in a daze. She stared straight ahead as though she were in a giant bubble that was shutting out the sounds of the world. Her mind started to slip.

*What'll we do? What'll we do? What'll we do, when we live in a shoe? Do I live in a shoe. No, the old lady lives in the shoe. What am I thinking? I'm going crazy. I've got to get a grip on myself or I'm going to lose my mind. I know, I know. I'll wait until the morning and ask Stacy. Oh, yes, that's it. He's lying. He's got to be lying. Lenny would never doing anything so debased.*

Liz went to bed that night totally numb with her mind in a turmoil. *What will I do if it's true? No it can't be true. I just won't believe it. But just what if it is? What'll I do? What'll I do What'll I do if I live in a shoe. Stop it! Stop it! Oh, please, God, let me sleep.* It took a long time for her to doze off. Nothing in her life had prepared her for anything like this. She was totally at a loss as to what to do. She loved Lenny and she knew he loved her, but her carousel was shattered into a million splinters, the horses lying on their sides -- dead and still.

Her own words from younger years came back to haunt her. She recalled talking to Carol after a little girl from Beeton had been abducted, raped and murdered. "I would kill any bastard who ever laid a hand on one of my kids. There would be no court case because he'd be dead before he made it to the stand." It was easy to say, until she was actually faced with the issue. If it had been a stranger, it would have been easier. But a husband, a common-law husband? What could she do?

*First things first*, she thought. She had to find out the truth. She assured herself that once she knew the truth she would know in which direction to go. With that thought soothing her, she was finally able to go to sleep.

The next morning after Lenny had gone to work and as the kids were getting ready for school, Liz called Stacy aside and very carefully broached the subject.

"Stacy, uh, Lenny said, uh something happened between you and him, uh, do you know what I mean?"

Stacy's face turned scarlet. She hung her head and nodded.

"Is it true?"

Stacy with her head hanging continued to nod.

A bomb exploded in Liz's brain. She couldn't breathe. She grabbed her chest. Then she wiped viciously at tears with the backs of her hands.

*Get a grip on yourself, Liz! You've got to think of her. You don't count right now.* She sniffed, dried her eyes and gathered Stacy into her arms.

Liz cuddled Stacy close, held on tightly and rocked her back and forth. Liz's mother-love swelled in her heart as she told her, *None of this is your fault.*

In her core Liz loved her kids, had always loved them. Her mind was blurred by alcohol, but she knew something had to be done and fast. Her babies were her most precious possession. What she didn't know was how difficult it was going to be to sort it all out.

After holding Stacy quietly for awhile, Liz let her go and encouraged her to finish getting ready for school. Liz sadly watched her walk away. At twelve, she was as tall as Liz. Once the kids were all off to school Liz wandered aimlessly around the fields all day in shock, trying with her non-functioning mind to figure out what to do.

As she tried to come to terms with it all, she imagined how a little child could blank out something so horrible by burying it deep in her subconscious. She felt like such a little child. She wished she could blank it out. She couldn't, but the knowledge of it in her mind and the feelings of it in her heart would never meet, leaving her divided in spirit for the rest of her life. She knew it all in her mind but somehow couldn't allow herself to feel it in her heart. It was too painful. So she put a shroud over her heart so as to never feel it, but she was left with the anguish of a "family" secret.

She was in a daze as she walked around. The question that replayed over and over in her mind was, *Where can we go?*

*To my parents'? No!* She could not tell her parents the truth. Alicia would *never* understand the mess she was in. *Can I tell my friends? They love me. No! I couldn't stand for them to know. I'm too ashamed.* Through a process of elimination, one by one, she dismissed the possibilities of where the kids and she could go. Now she cursed herself for putting her money into a term deposit.

Liz wandered all day tossing thoughts and ideas around in her head until she thought she was crazy.

"I'll go to the police," she muttered to herself. Then dismissed it. They would lock him up. She had heard horror stories about men guilty of child molesting who were killed in prison by other inmates. She didn't want that on her conscience. She was repulsed by the whole situation, but at the same time found that her feelings for Lenny had not automatically turned off as she thought they should. She had loved him so deeply and those feelings die hard. She had to think rationally. She had to do what was best for everyone involved, but especially for her Stacy, regardless of the repercussions to her or to Lenny.

She hated him for what he did, but she still loved him at the same time. It was insane. She had never been in such a turmoil in all her life. She had never ever felt so torn apart before. It was the worst thing that could ever happen in a family. Worse than a death. Her instincts told her that she had to do the best for her kids. Lenny was an adult, he had to take his chances and suffer the consequences of his actions.

All of a sudden, Liz knew what to do! The fog lifted and she was excited. Why hadn't she thought of it before? It was a way out for the time being.

There were no transition houses at that time. That would have been the ideal solution for the kids and her. It would have been somewhere she could go with four kids, an alcohol addiction, and no money, but that option was not available.

So her idea was perfect. The more she thought about it, the more she liked it. She walked to the neighbours and using their phone she called her doctor's number and made an appointment. In the meantime, she didn't drink and never let the kids out of her sight. She knew she could suffer through the two days until the appointment. Her doctor would advise her. Dr. Brown would know what to do. Besides, she would not be as emotionally involved as family and friends would. Being a woman, Liz felt Dr. Brown would deal sympathetically with her situation. Liz did an about face and returned to the house feeling satisfied that she had a way to solve her problem, if not the actual resolution.

When Liz arrived at the Doctor's office, she was shaking. She wondered how she would broach such a delicate subject. She felt dreadful shame for being in such a predicament. Several times she had to get a grip on herself so she wouldn't bolt out the door. She knew she had to stay. There was no way this could just be swept under the rug.

Finally she was ushered into the office by a pert little nurse. *What would she think if she knew?* Liz thought. She seemed so crisp and clean in her starched white uniform. Liz felt dirty and ashamed as they walked down the corridor. She felt as though she was walking the last mile. She was sure the pert little nurse would think she was deplorable if she knew. *Does it show on the outside? Can the nurse read the awful black secret I carry within? Why do I think I'm so bad? I didn't do anything Lenny is the perverse one. For some reason I feel just as guilty. Am I somehow to blame? Should I have known somehow? He doesn't look any different than any other man.* Those thoughts trailed behind her down the hallway, leaving slime from the slug that Liz was sure she was.

"Good morning, Liz. What can I do for you today?" Doctor Brown asked cheerfully, smiling in welcome.

"Well uh, I don't know where to start," Liz stated, embarrassment and shame pulsing it's way through her body.

"Just try starting at the beginning," Dr. Brown encouraged, reaching over and patting Liz's hand. Liz's inner struggle showed on the outside and the Doctor's eyes reflected compassion.

"Okay," Liz said shyly squirming in her seat while she was twisting the life out of an already shredded Kleenex.

"First of all, I need you to promise me that what I tell you will go no farther than this office. I need the strictest confidence," Liz said, wanting to protect her little family from outside investigations. Her daughter had been through enough already.

"Well sure, Liz. I promise, go on."

"You're sure?" The doctor nodded as Liz continued, "There's been a terrible thing happen in our family. I don't even know how to say this."

"Let me help you. I suspect you're talking about incest."

Hot tears instantly stung Liz's eyes as she nodded slowly, head down, unable to speak or look the doctor in the eye.

After what seemed like an eternity, Liz was finally able to utter the words, "Not exactly incest, I guess the proper term would be molesting. He was very drunk. I am just so ashamed about all of this."

"No, no, Liz, you have done the right thing," Dr. Brown said as she handed Liz a fresh Kleenex and continued, "How did you find out?"

"He told me. At first I thought he was lying, but then my daughter confirmed it. I just didn't know how to deal with it. I couldn't go to my family or friends."

"That would be very difficult. I'm glad you came here, but I'm not exactly sure what the next step should be. I know I promised you I wouldn't tell anyone, but would you mind if I involved my husband? He has more years of medical experience, and I would like to get his opinion of how to handle this situation."

"I guess not, as long as he promises not to involve outsiders. The whole mess is just too embarrassing for our whole family."

Doctor Brown left her office and returned within a brief period of time.

"Well, Liz, my husband and I are in agreement that it is a very rare thing when a perpetrator tells on himself. This is a good indication that Lenny is seeking help. It doesn't necessarily mean he is a pedophile. Sometimes men will molest in a drunken state because of insecurity. Does he know you're here?"

"Yes, he agreed I should come."

"Good then. Listen, we won't report this matter to the police, but we do want to go to family services to get counselling for your family. Are you agreeable to that?"

"Yes, oh, yes. I'm sure Lenny will agree. But what should we do in the meantime. The kids and I have nowhere to go. What if he does it again?"

"I highly doubt that he will because he told you about it himself. He knows you know, so he will be very careful. Just sit tight until you hear from me. I'm going to get in touch with a good psychiatrist for Lenny. We'll get this all sorted out for you," the doctor said as she hugged Liz and walked her to the door.

Liz felt as though a ten ton weight had been lifted off her shoulders as she walked out of the doctor's office. She was to wait until she heard from Dr. Brown who would set things up with family services.

Lenny was relieved. Liz was relieved. They didn't drink. They were afraid to drink. They waited patiently for the doctor's word. They had no phone, but Liz checked the mail box every day. A week went by and there was no word. Things were getting tense in the house. Lenny was as nervous as a cat on a hot tin roof and Liz was bouncing between feeling good about the solution and feeling just sick at heart about even being in his company. She guarded her little brood like a mother hen guards her chicks.

At intervals she felt as though the right thing to do would be to get out of there. But who would take in four kids and a woman with no job and no money? The only money she had was in the term deposit account and she couldn't get at it. She had thought she was so smart when she took out the term deposit, but now she wasn't so sure she had been. She could really have used the money. She was stuck between a rock and a hard place. Not only that, but she was suffering withdrawal from alcohol. The pressure was unbearable. The situation was like a barrel full of explosives with someone holding a match close to the wick.

That someone turned out to be Lenny when he came home one night from work with a 24 pack of beer. At first Liz was afraid to join him, but her addiction was stronger than she knew and she finally crumpled and gulped down the booze. It afforded a temporary escape from the tension.

No trouble developed from their drinking that night so in the next few weeks that followed they continued to drink to relieve the stress. Still no word came from the doctor. Their drinking escalated to drown the pressure and their pressures escalated due to the drinking.

For some unknown reason, the doctor never did get in touch with Liz and with the numbing effects of alcohol Liz didn't think to get in touch with the doctor. Once drinking again her wits were scattered. And she needed to drink.

So Liz just kept going round and round on a carousel of horror. The horses were drunk with their mad turning round and round. She needed to get off but didn't know how. She thought she had discovered the secret of the carousel, she thought it meant being in love when in actuality it was her addiction. She was addicted to feeling good. In the beginning, romance and alcohol had provided those good feelings for her.

But now, she was a mental wreck. She stayed drunk most of the time, thinking it was helping her cope, not realizing it was making matters worse. The alcohol was really debilitating her. It had its hooks deep into her and she was bleeding slowly through every puncture, her life draining out of her.

Liz longed for a release. In fact she wished for the old days when Dar and Carol had been her dearest friends. Then as if her wish was answered Dar and Arnie showed up on her door step. Dar and Arnie's drinking had increased like Lenny and Liz's so they were like birds of a feather. Birds of a feather flock together they say, and so, they did.

Arnie teasingly stated, "Well Lenny, I don't like you and you don't like me but what the hell, Wanna have a few beers?"

Arnie broke the ice, Lenny laughed, and they cracked open the 24 pak of Molson's Export Ale that Arnie had carried in under his arm.

Lenny and Arnie proceeded to get extremely drunk very quickly. Liz and Dar followed suit. The conversation drifted to the couples' past indiscretions and then escalated into a full-blown physical fight between Arnie and Dar and Lenny and Liz. Arnie cold cocked Dar and knocked her unconscious while Lenny picked Liz up over his head and threw her off the porch. By this time alcohol and drugs had so damaged Lenny's brain that he was beyond hope.

Liz scrambled to her feet to try to run to the neighbour's. Her shoes had flown off when Lenny threw her and her feet were bare. She was drunk, but the walk began to sober her some, and she slowly became aware of excruciating pain. She could hear a bone clicking in her foot as she walked. The more sober she became, the greater the pain became. She realized she would never make it the mile to the neighbours so she turned around and made her way back to the house, limping with every step.

Jimmy was awake by this time, and he volunteered to go to the neighbour's and phone the police. By the time the two officers arrived, Dar had come to and Arnie and Lenny had very conveniently passed out drunk. The police officers pleaded with Dar and Liz to lay charges. But being victims of guilt and feeling they had brought it on themselves, they refused.

The alcohol had definitely obscured Liz's clear thinking. The police did their best to try to convince her to lay charges but to no avail. She was intimidated by Lenny most of the time now and was afraid of what he might do.

The officers insisted on taking Liz to the hospital. She was afraid of going because it would mean leaving the kids alone with Lenny. The doctor said the molesting probably wouldn't happen again, but Liz didn't want to take the chance.

Dar insisted that Liz go. She didn't know what Lenny had done because Liz was too ashamed to tell her so she didn't understand Liz's reluctance and just kept insisting. Finally, Liz gave in, but she made Dar promise on her life she wouldn't leave the kids until she got home. Dar didn't know what was up, but she knew Liz well enough to know it was really important to her so she stayed.

Liz returned home from the hospital the next day, her left foot and lower leg in a cast. Arnie and Dar had stayed at the house, true to Dar's word. Arnie and Lenny were both very sorry. They always were when they sobered up. They were like Jekyll and Hyde. It was hard for Dar and Liz to stay mad at them when they were being so nice. So the two women forgave them and the foursome had a few more beers together before Arnie and Dar left.

Liz comforted herself with Vera's words -- *Walk a mile in another man's moccasins. People would probably think I'm so bad, but I wonder what they would do in my shoes. She pictured herself saying "What if it was your husband. Just think about it, the man you have loved for so many years. What would you do?"* Then the thoughts from her youth would plague her -- *No man will ever hit me and get away with it. If anybody ever touches one of my kids, he will die.* She would think these thoughts and then quiet them with another drink. She felt heartsick at not having the where-withal to stand behind her own beliefs.

Lenny and Liz drank non-stop and things continued to get worse at "Wuthering Heights". Three weeks passed after Lenny threw Liz off the porch and broke her foot. It was a Saturday afternoon and Lenny brought home a case of beer, Liz, eager to drown her troubles, joined him. Just as they opened their first beers Darlene showed up at the door.

Dar and Liz had hardly started to feel good, and Lenny was already stinking drunk. The girls were sitting at the kitchen table having a good laugh over old times and Lenny, on the couch in the living room, got suspicious.

As he came into the kitchen he slurred, "You two think you're so good. What are you laughing about. You better not be talking about me." He glared at them with black glassy eyes.

Fear prickled up Liz's spine. Those eyes meant trouble. She knew Lenny was gone again and that terrible stranger who took over his body when he got so drunk was back. He came to where Liz sat and grabbed her by both her arms and lifted her in the air as though he was going to toss her across the room and shook her like a rag doll.

She squirmed as hard as she could and broke free from his grasp. She hobbled out through the door as fast as she could on her cast to escape him. He grabbed her from behind as she fled. He lifted her up in the air and threw her off the porch. Her body bounced as it hit the ground while she tried desperately to hold her broken foot in the air so it wouldn't slam down too hard.

Darlene came running through the door screaming and slapping at Lenny. He tried to throw her off the porch as well, but Dar was bigger and heavier than Liz so he started to choke her instead. She fought back scratching and clawing at his face to no avail and her face started to turn blue.

Liz jumped up, ran to Lenny and started hitting him and pulling on his arms to free Dar. With the two of them wailing on him Dar was able to break free from his grasp. She ran to where the kids were playing ball and gathered them together all around her. "Run, quick, to the car!" she screamed as they all ran wildly to Dar's big white Buick.

"Get in, get in, lock the doors!" She yelled. They did.

Lenny was blind with rage. He had hold of Liz again. Dar ran to the corner of the house where several bricks were piled and she started throwing them at Lenny. He let go of Liz to chase Dar so Liz and Dar both raced frantically for the car. The kids, watching with eyes bugged out, quickly lifted the two front door locks.

Liz and Dar just made it into the car, and slammed down the locks as Lenny pounded on the windshield.

Dar started the ignition in a flash and roared the car backwards down the lane, leaving Lenny enveloped in a cloud of dust shaking his fists after them.

"No way are you going to live like this anymore. You're too good for the likes of him. You and the kids will stay with me," Dar said, shaking and sputtering.

Crying and blubbering, Liz nodded frantically.

Finally, a way out!

# Chapter 37
# Trapped on a Carousel of Horror

Liz, Dar and all seven kids climbed out of Dar's car and ran into Dar and Arnie's house. They were so relieved to be in a safe place.

Even though the seven kids had to sleep on mattresses on the floor in Dar and Arnie's tiny 2 bedroom house, Liz and her kids were happy to be there.

It was crowded but it was a peaceful weekend compared to life at "Wuthering Heights". And Arnie proved to be on his best behaviour with all of them in the house.

"I've got to go home and get some clothes for the kids and me. I don't want to bring all the kids. It would be faster if I just go myself. Will you watch them and can I borrow your car?" Liz asked Dar as she sat sipping her coffee late Monday morning.

"Oh, Liz, Do you think you should go out there by yourself. What if Lenny's home and he's drunk. He might kill you if nobody's there to stop him. Arnie'll be home at noon why don't you wait and I'll go with you?"

"I've already put you out enough. I'll be quick. Lenny'll be on the base working. He never takes time off work even if he's nearly dead with a hangover. I'll be okay."

"Well if you're sure, but be careful."

Liz finished her coffee and left. She drove out to "Wuthering Heights" with a sense of urgency. When she arrived she rushed up the stairs to the kids' rooms, an eerie feeling surrounding her. She was quickly gathering some clothes together in a bag when she glanced out the front bedroom window and spotted a black and white cab pulling in the lane.

"Oh, my God, it's Lenny. What's he doing home?" she muttered. "I can't get out of here without him seeing me. Oh, man, I hope he's not drunk."

She rushed down the stairs and entered the living room just as he came through the door. His eyes bugged open and a smile formed on his lips as he staggered in. "Princess! Have you come home to stay?" he slurred.

"Uh, no, I, uh, just came to get some clothes," she stuttered, nervously.

He doubled up his fist and punched the door. "I need you home, Liz. I can't live without you," he shouted.

Liz started to shake as his temper flared. "I, I, can't come home Lenny. It's no good between us anymore."

He glared at Liz, then crossed the room and took his rifle down from the rack on the wall. He loaded the gun, cocked it, turned around and walked to where Liz stood frozen as she watched him. He held the rifle, loaded and cocked, to Liz's head. "Well if I can't have you, nobody's going too."

The blood drained from Liz's face. She looked down the cold steel barrel. Her kids' faces flashed before her eyes. She sunk to her knees, and grabbed the barrel tightly in one hand as Lenny lowered it.

"P-l-e-a-s-e, Lenny, please don't, I beg of you. If you can't think of me, at least think of my kids. They need me. Then seeing his eyes glass over she started to pray, tears streaming down her face, "Our Father who art in heaven..."

"Stop it, Liz, stop it!" he cried as he raised the gun away from her head.

Driven by his fear of losing her and by his own guilt, Lenny planned to shoot Liz first and then turn the gun on himself. But looking at her on her knees begging for her life touched his heart and he couldn't do it. He lowered the gun and said, "You're right Liz, you don't deserve to die. It's me, I'm the one. I'm going to go to the ravine and shoot myself. Things can never be the same between us now. Too much has gone wrong. I love you but I can't figure a way out of all this mess. This'll be best."

Liz breathed a deep sigh of relief as he lowered the rifle and uncocked it. She cupped her hands over her face and sobbed as he went out the door, his head hanging like a beaten man. She was so relieved not to be looking down the barrel of that rifle that she didn't even care about what he was going to do. Out of desperation she hoped that he'd do the job. It seemed as though they were bound together in deep darkness. It was a hopelessness so bottomless that there was no other solution. The only escape seemed to be that one of them had to die. *Better him than me. He's the guilty party,* she thought, and then, *What am I thinking. He is a human being after all.*

She raced out the door after him. He'd already disappeared over the ridge. She ran with all her might down the cow path toward the ravine

A gun shot echoed through the ravine splitting the silent summer air. "Lenn-e-e-e-ey!" her scream reverberated through the forest; a blue jay cocked his head; a gopher stuck his head out of his hole; Lenny lay silent and still, hearing nothing.

Liz ran to where his body lay on the bank of the river beside the log jam; the log jam she had crawled on to see the fish he'd been so happy to show her. She collapsed to her knees in a stupor and laid her head on his chest. The blue jay chattered overhead. Blood trickled down the bank to the river turning the water red. Liz lay on Lenny's chest staring straight ahead, eyes like black glass marbles.

The sun was setting in a blaze of red as Dar raced down the path to the ravine in search of Liz. She passed through the tall elm and pine trees and came to the clearing by the river. "Oh, my God! Oh, my God! Arni-e-e-e," she screeched.

"Hello, Dar? This is Peter, Lenny's cousin. Could I speak with Liz?"

"She's kind of under the weather, if you know what I mean?"

"Yeah. I just wanted to let her know arrangements have been made for Lenny's funeral. It'll be next Friday at two o'clock at Pine Funeral Home in Alliston."

"Thanks for calling. I'm sure she'll want to know."

On Friday, Liz attended the funeral wearing a black silk dress and a black veil over her head to conceal her swollen face and eyes. It was her first sober day since Lenny had died.

After the funeral Liz gave up totally. She drank more and more. She equated the numbing effect of alcohol with coping, but the more she drank, the worse things got. Dar and Carol tried to help her, but they couldn't. Liz had the attitude, *Why get up? Every time I do I only get knocked down again, so I might as well stay down and avoid the pain of the fall.*

She moved out of Dar's into an apartment on Centre Street in Beeton and continued to drink her life away using her precious college fund to buy her booze. The kids looked out for one another until finally, one by one, they all moved away. Jimmy and Stacy went to Toronto to make their fortune and to get out of the house. They couldn't stand to watch the mother that they loved so much slowly killing herself. Liz hadn't wanted them to go at such young ages, 16 and 15, but they were determined and Liz didn't have the wherewithal to stop them. Then finally, Alicia and John, thoroughly disgusted with Liz, took Bonnie and Janie in.

August, 1977. Three years went by in a blur with Liz drinking constantly. Totally alone, she slipped farther and farther down the scale. She pulled away from all her friends. She was too ashamed to face them. She had totally exhausted her college fund, so she befriended Oggie and Ben, the town drunks, to get her supply of booze.

Ben had a long grey beard that was always yellow looking from nicotine. Oggie, a bald-headed, round faced, Danish man, was a little more clean cut but he had a severe drinking problem nonetheless.

Ben lived in a shack in a back alley in town. His house was a disaster. His water system had bunged up and his only water supply was a hose running constantly outside. His bathroom facility was an outhouse with part of the door missing so that when Liz sat down, even though her bottom half was concealed, she could see outside.

The old wooden table in the kitchen was always littered with dirty dishes covered with rotting food and mold. When he did get around to doing the dishes, he just put them under the hose until the running water eventually rinsed them clean.

His living room consisted of one couch and one easy chair, each with the batting showing through, and one small wood stove that heated the whole shack. From about halfway across the living room to the other side was his junk business. Piled to the ceiling was just about anything anyone could ever want. You name it, Ben had it. Car parts, broken down washing machines, toasters, appliances, it was all there in the pile. If anyone in town needed a part for anything, they would go to Ben. He had an inventory in his head and could go to the exact spot and find any given item.

Ben was a very kind man. He would give you the shirt off his back, but he was the town drunk. He was Liz's drinking companion. Despite his drunkeness she grew very fond of him. Even in his drunken state he was constantly reading the Bible. They would read it together and discuss it. Somehow it gave them some solace.

After spending some time with Liz and coming to trust her completely, he disclosed his tragic tale. He wept bitterly and confessed that as a young man he had killed a man in a jealous rage and disposed of his body in a well. Liz wept for the loss of the young man's life and for the loss of Ben's life. For as surely as he had killed the other man, he had given up his own life to the destitution of alcoholism. He would never be free from his crime and Liz knew he would die drunk. She hoped she would too.

She spent all of her time at Ben's. Broke and destitute, she knew that he always had a gallon of Calona Red laced with brandy to give it an extra kick. She was truly hooked and needed to drink and how she got her booze didn't matter, only that she got it.

Time went on, and Liz continued to drink with Ben and Oggie. She knew everyone was disgusted with her, but nothing could deter her. She hardly ate anymore. She weighed 85 pounds. She was covered in big open sores. She often wet herself while she was passed out drunk which always left her feeling so debased, but even that didn't stop her. She looked haggard. She was only 35, but her life was over. Subconsciously, she hoped she would just die and be with Edmund again.

During the winter of 1980, Liz nearly did die. With no money to speak of, she had neglected to fill the oil tank in the little one bedroom house she had moved into when all the kids had left. Janie, now thirteen, visited Liz and brought her food from grandma's when John and Alicia travelled to Beeton once a week to see old friends of theirs who were staying at the Simcoe Manor. Janie loved her mother with all her heart and just wouldn't give up on her.

On one of her visits Janie came in the back door calling, "Mom, mom." No answer. She searched around and finally found Liz passed out on her bed in the freezing cold house with no blankets on. Her breathing was very laboured. Janie raced back to Simcoe Manor and Alicia called an ambulance. Liz was hospitalized with pneumonia.

Bonnie called Jimmy and Stacy to come home. In the meantime, she and Janie visited Liz and with her in a sober state they tried desperately to convince her to quit drinking.

"Come on mom, you've got to pull yourself together. We love you," Bonnie muttered. "Janie needs you I do too." Her words struck a chord in Liz.

"Alright, alright, I'll try. When I get out of the hospital I'll slow right down."

"No, mom you've got to quit completely."

"Oh, I don't think that's necessary. I can slow down. I've done it before. Remember those times. I just need a little drink every once in a while, you know, for my nerves. It just got the best of me because I didn't have any money to get oil in the tank. That's what made me sick. You'll see. I'll get it under control."

Bonnie and Janie looked at each other with knowing looks in their eyes and screwed their faces up in disappointment.

# Chapter 38
# Baby Jason

Jimmy and Stacy came right home to visit Liz. Stacy would be staying home. She walked into Liz's hospital room with a very swollen mid-section. She was pregnant.

After learning about Stacy's pregnancy, Liz tried some controlled drinking when she was released from the hospital. She found it difficult to quit completely, but she did quit going to Ben's. With renewed health from her hospital stay she felt stronger and was able to control her drinking for awhile, and so she was able to convince all the kids to move back home. They rented a larger place, but Liz was definitely addicted, even though she didn't want to admit it to herself and eventually things just got worse again.

Also during the three years when Liz had withdrawn from society, Carol and Dar had both moved to Alberta. Carol had moved first. Then, Dar, watching Liz deteriorate and fearing for herself, left Arnie, quit drinking completely, and moved out west to Edmonton to be near Carol.

So when John and Alicia announced that they were going to retire in Creston, British Columbia, Liz decided to follow them with all her kids in the hopes that she could effect a final cure for her drinking. A geographic cure.

She did fine for awhile, even attaining a job through an incentive program with social services at the Creston Court House. As usual she excelled at the job and was quickly hired full-time until she was caught driving while impaired in the winter beater she had acquired.

Needless to say, that ended her new found career and opportunity to better herself. So in order to escape Alicia's constant nagging about her failure, she left Creston and moved to Trail, B.C. with all the kids. With the aid of social services they moved into a large one room apartment. But because it was too crowded for all of them, Jimmy left for Edmonton to stay with Carol until he found a job to care for himself. And Stacy was sent to an unwed mother's home in Kamloops by their social worker.

Then Liz felt she couldn't be alone so she gathered "friends" around her who drank like she did. A lot of her so-called friends were in the same predicament. They were not bad people any more than Liz was. Her core was good and their's were too. They were just victims of the demon alcohol, like she was.

The friends that Liz chose loved music the same as she did and they spent many hours at Liz's drinking to excess, playing guitars, singing out of tune and trying to have a good time. Thus went her life until the day a very important phone call came.

"Hello, Mrs. Carter, this is Mrs. French from the home. Your daughter Stacy has gone into labour. The house mother is with her so don't worry. She has been coached on labour and delivery and someone will be with her all the time."

"Oh, I want to be there!" Liz cried, excitement rising in her voice at the prospect of a new baby grandchild, her first. *I'm too young to be a grandmother. I'm only 36. Oh, what the heck, I'm so excited. I'm gonna have to clean up my act. I'll have to quit drinking. Yes, that's a must. I never drank when my kids were babies. Babies are so special and so clean and innocent. Yes, I'll quit drinking for sure. I'll be a model Grandma. Oh, this is too wonderful for words.* All these thoughts flooded through her mind in an instant, only to be crushed by Mrs French's next words.

"Uh, Mrs. Carter, you should know that Stacy is giving her child up. He's to be taken away immediately to a foster home pending adoption," she informed Liz, coldly.

"What? No way! Whose idea is this? Certainly not Stacy's. We'll just see about that," Liz shouted into the phone.

Liz was ready to do battle. She would do anything, give up anything, but not her first grandchild. The thought of a new baby in their lives delighted her and as though a bright light turned on realization started to dawn on her. *What has become of my life? Such a wonderful event and I am in no position to be of help. I feel just sick. I've even spent the college fund. Oh, man I can't even help financially.* Reality hit her like a ton of bricks, and then her mind started working again. She had to do something and fast. The next day, she went to see a lawyer.

"I'm sorry, Mrs. Carter, there's just nothing we can do. Grandparents have no rights. It's totally your daughter's decision."

"That's the point. I don't believe it is my daughter's decision. I believe she's been coerced by the people at the home."

Liz felt terrible. *What support can I provide?* With a sinking feeling she remembered the spent college funds. *What right do I have to demand? I never supported my own kids properly. I don't have a leg to stand on. What am I thinking, I'm nothing but a drunk anyway.* Her negative thinking almost convinced her to give up again. But on the other hand, she knew Stacy. She knew that Stacy would never get over it in years to come if she gave up her child. No! No matter what her situation was, something had to be done and it had to be done fast.

As if in answer to her last thought, the lawyer declared, "Well, Mrs. Carter, my only advice to you is that you work on your daughter. If you think they've swayed her, perhaps you can change her mind. If I were in your shoes, I would be on that phone and talking her ear off."

Liz wanted to reach over and kiss him for giving her the boost she needed. Encouraged by the lawyer's words, she proceeded to do just what he said. She spent days and tons of long distance phone calls persuading Stacy with all kinds of promises to support her.

Stacy wasn't budging. The women at the home had done a good job on her. During her stay, they had shown the girls films of teenage girls drinking and doing drugs and not caring for their babies properly. They had convinced her that it was best for the baby to give him up.

Liz knew Stacy and she knew different. She might have been a failure, but Stacy had the determination and confidence to overcome anything. She was not beaten down and weak like Liz. Liz also believed Stacy was the type who would never get over letting her baby go. So Liz fought tooth and nail, but to no avail.

By this time, Bonnie had started dating a nice young man named Darren who volunteered to take them all up to Kamloops to see the baby and Stacy at his expense. He drove the seven hour trip and paid for motel rooms for them all. He was a gem. Things were finally working out for Liz. They arrived three days after Jason had been born. By the time they got to the hospital, Stacy had returned to the home, but Jason was still in the nursery.

"Oh, Janie, Bonnie, look at that sweet little face. Isn't he the picture of innocence, so pure? Oh, can I please hold him?" Liz crooned to the stately nurse who held Liz's first little grandson. Completely sober for the first time in a long time, Liz beamed, a broad grin forming on her face. Then her face drooped and the grin quickly disappeared as the nurse coldly stated, "No, I'm sorry you are not allowed to hold the baby. He is to be given up for adoption."

Tears gushed from Liz's eyes. Her heart was ripped in two. Would this be the final price she had to pay for her debased life, to never hold her grandson in her arms, feel his soft skin beneath her fingers, sing lullabies to him, watch him sleep? Hadn't she paid enough already?

Liz left the hospital feeling bereft. But by the time she arrived at the Home she was busting with determination. Nobody but nobody was going to take that baby away. No matter what she had to do to prevent it, she was determined. Liz was bursting with new life.

"Stacy, can we go somewhere and talk privately?"

"Sure, Mom. We can go to the sitting room, but I'm telling you right now, I'm not changing my mind," Stacy said, her face tight and grim.

Stacy was determined, but Liz was more determined. She was willing to give up anything to help Stacy keep her child so she wouldn't have to go through the agony of wondering where is he? Who is he with? What does he look like now? Is he okay?

"Stacy I seriously think you should reconsider. I don't think that you're looking at all the angles here."

"Mom, don't start. I know what I'm doing. I don't want to hurt your feelings but if I keep him I won't have any help. I want to do something with my life. The housemother says I'm very smart and that I should do something with my brain. You always said you wanted us all to go to college and be something. Well, I will have a chance if I let Jason go. Please don't make it any harder than it already is."

"Oh, Stacy, I do want you to be something. I've never given up on that dream." Liz's determination started to slip as she thought about how she'd spent all the college funds, but then she took a deep breath and continued, "I just got sidetracked a little that's all. I'll look after Jason while you go back to school. Please come home and give me a chance."

"I don't know. They showed us films about babies being neglected by drinking and drugging teens. I don't want that to happen to Jason. You know how you drink. I don't want Jason in that kind of environment."

"Stacy I promise with all my heart I'll quit. I've been sober for a week now. Ever since I heard about Jason's birth, I just quit. It hasn't been easy, but after seeing his little face I know I'll make it this time. We can do so many things with him. Just think about it. We'll buy him everything he needs. Grandma will help us too, I'm sure. He's family. He's ours. We can watch him grow, all of us together. Come on Stacy. Bonnie and Janie help too. We'll be a family again. I can feel it in my bones. I'll get a bigger place. Everything will be alright. We all love him already. I promise on my life. You don't want to be wondering for years to come where he is? Is he alright? What does he look like? Do you?"

"Oh, Mom, no. I don't, but I don't know if I can trust you. You're drinking is so awful and nothing seems to deter you."

"This will!" Liz said, fully determined she would carry out her word.

Tears filled Stacy's eyes, then slowly trickled down her cheeks. She was confused. Liz was right. She didn't want to give Jason up any more than she wanted to fly to the moon, but she wanted what was best for him and for her. She had been convinced that adoption was the best. But now Liz was convincing her otherwise, and Stacy was believing her. It was easy to believe because Liz meant every word, with all her heart, she meant every word.

Liz threw her arms around Stacy and cuddled her close as her own tears flowed freely.

"I promise, pet. No more drinking for me. I'm so sorry for what I've put you through. It's over! From now on you'll see a sober Mom."

Stacy hugged her and nodded her head in agreement and a big smile broke through the tears like sunshine through a rainy sky. Liz could see the rainbow. The two left the sitting room arms around each other to head to the Housemother's office to tell her the good news.

With the determination only grandmothers understand, Liz had finally convinced Stacy to change her mind. She was delighted and bent on keeping her word. She would do everything in her power to support Stacy and keep Jason safe and well taken care of.

Once they were home, Liz borrowed money from Alicia to rent a bigger place and to help get things set up for the baby. Stacy and Liz had a wonderful time shopping at the large Eaton's store, picking out clothes, a stroller, a high chair, a crib, you name it, they bought it. Liz kept her promise to stay sober. Stacy got a job at a Boston Pizza for the summer to help with expenses and Liz cared for little Jason. She bathed him, fed him, sang to him, cuddled him and loved him. True to her word it was a new life. Three months went by, and Liz was in her glory. The kids were all back. They were a family again.

Then one night a knock came at the door. When Liz opened the door she saw several people carrying cases of beer and guitars.

"Hi, Liz, we haven't seen you around in months. What have you been doing with yourself?" said Paul, one of Liz's newfound friends.

"Oh, I have a new little grandson, and I quit drinking. Do you want to see him? I am the proud Grandma."

"Sure, do you mind if we bring the beer in."

"Well, uh, I guess, not. *I* can't drink though. I've got my Grandson to care for. His mother is working tonight and I promised her I wouldn't drink anymore."

Her biggest mistake was letting them in the door. Once again she found it hard to say no. All her sincere and well-intentioned promises went out the window as she joined her cohorts once they started to get drunk. She couldn't deal with the pressure of staying sober while everyone was getting drunk around her so she caved in to their invitation to have a beer. "Just one," she said, "to help me relax."

"Mom! Mom! Wake up right now! It's four o'clock in the morning. How long has Jason been crying? What's the matter with you? You promised." Stacy's furious voice penetrated Liz's alcoholic fog.

Liz fought the haze surrounding her sick mind and finally came to. "What, whatsa matter? Oh, the baby. He's crying. It's his two o'clock feeding," she said as she struggled to get up.

"Forget it! You're too late. I'll do it myself," Stacy hissed.

"W-What time is it?"

"Four o'clock in the morning. He's been crying for two hours. What the hell's the matter with you."

"Oh Stacy, I'm so sorry." Liz's heart broke at the realization of her own failing. Stacy was crying. The look in her eyes was of pure disgust at Liz, mixed with hopelessness for herself and Jason. Stacy looked beaten. She had taken Liz at her word, and Liz had failed her once again. The desperation in Stacy's words stung as they reached Liz's inner core, "How can you do this to me?"

"Stacy, I'm so sorry. I promise you I will do something about my drinking." Liz now knew the drinking problem was bigger than her. She had no power over it. She had never been able to admit before that she couldn't control it. Now, she knew better. With Stacy's pain and Jason's cries wringing her heart, Liz promised faithfully she would go to Alcoholics Anonymous.

Stacy made sure Liz went. She accompanied her to the A.A. club at noon that day with little Jason in his stroller. Arrangements were made for Liz to attend the meeting that night.

Sheila, from Alcoholics Anonymous arrived in a brand new blue Chev. Liz piled the two-month old Jason into the back seat in his bassinet. Stacy had to work so Liz was told she could bring Jason to the meeting.

They arrived at the parking lot at the back of the clubhouse, beneath the Cominco Hill, where several people were flocking to the door. As Liz went to open the car door a very handsome man reached for the handle and opened the door for her.

"Here let me help you carry that basket," he said cheerfully.

Liz felt like royalty as he took her hand and helped her to climb out of the small car. Then he pushed the seat ahead and reached in for the basket. As he was pulling the basket out another equally good looking young man came up to join them, "Need any help?" he asked as he extended his hand to Liz. "I'm Norm," he said as he warmly shook Liz's hand in greeting. She felt very flattered and cared about. She hadn't been treated so considerately by men for a long time.

"Oh, yeah, and I'm Mick," the other man said, smiling warmly.

They entered the old house that had been turned into a meeting place. They left Jason sleeping soundly in his bassinet on the kitchen table as they went into the meeting room. Liz's eyes bugged out as she took in the scene. Row on row of green and orange leather stacking chairs were filled with all kinds of people. She was amazed at the number of people and the looks of them. There were several women, some her age, some older, all dressed very respectably and lots of fine looking men. This was nothing like the meeting she had gone to years ago in Ontario. She was impressed.

"Could we open this meeting with a moment of silence for those who have helped us and for those whom we may help?" the chairman's solemn voice quoted.

As the crowd stood, Liz, hung over and looking beaten and forlorn, stumbled to her feet. She found the silence to be deafening and the moment to be an eternity. Her sick and broken mind raced back across the shattered years of her life. Some of the memories were so ugly and painful that she couldn't bear to think about them. But try as hard as she might, they kept popping up, until finally she turned her thoughts to rehearsing what she'd say when it came her turn to speak.

Then a statement made by an older man captured her attention instantly. She sat and listened intently as he spoke. "I never felt like I belonged anywhere, even in my own family. I always had *a haunting emptiness* inside." Those words echoed in her head as her heart related at once. She realized that she had always felt that way --- at home, at school, everywhere. She never felt like she belonged anywhere and there was always that horrible haunting emptiness that she equated as the need for a man. The only time she felt at ease and comfortable in her own skin was when she was drinking.

The chairman asked one person after another to speak. A lot of what was said escaped Liz's sick mind, but the kindness and the warmth in the room was etched deeply into her heart that night.

She had plenty to say, but when the chairman looked compassionately in her direction and said "Would you like to add anything?", the only thing that came out was, "My name is Elizabeth and I'm an alcoholic." Then from the depths of her soul a cry escaped her lips and her body shook with sobs. She felt like she had come home. The carousel with the drunk horses had made it's last turn.

## The End

# Epilogue

Liz fought with all her strengths against her addictions, and she won the battle. The years passed quickly, and her children became adults with children of their own. Liz won the battle against alcoholism, but she was losing the battle against cancer.

The family room in the hospital was dimly lit because the light bothered her eyes. Jimmy, Stacy, Bonnie, Janie, Jason and Bailee, her youngest child (that's a whole other story) were all huddled around her bed, hugging each other with tears streaming down their cheeks. As Liz looked at them, she reflected on the happy years of sobriety she had enjoyed with them.

She coughed and with great effort she whispered, "I love you all with all my heart." She looked at her babies, content that they had finished what she had set out to do, even though the outcome was not the same as her dreams had been. With the aid of government loans, each of the girls had realized their own dreams. Stacy went to nursing school, Bonnie took a course in child care and Janie became part owner of a popular restaurant chain, Jimmy was a master corporal in the army. Liz was so proud of how handsome he looked in his dress uniform. And Bailee was a cashier in a large grocery chain.

She was neither unhappy nor frightened. Yes, she was ready to go. They would be alright now. She tried to comfort them. "Try not to be too sad. In the twinkling of an eye I'll be where I've always longed to be."

She was so weak she could hardly lift her right arm. But she made the effort, reached over and with her fingers gently caressed the fading white scar tissue on her left upper arm. She looked down. They were still there, the initials E. B.

"Oh, look the wind is coming up. Quick open the window. I've always loved the wind. It's free and goes where ever it wants." Liz whispered. A warm breeze caressed her face oh so gently and then very faintly she thought she could hear the lilting music of the carousel. With that her eyes closed, her body went limp and she died with a peaceful smile on her face; her babies were okay and she was on her way to Edmund.

# About the Author

Kimberley Rose Dawson lives in a small, valley town amidst the mountains of Beautiful British Columbia with her two cats. She wrote CAROUSEL, based on the true story of Elizabeth Burgess' life struggle, in the hopes that it might help other women with addiction problems.

Ms. Dawson is busy writing again so watch for the sequel to CAROUSEL, *CAROUSEL - THE MISSING YEARS*, which continues with Elizabeth Burgess' story exactly where it left off in the last chapter of CAROUSEL. The story covers Elizabeth's fight to stay sober in spite of all her adversities, and her continuing struggle against her Carousel. Will she finally defeat the Carousel? Find out in *CAROUSEL - THE MISSING YEARS*.